NAN OF MUSIC MOUNTAIN

De Spain covered a hardly perceptible black object on the trail.

Nan of
Music Mountain

BY
Frank H. Spearman

Illustrated by
N. C. Wyeth

We are pleased to add *Nan of Music Mountain* to our list of Frank Spearman titles. The other Spearman titles now available from The Paper Tiger are his two collections of short stories, *Held for Orders* and *The Nerve of Foley*. Also available are three of his novels, *The Daughter of a Magnate*, *Whispering Smith*, and *Laramie Holds the Range*. We believe that these six titles represent the very best of Frank Spearman. If you enjoy any one of them, you likely will enjoy the others.

Originally published by Charles Scribner's Sons, 1916

Published by
The Paper Tiger, Inc.
335 Jefferson Avenue
Cresskill, NJ 07626
(201) 567-5620
www.papertig.com

ISBN 1-889439-09-6

TO MY SON

EUGENE LONERGAN SPEARMAN

CONTENTS

Contents

ILLUSTRATIONS

Nan of Music Mountain

CHAPTER I

FRONTIER DAY

LEFEVER, if there was a table in the room, could never be got to sit on a chair; and being rotund he sat preferably sidewise on the edge of the table. One of his small feet—his feet were encased in tight, high-heeled, ill-fitting horsemen's boots—usually rested on the floor, the other swung at the end of his stubby leg slowly in the air. This idiosyncrasy his companion, de Spain, had learned to tolerate.

But Lefever's subdued whistle, which seemed meditative, always irritated de Spain more or less, despite his endeavor not to be irritated. It was like the low singing of a tea-kettle, which, however unobtrusive, indicates steam within. In fact, John Lefever, who was built not unlike a kettle, and whose high, shiny forehead was topped by a pompadour shock of very yellow hair, never whistled except when there was some pressure on his sensibilities.

Nan of Music Mountain

The warm sun streaming through the windows of the private office of the division superintendent at Sleepy Cat, a railroad town lying almost within gunshot of the great continental divide, would easily have accounted for the cordial perspiration that illumined Lefever's forehead. Not that a perspiration is easily achieved in the high country; it isn't. None, indeed, but a physical giant, which Lefever was, could maintain so constant and visible a nervous moisture in the face of the extraordinary atmospheric evaporation of the mountain plateaus. And to de Spain, on this occasion, even the glistening beads on his companion's forehead were annoying, for he knew that he himself was properly responsible for their presence.

De Spain, tilted back in the superintendent's chair, sat near Lefever—Jeffries had the mountain division then—his elbows resting on the arms of the revolving-chair, and with his hands he gripped rather defiantly the spindles supporting them; his feet were crossed on the walnut rim of the shabby, cloth-topped table. In this attitude his chin lay on his soft, open collar and tie, his sunburnt lips were shut tight, and above and between his nervous brown eyes were two little, vertical furrows of perplexity and regret. He was looking at the dull-finish barrel of a new rifle, that lay across Lefever's lap. At intervals Lefever took the rifle up and, whistling softly, examined with care a fracture of the lever, the broken thumb-piece of which lay on the table between the two men.

From the Main Street side of the large room came the hooting and clattering of a Frontier Day celebration, and these noises seemed not to allay the discomfort apparent on the faces of the two men.

"It certainly is warm," observed Lefever, apropos of nothing at all.

"Why don't you get out of the sun?" suggested de Spain shortly.

Lefever made a face. "I am trying to keep away from that noise."

"Hang it, John," blurted out de Spain peevishly, "what possessed you to send for *me* to do the shooting, anyway?"

His companion answered gently—Lefever's patience was noted even among contained men— "Henry," he remonstrated, "I sent for you because I thought you could shoot."

De Spain's expression did not change under the reproach. His bronzed face was naturally amiable, and his mental attitude toward ill luck, usually one of indifference, was rarely more than one of perplexity. His features were so regular as to

3

Nan of Music Mountain

contribute to this undisturbed expression, and his face would not ordinarily attract attention but for his extremely bright and alive eyes—the frequent mark of an out-of-door mountain life—and especially for a red birthmark, low on his left cheek, disappearing under the turn of the jaw. It was merely a strawberry, so-called, but an ineradicable stamp, and perhaps to a less preoccupied man a misfortune. Henry de Spain, however, even at twenty-eight, was too absorbed in many things to give thought to this often, and after knowing him, one forgot about the birthmark in the man that carried it. Lefever's reproach was naturally provocative. "I hope now," retorted de Spain, but without any show of resentment, "you understand I can't."

"No," persisted Lefever good-naturedly, "I only realize, Henry, that this wasn't your day for the job."

The door of the outer office opened and Jeffries, the superintendent, walked into the room; he had just come from Medicine Bend in his car. The two men rose to greet him. He asked about the noise in the street.

"That noise, William, comes from all Calabasas and all Morgan's Gap," explained Lefever, still fondling the rifle. "The Morgans are celebrating our defeat. They put it all over us.

4

Frontier Day

We were challenged yesterday," he continued in response to the abrupt questions of Jeffries. "The Morgans offered to shoot us offhand, two hundred yards, bull's-eye count. The boys here— Bob Scott and some of the stage-guards—put it up to me. I thought we could trim them by running in a real gunman. I wired to Medicine Bend for Henry. Henry comes up last night with a brand-new rifle, presented, I imagine, by the Medicine Bend Black Hand Local, No. 13. This is the gun," explained Lefever feebly, holding forth the exhibit. "The lever," he added with a patient expletive, "broke."

"Give me the gun, John," interposed de Spain resignedly. "I'll lay it on the track to-night for a train to run over."

"It was a time limit, you understand, William," persisted Lefever, continuing to stick pins calmly into de Spain. "Henry got to shooting too fast."

"That wasn't what beat me," exclaimed de Spain curtly. And taking up the offending rifle he walked out of the room.

"Nor was it the most humiliating feature of his defeat," murmured Lefever, as the door closed behind his discomfited champion. "What do you think, William?" he grumbled on. "The Morgans ran in a girl to shoot against us—true as there's a God in heaven. They put up Nan

5

Morgan, old Duke Morgan's little niece. And
what do you think? She shot the fingers clean
off our well-known Black Hand scout. I never
before in my life saw Henry so fussed. The little
Music Mountain skirt simply put it all over him.
She had five bull's-eyes to Henry's three when the
lever snapped. He forfeited."

"Some shooting," commented Jeffries, rapidly
signing letters.

"We expected some when Henry unslung his
gun," Lefever went on without respecting Jeffries's
preoccupation. "As it is, those fellows have
cleaned up every dollar loose in Sleepy Cat, and
then some. Money? They could start a bank
this minute."

Sounds of revelry continued to pour in through
the street window. The Morgans were celebrating uncommonly. "Rubbing it in, eh, John?"
suggested Jeffries.

"Think of it," gasped Lefever, "to be beaten
by an eighteen-year-old girl."

"Now that," declared Jeffries, waking up as if
for the first time interested, "is exactly where you
made your mistake, John. Henry is young and
excitable——"

"Excitable!" echoed Lefever, taken aback.

"Yes, excitable—when a girl is in the ring—
why not? Especially a trim, all-alive, up-and-

coming, blue-eyed hussy like that girl of Duke Morgan's. She would upset any young fellow, John."

"A girl from Morgan's Gap?"

"Morgan's Gap, nothing!" responded Jeffries scornfully. "What's that got to do with it? Does that change the fire in the girl's eye, the curve of her neck, the slope of her shoulder, John, or the color of her cheek?" Lefever only stared. "De Spain got to thinking about the girl," persisted Jeffries, "her eyes and neck and pink cheeks rattled him. Against a girl you should have put up an old, one-eyed scout like yourself, or me, or Bob Scott.

"There's another thing you forget, John," continued Jeffries, signing even more rapidly. "A gunman shoots his best when there's somebody shooting at him—otherwise he wouldn't be a gunman—he would be just an ordinary, every-day marksman, with a Schuetzenverein medal and a rooster feather in his hat. That's why you shoot well, John—because you're a gunman, and not a marksman."

"That boy can shoot all around me, Jeff."

"For instance," continued Jeffries, tossing off signatures now with a rubber stamp, and developing his incontestable theory at the same time, "if you had put Gale Morgan up against Henry

7

at, say five hundred yards, and told them to shoot *at* each other, instead of against each other, you'd have got bull's-eyes to burn from de Spain. And the Calabasas crowd wouldn't have your money. John, if you want to win money, you must study the psychological."

There was abundance of raillery in Lefever's retort: "That's why you are rich, Jeff?"

"No, I am poor because I failed to study it. That is why I am at Sleepy Cat holding down a division. But now that you've brought Henry up here, we'll keep him."

"What do you mean, keep him?" demanded Lefever, starting in protest.

"What do I mean?" thundered Jeffries, who frequently thundered even when it didn't rain in the office. "I mean I need him. I mean the time to shoot a bear is when you see him. John, what kind of a fellow is de Spain?" demanded the superintendent, as if he had never heard of him.

"Henry de Spain?" asked Lefever, sparring innocently for time.

"No, Commodore George Washington, General Jackson, Isaac Watts de Spain," retorted Jeffries peevishly. "Don't you know the man we're talking about?"

"Known him for ten years."

Frontier Day

"Then why say 'Henry' de Spain, as if there were a dozen of him? He's the only de Spain in these parts, isn't he? What kind of a fellow is he?"

Lefever was ready; and as he sat in a chair sidewise at the table, one arm flung across the green baize, he looked every inch his devil-may-care part. Regarding Jeffries keenly, he exclaimed with emphasis: "Why, if you want him short and sharp, he's a man with a soft eye and a snapturtle jaw, a man of close squeaks and short-arm shots, always getting into trouble, always getting out; a man that can wheedle more out of a horse than anybody but an Indian; coax more shots out of a gun than anybody else can put into it —if you want him flat, that's Henry, as I size him."

Jeffries resumed his mildest tone: "Tell him to come in a minute, John."

De Spain himself expressed contemptuous impatience when Lefever told him the superintendent wanted him to go to work at Sleepy Cat. He declared he had always hated the town; and Lefever readily understood why he should especially detest it just now. Every horseman's yell that rang on the sunny afternoon air through the open windows—and from up the street and down there were still a good many—was one of

9

derision at de Spain's galling defeat. When he at length consented to talk with Jeffries about coming to Sleepy Cat, the interview was of a positive sort on the one side and an obstinate sort on the other. De Spain raised one objection after another to leaving Medicine Bend, and Jeffries finally summoned a show of impatience.

"You are looking for promotion, aren't you?" he demanded threateningly.

"Yes, but not for motion without the 'pro,'" objected de Spain. "I want to stick to the railroad business. You want to get me into the stage business."

"Temporarily, yes. But I've told you when you come back to the division proper, you come as my assistant, if you make good running the Thief River stages. Think of the salary."

"I have no immediate heirs."

"This is not a matter for joking, de Spain."

"I know that, too. How many men have been shot on the stages in the last six months?"

"Why, now and again the stages are held up, yes," admitted Jeffries brusquely; "that is to be expected where the specie shipments are large. The Thief River mines are rotten with gold just now. But you don't have to drive a stage. We supply you with good men for that, and good guards—men willing to take any kind of a chance if the pay is right. And the pay is right, and yours as general manager will be right."

"I have never as yet generally managed any stage line," remarked de Spain, poking ridicule at the title, "no matter how modest an outfit."

"You will never learn younger. There is a fascination," declared Jeffries, ignoring the fling, and tilting his chair eloquently back to give ease and conviction to his words, "about running a good stage line that no railroad business can ever touch. There is, of course, nothing in the Rocky Mountains, for that matter in the United States—nothing, I guess, in the world—that approaches the Thief River line in its opportunities. Every wagon we own, from the lightest to the heaviest, is built to order on our particular specifications by the Studebaker people." Here Jeffries pointed his finger sharply at de Spain as if to convict him of some dereliction. "You've seen them! You know what they are."

De Spain, bullied, haltingly nodded acquiescence.

"Second-growth hickory in the gears," continued Jeffries encouragingly, "ash tongues and boxes——"

"Some of those old buses look like ash-boxes," interposed de Spain irreverently.

But Jeffries was not to be stopped: "Timkin

springs, ball-bearing axles—why, man, there is no vehicle in the world built like a Thief River stage."

"You are some wagon-maker, Jeff," said de Spain, regarding him ironically.

Jeffries ignored every sarcasm. "This road, as you know, owns the line. And the net from the specie shipments equals the net on an ordinary railroad division. But we must have a man to run that line that can curb the disorders along the route. Calabasas Valley, de Spain, is a bad place."

"Is it?" de Spain asked as naïvely as if he had never heard of Calabasas, though Jeffries was nervily stating a fact bald and notorious to both.

"There are a lot of bad men there," Jeffries went on, "who are bad simply because they've never had a man to show them."

"The last 'general' manager was killed there, wasn't he?"

"Not in the valley, no. He was shot at Calabasas Inn."

"Would that make very much difference in the way he felt about it?"

Jeffries, with an effort, laughed. "That's all right, Henry! They won't get you." Again he extended his finger dogmatically: "If I thought they would, I wouldn't send you down there."

Frontier Day

"Thank *you*."

"You are young, ambitious: four thousand a year isn't hanging from every telegraph-pole; it is almost twice what they are paying me."

"You're not getting shot at."

"No man, Henry, knows the hour of his death. No man in the high country knows when he is to be made a target—that you well understand. Men are shot down in this country that have no more idea of getting killed than I have—or you have."

"Don't include me. I have a pretty good idea of getting killed right away—the minute I take this job."

"We have temporized with this Calabasas outfit long enough," declared Jeffries, dropping his mask at last. "Deaf Sandusky, Logan, and that squint-eyed thief, Dave Sassoon—all hold-up men, every one of them! Henry, I'm putting you in on that job because you've got nerve, because you can shoot, because I don't think they can get you—and paying you a whaling big salary to straighten things out along the Spanish Sinks. Do you know, Henry—" Jeffries leaned forward and lowered his tone. Master of the art of persuading and convincing, of hammering and pounding, of swaying the doubting and deciding the undecided, the strong-eyed mountain-man looked his best as he held the younger man under his

13

spell. "Do you know," he repeated, "I suspect that Morgan Gap bunch are really behind and beneath a lot of this deviltry around Calabasas? You take Gale Morgan: why, he trains with Dave Sassoon; take his uncle, Duke: Sassoon never is in trouble but what Duke will help him out." Jeffries exploded with a slight but forcible expletive. "Was there ever a thief or a robber driven into Morgan's Gap that didn't find sympathy and shelter with some of the Morgans? I believe they are in every game pulled on the Thief River stages."

"As bad as that?"

Jeffries turned to his desk. "Ask John Lefever."

De Spain had a long talk with John. But John was a poor adviser. He advised no one on any subject. He whistled, he hummed a tune, if his hat was on he took it off, and if it happened to be off, which was unusual, he put it on. He extended his arm, at times, suddenly, as if on the brink of a positive assertion. But he decided nothing, and asserted nothing. If he talked, he talked well and energetically; but the end of a talk usually found him and de Spain about where they began. So it was on this trying day—for Lefever was not able wholly to hide the upsetting of his confidence of victory, and his humiliation at the now more distant yells from the Calabasas and Morgan Gap victors.

But concerning the Morgans and their friends, Lefever, to whom Jeffries had rudely referred the subject at the close of his talk with de Spain, did abandon his habitual reticence. "Rustlers, thieves, robbers, coiners, outlaws!" he exclaimed energetically.

"Is this because they got your money to-day, John?" asked de Spain.

"Never mind my money. I've got a new job with nothing to do, and plenty of cash."

De Spain asked what the job was. "On the stages," announced Lefever. "I am now general superintendent of the Thief River Line."

"What does that mean?"

"It means that I act for the reorganization committee in buying alfalfa for the horses and smokeless pipes for the guards. I am to be your assistant."

"I'm not going to take that job, John."

"Yes, you are."

"Not if I know it. I am going back to Medicine Bend to-night." Lefever took off his hat and twirled it skilfully on one hand, humming softly the while. "John," asked de Spain after a pause, "who is that girl that shot against me this afternoon?"

15

"That," answered Lefever, thinking, shocked, of Jeffries's words, "was Nan Morgan."

"Who is she?"

"Just one of the Morgans; lives in the Gap with old Duke Morgan, her uncle; lived there as long as I can remember. Some shot, Henry."

"How can she live in the Gap," mused de Spain, "with an outfit like that?"

"Got nowhere else to live, I guess. I believe you'd better change your mind, Henry, and stay with us."

"No," returned de Spain meditatively, "I'm not going to stay. I've had glory enough out of this town for a while." He picked up his hat and put it on. Lefever thought it well to make no response. He was charged with the maintenance and operation of the stage-line arsenal at Sleepy Cat, and spent many of his idle moments toying with the firearms. He busied himself now with the mechanism of a huge revolver—one that the stage-driver, Frank Elpaso, had wrecked on the head of a troublesome negro coming in from the mines. De Spain in turn took off his hat, poked the crown discontentedly, and, rising with a loss of amiability in his features and manner, walked out of the room.

The late sun was streaming down the full length of Main Street. The street was still filled with

Frontier Day

loiterers who had spent the day at the fair, and
lingered now in town in the vague hope of seeing
a brawl or a fight before sundown—cattlemen and
cowboys from the northern ranges, sheepmen from
the Spider River country, small ranchers and
irrigators from the Bear basin, who picked their
steps carefully, and spoke with prudence in the
presence of roisterers from the Spanish Sinks,
and gunmen and gamblers from Calabasas and
Morgan's Gap. The Morgans themselves and
their following were out to the last retainer.

CHAPTER II

SLEEPY CAT has little to distinguish it in its
casual appearance from the ordinary mountain railroad town of the western Rockies. The
long, handsome railroad station, the eating-house,
and the various division-headquarters buildings
characteristic of such towns are in Sleepy Cat
built of local granite. The yard facilities, shops,
and roundhouses are the last word in modern railroad construction, and the division has not infrequently held the medal for safety records.

But more than these things go toward making
up the real Sleepy Cat. It is a community with
earlier-than-railroad traditions. Sleepy Cat has
been more or less of a settlement almost since the
day of Jim Bridger, and its isolated position in
the midst of a country of vast deserts, far mountain ranges, and widely separated watercourses
has made it from the earliest Western days a
rendezvous for hunters, trappers, emigrants, prospectors, and adventurers—and these have all, in
some measure, left their impress on the town.

Sleepy Cat lies prettily on a high plateau north

18

and east of the railroad, which makes a détour here to the north to round the Superstition Range; it is a county-seat, and this, where counties are as large as ordinary Eastern States, gives it some political distinction.

The principal street lies just north of the railroad, and parallels it. A modern and substantial hotel has for some years filled the corner above the station. The hotel was built by Harry Tenison soon after the opening of the Thief River gold-fields. Along Main Street to the west are strung the usual mountain-town stores and saloons, but to the north a pretty residence district has been built up about the court-house square. And a good water-supply, pumped from Rat River, a brawling mountain stream that flows just south of the town, has encouraged the care of lawns and trees.

Before de Spain had walked far he heard music from the open-air dancing-pavilion in Grant Street. Stirred by an idle curiosity, he turned the corner and stopped to watch the crowded couples whirling up and down the raised platform under paper lanterns and red streamers to the music of an automatic piano. He took his place in a fringe of onlookers that filled the sidewalk. But he was thinking as he stood, not of the boisterous dancing or the clumsy dancers, but of the broken lever and the defeat at the fair-grounds. It still rankled in his mind. While he stood thinking the music ceased.

A man, who appeared to be in authority, walked to the centre of the dancing-floor and made an announcement that de Spain failed to catch. The manager apparently repeated it to those of his patrons that crowded around him, and more than once to individual inquirers who had not caught the purport of what had been said. These late comers he pushed back, and when the floor had been well cleared he nodded to the boy operating the piano, and looked toward a young couple standing in an attitude of waiting at the head of the hall.

All eyes being turned their way, de Spain's attention as well was drawn toward them. The man was powerful in stature, and rather too heavy, but straight as an Indian. His small, reddish face was tanned by the sun and wind, and his manner as he stood with arms akimbo, his hands resting on his belt, facing his partner and talking to her, had the confidence of a man at ease with women. From the handsome hat which, as he turned to his partner for the dance, he sent spinning toward a table beside the piano, the soft brown shirt and flowing tie, down to the small, high-heeled and spurred boots, he wore the distinctive cowboy rig of the mountains, even to the heavy hip-holster, in which his revolver was slung. He was, in fact, rather too smartly dressed, too confident in manner to please de Spain, who was in no mood to be pleased anyway, and who could conceive a dislike for a man the instant he set eyes on him—and a liking as quickly. He seemed to recall, too, that this particular fellow had crowed the loudest when he himself forfeited the shooting-match earlier in the day.

But de Spain, unamiable as he now was, looked with unconcealed interest at the man's dancing partner. She, too, was browned by the mountain sun and air—a slight, erect girl, her head well set, and a delicate waist-line above a belted brown skirt, which just reached the tops of her small, high, tan riding-boots. She wore a soft, French-gray Stetson hat. Her dark-brown hair was deftly hidden under it, but troublesome ringlets strayed about her ears as if she had not seen a glass for hours, and these, standing first with one hand and then the other laid against her leather belt, she put up into place, and as if not wholly at ease with her surroundings. Instead of looking at her partner, who talked to her while waiting, her eyes, noticeably pretty, wandered about the platform, resting at moments on the closely drawn lines of spectators. They reflected

in their unrest the dissatisfied expression of her
face. A talkative woman standing just in front
of de Spain, told a companion that the man was
Gale Morgan, a nephew of Satterlee, laziest of the
Morgans. De Spain, who never had to look
twice at any woman, at once recognized in the
dancing partner the little Music Mountain girl
who had been his undoing at the target; the
woman added that Nan was, in some hazy degree,
Gale's cousin.

The energetic piano thumped the strains of a
two-step. Gale Morgan extended his arm toward
Nan; she looked very slight at his side. But
instead of taking her position, she drew back,
looking up and frowning as she seemed to speak
objectingly to Gale. De Spain saw her hesitation without catching its import. The talkative
woman near at hand was more divining. "Lord,
that Nan Morgan makes me tired," she exclaimed to her gum-chewing companion, "ever
see anything like her? First she wouldn't dance
unless the floor was cleared—Sleepy Cat folks
ain't good enough for them Music Mountain
cattle thieves! And now the music doesn't suit
her. Listen to that boob of a boy trying one
piece after another to get one to suit my outlaw
lady. Nerve!"

But while the impatient woman chafed the

right tune was found, and Nan Morgan's face, as she watched the manipulator of the piano, brightened. "Faster!" she cried under her breath, taking her position on her cousin's arm. Then, responding with a sort of fiery impatience to her partner's guiding, she caught the rapid step of the music, and together the two swept down the floor.

Whatever the impatience of the crowd over the finicky start, the spectators soon showed their admiration of the dancing with unrestrained handclapping, and followed with approving outcries. De Spain, standing apart, watched Nan's flying feet, wondering how she and her people could possibly be what they were painted, and whether they really were so or not. Every swaying step, every agile turn proved how sure she was of herself, and how perfectly her body answered to every exaction of the quick movement of the dance. Gale Morgan seemed the merest attendant for his partner, who, with quickened pulses, gave herself up more and more to the lively call of the music.

Once the two swung away out, near to de Spain's corner. As Nan whirled by, de Spain, either with the infection of the music or from her nearness to him, caught his breath. His eyes riveted themselves on her flushed face as she

passed—oblivious of his presence—and he recalled how in the morning she had handled her
rifle in the same quick, sure way. De Spain
could not dance at all; but no one could successfully accuse him of not knowing how to handle
any sort of a gun. It was only now, as she came
so very close to him for the first time since the
mortification of the morning, and he saw the
smoothness of her pink-brown cheeks, that he
could ungrudgingly give her full credit for shooting him down. He forgave her, unasked, the
humiliation she had put on him. He felt an impulse to go up to her—now that she had stopped
dancing—and congratulate her honestly, instead
of boorishly as he had done at the match, and to
say, unreservedly, that she was the better shot—
indeed, one of the best he had ever seen.

But while he thought all of this he did not stir
a step. The two dancers at once disappeared,
and a new and rougher party crowded out on the
floor.

"Now, isn't that a pretty bunch!" exclaimed
the critical woman again. "That's the Calabasas
gang. Look at those four men with the red neck-
erchiefs. Sandusky, that big fellow, with the
crooked jaw—Butch, they call him—and his
jaw's not half as crooked as Sandusky himself,
either. He couldn't lie in bed straight. And

The Thief River Stage Line

Harvey Logan, with his black hair plastered over his eyes. Why, for one drink those two fellows would turn loose on this crowd and kill half a dozen. And there's two of Duke Morgan's cowboys with them, boozing old Bull Page, and that squint-eyed Sassoon—he's worse than the others, that fellow—a fine bunch to allow in this town."

De Spain had excellent ears. He had heard of these Calabasas men—of Sandusky and of the little fellow, Logan. They had much more than a local reputation as outlaws; they were known from one end of the Superstition Range to the other as evil-doers of more than ordinary ruthlessness. De Spain, from force of habit, studied every detail of their make-up. Both showed more than traces of drink, and both securing partners joined rudely in the dancing. It had become second nature to de Spain to note even insignificant details concerning men, and he took an interest in and remarked how very low Logan carried his gun in front of his hip. Sandusky's holster was slung higher and farther back on the side. Logan wore a tan shirt and khaki. Sandusky, coatless, was dressed in a white shirt, with a red tie, and wore a soiled, figured waistcoat fastened at the bottom by a cut-glass button.

The Sleepy Cat gossip commented on how much money these men had been spending all day.

She wondered aloud, reckless apparently of consequences, who had been robbed, lately, to provide it. Her companion scolded her for stirring up talk that might make trouble; averred she didn't believe half the stories she heard; asserted that these men lived quietly at Calabasas, minding their own affairs. "And they're kind to poor folks, too." "Sure," grimaced the obdurate one, "with other people's money." De Spain had no difficulty in placing the two women. One was undoubtedly the wife of a railroad man, who hated the mountain outlaws, and the other was, with equal certainty, a town sympathizer with slandered men, and the two represented the two community elements in Sleepy Cat.

De Spain, discontented, turning again into Main Street, continued on toward the Thief River stage barn. He knew an old Scotch Medicine Bend barnman that worked there, a boyhood friend; but the man, McAlpin, was out. After looking the horses over and inspecting the wagons with a new but mild curiosity, awakened by Jeffries's proposal, de Spain walked back toward the station. He had virtually decided not to take the job that Jeffries painted as so attractive, and resolved now to take the night train back to Medicine Bend. Medicine Bend was his home. He knew every man, woman, and child in the town. Before the tragic death of his father, his mother had lived there, and de Spain had grown up in the town and gone to school there. He was a railroad man, anyway—a modest trainmaster— and not eager for stage-line management.

The prospect of reducing the Sinks to a law-and-order basis at his own proper risk could not be alluring to the most aggressive of law-and-order men—and de Spain was not aggressive. Yet within a moment of his sensible decision he was . to be hurried by a mere accident to an exactly contrary fate.

As he passed Grant Street again he encountered a party on horseback heading for the river bridge. Trotting their horses leisurely, they turned the corner directly in front of de Spain. There were five in the company. Three of the men were riding abreast and a little ahead. Of these, the middle horseman was a spare man of forty years, with a black military hat, and a frankly disreputable air. His face was drawn up into a one-sided smile, marked by a deep, vertical wrinkle running up, close to his nose, from the corner of his mouth almost to the inner corner of his eye. Satt Morgan's smile was habitual and lessened his stern aspect. At his right rode his cousin, Duke Morgan, older, shorter, and stouter. His square, heavy-jawed, smooth-shaven face was lighted by hard, keen eyes, and finished by an uncompromising chin. Duke was the real head of the clan, of which there were numerous branches in the Superstition Mountains, all looking with friendliness or enmity to the Morgans of Morgan's Gap.

The yellow-haired man riding on the left, with a red face and red-lidded, squinting eyes, was in stature something between the two Morgans, and about the age of the elder cousin. His shoulders slouched, and he showed none of the blood of his companions. But this man, David Sassoon, the Calabasas gambler, quondam cowboy, and chronic brawler, stood in some way close to the different Morgans, and was reputed to have got each of them, at different times, out of more than one troublesome affair, either by sheer force of arms, or through his resourceful cunning.

These men were followed by a younger man riding with a very young woman. De Spain knew none of the front-rank men, but he knew well Nan Morgan and her dancing partner.

They were talking together, and Nan seemed from her manner at odds with her companion. He appeared to be trying to laugh the situation off when he caught sight of de Spain pausing for them to pass. Gale's face lighted as he set eyes on him, and he spoke quickly to Nan. De Spain could not at first hear his words, but he needed no ears to interpret his laugh and the expression on his face. Nan, persistently importuned, looked around. She saw de Spain, much closer, it would seem, than she had expected to see a man looking directly at her, and her eyes rested on him only a moment. The substance of her cousin's words she apparently had not caught, and he repeated them in a louder voice: "There's your handsome Medicine Bend gunman!"

Nan, glancing again toward de Spain, seemed aware that he heard. She looked away. De Spain tightened up with a rage. The blood rushed to his face, the sarcasm struck in. If the birthmark could have deepened with humiliation it would have done so at the instant of the cold inspection of the girl's pretty eyes. But he cared less for Nan's inspection, cold as it was, than for the jibe of her satisfied cousin. Not content, Gale, calling ahead to the others, invited their attention to the man on the street corner. De Spain felt minded to hurl an insult at them in a body. It would have been four to one—rather awkward odds even if they were mounted—and there was a woman. But he only stood still, returning their inspection as insolently as silence could. Each face was faithfully photographed and filed in his memory, and his steady gaze fol-

lowed them until they rode down the hill and
clattered jauntily out on the swaying suspension
bridge that still crosses the Rat River at Grant
Street, and connects the whole south country—
the Spanish Sinks, the Thief River gold-fields, the
saw-toothed Superstition Range, Morgan's Gap,
and Music Mountain with Sleepy Cat and the
railroad.

De Spain, walking down Grant Street, watched
the party disappear among the hills across the
river. The encounter had stirred him. He already hated the Morgans, at least all except the
blue-eyed girl, and she, it was not difficult to
divine from her expression, was, at least, disdain-
ful of her morning rival.

Reaching the station platform while still busy
with his thoughts, de Spain encountered Jeffries
and Lefever.

"When are you coming up to take my job,
Henry?" demanded the superintendent without
any parley.

"I am not coming up," announced de Spain
bluntly.

"Not coming up, eh? All right, we'll find
somebody that will come up," retorted Jeffries.
"John," he added, "wire Medicine Bend to send
Farrell Kennedy here in the morning to see me."

"What's the reason that fellow sticks so close

to Medicine Bend?" demanded Jeffries, when Lefever joined him later in his office.

"Don't ask me," frowned Lefever perplexed. "Don't ask me. Henry is odd in some ways. You can't tell what's going on inside that fellow's head by looking at the outside of it." Jeffries grunted coldly at this bit of wisdom. "I'll tell you what I should think—if I had to think: Henry de Spain has never found out rightly who was responsible for the death of his father. He expects to do it, sometime; and he thinks sometime he's going to find out right there in Medicine Bend."

While they were talking the train was pulling out for Medicine Bend with de Spain on board.

It was a tedious ride, and de Spain was much too engaged with his thoughts to sleep. The Morgans were in his head, and he could not be rid of them. He recalled having been told that long ago some of these same Morgans lived on the Peace River above his father's ranch. Every story he had ever heard of their wild lives, for they were men sudden in quarrel and reckless of sequel, came back to his mind. He wondered what sort of a young girl this could be who lived among them—who *could* live among them—and be what she seemed at a glance to be—a fawn among mountain-wolves.

It was late when he reached Medicine Bend, and raining—a dismal kind of a night. Instead of going to his room, just across the street from the station, he went up-stairs and sat down with the train-despatchers. After an hour of indecision, marked by alternative fits of making up and unmaking his mind, he went, instead of going to bed, into the telegraph-room, where black-haired Dick Grady sat at a key.

"How about the fight to-night at Sleepy Cat?" Grady asked at once.

"What fight?" demanded de Spain perfunctorily.

"The Calabasas gang got to going again up there to-night. They say one of the Morgans was in it. Some town, that Sleepy Cat, eh, Henry?"

"What Morgan was in it?"

"Gale Morgan. A lot of stuff came in on it an hour ago. Was there anything started when you left?"

"I didn't hear of anything," responded de Spain. But his indifference to the subject was marked.

"What's the matter?" demanded the operator. "Aren't you well to-night?"

"Perfectly."

"Sleepy?"

32

The Thief River Stage Line

De Spain roused himself. "Dick, have you got a Sleepy Cat wire open?"

"What do you want?"

"Tell Jeffries I'll take that Thief River stage job."

CHAPTER III

FROM a car window at Sleepy Cat may be seen, stretching far down into the southwest a chain of towering peaks, usually snow-clad, that dominate the desert in every direction for almost a hundred miles. In two extended groups, separated by a narrow but well-defined break, they constitute a magnificent rampart, named by Spaniards the Superstition Mountains, and they stretch beyond the horizon to the south, along the vast depression known locally as the Spanish Sinks. The break on the eastern side of the chain comes about twenty miles southwest of Sleepy Cat, and is marked on the north by the most striking, and in some respects most majestic peak in the range—Music Mountain; the break itself has taken the name of its earliest white settlers, and is called Morgan's Gap. No railroad has ever yet penetrated this southern country, despite the fact that rich mines have been opened along these mountains, and are still being opened; but it lies to-day in much of the condition of primi-

34

tive savagery, and lawlessness, as the word is conventionally accepted, that obtained when the first rush was made for the Thief River goldfields.

It is not to be understood that law is an unknown equation between Calabasas and Thief River, or even between Calabasas and Sleepy Cat. But as statute law it suffers so many infractions as to be hardly recognizable in the ordinary sense. Business is done in this country; but business must halt everywhere with its means of communication, and in the Music Mountain country it still rests on the facilities of a stage line. The stage line is a big and vigorous affair, a perfectly organized railroad adjunct with the best horses, the best wagons, the best freighting outfits that money can supply.

But this is by no means, in its civilizing effect, a railroad. A railroad drives lawlessness before it—the Music Mountain country still leans on stage-line law. The bullion wagons still travel the difficult roads. They look for safety to their armed horsemen; the four and six horse stages look to the armed guard, the wayfarer must look to his horse—and it should be a good one; the mountain rancher to his rifle, the cattle thief to the moonless night, the bandit to his wits, the gunman to his holster: these include practically all of the people that travel the Spanish Sinks, except the Morgans and the Mormons. The Mormons looked to the Morgans for safety; the Morgans to themselves.

For many a year the Morgans have been almost overlords of the Music Mountain country. They own, or have laid claim to, an extended territory in the mountains, a Spanish grant. One of the first mountain Morgans married a Spanish girl, and during the early days, when the Morgans were not fighting some one out of court, they were fighting some one in court on their endless and involved titles.

But whether they won domain in lawsuit or lost it, one pearl of their holdings they never submitted to the jurisdiction of any tribunal other than their own arms. Morgan's Gap opens south of Music Mountain, less than ten miles west of Calabasas. It is a narrow valley where valleys are more precious than water—for the mountain valley means water—and this in a country where water is much more precious than life. And some of the best of this land at the foot of Music Mountain was the maternal inheritance of Nan Morgan.

At Calabasas the Thief River stage line maintains completely equipped relay barns. They are over twenty miles from Sleepy Cat, but nearly fifty the other way from Thief River. The un-

equal division is not due to what was desirable
when the route was laid out, but to the limit of
what man could do in the never-conquered desert.
This supplies at Calabasas a spring, to tempt the
unwary traveller still farther within its clutches.
A large number of horses are kept at Calabasas,
and the barn crews are quartered there in a company barrack. Along the low ridges and in the
shallow depressions about Calabasas Spring there
are a very few widely separated shacks, once built
by freighters and occupied by squatter outlaws
to be within reach of water. This gives the vicin-
ity something of the appearance of a poorly
sustained prairie-dog town. And except these
shacks, there is nothing between Calabasas, Thief
River, and the mountains except sunshine and
alkali. I say nothing, meaning especially nothing in the way of a human habitation.

But there is a queer inn at Calabasas. A pi-
oneer Thief River prospector, mad with thirst,
fought his way across the Sinks to the Calabasas
Spring, and wandered thence one day into Sleepy
Cat. In a delirium of gratitude he ordered built
at Calabasas what he termed a hotel, to provide
at that forbidden oasis for the luxurious comfort
of future thirst-mad wanderers. It was built of
lumber hauled a thousand miles, and equipped
with luxuries brought three thousand—a fearsome,

rambling structure, big enough for all the prospectors in the Rocky Mountains.

Having built this monument, creditable to his good-will rather than his good sense, the unfortunate man went really mad, and had the sorry distinction of being the first person to be put in the insane asylum at Bear Dance. It had never occurred to him that any one had any title to, or that any madder man would lay any claim to, so accursed a spot as Calabasas. But old Duke Morgan announced in due time that the hotel was built on Morgan land, and belonged to the Morgans. Nobody outside a madhouse could be found to dispute with Duke Morgan a title to land within ten miles of Morgan's Gap, and none but a lunatic would attempt to run a hotel at Calabasas, anyway. However, a solution of the difficulty was found: Duke's colorable title gave the cue to his retainers in the Gap, and in time they carted away piecemeal most of the main building, leaving for years the kitchen and the servants' quarters adjoining it to owls, lizards, scorpions, and spiders.

Meantime, to tap the fast-developing gold-fields, the freight route and stages had been put in, and the barns built at Calabasas. A need naturally developed for at least one feature of a hotel—a barroom. A newer lunatic answered the

The Spanish Sinks

call of civilization—a man only mildly insane stocked the kitchen range with liquors, and fitted up in a crude way the ice-boxes—where there never was ice—serving pantries, and other odd nooks for sleeping quarters. Here the thirsty stage passenger, little suspecting the origin of the facilities offered him for a drink, may choose strong drink instead of water—or rather, he is restricted to strong drink where water might once have been had—the spring being piped now half a mile to the barns for the horses. And this shack, as it is locally called, run by a Mexican, is still the inn at Calabasas. And it continues to contribute, through its stirring annals, to the tragic history of the continental divide.

It need hardly be said that Duke Morgan laid claim also to the Calabasas Spring. But on this the company, being a corporation, fought him. And after somewhat less of argument and somewhat more of siege and shooting, a compromise was reached whereby the company bought annually at an exorbitant price all of Duke, Satterlee, and Vance Morgan's hay, and as the Morgans had small rivers of water in the mountains, and never, except when crowded, drank water, a *modus vivendi* was arranged between the claimants. The only sufferer through this was the Mexican publican, who found every Morgan his landlord, and demanding from him tithes over the bar. But force is usually met with cunning, and such Morgans as would not pay in advance at Calabasas, when thirsty, often found the half-mad publican out of goods.

The Calabasas Inn stood in one of the loneliest canyons of the whole seventy miles between Sleepy Cat and Thief River; it looked in its depletion to be what it was, a sombre, mysterious, sun, wind, and alkali beaten pile, around which no one by any chance ever saw a sign of life. It was a ruin like those pretentious deserted structures sometimes seen in frontier towns—relics of the wide-open days, which stand afterward, stark and sombre, to serve as bats' nests or blind-pigs. The inn at Calabasas looked its part—a haunt of rustlers, a haven of nameless men, a refuge of road-agents.

The very first time de Spain made an inspection trip over the stage line with Lefever, he was conscious of the sinister air of this lonely building. He and Lefever had ridden down from the barn, while their horses were being changed, to look at the place. De Spain wanted to look over everything connected in any way, however remotely, with the operation of his wagons, and this joint, Lefever had told him, was where the freighters and drivers were not infrequently robbed of

their money. It was here that one of their own
men, Bill McCarty, once "scratched a man's
neck" with a knife—which, Bill explained, he just
"happened" to have in his hand—for cheating at
cards. Lefever pointed out the unlucky gambler's
grave as he and de Spain rode into the canyon
toward the inn.

Not a sign of any sort was displayed about the
habitation. No man was invited to enter, no
man warned to keep out, none was anywhere in
sight. The stage men dismounted, threw their
lines, pushed open the front door of the house and
entered a room of perhaps sixteen by twenty feet.
It had been the original barroom. A long, high,
elaborately carved mahogany bar, as much out of
keeping as it possibly could be with its surroundings, stretched across the farther side of the room.
The left end, as they faced the bar, was brought
around to escape a small window opening on a
court or patio to the rear of the room. Back of
the bar itself, about midway, a low door in the
bare wall gave entrance to a rear room. Aside
from this big, queer-looking piece of mahogany,
the low window at the left end of it, and the low
door at the back, the room presented nothing but
walls. Two windows flanking the front door
helped to light it, but not a mirror, picture, chair,
table, bottle, or glass was to be seen. De Spain

covered every feature of the interior at a glance. "Quiet around here, John," he remarked casually.

"This is the quietest place in the Rocky Mountains most of the time. But when it is noisy, believe me, it is noisy. Look at the bullet-holes in the walls."

"The old story," remarked de Spain, inspecting with mild-mannered interest the punctured plastering, "they always shoot high."

He walked over to the left end of the bar, noting the hard usage shown by the ornate mahogany, and spreading his hands wide open, palms down, on the face of it, glanced at the low window on his left, opening on the gravelled patio. He peered, in the semidarkness, at the battered door behind the bar.

"Henry," observed Lefever, "if you are looking for a drink, it would only be fair, as well as politic, to call the Mexican."

"Thank you, John, I'm not looking for one. And I know you don't drink."

"You want to know, then, where the Mexican keeps his gun?" hazarded Lefever.

"Not especially. I just want to know——"

"Everything."

"What's behind the bar. That's natural, isn't it?"

Very complete fittings and compartments told

The Spanish Sinks

of the labor spent in preparing this inner side for the convenience of the bartender and the requirements of exacting patrons, but nothing in the way of equipment, not so much as a pewter spoon, lay anywhere visible.

De Spain, turning, looked all around the room again. "You wouldn't think," he said slowly, "from looking at the place there was a road-agent within a thousand miles."

"You wouldn't think, from riding through the Superstition Mountains there was a lion within a thousand miles. I've hunted them for eleven years, and I never saw one except when the dogs drove 'em out; but for eleven years they saw me. If we haven't been seen coming in here by some of this Calabasas bunch, I miss my guess," declared Lefever cheerfully.

The batten door behind the bar now began to open slowly and noiselessly. Lefever peered through it. "Come in, Pedro," he cried reassuringly, "come in, man. This is no officer, no revenue agent looking for your license. Meet a friend, Pedro," he continued encouragingly, as the swarthy publican, low-browed and sullen, emerged very deliberately from the inner darkness into the obscurity of the barroom, and bent his one good eye searchingly on de Spain. "This," Lefever's left hand lay familiarly on the back of de Spain's shoulder, "is our new manager, Mr. Henry de Spain. Henry, shake hands with Mexico."

This invitation to shake hands seemed an empty formality. De Spain never shook hands with anybody; at least if he did so, he extended, through habit long inured, his left hand, with an excuse for the soreness of his right. Pedro did not even bat his remaining eye at the invitation. The situation, as Lefever facetiously remarked, remained about where it was before he spoke, and nothing daunted, he asked de Spain what he would drink. De Spain sidestepped again by asking for a cigar. Lefever, professing he would not drink alone, called for cigarettes. While Pedro produced them, from nowhere apparently, as a conjurer picks cards out of the air, the sound of galloping horses came through the open door. A moment later three men walked, single file, into the room. De Spain stood at the left end of the bar, and Lefever introduced him to Gale Morgan, to David Sassoon, and to Sassoon's crony, Deaf Sandusky, as the new stage-line manager. The later arrivals lined up before the bar, Sandusky next to Lefever and de Spain, so he could hear what was said. Pedro from his den produced two queer-looking bottles and a supply of glasses.

"De Spain," Gale Morgan began bluntly, "one

The Spanish Sinks

of our men was put off a stage of yours last week by Frank Elpaso." He spoke without any preliminary compliments, and his heavy voice was bellicose.

De Spain, regarding him undisturbed, answered after a little pause: "Elpaso told me he put a man off his stage last week for fighting."

"No," contradicted Morgan loudly, "not for fighting. Elpaso was drunk."

"What's the name of the man Elpaso put off, John?" asked de Spain, looking at Lefever.

Morgan hooked his thumb toward the man standing at his side. "Here's the man right here, Dave Sassoon."

Sassoon never looked a man in the face when the man looked at him, except by implication; it was almost impossible, without surprising him, to catch his eyes with your eyes. He seemed now to regard de Spain keenly, as the latter, still attending to Morgan's statement, replied: "Elpaso tells a pretty straight story."

"Elpaso couldn't tell a straight story if he tried," interjected Sassoon.

"I have the statement of three other passengers; they confirm Elpaso. According to them, Sassoon—" de Spain looked straight at the accused, "was drunk and abusive, and kept trying to put some of the other passengers off. Finally

45

he put his feet in the lap of Pumperwasser, our tank and windmill man, and Pumperwasser hit him."

Morgan, stepping back from the bar, waved his hand with an air of finality toward his inoffensive companion: "Here is Sassoon, right here—he can tell the whole story."

"Those fellows were miners," muttered Sassoon. His utterance was broken, but he spoke fast. "They'll side with the guards every time against a cattleman."

"There's only one fair thing to do, de Spain," declared Morgan. He looked severely at de Spain: "Discharge Elpaso."

De Spain, his hands resting on the bar, drew one foot slowly back. "Not on the showing I have now," he said. "One of the passengers who joined in the statement is Jeffries, the railroad superintendent at Sleepy Cat."

"Expect a railroad superintendent to tell the truth about a Calabasas man?" demanded Sassoon.

"I should expect him at least to be sober," retorted de Spain.

"Sassoon," interposed Morgan belligerently, "is a man whose word can always be depended on."

"To convey his meaning," intervened Lefever

cryptically. "Of course, I know," he asserted, earnest to the point of vehemence. "Every one in Calabasas has the highest respect for Sassoon. That is understood. And," he added with as much impressiveness as if he were talking sense, "everybody in Calabasas would be sorry to see Sassoon put off a stage. But Sassoon is off: that is the situation. We are sorry. If it occurs again——"

"What do you mean?" thundered Morgan, resenting the interference. "De Spain is the manager, isn't he? What we want to know is, what you are going to do about it?" he demanded, addressing de Spain again.

"There is nothing more to be done," returned de Spain composedly. "I've already told Elpaso if Sassoon starts another fight on a stage to put him off again."

Morgan's fist came down on the bar. "Look here, de Spain! You come from Medicine Bend, don't you? Well, you can't bully Music Mountain men—understand that."

"Any time you have a real grievance, Morgan, I'll be glad to consider it," said de Spain. "When one of your men is drunk and quarrelsome he will be put off like any other disturber. That we can't avoid. Public stages can't be run any other way."

"All right," retorted Morgan. "If you take that tack for your new management, we'll see how you get along running stages down in this country."

"We will run them peaceably, just as long as we can," smiled de Spain. "We will get on with everybody that gives us a chance."

Morgan pointed a finger at him. "I give you a chance, de Spain, right now. Will you discharge Elpaso?"

"No."

Morgan almost caught his breath at the refusal. But de Spain could be extremely blunt, and in the parting shots between the two he gave no ground.

"Jeffries put me here to stop this kind of rowdyism on the stages," he said to Lefever on their way back to the barn. "This is a good time to begin. And Sassoon and Gale Morgan are good men to begin with," he added.

As the horses of the two men emerged from the canyon they saw a slender horsewoman riding in toward the barn from the Music Mountain trail. She stopped in front of McAlpin, the barn boss, who stood outside the office door. McAlpin, the old Medicine Bend barnman, had been promoted from Sleepy Cat by the new manager. De Spain recognized the roan pony, but, aside

The Spanish Sinks

from that, a glance at the figure of the rider, as she sat with her back to him, was enough to assure him of Nan Morgan. He spurred ahead fast enough to overhear a request she was making of McAlpin to mail a letter for her. She also asked McAlpin, just as de Spain drew up, whether the down stage had passed. McAlpin told her it had. De Spain, touching his hat, spoke: "I am going right up to Sleepy Cat. I'll mail your letter if you wish."

She looked at him in some surprise, and then glanced toward Lefever, who now rode up. De Spain was holding out his hand for the letter. His eyes met Nan's, and each felt the moment was a sort of challenge. De Spain, a little self-conscious under her inspection, was aware only of her rather fearless eyes and the dark hair under her fawn cowboy hat.

"Thank you," she responded evenly. "If the stage is gone I will hold it to add something." So saying, she tucked the letter inside her blouse and spoke to her pony, which turned leisurely down the road.

"I'm trying to get acquainted with your country to-day," returned de Spain, managing with his knee to keep his own horse moving alongside Nan as she edged away.

She seemed disinclined to answer, but the silence

and the awkwardness of his presence drew at
length a dry disclaimer: "This is not my country."

"I understood," exclaimed de Spain, following
his doubtful advantage, "you lived out this way."

"I live near Music Mountain," returned Nan
somewhat ungraciously, using her own skill at the
same time to walk her horse away from her unwelcome companion.

"I've heard of Music Mountain," continued de
Spain, urging his lagging steed. "I've often
wanted to get over there to hunt."

Nan, without speaking, ruthlessly widened the
distance between the two. De Spain unobtru-
sively spurred his steed to greater activity. "You
must have a great deal of game around you. Do
you hunt?" he asked.

He knew she was famed as a huntress, but he
could make no headway whatever against her
studied reserve. He watched her hands, graceful
even in heavy gloves; he noticed the neck-piece
of her tan blouse, and liked the brown throat
and the chin set so resolutely against him. He
surmised that she perhaps felt some contempt for
him because she had outshot him, and he continued to ask about game, hoping for a chance in
some far-off time to redeem his marksmanship
before her and giving her every possible chance to

invite him to try the hunting around Music Mountain.

She was deaf to the broadest hints; and when at length she excused herself and turned her pony from the Sleepy Cat road into the Morgan Gap trail, de Spain had been defeated in every attempt to arouse the slightest interest in anything he had said. But, watching with regret, at the parting, the trim lines of her figure as she dashed away on the desert trail, seated as if a part of her spirited horse, he felt only a fast-rising resolution to attempt again to break through her stubborn reticence and know her better.

CHAPTER IV

FIRST BLOOD AT CALABASAS

NOTHING more than de Spain's announcement that he would sustain his stage-guards was necessary to arouse a violent resentment at Calabasas and among the Morgan following. Some of the numerous disaffected were baiting the stages most of the time. They bullied the guards, fought the passengers, and fomented discontent among the drivers. In all Thief River disturbances, whether a raid on cattlemen, a stage hold-up, a gun fight, or a tedious war of words, the Calabasas men, sometimes apparently for the mere maintaining of prestige, appeared to take leading rôles. After de Spain's declaration the grievance against Elpaso was made a general one along the line. His stage was singled out and ridden at times both by Sandusky and Logan— the really dangerous men of the Spanish Sinks— and by Gale Morgan and Sassoon to stir up trouble.

But old Frank Elpaso was far from being a fool. A fight with any one of these men meant

First Blood at Calabasas

that somebody would be killed, and no one could tell just who, Elpaso shrewdly reckoned, until the roll-call at the end of it. He therefore met truculence with diplomacy, threatening looks with flattery, and hard words with a long story. Moreover, all Calabasas knew that Elpaso, if he had to, would fight, and that the eccentric guard was not actually to be cornered with impunity. Even Logan, who, like Sandusky, was known to be without fear and without mercy, felt at least a respect for Elpaso's shortened shotgun, and stopped this side actual hostilities with him. When the June clean-up of the No. 2 Thief River mine came through—one hundred and six thousand dollars in gold bullion under double guard—and a Calabasas contingent of night-riders tried to stop the treasure, rumor along the Sinks had it that Elpaso's slugs, delivered at the right moment, were responsible for Deaf Sandusky's long illness at Bear Dance, and the failure of the subsequent masked attack on the up stage.

Sassoon, however, owing to the indignity now put upon him, also nourished a particular grievance against the meditative guard, and his was one not tempered either by prudence or calculation. His chance came one night when Elpaso had unwisely allowed himself to be drawn into a card game at Calabasas Inn. Elpaso was no-

toriously a stickler for a square deal at cards.
He was apparently the only man at Calabasas
that hoped for such a thing, and certainly the
only one so rash as to fight for it—yet he always
did. A dispute on this occasion found him without a friend in the room. Sassoon reached for
him with a knife.

McAlpin was the first to get the news at the
barn. He gave first aid to the helpless guard, and,
without dreaming he could be got to a surgeon
alive, rushed him in a light wagon to the hospital
at Sleepy Cat, where it was said that he must
have more lives than a wildcat. Sassoon, not
caring to brave de Spain's anger in town, went
temporarily into hiding. A second surgeon was
brought from Medicine Bend, and heroic efforts
were put forth to nurse again into life the feeble
spark the assassin had left in the unlucky guard.

Word of this cutting reached de Spain at Thief
River. He started for Calabasas, learned there
during a brief stop what he could—which was, of
course, next to nothing—of the affray, and posted
on to Sleepy Cat.

A conference was held in Jeffries's office. De
Spain, Lefever, and some of the division staff discussed the situation raised by the affair. De
Spain was instructed to see that Sassoon was
brought in and made an example of for the bene-

fit of his Calabasas friends. Accordingly, while the guard's life hung in the balance, the sheriff, Jim Druel, was despatched after Sassoon. A great deal of inquiry, much riding, and a lot of talk on Druel's part accomplished nothing.

Lefever spoiled with impatience to get after Sassoon. "The only way we'll ever get one of that gang is to go for him ourselves," said he. The sheriff's campaign did collapse. Sassoon could not be found although rumor was notorious that he continued to haunt Calabasas. Lefever's irritation grew. "Never mind, John," counselled de Spain, "forget about wanting him. Sometime one of us will stumble on him, and when we do we'll shackle him." The precaution was taken, meantime, to secure a warrant for the missing man, together with authority for either of the two to serve it. Elpaso, in the end, justified his old reputation by making a recovery— haltingly, it is true, and with perilous intervals of sinking, but a recovery.

It was while he still lay in the hospital and hope was very low that de Spain and Lefever rode, one hot morning, into Calabasas and were told by McAlpin that Sassoon had been seen within five minutes at the inn. To Lefever the news was like a bubbling spring to a thirsty man. His face beamed, he tightened his belt, shook out

his gun, and looked with benevolent interest on
de Spain, who stood pondering. "If you will
stay right here, Henry," he averred convincingly,
"I will go over and get Sassoon."

The chief stage-guard, Bob Scott, the Indian,
was in the barn. He smiled at Lefever's enthu-
siasm. "Sassoon," said he, "is slippery."

"You'd better let us go along and see you do
it," suggested de Spain, who with the business in
hand grew thoughtful.

"Gentlemen, I thank you," protested Lefever,
raising one hand in deprecation, the other resting
lightly on his holster. "We still have some *little*
reputation to maintain along the Sinks. Don't
let us make it a *posse* for *Sassoon*." No one opposed him further, and he rode away alone.

"It won't be any trouble for John to bring Sassoon in," murmured Scott, who spoke with a
smile and in the low tone and deliberate manner
of the Indian, "if he can find him."

With de Spain Scott remained in front of the
barn, saddled horses in hand. They could see
nothing of the scene of action, and de Spain was
forced in idleness to curb his impatience. Lefever rode down to the inn without seeing a living
thing anywhere about it. When he dismounted
in front he thought he heard sounds within the
barroom, but, pushing open the door and looking

First Blood at Calabasas

circumspectly into the room before entering, he was surprised to find it empty.

There was something, under the circumstances and in the stimulus of danger, almost uncanny in the silence, the absence of any life whatever about the place. Lefever walked cautiously inside; there seemed no need of caution. No one was there to confront or oppose him. Surveying the interior with a rapid glance, he walked to the left end of the bar and, gun in readiness, looked apprehensively behind it. Not so much as a strainer was to be seen underneath. He noticed, however, that the sash of the low window on his left, which looked into the patio, was open, and two heel-marks in the hard clay suggested that a man might have jumped through. Whether these were Sassoon's heels or another's, Lefever decided they constituted his clew, and, running out of the front door, he sprang into his saddle and rode to where he could signal de Spain and Scott to come up.

He told his story as they joined him, and the three returned to the inn. Scott rode directly to the rear. Lefever took de Spain in to the bar, showed him the open sash, and pointed to the heel-prints. De Spain stepped through the window, Lefever following. An examination showed the slide of a spur-rowel behind one heel-mark and indications of a hasty jump.

While they bent over the signs that seemed to connect their quarry with the place, a door opened across the courtyard, and Pedro appeared. He was curiously dense to all inquiries, and Lefever, convinced that Sassoon was somewhere at hand, revenged himself by searching the place.

In the dark kitchen a very old woman and a slovenly girl were at work. No one else was to be found anywhere.

De Spain, who was the more experienced tracker, thought he could follow the footprints to the arched opening across the patio. This was closed only by a swinging gate, and afforded easy escape from a pursuer. At some distance outside this gate, as de Spain threw it open, sat Bob Scott on his horse. De Spain made inquiry of Scott. No one had been seen. Returning to Lefever, who, greatly chagrined, had convinced himself that Sassoon had got away, de Spain called Scott into the patio.

A better tracker than either of his companions, Scott after a minute confirmed their belief that Sassoon must have escaped by the window. He then took the two men out to where some one, within a few minutes, had mounted a horse and galloped off.

"But where has he gone?" demanded Lefever,

pointing with his hand. "There is the road both ways for three miles." Scott nodded toward the snow-capped peak of Music Mountain. "Over to Morgan's, most likely. He knows no one would follow him into the Gap. Just for fun, now, let's see."

Dismounting, the Indian scrutinized the hoof-prints where the horse had stood. Getting into the saddle again, he led the way, bending over his horse's neck and stopping frequently to read the trail, half a mile out along the Gap road, until he could once more readily point out the hoof-prints to his companions. "That is Sassoon," he announced. "I know the heels. And I know he rides this horse; it belongs to Gale Morgan. Sassoon," Scott smiled sympathetically on Lefever, "is half-way to Morgan's Gap."

"After him!" cried Lefever hotly. De Spain looked inquiringly at the guard. Scott shook his head. "That would be all right, but there's two other Calabasas men in the Gap this afternoon it wouldn't be nice to mix with—Deaf Sandusky and Harvey Logan."

"We won't mix with them," suggested de Spain.

"If we tackle Sassoon, they'll mix with us," explained Scott. He reflected a moment. "They always stay at Gale Morgan's or Duke's. We might sneak Sassoon out without their getting on.

Sassoon knows he is safe in the Gap; but he'll hide even after he gets there. He takes two precautions for every other man's one. Sassoon is a wonder at hiding out. I've got the Thief River run this afternoon——"

De Spain looked at him. "Well?"

Scott's face softened into the characteristic smile—akin to a quiet grin—that it often wore. "If I didn't have to go through to-day, and the three of us could get to the Gap before daylight to-morrow morning, I would give Sassoon a run for his money in spite of the other fellows."

"Don't take your run this afternoon," directed de Spain. "Telephone Sleepy Cat for a substitute. Suppose we go back, get something to eat, and you two ride singly over toward the Gap this afternoon; lie outside under cover to see whether Sassoon or his friends leave before night —there's only one way out of the place, they tell me. Then I will join you, and we'll ride in before daylight, and perhaps catch him while everybody is asleep."

"If you do," predicted Scott, in his deliberate way of expressing a conclusion, "I think you'll get him."

It was so arranged.

CHAPTER V

ROUNDING UP SASSOON

D^E SPAIN joined his associates at dark outside the Gap. Neither Sassoon nor his friends had been seen. The night was still, the sky cloudless, and as the three men with a led horse rode at midnight into the mountains, the great red heart of the Scorpion shone afire in the southern sky. Spreading out when they rode between the mountain walls, they made their way without interruption silently toward their rendezvous, an aspen grove near which Purgatoire Creek makes its way out of the Gap and, cutting a deep gash along the edge of the range for a hundred miles, empties into the Thief.

Scott was the first to reach the trees. The little grove spreads across a slope half a mile wide between the base of one towering cliff, still bearing its Spanish name, El Capitan, and the gorge of the Purgatoire. To the east of this point the trails to Calabasas and to Sleepy Cat divide, and here Scott and Lefever received de Spain, who had ridden slowly and followed Scott's

injunctions to keep the red star to the right of
El Capitan all the way across the Sinks.

Securing their horses, the three stretched out
on the open ground to wait for daylight. De
Spain was wakeful, and his eyes rested with curiosity on the huge bulk of Music Mountain, rising
overwhelmingly above him. Through the Gap
that divided the great, sentinel-like front of El
Capitan, marking the northern face of the mountain rift, from Round Top, the south wall of the
opening, stars shone vividly, as if lighting the way
into the silent range beyond.

The breathing of his companions soon assured
de Spain that both were asleep. The horses were
quiet, and the night gave no sound save that
vaguely through the darkness came the faint brawl
of tiny cataracts tumbling down far mountain
heights. De Spain, lying on his side, his head
resting on his elbow, and his hands clasped at
the back of his neck, meditated first on how he
should capture Sassoon at daybreak, and then on
Nan Morgan and her mountain home, into which
he was about to break to drag out a criminal.
Sassoon and his malice soon drifted out of his
mind, but Nan remained. She stayed with him,
it seemed, for hours—appearing and disappearing,
in one aspect more alluring than another. Then
her form outlined in the mists that rose from the

Rounding Up Sassoon

hidden creek seemed to hover somewhere near until Scott's hand laid on the dreamer's shoulder drove it suddenly away. Day was at hand.

De Spain got up and shook off the chilliness and drowsiness of the night. It had been agreed that he, being less known in the Gap than either of his companions, could best attempt the difficult capture. It was strictly a *coup de main,* depending for its success on chance and nerve. The one that tried it might manage to bring out his man—or might be brought out himself. Between these alternatives there was not much middle ground, except that failing to find Sassoon, or in case he should be intercepted with his prisoner, the intruder, escaping single-handed from a shower of bullets, might still get away. But Morgan's Gap men were esteemed fairly good marksmen.

Bob Scott, who knew the recess well, repeated his explicit directions as to how de Spain was to reach Sassoon's shack. He repeated his description of its interior, told him where the bed stood, and even where Sassoon ordinarily kept his knife and his revolver. The western sky was still dark when de Spain, mounting, discussed the last arrangements with his scouts and, taking the bridle of the led horse, turned toward Round Top. At its narrowest point the Gap opening is barely two

63

miles wide, and the one road, in and out, lies among the rocks through this neck; toward it all trails inside the Gap converge. De Spain gave his horse his head—it was still too dark to distinguish the path—and depended on his towering landmarks for his general direction. He advanced at a snail's pace until he passed the base of El Capitan, when of a sudden, as he rode out from among high projecting rocks full into the opening, faint rays of light from the eastern dawn revealed the narrow, strangely enclosed and perfectly hidden valley before him. The eastern and southern sides still lay in darkness, but the stupendous cliffs frowning on the north and west were lighted somewhat from the east. The southern wall, though shrouded, seemed to rise in an unending series of beetling arêtes.

De Spain caught his breath. No description he had ever heard of the nook that screened the Morgans from the outside world had prepared him for what he saw. From side to side of the gigantic mountain fissure, it could hardly be, de Spain thought, more than a few thousand yards —so completely was his sense of proportion stunned by the frowning cliffs which rose, at points, half a mile into the sky. But it was actually several miles from wall to wall, and the Gap was more than as much in depth, as it ran back

Rounding Up Sassoon

to a mere wedge between unnamed Superstition peaks.

Every moment that he pushed ahead warned him that daylight would come suddenly and his time to act would be short. The trail he followed broadened into a road, and he strained his eyes for signs, first of life, and then of habitation. The little creek, now beside his way, flowed quietly albeit swiftly along, and his utmost vigilance could detect no living thing stirring; but a turn in the trail, marked by a large pine-tree and conforming to a bend of the stream, brought him up startled and almost face to face with a long, rambling ranch-house. The gable end of the two-story portion of the building was so close to him that he instantly reined up to seek hiding from its upper and lower windows.

From Scott's accurate description he knew the place. This was Duke Morgan's ranch-house, set as a fortress almost at the mouth of the Gap. To pass it unobserved was to compass the most ticklish part of his mission, and without changing his slow pace he rode on, wondering whether a bullet, if fired from any of the low, open windows —which he could almost throw his hat into as he trotted past—would knock him off his horse or leave him a chance to spur away. But no bullet challenged him and no sound came from the

65

silent house. He cantered away from the peril, thinking with a kind of awe of Nan, asleep, so close, under that roof—confident, too, he had not been seen—though, in matter of fact, he had been.

He quickened his pace. The place he wanted to reach was more than a mile distant. Other cabins back toward the north wall could be seen dimly to his right, but all were well removed from his way. He found, in due time, the ford in the creek, as Scott had advised, made it without mishap, scrambled up a steep and rocky path, and saw confronting him, not far ahead, a small, ruinous-looking cabin shack. Dismounting before this, he threw his lines, shook himself a little, and walked up to the cabin door. It was open.

The mild-minded conspirators who had planned the details of the abduction were agreed that if the effort could be made a success at all, there was but one way to effect it, and that was to act, in every step, openly. Any attempt to steal on Sassoon unawares would be a desperate one; while to walk boldly into his cabin at daybreak would be to do only what his companions were likely at any time to do, and was the course least calculated to lead to serious trouble. None of the three were unaware of the psychological action of that peculiar instinct of danger possessed by men habitually exposed to surprise—they knew how easily it may be aroused in a sleeper by the unusual happening about him, and how cunningly it is allayed by counterfeiting within his hearing the usual course of normal events.

De Spain, following the chosen policy, called gruffly to the cabin inmate. There was no answer. All had sounded extremely plausible to de Spain at the time he listened to Bob Scott's ingenious anticipation of the probabilities, and he had felt while listening to the subtle Indian that the job was not a complicated one.

But now, as he hitched his trouser band near to the butt of his revolver with his right hand, and laid his left on the jamb of the door with an effort to feel at home, stepped unevenly across the threshold, and tried to peer into the interior darkness, Scott's strategy did not, for some reason, commend itself quite so convincingly to him. There seemed, suddenly, a great many chances for a slip in the programme. De Spain coughed slightly, his eyes meantime boring the darkness to the left, where Sassoon's bed should be. The utmost scrutiny failed to disclose any sign of it or any sound of breathing from that corner. He took a few steps toward where the man should be asleep, and perceived beyond a doubt that there was no bed in the corner at all. He turned toward the other corner, his hand covering the butt of his gun. "Hello, Shike!" he called out in a slightly strained tone of camaraderie, addressing Sassoon by a common nickname. Then he listened. A trumpeting snore answered. No sound was ever sweeter to de Spain's ear. The rude noise cleared the air and steadied the intruder as if Music Mountain itself had been lifted off his nerves.

He tried again: "Where are you, Shike?" he growled. "What's this stuff on the floor?" he continued, shuffling his way ostentatiously to the other side of the room. But his noise-making was attended with the utmost caution. He had dropped, like a shot, flat on the floor and crawled, feeling his way, to the opposite side of the room, only to find, after much trouble, that the bed in the darkness was there, but it was empty. De Spain rose. For a moment he was nonplussed. An inside room remained, but Scott had said there was no bed within it. He felt his way toward the inner door. This was where he expected to find it, and it was closed. He laid a hand gingerly on the latch. "Where are you, Shike?" he demanded again, this time with an impatient expletive summoned for the occasion. A second fearful snore answered him. De Spain, relieved, almost laughed as he pushed the door open, though not sure whether a curse or a shot would greet him. He got neither. And a welcome surprise in the dim light came through a stuffy pane of glass at one end of the room. It revealed at the other end a man stretched asleep on a wall bunk—a man that would, in all likelihood, have heard the stealthiest sound had any effort been made to conceal it, but to whose ears the rough voices of a mountain cabin are mere sleeping-potions.

The sleeper was destined, a moment later, to a ruder awakening than even his companion outlaws ever gave him. Lying unsuspectingly on his back, he woke to feel a hand laid lightly on his shoulder. The instinct of self-preservation acted like a flash. His eyes opened and his hands struck out like cat's paws to the right and left: no knife and no revolver met them. Instead, in the semidarkness a strange face bent over him. His fists shot out together, only to be caught in a vise that broke his arms in two at the elbows, and forced them back against his throat. Like lightning, he threw up his knees, drew himself into a heap, and shot himself out, hands, arms, legs, back, everything into one terrific spring. But the sinewy vise above only gave for the shock, then it closed again relentlessly in. A knee, like an anvil, pushed inexorably into his stomach and

69

heart and lungs. Another lay across his right arm, and his struggling left arm he could not, though his eyes burst with the strain from their sockets, release from where, eagle-like claws gripped at his throat and shut off his breath.

Again and again, with the fury of desperation, Sassoon drew in his powerful frame, shot it out, twisted and struggled. Great veins swelled on his forehead, his breath burst in explosive gasps, he writhed from side to side—it was all one. After every effort the cruel fingers at his throat tightened. The heavy knee on his chest crushed more relentlessly. He lay still.

"Are you awake, Shike?" Sassoon heard from the gloom above him. But he could not place the voice. "You seem to move around a good deal in your sleep. If you're awake, keep still. I've come from Sleepy Cat to get you. Don't mind looking for your gun and knife. Two men are with me. You can have your choice. We've got a horse for you. You can ride away from us here inside the Gap, and take what hits you in the back, or you can go to Sleepy Cat with us and stand your trial. I'll read your warrant when the sun gets a little higher. Get up and choose quick."

Sassoon could not see who had subdued him, nor did he take long to decide what to do. Scott had predicted he would go without much fuss, and de Spain, now somewhat surprised, found Bob right in his forecast. With less trouble than he expected, the captor got his man sullenly on horseback, and gave him severely plain directions as to what not to do. Sassoon, neither bound nor gagged, was told to ride his horse down the Gap closely ahead of de Spain and neither to speak nor turn his head no matter what happened right or left. To get him out in this manner was, de Spain realized, the really ticklish part of the undertaking.

Fortune, however, seemed to favor his assurance in invading the lions' den. In the growing light the two men trotted smartly a mile down the trail without encountering a sign of life. When they approached the Morgan ranch-house de Spain again felt qualms. But he rode close to his prisoner, told him in restrained monologue what would happen if he made a noise, and even held him back in his pace as they trotted together past the Gap stronghold. Nevertheless, he breathed more freely when they left the house behind and the turn in the road put them out of range of its windows. He closed up the distance between himself and Sassoon, riding close in to his side, and looked back at the house. He looked quickly, but though his eyes were off his path and his prisoner for only a fraction of a second, when he looked ahead again he saw confronting him, not a hundred yards away, a motionless horseman.

CHAPTER VI

WITH a sudden, low command to Sassoon to check his horse, and without a movement that could be detected in the dawn ten yards away, de Spain with the thumb and finger of his right hand lifted his revolver from its scabbard, shifted his lines from his left hand to his right, rode closer to Sassoon and pressed the muzzle of the gun to his prisoner's side. "You've got one chance yet, Shike, to ride out of here alive," he said composedly. "You know I am a rustler—cousin of John Rebstock's. My name is 'Frenchy'; I belong in Williams Cache. I rode in last night from Thief River, and you are riding out with me to start me on to the Sleepy Cat trail. If you can remember that much——"

While he spoke to Sassoon his eyes were fixed on the rider halted in their path. De Spain stopped half-way through his sentence. The figure revealed in the half-light puzzled him at first. Then it confused and startled him. He saw it was not a man at all, but a woman—and a woman

73

than whom he would rather have seen six men.
It was Nan Morgan.

With her head never more decisively set under
her mannish hat, her waist never more attractively
outlined in slenderness, she silently faced de
Spain in the morning gray. His face reflected his
chagrined perplexity. The whole fabric of his
slender plot seemed to go to pieces at the sight
of her. At the mere appearance of his frail and
motionless foe a feeling of awkward helplessness
dissolved his easy confidence. He now reversed
every move he had so carefully made with his
hands and, resentfully eying Nan, rode in somewhat behind Sassoon, doing nothing further than
to pull his kerchief up about his neck, and wondering what would be likely to happen before the
next three minutes were up. Beyond that flash
the future held no interest for him—his wits had
temporarily failed.

Of one thing he felt assured, that it was in no
wise up to him to speak or do first. He could already see Nan's eyes. They were bent keenly first
on him, then on his companion, and again on him.
De Spain kept his face down as much as he dared,
and his hat had been pulled well over it from the
beginning. She waited so long before accosting
the two men that de Spain, who was ready to
hope any improbable thing, began to hope she

might let them pass unchallenged. He had resolved, if she did not speak to push past without even looking at her. They were now almost abreast. His fine resolution went smash overboard. The very instinctive knowledge that her eyes were bent on his made him steal a glance at her in spite of himself. The next instant he was shamefacedly touching his hat. Though nothing was lost on her, Nan professed not to see the greeting. He even continued to dream she did not recognize him. Her eyes, in fact, were directed toward Sassoon, and when she spoke her tone was dry with suspicion.

"Wait a moment, Sassoon. Where are you going?" she demanded. Sassoon hitched with one hand at his trousers band. He inclined his head sulkily toward his companion. "Starting a man on the trail for Sleepy Cat."

"Stop," she exclaimed sharply, for de Spain, pushing his own horse ahead, had managed without being observed, to kick Sassoon's horse in the flank, and the two were passing. Sassoon at the resolute summons stopped. De Spain could do no less; both men, halting, faced their suspicious inquisitor. She scrutinized de Spain keenly. "What is this man doing in the Gap?"

"He come up from Thief River last night," answered Sassoon monotonously.

75

Nan of Music Mountain

"What is he doing here with you?" persisted Nan.

"He's a cousin of John Rebstock's from Williams Cache," continued Sassoon. The yarn would have sounded decently well in the circumstances for which it was intended, but in the searching gaze of the eyes now confronting and clearly recognizing him, it sounded so grotesque that de Spain would fully as lief have been sitting between his horse's legs as astride his back.

"That's not true, Sassoon," said his relentless questioner. Her tone and the expression of her face boded no friendliness for either of the two she had intercepted.

De Spain had recovered his wits. "You're right," he interposed without an instant's hesitation. "It isn't true. But that's not his fault; he is under arrest, and is telling you what I told him to tell you. I came in here this morning to take Sassoon to Sleepy Cat. He is a prisoner, wanted for cutting up one of our stage-guards."

Nan, coldly sceptical, eyed de Spain. "And do you try to tell me"—she pointed to Sassoon's unbound hands—"that he is riding out of here, a free man, to go to jail?"

"I do tell you exactly that. He is my prisoner——"

"I don't believe either of you," declared Nan

scornfully. "You are planning something underhand together."

De Spain laughed coolly. "We've planned that much together, but not, I assure you, with his consent."

"I don't believe your stories at all," she declared firmly.

De Spain flushed. The irritation and the serious danger bore in on him. "If you don't believe me it's not my fault," he retorted. "I've told you the truth. Ride on, Sassoon."

He spoke angrily, but this in no wise daunted Nan. She wheeled her horse directly in front of them. "Don't you stir, Sassoon," she commanded, "until I call Uncle Duke."

De Spain spurred straight at her; their horses collided, and his knee touched hers in the saddle. "I'm going to take this man out of here," he announced in a tone she never had heard before from a man. "I've no time to talk. Go call your uncle if you like. We must pass."

"You shan't pass a step!"

With the quick words of defiance the two glared at each other. De Spain was taken aback. He had expected no more than a war of words—a few screams at the most. Nan's face turned white, but there was no symptom even of a whimper. He noticed her quick breathing, and felt, instinctively, the restrained gesture of her right hand as it started back to her side. The move steadied him. "One question," he said bluntly, "are you armed?"

She hated even to answer, and met his searching gaze resentfully, but something in his tone and manner wrung a reply. "I can defend myself," she exclaimed angrily.

De Spain raised his right hand from his thigh to the pommel of his saddle. The slight gesture was eloquent of his surrender of the issue of force. "I can't go into a shooting-match with you about this cur. If you call your uncle there will be bloodshed—unless you drop me off my horse right here and now before he appears. All I ask you is this: Is this kind of a cutthroat worth that? If you shoot me, my whole posse from Sleepy Cat is right below us in the aspens. Some of your own people will be killed in a general fight. If you want to shoot me, shoot—you can have the match all to yourself. If you don't, let us go by. And if I've told you one word that isn't true, call me back to this spot any time you like, and I'll come at your call, and answer for it."

His words and his manner confounded her for a moment. She could not at once make an answer, for she could not decide what to say. Then,

78

of a sudden, she was robbed of her chance to answer. From down the trail came a yell like a shot. The clatter of hoofs rang out, and men on horses dashed from the entrance of the Gap toward them. De Spain could not make them out distinctly, but he knew Lefever's yell, and pointed. "There they are," he exclaimed hurriedly. "There is the whole posse. They are coming!" A shot, followed closely by a second, rang out from below. "Go," he cried to Nan. "There'll be shooting here that I can't stop!" He slapped Sassoon's pony viciously with his hand, yelled loud in answer to Lefever, and before the startled girl could collect herself, de Spain, crouching in his saddle, as a fusillade cracked from Lefever's and Scott's revolvers, urged Sassoon's horse around Nan's, kicked it violently, spurred past her himself, and was away. White with consternation and anger, she steadied herself and looked after the fleeing pair. Then whirling in her saddle, she ran her pony back to the ranch-house to give the alarm.

Yelling like half a dozen men, Lefever and Scott, as de Spain and his prisoner dashed toward them, separated, let the pair pass, and spurred in behind to cover the flight and confront any pursuers. None at the moment threatened, but no words were exchanged until the whole party, riding fast, were well past El Capitan and out of the Gap.

For some unexpressed reason—so strong is the influence of tradition and reputation—no one of the three coveted a close encounter with the Morgans within its walls.

"It's the long heels for it now, boys," cried de Spain. His companions closed up again.

"Save your horses," cautioned Scott, between strides. "It's a good ways home."

"Make for Calabasas," shouted Lefever.

"No," yelled Scott. "They would stand us a siege at Calabasas. While the trail is open make for the railroad."

A great globe of dazzling gold burst into the east above the distant hills. But the glory of the sunrise called forth no admiration from the three men hurrying a fourth urgently along the Sleepy Cat trail. Between breaths de Spain explained his awkward meeting with Nan, and of the strait he was in when Lefever's strong lungs enabled him to get away unscratched. But for a gunman a narrow squeak is as good as a wide one, and no one found fault with the situation. They had the advantage—the only question was whether they could hold it. And while they continued to cast anxious glances behind, Scott's Indian eyes first perceived signs on the horizon that marked their pursuit.

"No matter," declared Lefever. "This is a

little fast for a fat man, anyway." He was not averse, either, to the prospect of a long-range exchange with the fighting mountaineers. All drew rein a little. "Suppose I cover the rear till we see what this is," suggested Lefever, limbering up as the other two looked back. "Push ahead with Sassoon. These fellows won't follow far."

"Don't be sure about that," muttered Scott. "Duke and Gale have got the best horses in the mountains, and they'd rather fight than eat. There they come now."

Dashing across a plain they themselves had just crossed, they could see three horsemen in hot chase. The pursued men rode carefully, and, scanning the ground everywhere ahead and behind, de Spain, Scott, and Lefever awaited the moment when their pursuers should show their hand. Scott was on the west of the line, and nearest the enemy.

"Who are they, Bob?" yelled Lefever.

Scott scrutinized the pursuers carefully. "One," he called back, "that big fellow on the right, is Deaf Sandusky, sure. Harvey Logan, likely, the middle man. The other I can't make out. Look!" he exclaimed, pointing to the foot-hills on their distant left. Two men, riding out almost abreast of them, were running their horses for a small canyon through which the trail led two miles ahead. "Some riding," cried Scott, watching the newcomers. "That farther man must be Gale Morgan. They are trying for the greasewood canyon, to cut us off."

"We can't stand for that," decided de Spain, surveying the ground around them. "There's not so much as a sage-brush here for cover."

Lefever pointed to his right; at some distance a dark, weather-beaten cone rose above the yellow desert. "Let's make a stand in the lava beds," he cried.

De Spain hesitated. "It takes us the wrong way." He pointed ahead. "Give them a run for that canyon, boys."

Urging their horses, the Sleepy Cat men rode at utmost speed to beat the flanking party to the trail gateway. For a few minutes it looked an even break between pursuers and pursued. The two men in the foot-hills now had a long angle to overcome, but they were doing a better pace than those of the Gap party behind, and half-way to the canyon it looked like a neck-and-neck heat for the narrow entrance. Lefever complained of the effort of keeping up, and at length reined in his horse. "Drop me here on the alkali, boys," he cried to the others. "I'll hold this end while you get through the canyon."

"No," declared de Spain, checking his pace.

Heels for It

"If one stays, all stay. This is as good a time as any to find out what these fellows mean."

"But not a very good place," commented Scott, as they slowed, looking for a depression.

"It's as good for us as it is for them," returned de Spain abruptly. "We'll try it right here."

He swung out of his saddle, Lefever and Scott after an instant's reconnoissance following. Sassoon they dismounted. Scott lashed his wrists together, while de Spain and Lefever unslung their carbines, got their horses down, and, facing the west and south, spread themselves on the ground.

The men behind lost nothing of the defensive movement of the pursued party, and slowed up in turn. For the moment the flankers were out of sight, but they must soon appear on the crest of a rise between them and the canyon. Lefever was first down and first ready with his rifle to cover the men behind. These now spread out and came on, as if for a rush.

Lefever, picking Logan, the foremost, sent a warning shot in front of him. De Spain fired almost at the same moment toward the big man making a détour to the right of the leader. The two bullets puffed in the distant alkali, and the two horsemen, sharply admonished, swerved backward precipitately. After a momentary circling indecision, the three rode closer together for a conference, dismounted, and opened a return fire on the little party lying to.

The strategy of their halt and their firing was not hard to penetrate. The men from the foot-hills were still riding for the canyon. No views were exchanged among Sassoon's captors, but all understood that this move must be stopped. Lefever and Scott, without words, merely left the problem to de Spain as the leader. He lay on the right of the line as they faced south, and this brought him nearest to the riders out of the foot-hills. Taking advantage of a lull in the firing, he pulled his horse around between himself and the attacking party, and in such a position that he could command with his rifle the fast-moving riders to the west.

Something of a predicament confronted him. He was loath to take a human life in the effort to get a cutthroat jailed, and hated even to cripple a beast for it, but the two men must be stopped. Nor was it easy to pick up the range offhand, but meaning that the Morgans, if they were Morgans, should understand how a rush would be met, he sent one shot after another, short, beyond, and ahead of the horsemen, to check them, and to feel the way for closer shooting if it should be necessary. The two dashed on

Heels for It

undaunted. De Spain perceived that warnings were wasted. He lowered his sights, and, waiting his chance as the leader of the foot-hill pursuers rode into a favorable range, he fired for his horse's head. The beast jumped convulsively and pitched forward, head down in a half somersault, throwing his rider violently to the ground. Scott and Lefever yelled loudly.

Out of the cloud of dust the man scrambled to his feet, looked coolly around, and brushed the alkali disgustedly from his eyes just as a second bullet from de Spain tore up the earth a few feet to one side of him. He jumped like a rabbit at this summons, and did not even make a further pretense at composure. Grabbing his hat from the ground, he ran like mad toward the hills. Meantime his mounted companion had turned about. De Spain sprang to his feet, jerked up his horse and cried: "Now for the canyon!" Pushing Sassoon into the saddle and profiting by the confusion, the railroad men rode hard for their refuge, and reached it without more molestation than an occasional shot from their distant pursuers on the main trail. De Spain and his scouts now felt assured of their escape. The foot-hills contingent was left far behind, and, though their remaining pursuers rode in at times with a show of rushing, the chase was a stern one, and could be checked whenever necessary. Halting at times in this way to breathe their horses, or to hold off the rear pursuit, de Spain with his two companions and their prisoner rode into Sleepy Cat, locked Sassoon up, and went to the Mountain House for breakfast.

CHAPTER VII

MAINTAINING A REPUTATION

THE abduction of Sassoon, which signalized de Spain's entry into the stage-line management, created a sensation akin to the exploding of a bomb under the range. The whole mountain country, which concentrates, sensibly, on but one topic at a time, talked for a week of nothing else. No such defiance of the traditions of the Morgan rule along the reaches of the Spanish Sinks had been attempted in years—and it was recalled more than once, when de Spain's feat was discussed at the ranches, on the trails, and in the haunts of gunmen in Calabasas, that no one of those who had ever braved the wrath of the Sink rulers had lived indefinitely to boast of it.

Experienced men, therefore, in the high country—men of that class who, wherever found, are old in the ways of the world, and not promptly moved by new or youthful adventure—dismissed the incident after hearing the details, with the comment or the conclusion that there would hardly be for de Spain more than one additional chapter to the story, and that this would be a short one. The most active Morgans—Gale, Duke, and the easy-going Satterlee—were indeed wrought to the keenest pitch of revengeful anger. No question of the right or wrong of the arrest was discussed—justification was not considered. It was an overwhelmingly insolent invasion—and worst of all, a successful invasion, by one who had nothing but cool impudence, not even a budding reputation to justify his assault on the life-long prestige of the Gap clan. Gale Morgan strode and rode the streets of Sleepy Cat looking for de Spain, and storming.

De Spain himself, somewhat surprised at the storm he had kicked up, heeded the counsel of Scott, and while the acute stage of the resentment raged along the trail he ran down for a few days to Medicine Bend to buy horses. Both Gale and Duke Morgan proclaimed, in certain public places in Sleepy Cat, their intention of shooting de Spain on sight; and as a climax to all the excitement of the week following his capture, the slippery Sassoon broke jail and, after a brief interval, appeared at large in Calabasas.

This feat of the Morgan satellite made a loud laugh at de Spain's expense. It mitigated somewhat the humiliation of Sassoon's friends, but it in no wise diminished their expressed resolve to punish de Spain's invasion. Lefever, who as the mixer among the stage men, kept close to the drift of public sentiment, decided after de Spain's return to Sleepy Cat that the stage-line authorities had gained nothing by Sassoon's capture.

"We ought to have thought of it before, Henry," he said frankly one night in Jeffries's office, "but we didn't think."

"Meaning just what, John?" demanded de Spain without real interest.

"Meaning, that in this country you can't begin on a play like pulling Sassoon out from under his friends' noses without keeping up the pace— without a second and third act. You dragged Sassoon by his hair out of the Gap; good. You surprised everybody; good. But you can't very well stop at that, Henry. You have raised hopes, you have led people to invest you with the faint glimmerings of a reputation. I say, the glimmerings, because such a feat by itself doesn't insure a permanent reputation, Henry. It is, so to say, merely a 'demand' reputation—one that men reserve the right to recall at any moment. And the worst of it is, if they ever do recall it, you are worse off than when before they extended the brittle bauble to you."

"Jingo, John! For a stage blacksmith you are some spieler." De Spain added an impatient, not to say contumelious exclamation concerning the substance of Lefever's talk. "I didn't ask them for a reputation. This man interfered with my guard—in fact, tried to cut his throat, didn't he?"

"Would have done it if Frank had been an honest man."

"That is all there is to it, isn't it? If Sassoon or anybody else gets in the way of the stages, I'll go after them again—that's all there is to it, isn't it?"

Lefever tapped the second finger of one fat hand gently on the table. "Practically; practically all, Henry, yes. You don't quite understand, but you have the right idea. What I am trying to hammer into your dense cocoanut is, that when a man has, gets, or is given a reputation out in this country, he has got to live up to it."

"What do you want me to do—back a horse and shoot two guns at once up and down Main Street, cowboy style?"

Lefever kept his patience without difficulty. "No, no. You'll understand."

"Scott advised me to run down to Medicine Bend for a few days to let the Morgans cool off."

"Right. That was the first step. The few days are a thing of the past. I suppose you know," continued Lefever, in as well-modulated a tone as he could assume to convey information that could not be regarded as wholly cheerful, "that they expect to get you for this Sassoon job."

De Spain flushed. But the red anger lasted only a moment. "Who are 'they'?" he asked after a pause.

"Deaf Sandusky, Logan, of course, the Calabasas bunch, and the Morgans."

De Spain regarded his companion unamiably. "What do they expect I'll be doing while they are getting me?"

Lefever raised a hand deprecatingly. "Don't be overconfident, Henry; that's your danger. I know you can take care of yourself. All I want to do is to get the folks here acquainted with your ability, without taking unnecessary chances. You see, people are not now asking questions of one another; they are asking them of themselves. Who and what is this newcomer— an accident or a genuine arrival? A common squib or a real explosion? Don't get excited," he added, in an effort to sooth de Spain's obvious irritation. "You have the idea, Henry. It's time to show yourself."

"I can't very well do business here without showing myself," retorted de Spain.

"But it is a thing to be managed," persisted

Lefever. "Now, suppose—since the topic is up —we 'show' in Main Street for a while."

"Suppose we do," echoed de Spain ungraciously.

"That will crack the début ice. We will call at Harry Tenison's hotel, and then go to his new rooms—go right to society headquarters first— that's my theory of doing it. If anybody has any shooting in mind, Tenison's is a quiet and orderly place. And if a man declines to eat anybody up at Tenison's, we put him down, Henry, as not ravenously hungry."

"One man I would like to see is that sheriff, Druel, who let Sassoon get out."

"Ready to interview him now?"

"I've got some telegrams to answer."

"Those will keep. The Morgans are in town. We'll start out and find somebody."

It was wet and sloppy outside, but Lefever was indifferent to the rain, and de Spain thought it would be undignified to complain of it.

When, followed by Lefever, he walked into the lobby of Tenison's hotel a few moments later the office was empty. Nevertheless, the news of the appearance of Sassoon's captor spread. The two sauntered into the billiard-hall, which occupied a deep room adjoining the office and opened with large plate-glass windows on Main Street. Every

Maintaining a Reputation

table was in use. A fringe of spectators in the chairs, ostensibly watching the pool games, turned their eyes toward de Spain—those that recognized him distinguishing him by nods and whispers to others.

Among several groups of men standing before the long bar, one party of four near the front end likewise engaged the interest of those keener loafers who were capable of foreseeing situations. These men, Satterlee Morgan, the cattleman; Bull Page, one of his cowboys; Sheriff Druel, and Judge Druel, his brother, had been drinking together. They did not see Lefever and his companion as the two came in through the rear lobby door. But Lefever, on catching sight of them, welcomed his opportunity. Walking directly forward, he laid his hand on Satt Morgan's shoulder. As the cattleman turned, Lefever, genially grasping his hand, introduced de Spain to each of the party in turn. What followed in the brief interval between the meeting of the six men and the sudden breaking up of the group a few moments later was never clearly known, but a fairly conclusive theory of it was afterward accepted by Sleepy Cat.

Morgan threw the brim of his weather-beaten hat back from his tanned face. He wore a mustache and a chin whisker of that variety designated in the mountains by the most opprobrious of epithets. But his smile, which drew his cheeks into wrinkles all about his long, round nose, was not unfriendly. He looked with open interest from his frank but not overtrustworthy eyes at de Spain. "I heard," he said in a good-natured, slightly nasal tone, "you made a sunrise call on us one day last week."

"And I want to say," returned de Spain, equally amiable, "that if I had had any idea you folks would take it so hard—I mean, as an affront intended to any of you—I never would have gone into the Gap after Sassoon. I just assumed— making a mistake as I now realize—that my scrap would be with Sassoon, not with the Morgans."

Satt's face wrinkled into a humorous grin. "You sure kicked up some alkali."

De Spain nodded candidly. "More than I intended to. And I say—without any intention of impertinence to anybody else—Sassoon is a cur. I supposed when I brought him in here after so much riding, that we had sheriff enough to keep him." He looked at Druel with such composure that the latter for a moment was nonplussed. Then he discharged a volley of oaths, and demanded what de Spain meant. De Spain did not move. He refused to see the angry sheriff. "That is where I made my second mistake," he

94

continued, speaking to Morgan and forcing his tone just enough to be heard. Druel, with more hard words, began to abuse the railroad for not paying taxes enough to build a decent jail. De Spain took another tack. He eyed the sheriff calmly as the latter continued to draw away and left de Spain standing somewhat apart from the rest of the group. "Then it may be I am making another mistake, Druel, in blaming you. It may not be your fault."

"The fault is, you're fresh," cried Druel, warming up as de Spain appeared to cool. The line of tipplers backed away from the bar. De Spain, stepping toward the sheriff, raised his hand in a friendly way. "Druel, you're hurting yourself by your talk. Make me your deputy again sometime," he concluded, "and I'll see that Sassoon stays where he is put."

"I'll just do that," cried Druel, with a very strong word, and he raised his hand in turn. "Next time you want him locked up, you can take care of him yourself."

The sharp crack of a rifle cut off the words; a bullet tore like a lightning-bolt across de Spain's neck, crashed through a mahogany pilaster back of the bar, and embedded itself in the wall. The shot had been aimed from the street for his head. The noisy room instantly hushed. Spectators

sat glued to their chairs. White-faced players
leaned motionless against the tables. De Spain
alone had acted; all that the bartenders could
ever remember after the single rifle-shot was seeing his hand go back as he whirled and shot
instantly toward the heavy report. He had
whipped out his gun and fired sidewise through
the window at the sound.

That was all. The bartenders breathed and
looked again. Men were crowding like mad
through the back doors. De Spain, at the cigar
case, looked intently into the rainy street, lighted
from the corner by a dingy lamp. The four men
near him had not stirred, but, startled and alert,
the right hand of each covered the butt of a revolver. De Spain moved first. While the pool
players jammed the back doors to escape, he spoke
to, without looking at, the bartender. "What's
the matter with your curtains?" he demanded,
sheathing his revolver and pointing with an expletive to the big sheet of plate glass. "Is this
the way you build up business for the house?"

Those close enough to the window saw that
the bare pane had been cut, just above the middle, by two bullet-holes. Curious men examined
both fractures when de Spain and Lefever had
left the saloon. The first hole was the larger. It
had been made by a high-powered rifle; the sec-

96

ond was from a bullet of a Colt's revolver; it was remarked as a miracle of gun-play that the two were hardly an inch apart.

In the street a few minutes later, de Spain and Lefever encountered Scott, who, with his back hunched up, his cheap black hat pulled well down over his ears, his hands in his trousers pockets and his thin coat collar modestly turned against the drizzling rain, was walking across the parkway from the station.

"Sassoon is in town," exclaimed Lefever with certainty after he had told the story. He waited for the Indian's opinion. Scott, looking through the water dripping from the brim of his seasoned derby, gave it in one word. "Was," he amended with a quiet smile.

"Let's make sure," insisted Lefever. "Supposing he might be in town yet, Bob, where is he?"

Scott gazed up the street through the rain lighted by yellow lamps on the obscure corners, and looked down the street toward the black reaches of the river. "If he's here, you'll find him in one of two places. Tenison's——"

"But we've just come from Tenison's," objected Lefever.

"I mean, across the street, up-stairs; or at Jim Kitchen's barn. If he was hurried to get away," added Scott reflectively, "he would slip up-stairs over there as the nearest place to hide; if he had time he would make for the barn, where it would be easy to cache his rifle."

Lefever took the lapel of the scout's coat in his hand. "Then you, Bob, go out and see if you can get the whole story. I'll take the barn. Let Henry go over to Tenison's and wait at the head of the stairs till we can get back there. It is just around the corner—second floor—a dark hall running back, opposite the double doors that open into an anteroom. Stay there, Henry, till we come. It won't be long, and if we don't get track of him you may spot your man yourself."

De Spain found no difficulty in locating the flight of marble stairs that led to the gambling-rooms. It was the only lighted entrance in the side street. No light shone at the head of the stairs, but a doorway on the left opened into a dimly lighted anteroom and this, in turn, through a large arch, opened on a large room brilliantly lighted by chandeliers—one in the centre and one near each corner. Around three sides of this room were placed the keno layouts, roulette-wheels, faro-tables, and minor gambling devices. Off the casino itself small card-rooms opened.

The big room was well filled for a wet night. The faro-tables were busy, and at the central table at the farther end of the room—the table designated as Tenison's, because, at the rare intervals in which the proprietor dealt, he presided at this table—a group watched silently a game in progress. De Spain took a place in shadow near one side of the archway facing the street-door and at times looked within for the loosely jointed frame, crooked neck, tousled forehead, and malevolent face of the cattle thief. He could find in the many figures scattered about the room none resembling the one he sought.

A man entering the place spoke to another coming out. De Spain overheard the exchange. "Duke got rid of his steers yet?" asked the first.

"Not yet."

"Slow game."

"The old man sold quite a bunch this time. The way he's playing now he'll last twenty-four hours."

De Spain, following the newcomer, strolled into the room and, beginning at one side, proceeded in leisurely fashion from wheel to wheel and table to table inspecting the players. Few looked at him and none paid any attention to his presence. At Tenison's table he saw in the dealer's chair the large, white, smooth face, dark eyes, and clerical expression of the proprietor, whose presence meant a real game and explained the interest of the idlers crowded about one player whom de Spain, without getting closer in among the onlookers than he wanted to, could not see.

Tenison, as de Spain approached, happened to look wearily up; his face showed the set lines of a protracted session. He neither spoke nor nodded to the newcomer, but recognized him with a mere glance. Then, though his eyes had rested for only an instant on the new face, he spoke in an impassive tone across the intervening heads: "What happened to your red tie, Henry?"

De Spain put up his hand to his neck, and looked down at a loose end hanging from his soft cravat. It had been torn by the bullet meant for his head. He tucked the end inside his collar. "A Calabasas man tried to untie it a few minutes ago. He missed the knot."

Tenison did not hear the answer. He had reverted to his case. De Spain moved on and, after making the round of the scattered tables, walked again through the archway into the anteroom, only to meet, as she stood hesitating and apparently about to enter the room, Nan Morgan.

CHAPTER VIII

THE GAMBLING-ROOM

THEY confronted each other blankly. To Nan's confusion was added her embarrassment at her personal appearance. Her hat was wet, and the limp shoulders of her khaki jacket and the front of her silk blouse showed the wilting effect of the rain. In one hand she clutched wet riding-gloves. Her cheeks, either from the cold rain or mental stress, fairly burned, and her eyes, which had seemed when he encountered her, fired with some resolve, changed to an expression almost of dismay.

This was hardly for more than an instant. Then her lips tightened, her eyes dropped, and she took a step to one side to avoid de Spain and enter the gambling-room. He stepped in front of her. She looked up, furious. "What do you mean?" she exclaimed with indignation. "Let me pass."

The sound of her voice restored his self-possession. He made no move to get out of her way, indeed he rather pointedly continued to obstruct her. "You've made a mistake, I think," he said evenly.

"I have not," she replied with resentment. "Let me pass."

"I think you have. You don't know where you are going," he persisted, his eyes bent uncompromisingly on hers.

She showed increasing irritation at his attempt to exculpate her. "I know perfectly well where I am going," she retorted with heat.

"Then you know," he returned steadily, "that you've no business to enter such a place."

His opposition seemed only to anger her. "I know where I have business. I need no admonitions from you as to what places I enter. You are impertinent, insulting. Let me pass!"

His stubborn opposition showed no signs of weakening before her resolve. "One question," he said, ignoring her angry words. "Have you ever been in these rooms before?"

He thought she quailed the least bit before his searching look. She even hesitated as to what to say. But if her eyes fell momentarily it was only to collect herself. "Yes," she answered, looking up unflinchingly.

Her resolute eyes supported her defiant word and openly challenged his interference, but he met her once more quietly. "I am sorry to hear it," he rejoined. "But that won't make any difference. You can't go in to-night."

"I will go in," she cried.

"No," he returned slowly, "you are not going in—not, at least, while I am here."

They stood immovable. He tried to reason her out of her determination. She resented every word he offered. "You are most insolent," she exclaimed. "You are interfering in something that is no concern of yours. You have no right to act in this outrageous way. If you don't stand aside I'll call for help."

"Nan!" De Spain spoke her name suddenly and threateningly. His words fell fast, and he checked her for an instant with his vehemence. "We met in the Gap a week ago. I said I was telling you the exact truth. Did I do it?"

"I don't care what you said or what you did——"

"Answer me," he said sharply, "did I tell you the truth?"

"I don't know or care——"

"Yes, you do know——"

"What you say or do——"

"I told you the truth then, I am telling it now. I will never see you enter a gambling-room as long as I can prevent it. Call for help if you like."

She looked at him with amazement. She

seemed about to speak—to make another protest. Instead, she turned suddenly away, hesitated again, put both her hands to her face,
burst into tears, and hurried toward the stairs.
De Spain followed her. "Let me take you to
where you are going?"

Nan turned on him, her eyes blazing through
her tears, with a single, scornful, furious word:
"No!" She quickened her step from him in such
confusion that she ran into two men just reaching the top of the stairs. They separated with
alacrity, and gave her passage. One of the men
was Lefever, who, despite his size, was extremely
nimble in getting out of her urgent way, and
quick in lifting his hat. She fairly raced down
the flight of steps, leaving Lefever looking after
her in astonishment. He turned to de Spain:
"Now, who the deuce was that?"

De Spain ignored his question by asking another: "Did you find him?" Lefever shook his
head. "Not a trace; I covered Main Street.
I guess Bob was right. Nobody home here,
Henry?"

"Nobody we want."

"Nothing going on?"

"Not a thing. If you will wait here for Bob,
I'll run over to the office and answer those telegrams."

The Gambling-Room

De Spain started for the stairs. "Henry," called Lefever, as his companion trotted hastily down, "if you catch up to her, kindly apologize for a fat man."

But de Spain was balked of an opportunity to follow Nan. In the street he ran into Scott. "Did you get the story?" demanded de Spain.

"Part of it."

"Was it Sassoon?"

Scott shook his head. "I wish it was."

"What do you mean?"

"Deaf Sandusky."

"Calabasas?"

Scott nodded. "You must have moved a couple of inches at the right nick, Henry. That man Sandusky," Bob smiled a sickly smile, "doesn't miss very often. He was bothered a little by his friends being all around you."

The two regarded each other for a moment in silence. "Why," asked de Spain, boiling a little, "should that damned, hulking brute try to blow *my* head off just now?"

"Only for the good of the order, Henry," grinned the scout.

"Nice job Jeff has picked out for me," muttered de Spain grimly, "standing up in these Sleepy Cat barrooms to be shot at." He drew in a good breath and threw up the wet brim of his hat. "Well, such is life in the high country, I suppose. Some fine day Mr. Sandusky will manage to get me—or I'll manage to get him—that all depends on how the happening happens. Anyway, Bob, it's bad luck to miss a man. We'll hang that much of a handicap on his beef-eating crop. Is he the fellow John calls the butcher?" demanded de Spain.

"That's what everybody calls him, I guess."

The two rejoined Lefever at the head of the stairs and the three discussed the news. Even Lefever seemed more serious when he heard the report. Scott, when asked where Sandusky now was, nodded toward the big room in front of them.

Lefever looked toward the gambling-tables. "We'll go in and look at him." He turned to Scott to invite his comment on the proposal. "Think twice, John," suggested the Indian. "If there's any trouble in a crowd like that, somebody that has no interest in de Spain or Sandusky is pretty sure to get hurt."

"I don't mean to start anything," explained Lefever. "I only want de Spain to look at him."

But sometimes things start themselves. Lefever found Sandusky at a faro-table. At his side sat his partner, Logan. Three other players, together with the onlookers, and the dealer—whose tumbled hair fell partly over the visor that pro-

The Gambling-Room

tected his eyes from the glare of the overhead light—made up the group. The table stood next to that of Tenison, who, white-faced and impassive under the heat and light, still held to his chair.

Lefever took a position at one end of the table, where he faced Sandusky, and de Spain, just behind his shoulder, had a chance to look the two Calabasas men closely over. Sandusky again impressed him as a powerful man, who, beyond an ample stomach, carried his weight without showing it. What de Spain most noted, as it lay on the table, was the size and extreme length of the outlaw's hand. He had heard of Sandusky's hand. From the tips of the big fingers to the base of the palm, this right hand, spread over his chips, would cover half again the length of the hand of the average man.

De Spain credited readily the extraordinary stories he had heard of Sandusky's dexterity with a revolver or a rifle. That he should so lately have missed a shot at so close range was partly explained now that de Spain perceived Sandusky's small, hard, brown eyes were somewhat unnaturally bright, and that his brows knit every little while in his effort to collect himself. But his stimulation only partly explained the failure; it was notoriously hard to upset the powerful outlaw with alcohol. De Spain noted the coarse,

107

straw-colored hair—plastered recently over the forehead by a barber—the heavy, sandy mustache, freshly waxed by the same hand, the bellicose nostrils of the Roman nose, the broad, split chin, and mean, deep lines of a most unpromising face. Sandusky's brown shirt sprawled open at the collar, and de Spain remembered again the flashy waistcoat, fastened at the last buttonhole by a cut-glass button.

At Sandusky's side sat his crony in all important undertakings—a much smaller, sparer man, with aggressive shoulders and restless eyes. Logan was the lookout of the pair, and his roving glance lighted on de Spain before the latter had inspected him more than a moment. He lost no time in beginning on de Spain with an insolent question as to what he was looking at. De Spain, his eye bent steadily on him, answered with a tone neither of apology nor pronounced offense: "I am looking at you."

Lefever hitched at his trousers cheerily and, stepping away from de Spain, took a position just behind the dealer. "What are you looking at me for?" demanded Logan insolently.

De Spain raised his voice to match exactly the tone of the inquiry. "So I'll know you next time."

Logan pushed back his chair. As he turned

his legs from under the table to rise, a hand
rested on his shoulder. He looked up and saw
the brown face and feeble smile of Scott. Logan
with his nearest foot kicked Sandusky. The big
fellow looked up and around. Either by chance
or in following the sound of the last voice, his
glance fell on de Spain. He scrutinized for a
suspicious instant the burning eyes and the red
mark low on the cheek. While he did so—comprehension dawning on him—his enormous hands,
forsaking the pile of chips with which both had
been for a moment busy, flattened out, palms
down, on the faro-table. Logan tried to rise.
Scott's hand rested heavily on him. "What's
the row?" demanded Sandusky in the queer tone
of a deaf man. Logan pointed at de Spain.
"That Medicine Bend duck wants a fight."

"With a man, Logan; not with a cub," retorted
de Spain, matching insult with insult.

"Maybe I can do something for you," interposed Sandusky. His eyes ran like a flash around
the table. He saw how Lefever had pre-empted
the best place in the room. He looked up and
back at the man standing now at his shoulder,
and almost between Logan and himself. It was
the Indian, Scott. Sandusky felt, as his faculties
cleared and arranged themselves every instant,
that there was no hurry whatever about lifting

his hand; but he could not be faced down without
a show of resistance, and he concluded that for
this occasion his tongue was the best weapon.
"If I can," he added stiffly, "I'm at your service."

De Spain made no answer beyond keeping his
eyes well on Sandusky's eyes. Tenison, over-
hearing the last words, awoke to the situation
and rose from his case. He made his way through
the crowd around the disputants and brusquely
directed the dealer to close the game. While
Sandusky was cashing in, Tenison took Logan
aside. What Tenison said was not audible, but it
sufficed to quiet the little fellow. The only thing
further to be settled was as to who should leave
the room last, since neither party was willing to
go first. Tenison, after a formal conference with
Lefever and Logan, offered to take Sandusky
and Logan by a private stairway to the billiard-
room, while Lefever took de Spain and Scott out
by way of the main entrance. This was arranged, and when the railroad men reached the
street rain had ceased falling.

Scott warned de Spain to keep within doors,
and de Spain promised to do so. But when they
left him he started out at once to see whether he
could not, by some happy chance, encounter Nan.

CHAPTER IX

A CUP OF COFFEE

HE was willing, after a long and bootless search, to confess to himself that he would rather see Nan Morgan for one minute than all women else in the world for a lifetime. The other incidents of the evening would have given any ordinary man enough food for reflection—indeed they did force de Spain to realize that his life would hang by a slender thread while he remained at Sleepy Cat and continued to brave the rulers of the Sinks.

But this danger, which after all was a portion of his responsibility in freeing his stages from the depredations of the Calabasas gang, failed to make on him the moving impression of one moment of Nan Morgan's eyes. She could upset him completely, he was forced to admit, by a glance, a word, a gesture—a mere turn of her head. There was in the whole world nothing he wanted to do so much as in some way to please her—yet it seemed his ill luck to get continually deeper into her bad graces. It had so stunned and angered him to meet her intent on entering

a gambling-hall that he was tormented the whole
night. Association with outlaws—what might it
not do for even such a girl? While her people
were not all equally reprobate, some of them at
least were not far better than the criminals of
Calabasas. To conceive of her gambling pub-
licly in Sleepy Cat was too much. He had even
taken a horse, after cautiously but persistently
haunting the streets for an hour, and ridden across
the river away out on the mountain trail, hoping
to catch a sight of her.

On his way back to town from this wild-goose
chase, he heard the sound of hoofs. He was
nearing the river and he turned his horse into a
clump of trees beside the bridge. The night was
very dark, but he was close to the trail and had
made up his mind to speak to Nan if it were she.
In another moment his ear told him there were
two horses approaching. He waited for the
couple to cross the bridge, and they passed him
so close he could almost have touched the nearer
rider. Then he realized, as the horse passing beside him shied, that it was Sandusky and Logan
riding silently by.

For a week de Spain spent most of his time in
Sleepy Cat trying to catch sight of Nan. His
reflection on the untoward incidents that had set
them at variance left him rebellious. He medi-

A Cup of Coffee

tated more about putting himself right with her than about all his remaining concerns together. A strange fire had seized him—that fire of the imagination which scorns fair words and fine reasoning, but which, smothered, burns in secret until, fanned by the wind of accident, it bursts out the more fiercely because of the depths in which it has smouldered.

Every day that de Spain rode across the open country, his eyes turned to the far range and to Music Mountain. The rounded, distant, immutable peak—majestic as the sun, cold as the stars, shrouding in its unknown fastnesses the mysteries of the ages and the secrets of time—meant to him now only this mountain girl whom its solitude sheltered and to whom his thoughts continually came back.

Within two weeks he became desperate. He rode the Gap trail from Sleepy Cat again and again for miles and miles in the effort to encounter her. He came to know every ridge and hollow on it, every patch and stone between the lava beds and the Rat River. And in spite of the counsels of his associates, who warned him to beware of traps, he spent, under one pretext or another, much of the time either on the stages to and from Calabasas or in the saddle toward Morgan's Gap, looking for Nan.

Killing time in this way, after a fruitless ride, his persistence was one day most unexpectedly rewarded at the Calabasas barns. He had ridden through a hot sun from Sleepy Cat, passing the up stage half-way to Calabasas, and had struck from there directly out on the Sinks toward Morgan's Gap. Riding thence around the lower lava beds, he had headed for Calabasas, where he had an appointment to meet Scott and Lefever at five o'clock. When de Spain reached the Calabasas barn, McAlpin, the barn boss, was standing in the doorway. "You'd never be comin' from Sleepy Cat in the saddle!" exclaimed McAlpin incredulously. De Spain nodded affirmatively as he dismounted. "Hot ride, sir; a hot day," commented McAlpin, shaking his head dubiously as he called a man to take the horse, unstrapped de Spain's coat from the saddle, and followed the manager into the office.

The heat was oppressive, and de Spain unbuckled his cartridge-belt, slipped his revolver from the holster, mechanically stuck it inside his trousers waistband, hung the heavy belt up under his coat, and, sitting down, called for the stage report and asked whether the new blacksmith had sobered up. When McAlpin had given him all minor information called for, de Spain walked with him out into the barn to inspect the

A Cup of Coffee

horses. Passing the very last of the box-stalls, the manager saw in it a pony. He stopped. No second glance was needed to tell him it was a good horse; then he realized that this wiry, sleek-legged roan, contentedly munching at the moment some company hay, was Nan Morgan's.

McAlpin, talking volubly, essayed to move on, but de Spain, stubbornly pausing, only continued to look at the handsome saddle-horse. McAlpin saw he was in for it, and resigned himself to an inquisition. When de Spain asked whose horse it was, McAlpin was ready. "That little pony is Nan Morgan's, sir."

De Spain made no comment. "Good-looking pony, sir," ventured McAlpin half-heartedly.

"What's it doing here?" demanded de Spain coldly.

Before answering, the barn boss eyed de Spain very carefully to see how the wind was setting, for the pony's presence confessed an infraction of a very particular rule. "You see," he began, cocking at his strict boss from below his visorless cap a questioning Scotch eye, "I like to keep on good terms with that gang. Some of them can be very ugly. It's better to be friends with them when you can—by stretching the barn rules a little once in a while—than to have enemies of 'em all the time—don't you think so, sir?"

"What's her horse doing here?" asked de Spain, without commenting on the long story, but also without showing, as far as the barnman could detect, any growing resentment at the infraction of his regulations.

McAlpin made even the most inconsequential approaches to a statement with a keen and questioning glance. "The girl went up to the Cat on the early stage, sir. She's coming back this afternoon."

"What is she riding away over here to Calabasas for to take the stage, instead of riding straight into Sleepy Cat?"

Once more McAlpin eyed him carefully. "The girl's been sick."

"Sick?"

"She ain't really fit to ride a step," confided the Scotch boss with growing confidence. "But she's been going up two or three times now to get some medicine from Doc Torpy—that's the way of it. There's a nice girl, sir—in a bunch o' ruffians, I know—though old Duke, she lives with, he ain't a half-bad man except for too many cards; I used to work for him—but I call her a nice girl. Do you happen to know her?"

De Spain had long been on guard. "I've spoken with her in a business way one or twice, Jim. I can't really say I know her."

A Cup of Coffee

"Nice girl. But that's a tough bunch in that Gap, sure as you're alive; yes, sir."

De Spain was well aware the canny boss ought to know. McAlpin had lived at one time in the Gap, and was himself reputed to have been a hardy and enduring rider on a night round-up.

"Anything sick, Jim?" asked de Spain, walking on down the barn and looking at the horses. It was only the second time since he had given him the job that de Spain had called the barn boss "Jim," and McAlpin answered with the rising assurance of one who realizes he is "in" right. "Not so much as a sore hoof in either alley, Mr. de Spain. I try to take care of them, sir."

"What are we paying you, Jim?"

"Twenty-seven a week, sir; pretty heavy work at that."

"We'll try to make that thirty-two after this week."

McAlpin touched his cap. "Thank you kindly, sir, I'm sure. It costs like hell to live out here, Mr. de Spain."

"Lefever says you live off him at poker."

"Ha, ha! Ha, ha, sir! John will have his joke. He's always after me to play poker with him—I don't like to do it. I've got a family to support—he ain't. But by and far, I don't think John and me is ten dollars apart, year in and year

out. Look at that bay, sir! A month ago Elpaso said that horse was all in—look at him now.
I manage to keep things up."

"What did you say," asked de Spain indifferently, "had been the matter with Nan Morgan?"
Her name seemed a whole mouthful to speak, so
fearful was he of betraying interest.

"Why, I really didn't say, sir. And I don't
know. But from what she says, and the way she
coughs, I'm thinking it was a touch of this p-new-
monia that's going around so much lately, sir."

His listener recalled swiftly the days that had
passed since the night he had seen her wet through
in the cold rain at Sleepy Cat. He feared Jim's
diagnosis might be right. And he had already
made all arrangements to meet the occasion now
presenting itself. Circumstances seemed at last
to favor him, and he looked at his watch. The
down stage bringing Nan back would be due in
less than an hour.

"Jim," he said thoughtfully, "you are doing
the right thing in showing some good-will toward
the Morgans."

"Now, I'm glad you think that, sir."

"You know I unintentionally rubbed their
backs the wrong way in dragging Sassoon out."

"They're jealous of their power, I know—very
jealous."

A Cup of Coffee

"This seems the chance to show that I have no real animosity myself toward the outfit."

Since de Spain was not looking at him, McAlpin cocked two keen and curious eyes on the sphinx-like birthmark of the very amiable speaker's face. However, the astute boss, if he wondered, made no comment. "When the stage comes in," continued de Spain quietly, "have the two grays— Lady and Ben—hitched to my own light Studebaker. I'll drive her over to the Gap myself."

"The very thing," exclaimed McAlpin, staring and struggling with his breath.

"In some way I've happened, both times I talked with her, to get in wrong—understand?" McAlpin, with clearing wits, nodded more than once. "No fault of mine; it just happened so. And she may not at first take kindly to the idea of going with me."

"I see."

"But she ought to do it. She will be tired— it's a long, dusty ride for a well woman, let alone one that has been ill."

"So it is, so it is!"

De Spain looked now shamelessly at his ready-witted aid. "See that her pony is lame when she gets here—can't be ridden. But you'll take good care of him and send him home in a few days— get it?"

McAlpin half closed his eyes. "He'll be so lame it would stagger a cowboy to back him ten feet—and never be hurt a mite, neither. Trust me!"

"No other horse that she could ride, in the barn?"

"No horse she could ride between Calabasas and Thief River."

"If she insists on riding *something*, or even walking home," continued de Spain dubiously, for he felt instinctively that he should have the task of his life to induce Nan to accept any kind of a peace-offering, "I'll ride or walk with her anyway. Can you sleep me here to-night, on the hay?"

"Sleep you on a hair mattress, sir. You've got a room right here up-stairs, didn't you know that?"

"Don't mind the bed," directed de Spain prudently. "I like the hay better."

"As you like; we've got plenty of it fresh up-stairs, from the Gap. But the bed's all right, sir; it is, on me word."

With arrangements so begun, de Spain walked out-of-doors and looked reflectively up the Sleepy Cat road. One further refinement in his appeal for Nan's favor suggested itself. She would be hungry, possibly faint in the heat and dust, when

A Cup of Coffee

she arrived. He returned to McAlpin: "Where can I get a good cup of coffee when the stage comes in?"

"Go right down to the inn, sir. It's a new chap running it—a half-witted man from Texas. My wife is cooking there off and on. She'll fix you up a sandwich and a cup of good coffee."

It was four o'clock, and the sun beat fiercely on the desert. De Spain walked down to the inn unmindful of the heat. In summer rig, with his soft-shirt collar turned under, his forearms bare, and his thoughts engaged, he made his way rapidly on, looking neither to the right nor the left.

As he approached the weather-beaten pile it looked no more inviting in sunshine than it had looked in shadow; and true to its traditions, not a living being was anywhere to be seen. The door of the office stood ajar. De Spain, pushing it all the way open, walked in. No one greeted him as he crossed the threshold, and the unsightly room was still bare of furnishings except for the great mahogany bar, with its two very large broken mirrors and the battered pilasters and carvings.

De Spain pounded on the bar. His effort to attract attention met with no response. He walked to the left end of the bar, lifted the handrail that enclosed the space behind it, and pushed open the door between the mirrors leading to the back room. This, too, was empty. He called out—there was no response. He walked through a second door opening on an arcaded passageway toward the kitchen—not a soul was in sight. There was a low fire in the kitchen stove, but Mrs. McAlpin had apparently gone home for a while. Walking back toward the office, he remembered the covered way leading to a patio, which in turn opened on the main road. He perceived also that at the end next the office the covered way faced the window at the end of the long bar.

Irritated at the desertion of the place, due, he afterward learned, to the heat of the afternoon, and disappointed at the frustration of his purpose, he walked back through the rear room into the office. As he lifted the hand-rail and, passing through, lowered it behind him, he took out his watch to see how soon the stage was due. While he held the timepiece in his hand he heard a rapid clatter of hoofs approaching the place. Thinking it might be Scott and Lefever arriving from the south an hour ahead of time, he started toward the front door—which was still open—to greet them. Outside, hurried footsteps reached the door just ahead of him and a large man, stepping quickly into the room, confronted de Spain.

A Cup of Coffee

ne of the man's hands rested lightly on his right
le. De Spain recognized him instantly; the
nall, drooping head, carried well forward, the
:en eyes, the long hand, and, had there still
:en a question in his mind, the loud-patterned,
abby waistcoat would have proclaimed beyond
ubt—Deaf Sandusky.

CHAPTER X

THE GLASS BUTTON

EVEN as the big fellow stepped lightly just inside and to the left—as de Spain stood—of the door and faced him, the encounter seemed to de Spain accidental. While Sandusky was not a man he would have chosen to meet at that time, he did not at first consider the incident an eventful one. But before he could speak, a second man appeared in the doorway, and this man appeared to be joking with a third, behind him. As the second man crossed the threshold, de Spain saw Sandusky's high-voiced little fighting crony, Logan, who now made way, as he stepped within to the right of the open door, for the swinging shoulders and rolling stride of Gale Morgan.

Morgan, eying de Spain with insolence, as was his wont, closed the door behind him with a bang. Then he backed his powerful frame significantly against it.

A blind man could have seen the completeness of the snare. An unpleasant feeling flashed across de Spain's perception. It was only for the immeasurable part of a second—while uncertainty was resolving itself into a rapid certainty. When Gale Morgan stepped into the room on the heels of his two Calabasas friends, de Spain would have sold for less than a cup of coffee all his chances for life. Nevertheless, before Morgan had set his back fairly against the door and the trap was sprung, de Spain had mapped his fight, and had already felt that, although he might not be the fortunate man, not more than one of the four within the room would be likely to leave it alive.

He did not retreat from where he halted at the instant Sandusky entered. His one slender chance was to hug to the men that meant to kill him. Morgan, the nearest, he esteemed the least dangerous of the three; but to think to escape both Sandusky and Logan at close quarters was, he knew, more than ought to be hoped for.

While Morgan was closing the door, de Spain smiled at his visitors: "That isn't necessary, Morgan: I'm not ready to run." Morgan only continued to stare at him. "I need hardly ask," added de Spain, "whether you fellows have business with me?"

He looked to Sandusky for a reply; it was Logan who answered in shrill falsetto: "No. We don't happen to have business that I know of. A friend of ours may have a little, maybe!" Logan,

lifting his shoulders with his laugh, looked toward
his companions for an answer to his joke.

De Spain's smile appeared unruffled: "You'll
help him transact it, I suppose?"

Logan, looking again toward Sandusky, grinned:
"He won't need any help."

"Who is your friend?" demanded de Spain
good-naturedly. Logan's glance misled him; it
did not refer to Sandusky. And even as he asked
the question de Spain heard through the half-open
window at the end of the bar the sound of hoofs.
Hoping against hope for Lefever, the interruption cheered him. It certainly did not seem that
his situation could be made worse.

"Well," answered Logan, talking again to his
gallery of cronies, "we've got two or three friends
that want to see you. They're waiting outside
to see what you'll look like in about five minutes—ain't they, Gale?"

Some one was moving within the rear room.
De Spain felt hope in every footfall he heard, and
the mention this time of Morgan's name cleared
his plan of battle. Before Gale, with an oath,
could blurt out his answer, de Spain had resolved
to fight where he stood, taking Logan first and
Morgan as he should jump in between the two.
It was at the best a hopeless venture against Sandusky's first shot, which de Spain knew was al-

most sure to reach a vital spot. But desperate men cannot be choosers.

"There's no time for seeing me like the present," declared de Spain, ignoring Morgan and addressing his words to Logan. "Bring your friends in. What are you complaining about, Morgan?" he asked, resenting the stream of abuse that Gale hurled at him whenever he could get a word in. "I had my turn at you with a rifle the other day. You've got your turn now. And I call it a pretty soft one, too—don't you, Sandusky?" he demanded suddenly of the big fellow.

Sandusky alone through the talk had kept an unbroken silence. He was eating up de Spain with his eyes, and de Spain not only ached to hear him speak but was resolved to make him. Sandusky had stood motionless from the instant he entered the room. He knew all about the preliminary gabble of a fight and took no interest in it. He did *not* know all about de Spain, and being about to face his bullets he had prudence enough to wonder whether the man could have brought a reputation to Sleepy Cat without having done something to earn it. What Sandusky was sensibly intent on was the determination that he should not contribute personally to the further upbuilding of anybody's reputation. His eyes

with this resolve shining in them rested intently
on de Spain, and at his side the long fingers
of his right hand beat a soft tattoo against his
pistol holster. De Spain's question seemed to
arouse him. "What's your name?" he demanded
bluntly. His voice was heavy and his deafness
was reflected in the strained tone.

"It's on the butt of my gun, Sandusky."

"What's that he says?" demanded the man
known as the butcher, asking the question of
Logan, but without taking his eyes off his shifty
prey.

Logan raised his voice to repeat the words and
to add a ribald comment.

"You make a good deal of noise," muttered
Sandusky, speaking again to de Spain.

"That ought not to bother you much, Sandusky," shouted de Spain, trying to win a smile
from his taciturn antagonist.

"His noise won't bother anybody much longer,"
put in Logan, whose retorts overflowed at every
interval. But there was no smile even hinted at
in the uncompromising vigilance of Sandusky's
expressionless face. De Spain discounted the next
few mintues far enough to feel that Sandusky's
first shot would mean death to him, even if he
could return it.

"I'll tell you, de Spain," continued Logan,

"we're going to have a drink with you. Then we're going to prepare you for going back where you come from—with nice flowers."

"I guess you thought you could come out here and run over everybody in the Spanish Sinks," interposed Morgan, with every oath he could summon to load his words.

"Keep out, Morgan," exclaimed Logan testily. "I'll do this talking."

De Spain continued to banter. "Gentlemen," he said, addressing the three together and realizing that every moment wasted before the shooting added a grain of hope, "I am ready to drink when you are."

"He's ready to drink, Tom," roared Morgan in the deaf man's ear.

"I'm ready," announced Sandusky in hollow voice.

Still regarding de Spain with the most businesslike expression, the grizzled outlaw took a guarded step forward, his companions following suit. De Spain, always with a jealous regard for the relative distance between him and his self-appointed executioners, moved backward. In crossing the room, Sandusky, without objection from his companions, moved across their front, and when the four lined up at the bar their positions had changed. De Spain stood at the extreme left, Sandusky next, Logan beside him, and Gale Morgan, at the other end of the line, pretended to pound the bar for service. De Spain, following mountain etiquette in the circumstances, spread his open hands, palms down, on the bar. Sandusky's great palms slid in the same fashion over the checked slab in unspoken recognition of the brief armistice. Logan's hands came up in turn, and Morgan still pounded for some one to serve.

De Spain in the new disposition weighed his chances as being both better and worse. They had put Sandusky's first shot at no more than an arm's length from his prey, with Logan next to cover the possibility of the big fellow's failing to paralyze de Spain the first instant. On the other hand, de Spain, trained in the tactics of Whispering Smith and Medicine Bend gunmen, welcomed a short-arm struggle with the worst of his assailants closest at hand. One factor, too, that he realized they were reckoning with, gave him no concern. No men in the mountains understood better or were more expert in the technicalities of the law of self-defense than the gunmen of Calabasas. The killing of de Spain they well knew would, in spite of everything, raise a hornet's nest in Sleepy Cat, and they wished to be prepared for it. Their manœuvring on this score caused no disquiet to their slender, compactly built victim. "You'll wait a long time, if you wait for service here, Morgan," he said, commenting with composure on Morgan's impatience. Logan looked again at his two companions and laughed.

Every hope de Spain had of possible help from the back room died with that laugh. Then the door behind the bar slowly opened, and the scarfeatured face of Sassoon peered cautiously from the gloom. The horse thief, stooping, walked in with a leer directed triumphantly at the railroad man.

If it were possible to deepen it, the sinister spot on de Spain's face darkened. Something in his blood raged at the sight of the malevolent face. He glanced at Logan. "This," he smiled faintly, nodding toward Sassoon as he himself took a short step farther to the left, "is your drink, Harvey, is it?"

"No," retorted Logan loudly, "this is *your* drink."

"I'll take Sassoon," assented de Spain, good-natured again and shifting still another step to the left. "What do you fellows want now?"

"We want to punch a hole through that strawberry," said Logan, "that beauty-mark. Where did you get it, de Spain?"

"I might as well ask where you get your gall, Harvey," returned de Spain, watching Logan hunch Sandusky toward the left that both might crowd him closer. "I was born with my beauty-mark—just as you were born with your damned bad manners," he added composedly, for in hugging up to him his enemies were playing his game. "You can't help it, neither can I," he went on. "Somebody is bound to pay for putting that mark on me. Somebody is bound to pay for your manners. Why talk about either? Sassoon, set out for your friends—or I will. Spread, gentlemen, spread."

He had reached the position on which he believed his life depended, and stood so close to the end of the bar that with a single step, as he uttered the last words, he turned it. Sandusky pushed close next him. De Spain continued to speak without hesitation or break, but the words seemed to have no place in his mind. He was thinking only, and saw only within his field of vision, a cut-glass button that fastened the bottom of Sandusky's greased waistcoat.

"You've waited one day too long to collect for your strawberry, de Spain," cried Logan shrilly. "You've turned one trick too many on the Sinks, young fellow. If the man that put your mark on you ain't in this room, you'll never get him."

The Glass Button

"Which means, I take it, you're going to try to get me," smiled de Spain.

"No," bellowed Morgan, "it means we have got you."

"You are fooling yourself, Harvey." De Spain addressed the warning to Logan. "And you, too, Sandusky," he added.

"We'll take care of that," grinned Logan. Sandusky kept silence.

"You are jumping into another man's fight," protested de Spain steadily.

"Sassoon's fight is our fight," interrupted Morgan.

"I advise you," said de Spain once more, looking with the words at Sandusky and his crony, "to keep out of it."

"Sandusky," yelled Logan to his partner, "he advises me and you to keep out of this fight," he shrilly laughed.

"Sure," assented Sandusky, but with no variation in tone and his eyes on de Spain.

Logan, with an oath, leaned over the bar toward Sassoon, and pointed contemptuously toward the end of the bar. "Shike!" he cried, "step through the rail and take that man's gun."

De Spain, looking from one to the other of the four faces confronting him, laughed for the first time. But he was looking without seeing what

133

he seemed to look at. In reality, he saw only a
cut-glass button. He was face to face with taking
a man's life or surrendering his own, and he knew
the life must be taken in such a way as instantly
to disable its possessor. These men had chosen
their time and place. There was nothing for it
but to meet them. Sassoon was stepping toward
him, though very doubtfully. De Spain laughed
again, dryly this time. "Go slow, Sassoon," he
said. "That gun is loaded."

"If you want terms, hand over your gun to
Sassoon," cried Logan.

"Not till it's empty," returned de Spain. "Do
you want to try taking it?" he demanded of Logan, his cheeks burning a little darker.

Logan never answered the question. It was
not meant to be answered. For de Spain asked it
only to cover the spring he made at that instant
into Sandusky's middle. Catlike though it was,
the feint did not take the big fellow unprepared.
He had heard once, when or where he could not
tell, but he had never forgotten the hint, that de
Spain, a boxer, was as quick with his feet as with
his hands. The outlaw whirled. Both men shot
from the hip; the reports cracked together. One
bullet grazing the fancy button smashed through
the gaudy waistcoat: the other, as de Spain's
free hand struck at the muzzle of the big man's

Hugging his shield, de Spain threw his second shot over
Sandusky's left shoulder.

gun, tore into de Spain's foot. Sandusky, convulsed by the frightful shock, staggered against de Spain's arm, the latter dancing tight against him. Logan, alive to the trick but caught behind his partner, fired over Sandusky's right shoulder at de Spain's head, flattened sidewise against the gasping outlaw's breast. Hugging his shield, de Spain threw his second shot over Sandusky's left shoulder into Logan's face. Logan, sinking to the floor, never moved again. Supporting with extraordinary strength the unwieldy bulk of the dying butcher, de Spain managed to steady him as a buffer against Morgan's fire until he could send a slug over Sandusky's head at the instant the latter collapsed. Morgan fell against the bar.

Sandusky's weight dragged de Spain down. For an instant the four men sprawled in a heap. Sassoon, who had not yet got an effective shot across at his agile enemy, dropping his revolver, dodged under the rail to close. De Spain, struggling to free himself from the dying man, saw, through a mist, the greenish eyes and the thirsty knife. He fired from the floor. The bullet shook without stopping his enemy, and de Spain, partly caught under Sandusky's body, thought, as Sassoon came on, the game was up. With an effort born of desperation, he dragged himself from under the twitching giant, freed his revolver, rolled away,

and, with his sight swimming, swung the gun at
Sassoon's stomach. He meant to kill him. The
bullet whirled the white-faced man to one side
and he dropped, but pulled himself, full of fight,
to his knees and, knife in hand, panted forward.
De Spain rolling hastily from him, staggered to
his feet and, running in as Sassoon tried to strike,
beat him senseless with the butt of his gun.

His own eyes were streaming blood. His head
was reeling and he was breathless, but he remembered those of the gang waiting outside. He still
could see dimly the window at the end of the bar.
Dashing his fingers through the red stream on
his forehead, he ran for the window, smashed
through the sash into the patio and found Sassoon's horse trembling at the fusillade. Catching
the lines and the pommel, he stuck his foot up
again and again for the stirrup. It was useless;
he could not make it. Then, summoning all of
his fast-ebbing strength, he threw himself like a
sack across the horse's back, lashed the brute
through the open gateway, climbed into the saddle, and spurred blindly away.

CHAPTER XI

AFTER THE STORM

IT was well along toward midnight of the same day when two horsemen, after having ridden circumspectly around the outbuildings and corrals, dismounted from their horses at some little distance from the door of the Calabasas Inn. They shook out their legs as men do after a long turn in the saddle and faced each other in a whispered colloquy. An overcast sky, darkening the night, concealed the alkali crusting the riders and their horses; but the hard breathing of the latter in the darkness told of a pace forced for some hours.

"Find your feet before you go in, Pardaloe," suggested the heavier of the two men guardedly to the taller one.

"Does this man know you?" muttered the man addressed as Pardaloe, stamping in the soft dust and shifting slightly a gun harness on his breast.

"Pedro knows me," returned Lefever, the other man, "but McAlpin says there is a new man here, a half-wit. They all belong to the same gang—coiners, I believe, every one of them. They work here and push in Texas."

"Can you spot the room when you get upstairs, where we saw that streak of light a minute ago?" demanded Pardaloe, gazing at the black front of the building.

"I can spot every foot of the place, up-stairs and down, in the dark," declared Lefever, peering through the inky night at the ruinous pile.

Instead of meeting de Spain, as appointed, Lefever had come in from the Thief River stage with Scott three hours late only to learn of the fight at the Inn and de Spain's disappearance. Jeffries had already sent a party, of whom Pardaloe, a man of Farrell Kennedy's from Medicine Bend, had been picked up as one, down from Sleepy Cat, to look for the missing man, and for hours the search had gone forward.

"Suppose you go back to the barn," suggested Pardaloe, "and wait there while I go in and have a little talk with the landlord."

"Why, yes, Pardaloe. That's an idea," assented Lefever feebly. Then he laid the first two fingers of his fat right hand on the lapel of his companion's coat: "Where should you like your body sent?" he asked in feigned confidence. "Concerning these little details, it's just as well to know your wishes now."

"You don't suppose this boob will try to fight, do you, when he knows Jeffries will burn the shack over his head if another railroad man is attacked in it?" demanded Pardaloe.

"The most ruinous habit I have had in life—and first and last I have contracted many—has been, trusting other people," observed Lefever. "A man shouldn't trust anybody—not even himself. We can burn the boob's shack down—of course: but if you go in there alone the ensuing blaze would be of no particular interest to you."

"All right. We go in together."

"Not exactly that, either. You go first. Few of these forty-four bullets will go through two men at once."

Ignoring Lefever's pleasantry, Pardaloe, pulling his hat brim through force of habit well over his eyes, shook himself loose and, like a big cat walking in water, stepped toward the door. He could move his tall, bony frame, seemingly covered only with muscles and sinews, so silently that in the dark he made no more sound than a spectre. But once before the door, with Lefever close at hand, he pounded the cracked panels till the windows shook. Some time elapsed before there was any response. The pounding continued till a flickering light appeared at a window. There was an ill-natured colloquy, a delay, more impatience, and at length the landlord reluctantly opened the door.

Nan of Music Mountain

He held in his hand an oil-lamp. The chimney
had been smoked in such a way that the light of
the flame was thrown forward and not back.
Lefever in the background, nothing disturbed,
threw a flash-light back at the half-dressed innkeeper. His hair was tumbled sleepily across his
forehead and his eyes—one showing a white scar
across the pupil—set deep in retreating orbits,
blinked under heavy brows. "What do you
want?" he demanded. Pardaloe, without answering, pushed through the half-open door into
the room.

"We're staying here to-night," announced Pardaloe, as simply as possible. Lefever had already
edged into the doorway, pushing the stubborn
innkeeper aside by sheer bulk of weight and size.

The sleepy man gave ground stubbornly.
"I've got no beds," he growled surlily. "You
can't stay here."

Lefever at once assumed the case for the intruders. "I could sleep this minute standing on
my head," he declared. "And as for staying
here, I can't stay anywhere else. What's your
name, son?" he demanded, buttonholing in his
off-hand way the protesting man.

"My name is Philippi," answered the one-eyed
defiantly.

"Regards to Brutus, my dear fellow," retorted

After the Storm

Lefever, seizing the man's hand as if happily surprised.

"You can't crowd in here, so you might as well move on," declared Philippi gruffly. "This is no hotel."

Lefever laughed. "No offense, Philippi, but would it be indiscreet to ask which side of your face hurts the most when you smile?"

"If you've got no beds, we won't bother you long," interposed Pardaloe.

"I'd like a pitcher of ice-water, anyway," persisted Lefever. "Sit down, noble Greek; we'll talk this over."

"Who are you fellows?" demanded Philippi, looking from one to the other.

"I am a prospector from the Purgatoire," answered Pardaloe.

Philippi turned his keen eye on Lefever. "You a railroad man?"

"No, sir," declared Lefever, dusting the alkali vigorously from his coat sleeve.

"What are you?"

John looked as modest as it was possible for him to look. "Few people ask me that, but in matter of fact I am an *objet d'art*."

"What's that?"

"Different things at different times to different men, Philippi," answered Lefever simply, exploring, while he spoke, different corners of the room with his flash-light. "At this moment—" he stopped suddenly, then resumed reassuringly— "I want a drink."

"Nothing doing," muttered the landlord sulkily.

Lefever's flash-light focussed on a United States license hanging back of the bar. "Is that a mere frame-up, Philippi?" he demanded, walking significantly toward the vender's authority.

"Nothing in the house to-night."

"Then," announced Lefever calmly, "I arrest you."

Philippi started. "Arrest me?"

"For obtaining a thirst under false pretenses. Come, now, before we slip the irons on, get us something to eat. I'll go up-stairs and pick out a room to sleep in."

"I tell you," insisted Philippi profanely, "there are no rooms for you to sleep in up-stairs."

"And I," retorted Lefever, "tell you there are. Anyway, I left a sewing-machine up-stairs here three years ago, and promised to keep it oiled for the lady. This is a good time to begin."

With Lefever making the old steps creak, ahead, and Pardaloe, with his long, soft, pigeon-toed tread close behind, the unwilling landlord was taken up the stairs, and the two men thoroughly searched the house. Lefever lowered his

After the Storm

voice when the hunt began through the bedrooms
—few of which contained even a bed—but he
kept up a running fire of talk that gave Philippi
no respite from anxiety.

Outside the kitchen quarters, which likewise
were rigorously searched, not a soul could be
found in the house. One room only, over the
kitchen, gave hope of uncovering something.
The party reached the door of this room through
a narrow, tortuous passageway along an attic
gable. The door was locked. Philippi told them
it belonged to a sheep-herder who did not use it
often. He protested he had no key. Pardaloe
knocked and, getting no response, tried unsuc-
cessfully to force the lock. Lefever motioned him
aside and, after knocking loudly on the door himself, laid his shoulder against it. The door
creaked and sprung in crazy protest. The panels
cracked, the stubborn frame gave, and with a
violent crash Lefever pushed completely through
the locked barrier and threw his flash-light inside.
Pardaloe, urging the unwilling Philippi ahead,
followed.

The room, unfinished under the rafters, was
destitute of furnishings, and bore traces of long
disuse. Stretched on the floor toward the middle
of it, and side by side, lay two men. One of them
was very large, the other not more than half his

143

companion's size. Lefever kneeling over the man nearest the door listened for signs of breathing, and laid his head to the man's heart. Having completed his examination, he went around to the other—Pardaloe and Philippi silently watching—and looked him over with equal care. When he had done, he examined, superficially, the wounds of each man. Rising, he turned toward Philippi. "Were these men dead when you brought them up here?"

"I didn't bring 'em up," growled Philippi.

"You know them, Pardaloe?" asked Lefever. Pardaloe answered that he did. Lefever turned sharply on Philippi. "Where were you when this fight was going on?"

"Down at the stage barn."

"Getting your alibi ready. But, of course, you know that won't let you out, Philippi. Your best chance is to tell the truth. There were two others with this pair—where are Gale Morgan and Sassoon?"

"Satt Morgan was here with hay to-day. He took them over this evening to Music Mountain."

"Where were they hit?"

"Morgan was hit in the shoulder, as far as I heard. Sassoon was hit in the side, and in the neck."

"Where is de Spain?"

After the Storm

"Dead, I reckon, by this time."

"Where's his body?"

"I don't know."

"Why do you think he is dead?"

"Sassoon said he was hit in the head."

"Yet he got away on horseback!"

"I'm telling you what Sassoon said; I didn't see him."

Lefever and Pardaloe rode back to the stage barn. "Certainly looks blue for Henry," muttered Lefever, after he had gone over with Pardaloe and McAlpin all of the scant information that could be gathered. "Bob Scott," he added gloomily, "may find him somewhere on the Sinks."

At Sleepy Cat, Jeffries, wild with impatience, was on the telephone. Lefever, with McAlpin and Pardaloe standing at his side, reported to the superintendent all he could learn. "He rode away—without help, of course," explained Lefever to Jeffries in conclusion. "What shape he is in, it's pretty hard to say, Jeffries. Three more of the bunch, Vance Morgan, Bull Page, and a lame man that works for Bill Morgan, were waiting in the saddle at the head of the draw between the barn and the hotel for him if he should get away from the inn. Somehow, he went the other way and nobody saw hide nor hair of him, so far

as I can learn. If he was able to make it, Jeff, he
would naturally try for Sleepy Cat. But that's a
pretty fair ride for a sound man, let alone a man
that's hit—and everybody claims he was hit. If
he wasn't hit he should have been in Sleepy Cat
long before this. You say you've had men out
across the river?"

"Since dark," responded Jeffries. "But, John,"
he asked, "could a man hit in the way de Spain
was hit, climb into a saddle and make a get-
away?"

"Henry might," answered Lefever laconically.

Scott, with two men who had been helping him,
rode in at two o'clock after a fruitless search to
wait for light. At daybreak they picked up the
trail. Studying carefully the room in which the
fight had taken place, they followed de Spain's
jump through the broken sash into the patio.
Blood that had been roughly cleaned up marked
the spot where he had mounted the horse and
dashed through an open corral gate down the
south trail toward Music Mountain. There was
speculation as to why he should have chosen a
route leading directly into the enemy's country,
but there was no gainsaying the trail—occasional
flecks of blood blazed the direction of the fleeing
hoofs. These led—not as the trailers hoped they
would, in a wide détour across easy-riding coun-

try toward the north and the Sleepy Cat stage road—but farther and farther south and west into extremely rough country, a no man's land, where there was no forage, no water, and no habitation. Not this alone disquieted his pursuers; the trail as they pursued it showed the unsteady riding of a man badly wounded.

Lefever, walking his horse along the side of a ridge, shook his head as he leaned over the pony's shoulder. Pardaloe and Scott rode abreast of him. "It would take some hit, Bob, to bring de Spain to this kind of riding."

Beyond the ridge they found where he had dismounted for the first time. Here Scott picked up five empty shells ejected from de Spain's revolver. They saw more than trace enough of how he had tried to stanch the persistent flow from his wounds. He seemed to have worked a long time with these and with some success, for his trail thereafter was less marked by blood. It was, however, increasingly unsteady, and after a time it reached a condition that led Scott to declare de Spain was no longer guiding Sassoon's pony; it was wandering at will.

Confirmation, if it were needed, of the declaration could soon be read in the trail by all of them. The horse, unrestrained by its rider, had come almost completely about and headed again for

Music Mountain. Within a few miles of the snow-covered peak the hoof-prints ran directly into the road from Calabasas to Morgan's Gap and were practically lost in the dust of the wagon road.

"Here's a go," muttered Pardaloe at fault, after riding back and forth for a mile in an effort to pick the horse up again.

"Remember," interposed Scott mildly, "he is riding Sassoon's horse—the brute is naturally heading for home."

"Follow him home, then," said Lefever unhesitatingly.

Scott looked at his companion in surprise: "Near home, you mean, John," he suggested inoffensively. "For three of us to ride into the Gap this morning would be some excitement for the Morgans. I don't think the excitement would last long—for us."

The three were agreed, however, to follow up to the mouth of the Gap itself and did follow. Finding no trace of de Spain's movements in this quest, they rode separately in wide circles to the north and south, but without picking up a hoof-print that led anywhere or gave them any clew to the whereabouts of the missing man.

"There is one consolation," muttered Lefever, as they held to what each felt to be an almost hopeless search. "As long as Henry can stick to a saddle he can shoot—and the Morgans after yesterday afternoon will think twice before they close in on him, if they find him."

Scott shook his head: "That brings us up against another proposition, John. De Spain hasn't got any cartridges."

Lefever turned sharply: "What do you mean?"

"His belt is in the barn at Calabasas, hanging up with his coat."

"Why didn't you tell me that before," demanded Lefever indignantly.

"I've been hoping all the time we'd find Henry and I wouldn't have to tell you."

In spite of the hope advanced by Lefever that de Spain might by some chance have cartridges in his pocket, Scott's information was disquieting. However, it meant for de Spain, they knew, only the greater need of succor, and when the news of his plight was made known later in the day to Jeffries, efforts to locate him were redoubled.

For a week the search continued day and night, but each day, even each succeeding hour, reduced the expectation of ever seeing the hunted man alive. Spies working at Calabasas, others sent in by Jeffries to Music Mountain among the Morgans, and men from Medicine Bend haunting Sleepy Cat could get no word of de Spain. Fairly accurate reports accounted for Gale Morgan, nursing a wound at home, and for Sassoon, badly wounded and under cover somewhere in the Gap. Beyond this, information halted.

Toward the end of the week a Mexican sheepherder brought word in to Lefever that he had seen in Duke Morgan's stable, Sassoon's horse— the one on which de Spain had escaped. He averred he had seen the blood-stained Santa Fe saddle that had been taken off the horse when the horse was found at daybreak of the day following the fight, waiting at Sassoon's corral to be cared for. There could be, it was fairly well ascertained, no mistake about the horse: the man knew the animal; but his information threw no light on the fate of its missing rider.

Though Scott had known first of de Spain's helpless condition in his desperate flight, as regarded self-defense, the Indian was the last to abandon hope of seeing him alive again. One night, in the midst of a gloomy council at Jeffries's office, he was pressed for an explanation of his confidence. It was always difficult for Scott to explain his reasons for thinking anything. Men with the surest instinct are usually poorest at reasoning a conviction out. But, Bob, cross-examined and harried, managed to give some explanation of the faith that was in him. "In the

After the Storm

first place," he said, "I've ridden a good deal with that man— pretty much all over the country north of Medicine Bend. He is as full of tricks as a nut's full of meat. Henry de Spain can hide out like an Indian and doctor himself. Then, again, I know something about the way he fights; up here, they don't. If those four fellows had ever seen him in action they never would have expected to get out of a room alive, after a show-down with Henry de Spain. As near as I can make out from all the talk that's floating around, what fooled them was seeing him shoot at a mark here one day in Sleepy Cat."

Jeffries didn't interrupt, but he slapped his knee sharply.

"You might just as well try to stand on a box of dynamite, and shoot into it, and expect to live to tell it," continued Scott mildly, "as to shoot into that fellow in a room with closed doors and expect to get away with it. The only way the bunch can ever kill that man, without getting killed themselves, is to get him from behind; and at that, John, the man that fires the gun," murmured the scout, "ought to be behind a tree.

"You say he is hit. I grant it," he concluded. "But I knew him once when he was hit to lie out in the bush for a week. He got cut off once from Whispering Smith and Kennedy after a

151

scrimmage outside Williams Cache two years ago."

"You don't believe, then, he's dead, Bob?" demanded Jeffries impatiently.

"Not till I see him dead," persisted Scott unmoved.

CHAPTER XII

ON MUSIC MOUNTAIN

DE SPAIN, when he climbed into Sassoon's saddle, was losing sight and consciousness. He knew he could no longer defend himself, and was so faint that only the determination of putting distance between him and any pursuers held him to the horse after he spurred away. With the instinct of the hunted, he fumbled with his right hand for his means of defense, and was relieved to find his revolver, after his panicky dash for safety, safe in its place. He put his hand to his belt for fresh cartridges. The belt was gone.

The discovery sent a shock through his failing faculties. He could not recollect why he had no belt. Believing his senses tricked him, he felt again and again for it before he would believe it was not buckled somewhere about him. But it was gone, and he stuck back in his waistband his useless revolver. One hope remained—flight, and he spurred his horse cruelly.

Blood running continually into his eyes from the wound in his head made him think his eyes were gone, and direction was a thing quite beyond his power to compass. He made little effort to guide, and his infuriated horse flew along as if winged.

A warm, sticky feeling in his right boot warned him, when he tried to make some mental inventory of his condition, of at least one other wound. But he found he could inventory nothing, recollect next to nothing, and all that he wanted to do was to escape. More than once he tried to look behind, and he dashed his hand across his red forehead. He could not see twenty feet ahead or behind. Even when he hurriedly wiped the cloud from his eyes his vision seemed to have failed, and he could only cling to his horse to put the miles as fast as possible between himself and more of the Morgans.

A perceptible weakness presently forced him to realize he must look to his wounded foot. This he did without slackening speed. The sight of it and the feeling inside his torn and blood-soaked boot was not reassuring, but he rode on, sparing neither his horse nor his exhaustion. It was only when spells of dizziness, recurring with frequency, warned him he could not keep the saddle much longer, that he attempted to dismount to stanch the drip of blood from his stirrup.

Before he slackened speed he tried to look behind to reconnoitre. With relief he perceived his sight to be a trifle better, and in scanning the horizon he could discover no pursuers. Choosing a secluded spot, he dismounted, cut open his boot, and found that a bullet, passing downward, had torn an artery under the arch of the foot. Making a rude tourniquet, he succeeded in checking pretty well the spurting flow that was sapping his strength. After he had adjusted the bandage he stood up and looked at it. Then he drew his revolver again and broke it. He found five empty shells in the chambers and threw them away. The last cartridge had not been fired. He could not even figure out how he had happened to have six cartridges in the cylinder, for he rarely loaded more than five. Indeed, it was his fixed habit—to avoid accidents—never to carry a cartridge under the hammer of his gun— yet now there had been one. Without trying to explain the circumstance, he took fresh stock of his chances and began to wonder whether he might yet escape and live.

He climbed again into the saddle, and, riding to a ridge, looked carefully over the desert. It was with an effort that he could steady himself, and the extent of his weakness surprised him. What further perplexed him as he crossed a long divide, got another good view and saw no pursuit threatening in any direction, was to identify the country he was in. The only landmark anywhere in sight that he could recognize was Music Mountain. This now lay to the northwest, and he knew he must be a long way from any country he was familiar with. But there was no gainsaying, even in his confused condition, Music Mountain. After looking at it a long time he headed with some hesitation cautiously toward it, with intent to intercept the first trail to the northeast. This would take him toward Sleepy Cat.

As his eyes continued to sweep the horizon he noted that the sun was down and it was growing dark. This brought a relief and a difficulty. It left him less in fear of molestation, but made it harder for him to reach a known trail. The horse, in spite of the long, hard ride seemed fresh yet, and de Spain, with one cartridge would still have laughed at his difficulties had he not realized, with uneasiness, that his head was becoming very light. Recurring intervals of giddiness foreshadowed a new danger in his uncharted ride. It became again a problem for him to keep his seat in the saddle. He was aware at intervals that he was steadying himself like a drunken man. His efforts to guide the horse only bewildered the beast, and the two travelled on maudlin curves and doubled back on their track

On Music Mountain

until de Spain decided that his sole chance of reaching any known trail was to let go and give the horse his head.

A starless night fell across the desert. With danger of pursuit practically ended, and only a chance encounter to fear, de Spain tried to help himself by walking the horse and resting his bleeding foot in front of the pommel, letting the pony pick his way as he chose. A period of unconsciousness, a blank in de Spain's mind, soon followed the slowing up. He came to himself as he was lurching out of the saddle. Pulling himself together, he put the wet foot in the stirrup again and clung to the pommel with his hands. How long he rode in this way, or how far, he never knew. He was roused to consciousness by the unaccustomed sound of running water underneath his horse's feet.

It was pitch dark everywhere. The horse after the hard experience of the evening was drinking a welcome draft. De Spain had no conception of where he could be, but the stream told him he had somehow reached the range, though Music Mountain itself had been swallowed up in the night. A sudden and uncontrollable thirst seized the wounded man. He could hear the water falling over the stones and climbed slowly and painfully out of the saddle to the ground. With

the lines in his left hand he crawled toward the
water and, lying flat on the ground beside the
horse, put his head down to drink. The horse,
meantime, satisfied, lifted his head with a gulp,
rinsed his mouth, and pulled backward. The
lines slipped from de Spain's hand. Alarmed,
the weakened man scrambled after them. The
horse, startled, shied, and before his rider could
get to his feet scampered off in a trot. While de
Spain listened in consternation, the escaped horse,
falling into an easy stride, galloped away into the
night.

Stunned by this new misfortune, and listening
gloomily to the retreating hoof-beats, de Spain
pondered the situation in which the disaster left
him. It was the worst possible blow that could
have fallen, but fallen it had, and he turned with
such philosophy as he could to complete the
drink of water that had probably cost him his
life. At least, cold water never tasted sweeter,
never was so grateful to his parched tongue, and
since the price of the draft might be measured
by life itself, he drank extravagantly, stopping at
times to rest and, after breathing deeply, to drink
again.

When he had slaked a seemingly unquench-
able craving, he dashed the running water, first
with one hand and then the other, over his face.

On Music Mountain

He tried feebly to wash away some of the alkali that had crusted over the wound in the front of his head and was stinging and burning in it. There was now nothing to do but to secrete himself until daylight and wait till help should reach him—it was manifestly impossible for him to seek it.

Meantime, the little stream beside him offered first aid. He tried it with his foot and found it slight and shallow, albeit with a rocky bed that made wading in his condition difficult. But he felt so much better he was able to attempt this, and, keeping near to one side of the current, he began to follow it slowly up-stream. The ascent was at times precipitous, which pleased him, though it depleted his new strength. It was easy in this way to hide his trail, and the higher and faster the stream took him into the mountains the safer he would be from any Calabasas pursuers. When he had regained a little strength and oriented himself, he could quickly get down into the hills.

Animated by these thoughts, he held his way up-stream, hoping at every step to reach the gorge from which the flow issued. He would have known this by the sound of the falling water, but, weakening soon, he found he must abandon hope of getting up to it. However, by resting

159

and scrambling up the rocks, he kept on longer than he would have believed possible. Encountering at length, as he struggled upward, a ledge and a clump of bushes, he crawled weakly on hands and knees into it, too spent to struggle farther, stretched himself on the flattened brambles and sank into a heavy sleep.

He woke in broad daylight. Consciousness returned slowly and he raised himself with pain from his rough couch. His wounds were stiff, and he lay for a long time on his back looking up at the sky. At length he dragged himself to an open space near where he had slept and looked about. He appeared to be near the foot of a mountain quite strange to him, and in rather an exposed place. The shelter that had served him for the night proved worthless in daylight and, following his strongly developed instinct of self-preservation, de Spain started once more up the rocky path of the stream. He clambered a hundred feet above where he had slept before he found a hiding-place. It was at the foot of a tiny waterfall where the brook, striking a ledge of granite, had patiently hollowed out a shallow pool. Beside this a great mass of frost-bitten rock had fallen, and one of the bowlders lay tilted in such a way as to roof in a sort of cave, the entrance to which was not higher than a man's knee. De Spain crawled into this refuge. He conceived that from this high, open ledge he could show a small signal-fire at night, and if it were answered by his enemies he had a semblance of a retreat under the fallen rock, a hunting-knife, and one lone cartridge to protect himself with. A mountain-lion might have to be reckoned with; and if a pursuer should follow him under the rock his only chance would lie in getting hold, after a fight, of the man's loaded revolver or ammunition-belt. Such a hope involved a great deal of confidence, but de Spain was an optimist—most railroad men are.

The outlook was, in truth, not altogether cheerful—some would have called it, for a wounded man, desperate—but it had some slight consolations and de Spain was not given to long-range forebodings. The rising sun shone in a glory of clearness, and the cool night air rolling up the mountain was grateful and refreshing. Lying flat on the rock, he stretched his head forward and drank deeply of the ice-cold pool beside which he lay. The violent exertion of reaching the height had started the ruptured artery anew, and his first work was crudely to cleanse the wound and attempt to rebandage it. He was hungry, but for this there was only one alleviation—sleep—and, carefully effacing all traces of his presence on the ledge, he crawled into his rock retreat and fell again into a heavy slumber.

It was this repose that proved his undoing. He woke to consciousness so weak he could scarcely lift his head. It was still day. A consuming thirst assailed him, but he lacked the strength to crawl out of his cave, and, looking toward his bandaged foot, he was shocked at the sight of how it had bled while he slept. When he could rally from his discouragement he rewound the bandages and told himself what a fool he had been to drag his foot up the rocks before the wound had had any chance to heal. He resolved, despite his thirst, to lie still all day and give the artery absolute quiet. It required only a little stoicism; the stake was life.

Toward afternoon his restlessness increased, but he clung to his resolve to lie still. By evening he was burning with thirst, and when morning came after a feverish night, with his head on fire and his mouth crusted dry, he concluded rightly that one or both of his wounds had become infected.

De Spain understood what it meant. He looked regretfully at the injured foot. Swollen out of shape and angry-looking, the mere appearance would have told him, had the confirmation been needed, that his situation was becoming critical. This did not so much disconcert him as it surprised him and spurred him mentally to the necessity of new measures. He lay a long time thinking. Against the infection he could do little. But the one aid at his hand was abundance of cold water to drink and bathe his wound in, and to this he resolved now to drag himself. To crawl across the space that separated him from the pool required all the strength he could summon. The sun was already well up and its rays shot like spectrum arrows through the spray of the dainty cataract, which spurted in a jewelled sheet over a rocky ledge twenty feet above and poured noisily down from the broad pool along jagged bowlders below.

Crawling, choking with thirst, slowly forward, he reached the water, and, reclining on his side and one elbow, he was about to lean down to drink when he suddenly felt, with some kind of an instinctive shock, that he was no longer alone on the ledge. He had no interest in analyzing the conviction; he did not even question it. Not a sound had reached his ears. Only a moment before he had looked carefully all around. But the field of his vision was closely circumscribed by the walls about him. It was easy for an invader to come on his retreat unawares—at

163

all events, somebody, he was almost sure, stood behind him. The silence meant an enemy. The first thing to expect was a bullet. It would probably be aimed at the back of his head. At least he knew this was the spot to aim for to kill a man instantly and painlessly—yet he shrank from that anticipated crash.

And it was this thought that cost the defenseless man at the moment the most pain—that feeling, in advance, of the blow of the bullet that should snuff out his life. Defense was out of the question; he was as helpless as a baby. An impulse in his fingers to clutch his revolver he restrained at once—it could only hasten his death. He wondered, as the seconds passed, why his executioner hesitated to shoot, but he could not rid himself of the mental horror of being shot in the base of the brain. Anywhere else he would have almost welcomed a bullet; anywhere else it might have given him one chance for life through rolling over after he was struck in an attempt to kill his assailant.

His thoughts, working in flashes of lightning, suggested every possible trick of escape, and as rapidly rejected each. There was nothing for it but to play the part, to take the blow with no more than a quiver when it came. He had once seen a man shot in just that way. Braced to such a determination, de Spain bent slowly downward, and, with eyes staring into the water for a reflection that might afford a glimpse of his enemy, he began to drink. A splash above his head frightened him almost to death. It was a water-ousel dashing into the foaming cataract and out again, and the spray falling from the sudden bath wrecked the mirror of the pool. De Spain nearly choked. Each mouthful of water was a struggle. The sense of impending death had robbed even the life-giving drafts of their tonic; each instant carried its acute sensation of being the last. At length, his nerves weakened by hunger and exposure, revolted under the strain. Suppose it should be, after all, a fantasy of his fever that pictured so vividly an enemy behind. With an effort that cost more mental torture than he ever had known, he drew back on his elbow from the pool, steadied himself, turned his head to face his executioner, and confronted Nan Morgan.

CHAPTER XIII

SHE stood beside the rock from which the ledge was reached from below, and as if she had just stepped up into sight. Her rifle was so held in both hands that it could be fired from her hip, and at such close quarters with deadly accuracy. As she stood with startled eyes fixed on his haggard face, her slender neck and poised head were very familiar to de Spain.

And her expression, while it reflected her horrified alarm, did not conceal her anger and aversion at the sight of him. Unaware of the forbidding spectacle he presented, de Spain, swept by a brainstorm at the appearance of this Morgan —the only one of all the Morgans he had not fancied covering him and waiting to deliver his death-warrant—felt a fury sweep over him at the thought of being shot by a woman. The wild idea that she meant to kill him, which in a rational moment would never have entered his mind, now in his delirium completely obsessed him. Working, as it were, mechanically, even the instinct of self-defense asserted itself against

166

Parley

her. But enough of reason remained in his disordered senses to tell him that self-defense was out of the question. Whatever she meant to do, he could no more fire at this girl, even had he a chance—and he realized he was at her mercy —than he could at his sister; and he lay with his eyes bent on hers, trying to read her purpose.

She stood guarded, but motionless with surprise. De Spain turned himself slowly and, sitting up, waited for her to speak. There was little to hope for, he thought, in her expression. And all of his duplicity seemed to desert him before her cold resolution. The tricks he would have tried, at bay before a man, he felt no inclination to attempt. He read in her set face only abhorrence and condemnation, and felt in no way moved to argue her verdict. "I suppose," he said, at length, not trying to disguise his bitter resentment of her presence, "you've come to finish me."

His shirt stained and tattered for bandages, his hair matted in blood on his forehead, his eyes inflamed and sunken, his lips crusted and swollen, the birthmark fastened vividly on his cheek made him a desperate sight. Regarding him steadily, Nan, as bewildered as if she had suddenly come on a great wounded beast of prey still dangerous, made no response to his words. The two stared

at each other defiantly and for another moment
in silence. "If you are going to kill me," he continued, looking into her eyes without any thought
of appeal, "do it quick."

Something in his long, unyielding gaze impelled
her to break the spell of it. "What are you doing
here?" she demanded with anger, curbing her
voice to control her excitement as best she could.

De Spain, still looking at her, answered only
after a pause. "Hiding," he said harshly.

"Hiding to kill other men!" Nan's accusation
as she clutched her rifle was almost explosive.

He regarded her coolly, and with the interval
he had had for thinking, his wits were clearing.
"Do I look like a man hunting for a fight? Or,"
he added, since she made no answer, "like a man
hunting for a quiet spot to die in? How," he
went on slowly, delirium giving place to indignation, "can you say I'm hiding here to kill other
men? That's what your people tell you, is it?"

"I know you are a murderer."

In spite of his weakness he flushed. "No," he
exclaimed sharply, "I'm not a murderer. If you
think it"—he pointed contemptuously to her
side—"you have your rifle—use it!"

"My rifle is to defend myself with. I am not
a public executioner," she answered scornfully.

"You need no rifle to defend yourself from me

Parley

—though I am a murderer. And if you're not a public executioner, leave me—I'm dying fast enough."

"You came here to hide to kill somebody!" she exclaimed, as if the thought were a sudden explanation.

"What do you mean by 'here'? I might better ask why you came here," he retorted. "I don't know where I am. Do I look as if I came here by choice?" He paused. "Listen," he said, quite master of himself, "I'll tell you why I came. I shall never get away alive, anyway—you can have the truth if you want it. I got off my horse in the night to get a drink. He bolted. I couldn't walk. I climbed up here to hide till my wounds heal. Now, I've told you the truth. Where am I?"

The grip of her hands on the rifle might have relaxed somewhat, but she saw his deadly revolver in its accustomed place and did not mean to surrender her command of him. Nor would she tell him where he was. She parried his questions. He could get no information of any sort out of her. Yet he saw that something more than his mere presence detained and perplexed her. Her prompt condemnation of him rankled in his mind, and the strain of facing her suspicion wore on him. "I won't ask you anything more," he said

at length. "You do right to give me no information. It might help me save my life. I can't
talk any longer. You know you think I've no
right to live—that's what you think, isn't it?
Why don't you shoot?" She only stared at him.
"Why don't you answer?" he demanded recklessly.

Nan summoned her resolution. "I know you
tried to kill my cousin," she said hotly, after he
had taunted her once more. "And I don't know
you won't try it again as soon as you are able.
And I am going to think what to do before I
tell you anything or do anything."

"You know I tried to kill your cousin! You
know nothing of the kind. Your cousin tried to
kill me. He's a bully and a coward, a man that
doesn't know what fair fighting means. Tell
him that for me."

"You are safe in abusing him when he's not
here."

"Send him to me! This is no place for a woman
that calls me what you call me—send your cousin
and all his friends!" His voice shook with anger.
"Tell him I'm wounded; tell him I've had nothing to eat since I fought him before. And if he's
still afraid"—de Spain drew and broke his revolver almost like a flash. In that incredibly
quick instant she realized he might have threat-

ened her life before she could move a muscle
—"tell your fine cousin I've got one cartridge
left—just one!" So saying, he held in one hand
the loaded cartridge and in the other the empty
revolver.

"You think little of bloodshed, I know," she
returned unpleasantly.

"I think a whole lot," he drawled in painful
retort, "of fair fighting."

"And I'm a woman—you do well to taunt me
with that."

"I did not taunt you with it. You are hate-
fully unjust," he protested sullenly.

"You've asked me to go—I'm going. How
much of what you tell me is true, I don't know.
But I can believe my own eyes, and I believe you
are not in condition to do much injury, even if
you came here with that intention. You will
certainly lose your life if you move from your
hiding-place."

She started away. He leaned toward her.
"Stop," he said peremptorily, raising himself
with a wrenching effort. Something in the stern
eye held her. His extended hand pointed toward
her as arbitrarily as if, instead of lying helpless
at her feet, he could command her to his bidding.
"I want to ask you a question. I've told you the
truth. I have just one cartridge. If you are

going to send your cousin and his men here, it's only fair I should know it now—isn't it?"

Her face was hard in spite of the weakness he struggled to conceal. It annoyed her to think he had surmised she was revolving in her mind what to do. He was demanding an answer she had not yet given to herself.

"My cousin is wounded," she said, pausing. And then with indecision: "If you stay here quietly you are not likely to be molested."

She stepped down from the ledge as noiselessly as she had come. Shaken by the discovery she had so unexpectedly made, Nan retreated almost precipitately from the spot. And the question of what to do worried her as much as it worried de Spain. The whole range had been shaken by the Calabasas fight. Even in a country where appeal to arms was common, where men were ready to snuff out a life for a word, or kill for a mess of pottage—to settle for the least grave offense a dispute with a shot—the story of the surprising, unequal, and fatal encounter of the Calabasas men with de Spain, and of his complete disappearance after withstanding almost unheard-of odds, was more than a three days' wonder; nothing else was talked of for weeks. Even the men in Morgan's Gap, supposed to be past masters of the game played in the closed room at Calabasas, had been stunned by the issue of the few minutes with Jeffries's new man.

Nan, who had heard but one side of the story, pictured the aggressor from the tale of the two who lived to tell of the horribly sharp action with him. Morning, noon, and night she had heard nothing but the fight at Calabasas discussed by the men that rode in and out of the Gap—and in connection with it, de Spain's unexplained flight and disappearance. Those that knew the real story of the conspiracy to kill him did not talk much, after the disastrous outcome, of that part of the affair. But Nan's common sense whispered to her, whatever might be said about de Spain's starting the fight, that one man locked in a room with four enemies, all dangerous in an affray, was not likely to begin a fight unless forced to—none, at least, but a madman would do so. She had heard stories, too, of de Spain's drinking and quarrelling, but none that told them had ever seen him under the influence of drink or had had a quarrel with him except Gale and Sassoon—and these two were extremely quarrelsome.

Unhappy and irresolute, Nan, when she got home, was glad of an excuse to ride to Calabasas for a packet of dressings coming by stage from Sleepy Cat for Gale, who lay wounded at Satt

Morgan's; and, eating a hasty luncheon, she ordered her horse and set out.

Should she tell her Uncle Duke of finding de Spain? Whenever she decided that she must, something in the recollection of de Spain's condition unsettled her resolution. Tales enough of his bloodthirstiness, his merciless efficiency, his ever-ready craft and consummate duplicity were familiar to her—most of them made so within the last three days—for no one in her circle any longer professed to underrate the demonstrated resourcefulness of the man.

Yet only a few of these stories appealed to Nan's innate convictions of truth and justice. She lived among men who were, for the most part, not truthful or dependable even in small things —how could they be relied on to tell the truth about de Spain's motives and conduct? As to his deadly skill with arms, no stories were needed to confirm this, even though she herself had once overcome him in a contest. The evidence of this mastery had now a fatal pre-eminence among the tragedies of the Spanish Sinks. Where he lay he could, if he meditated revenge on her people, murder any of them, almost at will. To spare his life imperilled to this extent theirs— but surely he lay not far from death by exhaustion. Weighed against all she had ever listened to concerning his deceit was the evidence of her own sight. She had seen men desperately ill, and men desperately stricken. This man was either both or she could never again believe her senses. And if he was not helped soon he would die.

But who was to help him? Certainly none of his friends could know where he was hidden or of his plight—no help could come from them unless she told them. If she told them they would try to reach him. That would mean an appalling—an unthinkable—fight. If she told her uncle, could she keep him from killing de Spain? She believed not. He might promise to let him go. But she knew her uncle's ferocious resentment, and how easy it would be for him to give her fine words and, in spite of them, for de Spain to be found dead some morning where he lay— there were plenty of men available for jobs such as that.

All came back to one terrifying alternative: Should she help this wretched man herself? And if he lived, would he repay her by shooting some one of her own kin?

The long ride to Calabasas went fast as the debate swept on, and the vivid shock of her strange experience recurred to her imagination.

She drew up before the big barn. Jim McAlpin

was coming out to go to supper. Nan asked for her package and wanted to start directly back again. McAlpin refused absolutely to hear of it. He looked at her horse and professed to be shocked. He told her she had ridden hard, urged her to dismount, and sent her pony in to be rubbed, assuring Nan heartily there was not a man, outside the hostlers, within ten miles. While her horse was cared for, McAlpin asked, in his harmless Scotch way, about Gale.

Concerning Gale, Nan was non-committal. But she listened with interest, more or less veiled, to whatever running comment McAlpin had to offer concerning the Calabasas fight. "And I was sorry to see Gale mixed up in it," he concluded, in his effort to draw Nan out, "sorry. And sorrier to think of Henry de Spain getting killed that way. Why, I knowed Henry de Spain when he was a baby in arms." He put out his hand cannily. "I worked for his father before he was born." His listener remained obdurate. There was nothing for it except further probing, to which, however, Jim felt abundantly equal. "Some say," he suggested, looking significantly toward the door of the barn, and significantly away again, "that Henry went down there to pick a fight with the boys. But," he asserted cryptically, "I happen to know *that* wasn't so."

Parley

"Then what did he go down there for?" demanded Nan indignantly, but not warily.

McAlpin, the situation now in hand, took his time to it. He leaned forward in a manner calculated to invite confidence without giving offense. "Miss Nan," said he simply, "I worked for your Uncle Duke for five years—you know that." Nan had, at least, heard it fifty times. "I think a good deal of him—I think a good deal of you, so does the missus, so does little Loretta—she's always asking about you, the child is—and I hear and see a good deal here that other people don't get next to—they can't. Now Henry de Spain was here, with me, sitting right there where you are sitting, Miss Nan, in that chair," declared McAlpin with an unanswerable finger, "not fifteen minutes before that fight began, he was there. I told you he never went down there to fight. Do you want the proof? I'll tell you—I wouldn't want anybody else to know—will you keep it?"

Nan seemed indifferent. "Girls are not supposed to keep secrets," she said obstinately.

Her narrator was not to be balked. He pointed to the coat-rack on the wall in front of them both. "There is Henry de Spain's coat. He hung it there just before he went down to the inn. Under it, if you look, you'll find his belt of cartridges. Don't take my word—look for yourself."

Nan of Music Mountain

Giving this information time to sink in, Mc-
Alpin continued. Nan's eyes had turned, despite her indifference, to the coat; but she was
thinking more intently about the belt which
McAlpin asserted hung under it. "You want to
know what he did go down to the hotel for that
afternoon? I happen to know that, too," averred
McAlpin, sitting down, but respectfully, on the
edge of the chair. "First I want to say this: I
worked for your Uncle Duke five years."

He paused to give Nan a chance to dispute
the statement if she so desired. Then taking her
despairing silence as an indorsement of his position in giving her a confidence, he went on:
"Henry de Spain is dead," he said quietly. She
eyed him without so much as winking. "I
wouldn't tell it if he wasn't. Some of the boys
don't believe he is. I'm not a pessimist—not a
bit—but I'm telling you it's a physical impossi-
bility for a man to take the fire of four revolvers
in the hands of four men like those four men, at
arm's length, and live. Henry de Spain is the
cleverest man with a gun that ever rode the
Spanish Sinks, but limits is limits; the boy's
dead. And he was always talking about you.
It's God's truth, and since he's dead it harms
no one to tell it to you, though I'd never breathe
it to another. He was fairly gone on you. Now

178

that's the fair truth: the man was gone on you.
I knowed it, where others didn't know it. I was
the only one he could always ask about whether
you'd been here, and when; and when you might
be expected coming again—and all such things
like that.

"You don't have to knock me down, Miss
Nan, to put me wise about a man's being keen
on a girl. I'm a married man," declared McAlpin with modest pride. "He thought all the
time he was fooling me, and keeping covered.
Why, I laughed to myself at his tricks to get information without letting on! Now, that afternoon he came in here kind of moody. It was an
anniversary for him, and a hard one—the day his
father was shot from ambush—a good many
years ago, but nary one of us had forgot it. Then
he happened to see your pony—this same pony
you're riding to-day—a-standing back there in
the box-stall. He asked me whose it was; and
he asked me about you, and, by jinx! the way he
perked up when I told him you were coming in
on the stage that afternoon! When he heard
you'd been sick, he was for going down to the
hotel to get a cup of coffee—for you!" McAlpin,
like any good story-teller, was already on his feet
again. "He did it," he exclaimed, "and you
know what *he* got when he stepped into the bar-

room." He took hold of de Spain's coat and held it aside to enter his exhibit. "There," he concluded, "is his cartridge-belt, hanging there yet. The boy is dead—why shouldn't I tell you?"

Nan rode home much more excited, more bewildered than when she had ridden over. What should she do? It was already pretty clear to her that de Spain had not ridden unarmed to where she found him to ambush any of the Morgans. He was not dead; but he was not far from it if McAlpin was right and if she could credit her own senses in looking at him. What ought she to do?

Other things McAlpin had said crowded her thoughts. Strangest shock of all that this man of all other men should profess to care for her. She had shown anger when McAlpin dared speak of it; at least, she thought she had. And she still did not know how, sufficiently, to resent the thought of such audacity on de Spain's part; but recalling all she could of his words and actions, she was forced to confess to herself that McAlpin's assertions were confirmed in them— and that what McAlpin had said interpreted de Spain's unvarying attitude toward her. This was, to say the least, a further awkward complication for her feelings. She already had enough to confuse them.

CHAPTER XIV

NAN DRIFTS

WITHOUT going in to speak to Gale, whom Bull Page, his nurse, reported very cross but not hurt much, Nan left her packet for him and rode home. Her uncle Duke was in town. She had the house to herself, with only Bonita, the old Mexican serving-woman, and Nan ate her late supper alone.

The longer she pondered on de Spain and his dilemma—and her own—the more she worried. When she went to bed, up-stairs in her little gable room, she thought sleep—never hard for her to woo—would relieve her of her anxiety for at least the night. But she waited in vain for sleep. She was continually asking herself whether de Spain was really very badly hurt, or whether he might be only tricking her into thinking he was. Assailed by conflicting doubts, she tossed on her pillow till a resolve seized her to go up again to his hiding-place and see what she could see or hear—possibly, if one were on foot, she could uncover a plot.

She dressed resolutely, buckled a holster to

her side, and slipping a revolver—a new one that
Gale had given her—into it for protection, she
walked softly down-stairs and out of doors.

The night air was clear with a three-quarter
moon well up in the sky. She took her way
rapidly along the trail to the mountain, keeping
as much as possible within the great shadows
cast by the towering peaks. Not a sound met
her acute listening as she pressed on—not a living
thing seemed to move anywhere in the whole
great Gap, except this slender-footed, keen-eyed
girl, whose heart beat with apprehension of wiles,
stratagems, and ambush concerning the venture
she was making.

Breathing stealthily and keyed to a tense feeling of uncertainty and suspicion, Nan at length
found herself below the ledge where de Spain
was in hiding. She stopped and, with the craft
of an Indian, stood perfectly still for a very long
time before she began to climb up to where the
enemy lay. Hearing no sound, she took courage
and made the ascent. She reached without adventure the corner of the ledge where she had
first seen him, and there, lying flat, listened again.

Hearing only the music of the little cascade,
she swept the ledge as well as she could with her
eyes, but it was now so far in shadow as to lie in
impenetrable darkness. Hardly daring to breathe,

she crept and felt her way over it with her hands, discovering nothing until she had almost reached de Spain's retreat at the farther side. Then her heart stopped in an agony of fear—underneath the overhanging wall she heard voices.

To attempt to escape was as dangerous as to lie still. Had she dared, she would have retreated at once the way she came. Since she dared not, she was compelled to hear what was said, and, indeed, was eager to hear. De Spain had confederates, then, and had tricked her, after all. Whatever his plot, she was resolved to know it, and instead of retreating she took her revolver in hand and drew herself nearer. When she had gained her new position the mutterings, which had been indistinct, became audible. It was not two voices she had heard, but one—de Spain, she judged, was talking in his sleep.

But a moment later this explanation failed to satisfy her. The mutterings were too constant and too disconnected to be mistaken for sleep-talking—it dawned on Nan that this must be delirium. She could hear de Spain throwing himself from side to side, and the near and far sounds, as if of two voices, were explained. It was possible now for her to tell herself she was mistress of the situation. She crept nearer.

He was babbling in the chill darkness about

ammunition, urging men to make haste, warning
them of some one coming. He turned on the
rock floor ceaselessly, sometimes toward her,
sometimes from her, muttering of horses, water,
passengers, wheels, wrecks. He made broken
appeals to be chopped out, directed men where
to use their axes. Nan listened to his ravings,
overcome by the revelation of his condition.
Once her uncle had lain sick of a fever and had
been delirious; but that, her sole experience, was
nothing to this. Once de Spain threw out a
groping hand and, before she could escape, caught
her skirt. Nan tried to pull away. His grip
did not loosen. She took his hand in hers and,
while he muttered meaningless words, forced his
fingers open and drew away. His hand was dry
and burning hot.

She told herself he must die if he remained
longer unaided, and there were unpleasant possi-
bilities, if he died where he lay. Such a death,
so close to her own home might, if it were ever
known, throw suspicion on her uncle and arouse
the deeper resentment of the wounded man's
friends. If the least of pity played a part in
suggesting that her safest course was to help de
Spain, Nan kept its promptings as much as she
could in the penumbra of her thoughts. She
did not want to pity or to help him, she con-

vinced herself; but she did not want his death laid to a Morgan plot—for none of his friends would ever believe de Spain had found his way alive and alone to where he lay.

All of this Nan was casting up in her mind as she walked home. She had already decided, but without realizing it, what to do, and was willing to assume that her mind was still open.

Toward daylight of the morning, de Spain dreamed he was not alone—that a figure moved silently in the faintness of the dawn—a figure he struggled to believe a reality, but one that tricked his wandering senses and left him, at the coming of another day, weaker, with failing courage, and alone.

But when he opened his eyes later, and with a clearer head, he found food and drink near. Unable to believe his sight, he fancied his wavering senses deceiving him, until he put out his hand and felt actually the substance of what he saw. He took up a bottle of milk incredulously, and sipped at it with the caution of a man not unused to periods of starvation. He broke eggs and swallowed them, at intervals, hungrily from the shell; and meat he cached, animal-like, in near-by crannies and, manlike, in his pockets.

He was determined, if she should come again, to intercept his visitor. For forty-eight hours

he tried cat-naps with an occasional sandwich
to keep up his strength. Nan returned unseen,
and disappeared despite his watchfulness. A new
supply of food proved she had been near, but that
it would be hard to time her coming.

When she did come, the third time, an innocent
snare discovered her presence. It was just before day, and de Spain had so scattered small
obstacles—handfuls of gravel and little chips of
rock—that should she cross the ledge in the dark
she could hardly escape rousing him.

The device betrayed her. "I'm awake," announced de Spain at once from his retreat. When
she stopped at the words he could not see her;
she had flattened herself, standing, against a wall
of the ledge. He waited patiently. "You give
me no chance to thank you," he went on after a
pause. Nan, drawing nearer, put down a small
parcel. "I don't need any thanks," she replied
with calculated coolness. "I am hoping when
you are well enough you will go away, quietly, in
the night. That will be the only way you can
thank me."

"I shall be as glad to go as you can be to
have me," rejoined de Spain. "But that won't
be thanking you as I am going to. If you think
you can save my life and refuse my thanks as I
mean to express them—you are mistaken. I will

be perfectly honest. Lying out here isn't just what I'd choose for comfort. But if by doing it I could see you once in two or three days——"

"You won't see me again."

"No news could be worse. And if I can't, I don't know how I'm going to get out at all. I've no horse—you know that. I can't stand on my foot yet; if you had a light you might see for yourself. I think I showed you my gun. If you could tell me where I am——"

He halted on the implied question. Nan took ample time to reply.

"Do you mean to tell me you don't know where you are?" she asked, and there was a touch of vexed incredulity in her tone.

De Spain seemed unmoved by her scepticism. "I can't tell you anything else," he said simply. "You couldn't have any idea I crawled up here for the fun of it."

"I've been trying to think," she returned, and he perceived in the hardness of her voice how at bay she felt in giving him the least bit of information, "whether I ought to tell you anything at all——"

"I couldn't very decently take any unfair advantage after what you've done, could I?"

"Then—you are in Morgan's Gap," she said swiftly, as if she wanted it off her mind.

Nan of Music Mountain

There was no movement of surprise, neither was there any answer. "I supposed, when I found you here, you knew that," she added less resolutely; the darkness and silence were plainly a strain.

"I know you are telling the truth," he responded at length. "But I can hardly believe it. That's the reason, of course, you *did* find me. I rode a good many miles that night without knowing where I was or what I was doing. I certainly never figured on winding up here. How could I get in here without being stopped?"

"Everybody inside the Gap was outside hunting for you, I suppose."

"There isn't much use asking where I am, in the Gap. I never was inside but once. I shouldn't know if you did tell me."

"You are at the foot of Music Mountain, about a mile from where I live."

"You must have thought I meant to raid your house. I didn't. I was hit. I got mixed up in trying to get away. You want me out of here?"

"Very much."

"No more than I want to get out. Perhaps by to-morrow I could walk a few miles. I should have to assassinate somebody to get some ammunition."

"It wouldn't be hard for you to do that, I presume."

Her words and her tone revealed the intensity of her dislike and the depth of her distrust.

He was silent for a moment. Then he said, without resentment: "You are ashamed already of saying that, aren't you?"

"No, I am not," she answered defiantly.

"Yes, you are. You know it isn't true. If you believed it you never would have brought food here to save my life."

"I brought it to save some of my own people from possible death at your hands—to prevent another fight—to see if you hadn't manhood enough after being helped, to go away, when you were able to move, peaceably. One cartridge might mean one life, dear to me."

"I know whose life you mean."

"You know nothing about what I mean."

"I know better than you know yourself. If I believed you, I shouldn't respect you. Fear and mercy are two different things. If I thought you were only afraid of me, I shouldn't think much of your aid. Listen—I never took the life of any man except to defend my own——"

"No murderer that ever took anybody's life in this country ever said anything but that."

"Don't class me with murderers."

"You are known from one end of the country to the other as a gunman."

He answered impassively: "Did these men who

call me a gunman ever tell you why I'm one?"
She seemed in too hostile a mood to answer. "I
guess not," he went on. "Let me tell you now.
The next time you hear me called a gunman
you can tell them."

"I won't listen," she exclaimed, restive.

"Yes, you will listen," he said quietly; "you
shall hear every word. My father brought sheep
into the Peace River country. The cattlemen
picked on him to make an example of. He went
out, unarmed, one night to take care of the horses.
My mother heard two shots. He didn't come
back. She went to look for him. He was lying
under the corral gate with a hole smashed
through his jaw by a rifle-bullet that tore his
head half off." De Spain did not raise his voice
nor did he hasten his words. "I was born one
night six months after that," he continued. "My
mother died that night. When a neighbor's wife
took me from her arm and wrapped me in a
blanket, she saw I carried the face of my father
as my mother had seen it the night he was murdered. That," he said, "is what made me a
'gunman.' Not whiskey—not women—not cards
—just what you've heard. And I'll tell you
something else you may tell the men that call
me a gunman. The man that shot down my
father at his corral gate I haven't found yet. I

expect to find him. For ten years I've been getting ready to find him. He is here—in these mountains. I don't even know his name. But if I live, I'll find him. And when I do, I'll tear open his head with a soft bullet in the way he tore my father's open. After I get through with that man"—he hesitated—"they may call me whatever they like."

The faint ghostliness of the coming day, writing its warning in the eastern sky, the bitter chill of the dying night, the slow, hard, impassive utterance, the darkness in which she stood listening to an enemy she could not see, the loneliness and danger of her situation combined to impress on the unwilling listener the picture of the murder, the tragic birth, and the mother's death. "You want me out of the Gap," de Spain concluded, his voice unchanged. "I want to get out. Come back, once more, in the daytime. I will see what I can do with my foot by that time." He paused. "Will you come?"

She hesitated. "It would be too dangerous for me to come up here in the daytime. Trouble would follow."

"Come at dusk. You know I am no murderer."

"I don't know it," she persisted stubbornly. It was her final protest.

"Count, some day, on knowing it."

CHAPTER XV

CROSSING A DEEP RIVER

A GRIZZLY bear hidden among the hay-
stacks back of the corral would have given
Nan much less anxiety than de Spain secreted
in the heart of the Morgan stronghold. But as
she hurried home, fearful of encountering an early
rider who should ask questions, it seemed as if
she might, indeed, find some way of getting rid
of the troublesome foe without having it on her
conscience that she had starved a wounded man
to death, or that he had shot some one of her
people in getting away.

Her troubled speculations were reduced now
almost to wondering when de Spain would leave,
and, disinclined though she felt to further parley,
she believed he would go the sooner if she were
to consent to see him again. Everything he had
said to her seemed to unsettle her mind and to
imperil impressions concerning him that she felt
it dangerous, or at least treasonable, to part with.
To believe anything but the worst of a man whom
she heard cursed and abused continually by her

uncles, cousins, and their associates and retainers, seemed a monstrous thing—and every effort de Spain made to dislodge her prejudices called for fresh distrust on her part. What had most shaken her convictions—and it would come back to her in spite of everything she could do to keep it out of her mind—was the recollection of the murder of his father, the tragic death of his mother. As for the facts of his story, somehow she never thought of questioning them. The seal of its dreadful truth he carried on his face.

That day Nan washed her hair. On the second day—because there were no good reasons for it —she found herself deciding conscientiously to see de Spain for the last time, and toward sunset. This was about the time he had suggested, but it really seemed, after long thought, the best time. She began dressing early for her trip, and with constantly recurring dissatisfaction with her wardrobe—picking the best of her limited stock of silk stockings, choosing the freshest of her few pairs of tan boots. All of her riding-skirts looked shabby as she fretfully inspected them; but Bonita pressed out the newest one for the hurried occasion, while Nan used the interval, with more than usual care, on her troublesome hair—never less tractable, it seemed, in her life. Nothing, in truth, in her appearance, satisfied her, and she was obliged at last to turn from her glass with the hateful sigh that it made no difference anyway.

De Spain was sitting with his back against a rock, and his knees drawn up, leaning his head on his right hand and resting his elbow on the knee. His left arm hung down over his left knee, and the look on his face was one of reflection and irresolution rather than of action and decision. But he looked so restored after his brief period of nourishment that Nan, when she stepped up on the ledge at sunset, would not have known the wreck she had seen in the same place the week before.

His heart jumped at the sight of her young face, and her clear, courageous eyes surveyed him questioningly as he scrambled to his feet.

"I am going to tramp out of here to-morrow night," he confided to her after his thanks. "It is Saturday; a lot of your men will be in Sleepy Cat—and they won't all be very keen-sighted on their way back. I can get a good start outside before daylight."

She heard him with relief. "What will you do then?" she asked.

"Hide. Watch every chance to crawl a mile nearer Calabasas. I can't walk much, but I ought to make it by Sunday night or Monday

194

Crossing a Deep River

morning. I may see a friend—perhaps I may see
the other fellow's friend, and with my lone cartridge I may be able to bluff him out of a horse,"
he suggested, gazing at the crimson tie that
flowed from Nan's open neck. "By the way,"
he added, his glance resting on her right side as
he noticed the absence of her holster, "where is
your protector to-day?" She made no answer.
"Fine form," he said coldly, "to come unarmed
on an errand of mercy to a desperado."

Nan flushed with vexation. "I came away in
such a hurry I forgot it," she replied lamely.

"A forget might cost you your life."

"Perhaps you've forgotten you left a cartridge-
belt behind once yourself," she returned swiftly.
The retort startled him. How could she know?
But he would not, at first, ask a question, though
her eyes told him she knew what she was talking
about. They looked at each other a moment in
silence.

De Spain, convicted, finally laid his fingers
over the butt of his empty revolver. "How did
you find that out?"

She tossed her head. They were standing only
a few feet apart, de Spain supporting himself now
with his left hand high up against the wall; Nan,
with her shoulder lightly against it; both had become quizzical. "Other people forget, too, then,"

was all she said, fingering the loosened tie as the breeze from the west blew it toward her shoulder.

"No," he protested, "I didn't forget; not that time. I went over to the joint to get a cup of coffee and expected to be back within five minutes, never dreaming of walking into a bear trap." He drew his revolver and, breaking it negligently, took out the single cartridge. "Take this." He held the cartridge in his left hand and took two halting steps toward her—"since you are unarmed, I will be, too. Not that this puts us on an even footing. I don't mean that. Nothing would. You would be too much for me in any kind of a contest, armed or unarmed."

"What do you mean?" she demanded to hide her confusion. And she saw that each step he took cost pain, skilfully concealed.

"I mean," he said, "you are to take this cartridge as a remembrance of my forgetfulness and your adventure."

She drew back. "I don't want it."

"Take it."

He was persistent. She allowed him to drop the loaded shell into her hand. "Now," he continued, replacing his gun, "if I encounter any of your people in an attempt to break through a line, and somebody gets killed, you will know,

Crossing a Deep River

when you hear the story, that *this* time, at least, *I* didn't 'start it.'"

"All the same——" She hesitated. "I don't think that's exactly right. You need not shoot my people, even if you meet them. There are plenty of others you might meet——"

He put her objections aside, enjoying being so near her and happy that she made no retreat. "My reputation," he insisted, "has suffered a little in Morgan's Gap. I mean that at least one who makes her home under Music Mountain shall know differently of me. What's that?" He heard a sound. "Listen!"

The two, looking at each other, strained their ears to hear more through the rush of the falling water. "Some one is coming," said de Spain. Nan ran lightly to where she could peep over the ledge. Hardly pausing as she glanced down, she stepped quickly back. "I'll go right on up the mountain to the azalea fields," she said hastily.

He nodded. "I'll hide. Stop. If you are questioned, you don't know I'm here. You must say so for your own sake, not for mine."

She was gone before he had finished. De Spain drew quickly back to where he could secrete himself. In another moment he heard heavy footsteps where he had stood with his visitor. But the footsteps crossed the ledge, and their

sound died away up the path Nan had taken.
De Spain could not see the intruder. It was
impossible to conjecture who he was or what
his errand, and de Spain could only await whatever should develop. He waited several minutes
before he heard any sign of life above. Then
snatches of two voices began to reach him. He
could distinguish Nan's voice and at intervals
the heavier tones of a man. The two were descending. In a few moments they reached the
ledge, and de Spain, near at hand, could hear
every word.

"Hold on a minute," said the man roughly.
His voice was heavy and his utterance harsh.

"I must get home," objected Nan.

"Hold on, I tell you," returned her companion.
De Spain could not see, but he began already to
feel the scene. "I want to talk to you."

"We can talk going down," parried Nan.

De Spain heard her hurried footfalls. "No,
you don't," retorted her companion, evidently
cutting off her retreat.

"Gale Morgan!" There was a blaze in Nan's
sharp exclamation. "What do you mean?"

"I mean you and I are going to have this out
right here, before we leave this ledge."

"I tell you, I want to go home."

"You'll go home when I say so."

Crossing a Deep River

"How dare you stop me!"

"I'll show you what I dare, young lady. You've been backing and filling with me for two years. Now I want to know what you're going to do."

"Gale! Won't you have a little sense? Come along home with me, like a good fellow, and I'll talk things over with you just as long as you like."

"You'll talk things over with me right here, and as long as *I* like," he retorted savagely. "Every time I ask you to marry me you've got some new excuse."

"It's shameful for you to act in this way, Gale." She spoke low and rapidly to her enraged suitor. De Spain alone knew it was to keep her humiliation from his own ears, and he made no effort to follow her quick, pleading words. The moment was most embarrassing for two of the three involved. But nothing that Nan could say would win from her cousin any reprieve.

"When you came back from school I told Duke I was going to marry you. He said, all right," persisted her cousin stubbornly.

"Gale Morgan, what Uncle Duke said, or didn't say, has nothing whatever to do with *my* consent."

"I told you I was going to marry you."

"Does that bind me to get married, when I don't want to?"

"You said you'd marry me."

Nan exploded: "I never, never said so in this world." Her voice shook with indignation. "You know that's a downright falsehood."

"You said you didn't care for anybody else," he fairly bellowed. "Now I want to know whether you'll marry me if I take you over to Sleepy Cat to-morrow?"

"No!" Nan flung out her answer, reckless of consequence. "I'll never marry you. Let me go home."

"You'll go home when I get through with you. You've fooled me long enough."

Her blood froze at the look in his face. "How dare you!" she gasped. "Get out of my way!"

"You damned little vixen!" He sprang forward and caught her by the wrist. "I'll take the kinks out of you. You wouldn't marry me your way, now you'll marry me mine."

She fought like a tigress. He dragged her struggling into his arms. But above her half-stifled cries and his grunting laugh, Morgan heard a sharp voice: "Take your hands off that girl!"

Whirling, with Nan in his savage arms, the half-drunken mountaineer saw de Spain ten feet away, his right hand resting on the grip of his revolver. Stunned, but sobered by mortal danger, Morgan greeted his enemy with an oath.

Crossing a Deep River

"Stand away from that girl!" repeated de Spain harshly, backing the words with a step forward. Morgan's grasp relaxed. Nan, jerking away, looked at de Spain and instantly stepped in front of her cousin, on whom de Spain seemed about to draw.

"What are you doing here?" demanded Morgan, with an enraged oath.

"I left some business with you the other day at Calabasas half finished," said de Spain. "I'm here this afternoon to clean it up. Get away from that girl!"

His manner frightened even Nan. The quick step to the side and back—poising himself like a fencer—his revolver restrained a moment in its sheath by an eager right arm, as if at any instant it might leap into deadly play.

Shocked with new fear, Nan hesitated. If it was play, it was too realistic for the nerves even of a mountain girl. De Spain's angry face and burning eyes photographed themselves on her memory from that moment. But whatever he meant, she had her part to do. She backed, with arms spread low at her sides, directly against her cousin. "You shan't fight," she cried at de Spain.

"Stand away from that man!" retorted de Spain sternly.

"You shan't kill my cousin. What do you mean? What are you doing here? Leave us!"

"Get away, Nan, I tell you. I'll finish him," cried Morgan, puncturing every word with an oath.

She whirled and caught her cousin in her arms. "He will shoot us both if you fire. Take me away, Gale. You coward," she exclaimed, whirling again with trembling tones on de Spain, "would you kill a woman?"

De Spain saw the danger was past. It needed hardly an instant to show him that Morgan had lost stomach for a fight. He talked wrathfully, but he made no motion to draw. "I see I've got to chase you into a fight," said de Spain contemptuously, and starting gingerly to circle the hesitating cousin. Nan, in her excitement, ran directly toward the enemy, as if to cut off his movement.

"Don't you dare put me in danger," she cried, facing de Spain threateningly. "Don't you dare fight my cousin here."

"Stand away from me," hammered de Spain, eying Morgan steadily.

"He is wounded now," stormed Nan, so fast she could hardly frame the words. "You shan't kill him. If you are a man, don't shoot a wounded man and a woman. You shan't shoot. Gale! protect yourself!" Whirling to face her cousin,

"Stand away from that girl!" repeated de Spain harshly,
backing the words with a step forward.

she took the chance to back directly against de Spain. Both hands were spread open and partly behind her, the palms up, as if to check him. In the instant that she and de Spain were in contact he realized, rather than saw—for his eyes never released Morgan's eyes—what she was frantically slipping to him—the loaded cartridge. It was done in a flash, and she was running from him again. Her warm fingers had swept across his own. She had returned to him, voluntarily, his slender chance for life. But in doing it she had challenged him to a new and overwhelming interest in life itself. And again, in front of her cousin, she was crying out anew against the shedding of blood.

"I came up here to fight a man. I don't fight women," muttered de Spain, maintaining the deceit and regarding both with an unpromising visage. Then to Morgan. "I'll talk to you later. But you've got to fight or get away from here, both of you, in ten seconds."

"Take me away, Gale," cried Nan. "Leave him here—take me home! Take me home!"

She caught her cousin's arm. "Stay right where you are," shouted Morgan, pointing at de Spain, and following Nan as she pulled him along. "When I come back, I'll give you what you're looking for."

"Bring your friends," said de Spain tauntingly.
"I'll accommodate four more of you. Stop!"
With one hand still on his revolver he pointed the
way. "Go down that trail first, Morgan. Stay
where you are, girl, till he gets down that hill.
You won't pot me over her shoulder for a while
yet. Move!"

Morgan took the path sullenly, de Spain covering every step he took. Behind de Spain Nan
stood waiting for her cousin to get beyond ear-
shot. "What," she whispered hurriedly to de
Spain, "will you do?"

Covering Morgan, who could whirl on him at
any turn in the descent, de Spain could not look
at her in answering. "Looks pretty rocky,
doesn't it?"

"He will start the whole Gap as soon as he
gets to his horse."

He looked at the darkening sky. "They won't
be very active on the job before morning."

Morgan was at a safe distance. De Spain
turned to Nan. He tried to speak out to her,
but she sternly smothered his every effort. Her
cheeks were on fire, she breathed fast, her eyes
burned.

"It looks," muttered de Spain, "as if I should
have to climb Music Mountain to make a get-
away."

Crossing a Deep River

"There is no good place to hide anywhere above here," said Nan, regarding him intently.

"Why look so hard at me, then?" he asked. "If this is the last of it, I can take it here with our one lone cartridge."

Her eyes were bent on him as if they would pierce him through. "If I save your life—" still breathing fast, she hesitated for words—"you won't trick me—ever—will you?"

Steadily returning her appealing gaze, de Spain answered with deliberation. "Don't ever give me a chance to trick you, Nan."

"What do you mean?" she demanded, fear and distrust burning in her tone.

"My life," he said slowly, "isn't worth it."

"You know—" He could see her resolute underlip, pink with fresh young blood, quiver with intensity of feeling as she faltered. "You know what every man says of every girl—foolish, trusting, easy to deceive—everything like that."

"May God wither my tongue before ever it speaks to deceive *you*, Nan."

"A while ago you frightened me so——"

"Frightened you! Great God!" He stepped closer and looked straight down into her eyes. "If you had raised just one finger when I was bluffing that fellow, I'd have calmed down and eaten out of your little hand, by the hour!"

"There's not a moment to lose," she said
swiftly. "Listen: a trail around this mountain
leads out of the Gap, straight across the face of
El Capitan."

"I can make it."

"Listen! It is terribly dangerous——"

"Whatever it is it's a concrete boulevard to a
man in my fix."

"It is half a mile—only inches wide in places—
up and down—loose rock——"

"Some trail!"

"If you slip it's a thousand feet——"

"A hundred would be more than plenty."

"A good climber can do it—I have done it.
I'd even go with you, if I could."

"Why?"

She shook her head angrily at what he dared
show in his eyes. "Oh, keep still, listen!"

"I know you'd go, Nan," he declared unper-
turbed. "But believe me, I never would let you."

"I can't go, because to do any good I must
meet you with a horse outside."

He only looked silently at her, and she turned her
eyes from his gaze. "See," she said, taking him
eagerly to the back of the ledge and pointing,
"follow that trail, the one to the east—you can't
get lost; you can reach El Capitan before dark—
it's very close. Creep carefully across El Capitan

on that narrow trail, and on the other side there is a wide one clear down to the road—oh, do be careful on El Capitan."

"I'll be careful."

"I must watch my chance to get away from the corral with a horse. If I fail it will be because I am locked up at home, and you must hide and do the best you can. How much they will surmise of this, I don't know."

"Go now, this minute," he said, restraining his words. "If you don't come, I shall know why."

She turned without speaking and, fearless as a chamois, ran down the rocks. De Spain, losing not a moment, hobbled rapidly up along the granite-walled passage that led the way to his chance for life.

CHAPTER XVI

A VENTURE IN THE DARK

PUSHING his way hastily forward when he could make haste; crawling slowly on his hands and knees when held by opposing rock; feeling for narrow footholds among loose and treacherous fragments; flattening himself like a leech against the face of the precipice when the narrowing ledge left him only inches under foot; clinging with torn hands to every favoring crevice, and pausing when the peril was extreme for fresh strength, de Spain dragged his injured foot across the sheer face of El Capitan in the last shadows of the day's failing light.

Half-way across, he stopped to look down. Far below lay the valley shrouded in night. Where he stood, stars, already bright, lighted the peaks. But nowhere in the depths could he see any sign of life. Spent by his effort, de Spain reached the rendezvous Nan had indicated, as nearly as the stars would tell him, by ten o'clock. He fell asleep in the aspen grove. Horsemen passing not a hundred yards away roused him.

A Venture in the Dark

He could not tell how many or who they were, but from the sounds he judged they were riding into the Gap. The moon was not yet up, so he knew it was not much after midnight. The ground was very cold, and he crawled farther on toward the road along which Nan had said he might look for her. It was only after a long and doubtful hour that he heard the muffled footfalls of a horse. He stood concealed among the smaller trees until he could distinguish the outlines of the animal, and his eye caught the figure of the rider.

De Spain stepped out of the trees, and, moving toward Nan, caught her hand and helped her to the ground.

She enjoined silence, and led the horse into the little grove. Stopping well within it, she stooped and began rearranging the mufflers on the hoofs.

"I'm afraid I'm too late," she said. "How long have you been here?" She faced de Spain with one hand on the pony's shoulder.

"How could you get here at all?" he asked, reaching clandestinely for her other hand.

"I got terribly frightened thinking of your trying El Capitan. Did you have any falls?"

"You see I'm here—I've even slept since. You! How could you get here at all with a horse?"

"If I'm only not too late," she murmured, drawing her hand away.

"I've loads of time, it's not one o'clock."

"They are hiding on both trails outside watching for you—and the moon will be up—" She seemed very anxious. De Spain made light of her fears. "I'll get past them—I've got to, Nan. Don't give it a thought."

"Every corner is watched," she repeated anxiously.

"But I tell you I'll dodge them, Nan."

"They have rifles."

"They won't get a chance to use them on me."

"I don't know what you'll think of me—" He heard the troubled note in her voice.

"What do you mean?"

She began to unbutton her jacket. Throwing back the revers she felt inside around her waist, unfastened after a moment and drew forth a leathern strap. She laid it in de Spain's hands. "This is yours," she said in a whisper.

He felt it questioningly, hurriedly, then with amazement. "Not a cartridge-belt!" he exclaimed.

"It's your own."

"Where—?" She made no answer. "Where did you get it, Nan?" he whispered hurriedly.

A Venture in the Dark

"Where you left it."

"How?" She was silent. "When?"

"To-night."

"Have you been to Calabasas and back to-night?"

"Everybody but Sassoon is in the chase," she replied uneasily—as if not knowing what to say, or how to say it. "They said you should never leave the Gap alive—they are ready with traps everywhere. I didn't know what to do. I couldn't bear—after what—you did for me to-night—to think of your being shot down like a dog, when you were only trying to get away."

"I wouldn't have had you take a ride like that for forty belts!"

"McAlpin showed it to me the last time I was at the stage barn, hanging where you left it." He strapped the cartridges around him.

"You should never have taken that ride for it. But since you have—" He had drawn his revolver from his waistband. He broke it now and held it out. "Load it for me, Nan."

"What do you mean?"

"Put four more cartridges in it yourself. Except for your cartridge, the gun is empty. When you do that you will know none of them ever will be used against your own except to protect my life. And if you have any among them whose life ought to come ahead of mine—name him, or them, now. Do as I tell you—load the gun."

He took hold of her hands and, in spite of her refusals, made her do his will. He guided her hand to draw the cartridges, one after another, from his belt, and waited for her to slip them in the darkness into the empty cylinder, to close the breech, and hand the gun back.

"Now, Nan," he said, "you know me. You may yet have doubts—they will all die. You will hear many stories about me—but you will say: 'I put the cartridges in his revolver with my own hands, and I know he won't abuse the means of defense I gave him myself.' There can never be any real doubts or misunderstandings between us again, Nan, if you'll forgive me for making a fool of myself when I met you at Tenison's. I didn't dream you were desperate about the way your uncle was playing; I pieced it all together afterward." He waited for her to speak, but she remained silent.

"You have given me my life, my defense," he continued, passing from a subject that he perceived was better left untouched. "Who is nearest and dearest to you at home?"

"My Uncle Duke."

"Then I never will raise a hand against your Uncle Duke. And this man, to-night—this cousin —Gale? Nan, what is that man?"

A Venture in the Dark

"I hate him."

"Thank God! So do I!"

"But he is a cousin."

"Then I suppose he must be one of mine."

"Unless he tries to kill you."

"He won't be very long in trying that. And now, what about yourself? What have you got to defend yourself against him, and against every other drunken man?"

She laid her own pistol without a word in de Spain's hand. He felt it, opened, closed, and gave it back. "That's a good defender—when it's in reach. When it's at home it's a poor one."

"It will never be at home again except when I am."

"Shall I tell you a secret?"

"What is it?" asked Nan unsuspectingly.

"We are engaged to be married." She sprang from him like a deer. "It's a dead secret," he said gravely; "nobody knows it yet—not even you."

"You need never talk again like that if you want to be friends with me," she said indignantly. "I hate it."

"Hate it if you will; it's so. And it began when you handed me that little bit of lead and brass on the mountain to-night, to defend your life and mine."

"I'll hate you if you persecute me the way

213

Gale does. The moon is almost up. You must go."

"What have you on your feet, Nan?"

"Moccasins." He stooped down and felt one with his hand. She drew her foot hastily away. "What a girl to manage!" he exclaimed.

"I'm going home," she said with decision.

"Don't for a minute yet, Nan," he pleaded. "Think how long it will be before I can ever see you again!"

"You may never see anybody again if you don't realize your danger to-night. Can you ride with a hackamore?"

"Like a dream."

"I didn't dare bring anything else."

"You haven't told me," he persisted, "how you got away at all." They had walked out of the trees. He looked reluctantly to the east. "Tell me and I'll go," he promised.

"After I went up to my room I waited till the house was all quiet. Then I started for Calabasas. When I came back I got up to my room without being seen, and sat at the window a long time. I waited till all the men stopped riding past. Then I climbed through the window and down the kitchen roof, and let myself down to the ground. Some more men came past, and I hid on the porch and slipped over to the horse

A Venture in the Dark

barns and found a hackamore, and went down to the corral and hunted around till I found this little pinto—she's the best to ride bareback."

"I could ride a razorback—why take all that trouble for me?"

"If you don't start while you have a chance, you undo everything I have tried to do to avoid a fight."

The wind, stirring softly, set the aspen leaves quivering. The stars, chilled in the thin, clear night air, hung diamond-like in the heavens and the eastern sky across the distant desert paled for the rising moon. The two standing at the horse's head listened a moment together in the darkness. De Spain, leaning forward, said something in a low, laughing voice. Nan made no answer. Then, bending, he took her hand and, before she could release it, caught it up to his lips.

For a long time after he had gone she stood, listening for a shot—wondering, breathless at moments, whether de Spain could get past the waiting traps. The moon came up, and still lingering, torn with suspense, she watched a drift of fleecy clouds darken it. She scanned anxiously the wrinkled face of the desert which, with a woman's craft, hides at night the accidents of

age. It seemed to Nan as if she could overlook
every foot of the motionless sea for miles before
her; but she well knew how much it could conceal of ambush and death even when it professed
so fairly to reveal all. Strain her ears as she
would, the desert gave back no ripple of sound.
No shot echoed from its sinister recesses—not even
the clatter of retreating hoofs.

De Spain, true to all she had ever heard of his
Indian-like stealth, had left her side unabashed
and unafraid—living, laughing, paying bold court
to her even when she stubbornly refused to be
courted—and had made himself in the twinkling
of an eye a part of the silence beyond—the silence
of the night, the wind, the stars, the waste of sand,
and of all the mystery that brooded upon it.   She
would have welcomed, in her keen suspense, a
sound of some kind, some reminder that he yet
lived and could yet laugh; none came.

When it seemed as if an hour must have passed
Nan felt her way noiselessly home.   She regained
her room as she had left it, through her east window, and, throwing herself across her bed, fell
into a heavy sleep.

Day was breaking when the night boss, standing in the doorway at the Calabasas barns, saw a
horseman riding at a leisurely pace up the Thief

A Venture in the Dark

River road. The barnman scrutinized the approaching stranger closely. There was something strange and something familiar in the outlines of the figure. But when the night-rider had dismounted in front of the barn door, turned his horse loose, and, limping stiffly, walked forward on foot, the man rubbed his eyes hard before he could believe them. Then he uttered an incredulous greeting and led Henry de Spain into the barn office.

"There's friends of yours in your room upstairs right now," he declared, bulging with shock. De Spain, sitting down, forbade the barnman to disturb them, only asking who they were.

When he had asked half a dozen more leisurely questions and avoided answering twice as many, the barnman at de Spain's request helped him up-stairs. Beside himself with excitement, the night boss turned, grinning, as he laid one hand on the door-knob and the other on de Spain's shoulder.

"You couldn't have come," he whispered loudly, "at a better time."

The entryway was dark, and from the silence within the room one might have thought its occupants, if there were such, wrapped in slumber. But at intervals a faint clicking sound could be heard. The night man threw open the door. By

217

the light of two stage dash-lamps, one set on the
dresser and the other on a window-ledge, four
men sat about a rickety table in a life-and-death
struggle at cards. No voice broke the tense silence, not even when the door was thrown broadly
open.

No one—neither Lefever, Scott, Frank Elpaso,
nor McAlpin—looked up when de Spain walked
into the room and, with the night man tiptoeing
behind, advanced composedly toward the group.
Even then his presence would have passed unnoticed, but that Bob Scott's ear mechanically recorded the limping step and transmitted to his
trained intelligence merely notice of something
unusual.

Scott, picking up his cards one at a time as
Lefever dealt, raised his eyes. Startling as the
sight of the man given up for dead must have
been, no muscle of Bob Scott's body moved. His
expression of surprise slowly dissolved into a grin
that mutely invited the others, as he had found
out for himself, to find out for themselves.

Lefever finished his deal, threw down the pack,
and picked up his hand. His suspicious eyes
never rose above the level of the faces at the
table; but when he had thumbed his cards and
looked from one to the other of the remaining
players to read the weather-signals, he perceived

A Venture in the Dark

on Scott's face an unwonted expression, and looked to where the scout's gaze was turned for an explanation of it. Lefever's own eyes at the sight of the thinned, familiar face behind Elpaso's chair, starting, opened like full moons. The big fellow spread one hand out, his cards hidden within it, and with the other hand prudently drew down his pile of chips. "Gentlemen," he said lightly, "this game is interned." He rose and put a silent hand across the table over Elpaso's shoulder. "Henry," he exclaimed impassively, "one question, if you please—and only one: How in thunder did you do it?"

CHAPTER XVII

STRATEGY

ONE week went to repairs. To a man of action such a week is longer than ten years of service. But chained to a bed in the Sleepy Cat hospital, de Spain had no escape from one week of thinking, and for that week he thought about Nan Morgan.

He rebelled at the situation that had placed him at enmity with her kinsfolk, yet he realized there was no help for this. The Morgans were a law unto themselves. Hardened men with a hardened code, they lived in their fastness like Ishmaelites. Counselled by their leader, old Duke Morgan, brains of the clan and influential enough to keep outside the penalties of the law themselves, their understanding with the outlaws of the Sinks was apparently complete, and the hospitality of one or another of their following within the Gap afforded a refuge for practically any mountain criminal.

But none of these reflections lightened de Spain's burden of discontent. One thought alone possessed him—Nan; her comely body, which he worshipped to the tips of her graceful fingers; her alert mind, which he saw reflected in the simplest thought she expressed; her mobile lips, which he followed to the least sound they gave forth! The longer he pictured her, figured as she had appeared to him like a phantom on Music Mountain, the more he longed to be back at the foot of it, wounded again and famished. And the impulse that moved him the first moment he could get out of bed and into a saddle was to spur his way hard and fast to her; to make her, against a score of burly cousins, his own; and never to release her from his sudden arms again.

With de Spain, to think was to do; at least to do something, but not without further careful thinking, and not without anticipating every chance of failure. And his manner was to cast up all difficulties and obstacles in a situation, brush them aside, and have his will if the heavens fell. Such a temperament he had inherited from his father's fiery heart and his mother's suffering, close-set lips as he had remembered them in the little pictures of her; and he now set himself, while doing his routine work every day, to do one particular thing—to see, talk to, plead with, struggle with the woman, or girl, rather—child even, to his thoughts, so fragile she was—this girl who had given him back his life against her own marauding relatives.

For many days Nan seemed a match for all the wiles de Spain could use to catch sight of her. He spent his days riding up and down the line on horseback; driving behind his team; on the stages; in and out of the streets of Sleepy Cat —nominally looking for stock, for equipment, for supplies, or frankly for nothing—but always looking for Nan.

His friends saw that something was absorbing him in an unusual, even an extraordinary way, yet none could arrive at a certain conclusion as to what it was. When Scott in secret conference was appealed to by Jeffries, he smiled foolishly, at a loss, and shook his head.

Lefever argued with less reticence. "It stands to reason, Jeffries. A man that went through that ten minutes at Calabasas would naturally think a good deal about what he is getting out of his job, and what his future chances are for being promoted any minute, day or night, by a forty-five."

"Perhaps his salary had better be raised," conceded Jeffries reflectively.

"I figure," pursued Lefever, "that he has already saved the company fifty thousands in depredations during the next year or two. The Calabasas gang is busted for five years—they would eat out of his hand—isn't that so, Bob?"

"The Calabasas gang, yes; not the Morgans."

John's eyes opened on Scott with that solemnity he could assume to bolster a baldly unconvincing statement. "Not now, Bob. Not now, I admit; but they will."

Scott only smiled. "What do *you* make out of the way he acts?" persisted Lefever, resenting his companion's incredulity.

"I can't make anything of it," premised Bob, "except that he has something on his mind. If you'll tell me what happened from the time he jumped through the window at Calabasas till he walked into his room that night at the barn, I'll tell you what he's thinking about."

"What do you mean, what happened?"

"Henry left some things out of his story."

"How do you know?"

"I heard him tell it."

Jeffries, acting without delay on the suspicion that de Spain was getting ready to resign, raised his salary. To his surprise, de Spain told him that the company was already paying him more than he was worth and declined the raise; yet he took nobody whomsoever into his confidence.

However, the scent of something concealed in de Spain's story had long before touched Lefever's own nostrils, and he was stimulated by mere pride to run the secret down. Accordingly, he set himself to find, in a decent way, something in the nature of an explanation.

De Spain, in the interval, made no progress in his endeavor to see Nan. The one man in the country who could have surmised the situation between the two—the barn boss, McAlpin—if he entertained suspicions, was far too pawky to share them with any one.

When two weeks had passed without de Spain's having seen Nan or having heard of her being seen, the conclusion urged itself on him that she was either ill or in trouble—perhaps in trouble for helping him; a moment later he was laying plans to get into the Gap to find out.

Nothing in the way of a venture could be more foolhardy—this he admitted to himself—nothing, he consoled himself by reflecting, but something stronger than danger could justify it. Of all the motley Morgan following within the mountain fastness he could count on but one man to help him in the slightest degree—this was the derelict, Bull Page. There was no choice but to use him, and he was easily enlisted, for the Calabasas affair had made a heroic figure of de Spain in the bar-rooms. De Spain, accordingly, lay in wait for the old man and intercepted him one day on the road to Sleepy Cat, walking the twenty miles patiently for his whiskey.

"You must be the only man in the Gap, Bull, that can't borrow or steal a horse to ride," remarked de Spain, stopping him near the river bridge.

Page pushed back the broken brim of his hat and looked up. "You wouldn't believe it," he said, imparting a cheerful confidence, "but ten years ago I had horses to lend to every man 'tween here and Thief River." He nodded toward Sleepy Cat with a wrecked smile, and by a dramatic chance the broken hat brim fell with the words: "They've got 'em all."

"Your fault, Bull."

"Say!" Up went the broken brim, and the whiskied face lighted with a shaking smile, "you turned some trick on that Calabasas crew—some fight," Bull chuckled.

"Bull, is old Duke Morgan a Republican?"

Bull looked surprised at the turn of de Spain's question, but answered in good faith: "Duke votes 'most any ticket that's agin the railroad."

"How about picking a couple of good barnmen over in the Gap, Bull?"

"What kind of a job y' got?"

"See McAlpin the next time you're over at

Calabasas. How about that girl that lives with Duke?"

Bull's face lighted. "Nan! Say! she's a little hummer!"

"I hear she's gone down to Thief River teaching school."

"Came by Duke's less'n three hours ago. Seen her in the kitchen makin' bread."

"They're looking for a school-teacher down there, anyway. Much sickness in the Gap lately, Bull?"

"On'y sickness I knowed lately is what you're responsible for y'self," retorted Bull with a grin. "Pity y' left over any chips at all from that Calabasas job, eh?"

"See McAlpin, Bull, next time you're over Calabasas way. Here"—de Spain drew some currency from his pocket and handed a bill to Page. "Go get your hair cut. Don't talk too much—wear your whiskers long and your tongue short."

"Right-o!"

"You understand."

"Take it from old Bull Page, he's a world's wonder of a sucker, but he knows his friends."

"But remember this—you don't know me. If anybody knows you for a friend of mine, you are no good to me. See?"

Bull was beyond expressing his comprehension

in words alone. He winked, nodded, and screwed his face into a thousand wrinkles. De Spain, wheeling, rode away, the old man blinking first after him, and then at the money in his hand. He didn't profess to understand everything in the high country, but he could still distinguish the principal figures at the end of a bank-note. When he tramped to Calabasas the next day to interview McAlpin he received more advice, with a strong burr, about keeping his own counsel, and a little expense money to run him until an opening presented itself on the pay-roll.

But long before Bull Page reached Calabasas that day de Spain had acted. When he left Bull at the bridge, he started for Calabasas, took supper there, ordered a saddle-horse for one o'clock in the morning, went to his room, slept soundly and, shortly after he was called, started for Music Mountain. He walked his horse into the Gap and rode straight for Duke Morgan's fortress. Leaving the horse under a heavy mountain-pine close to the road, de Spain walked carefully but directly around the house to the east side. The sky was cloudy and the darkness almost complete. He made his way as close as he could to Nan's window, and raised the soft, crooning note of the desert owl.

After a while he was able to distinguish the outline of her casement, and, with much patience and some little skill remaining from the boyhood days, he kept up the faint call. Down at the big barn the chained watch-dog tore himself with a fury of barking at the intruder, but mountain-lions were common in the Gap, and the noisy sentinel gained no credit for his alarm. Indeed, when the dog slackened his fierceness, de Spain threw a stone over his way to encourage a fresh outburst. But neither the guardian nor the intruder was able to arouse any one within the house.

Undeterred by his failure, de Spain held his ground as long as he dared. When daybreak threatened, he withdrew. The following night he was in the Gap earlier, and with renewed determination. He tossed a pebble into Nan's open window and renewed his soft call. Soon, a light flickered for an instant within the room and died out. In the darkness following this, de Spain thought he discerned a figure outlined at the casement. Some minutes later a door opened and closed. He repeated the cry of the owl, and could hear a footstep; the next moment he whispered her name as she stood before him.

"What is it you want?" she asked, so calmly that it upset him. "Why do you come here?"

Where he stood he was afraid of the sound of her voice, and afraid of his own. "To see you," he said, collecting himself. "Come over to the pine-tree."

Under its heavy branches where the darkness was most intense, he told her why he had come—because he could not see her anywhere outside.

"There is nothing to see me about," she responded, still calm. "I helped you because you were wounded. I was glad to see you get away without fighting—I hate bloodshed."

"But put yourself in my place a little, won't you? After what you did for me, isn't it natural I should want to be sure you are well and not in any trouble on my account?"

"It may be natural, but it isn't necessary. I am in no trouble. No one here knows I even know you."

"Excuse me for coming, then. I couldn't rest, Nan, without knowing something. I was here last night."

"I know you were."

He started. "You made no sign."

"Why should I? I suspected it was you. When you came again to-night I knew I should have to speak to you—at least, to ask you not to come again."

"But you will be in and out of town sometimes, won't you, Nan?"

"If I am, it will not be to talk with you."

The words were spoken deliberately. De Spain was silent for a moment. "Not even to speak to me?" he asked.

"You must know the position I am in," she answered. "And what a position you place me in if I am seen to speak to you. This is my home. You are the enemy of my people."

"Not because I want to be."

"And you can't expect them not to resent any acquaintance on my part with you."

He paused before continuing. "Do you count Gale Morgan as one of your people?" he asked evenly.

"I suppose I must."

"Don't you think you ought to count all of your friends, your well-wishers, those who would defend you with their lives, among your people?" She made no answer. "Aren't they the kind of people," he persisted, "you need when you are in trouble?"

"You needn't remind me I should be grateful to you——"

"Nan!" he exclaimed.

"For I am," she continued, unmoved. "But——"

"It's a shame to accuse me in that way."

"You were thinking when you spoke of what happened with Gale on Music Mountain."

Strategy

"I wish to God you and I were on Music Mountain again! I never lived or did anything worth living for, till you came to me that day on Music Mountain. It's true I was thinking of what happened when I spoke—but not to remind you you owed anything to me. You don't; get that out of your head."

"I do, though."

"I spoke in the way I did because I wanted to remind you of what might happen some time when I'm not near."

"I shan't be caught off my guard again. I know how to defend myself from a drunken man."

He could not restrain all the bitterness he felt. "That man," he said deliberately, "is more dangerous sober than drunk."

"When I can't defend myself, my uncle will defend me."

"Ask him to let me help."

"He doesn't need any help. And he would never ask you, if he did. I can't live at home and know you; that is why I ask you not to come again."

He was silent. "Don't you think, all things considered," she hesitated, as if not knowing how easiest to put it, "you ought to be willing to shake hands and say good-by?"

"Why, if you wish it," he answered, taken aback. And he added more quietly, "yes, if you say so."

"I mean for good."

"I—" he returned, pausing, "don't."

"You are not willing to be fair."

"I want to be fair—I don't want to promise more than human nature will stand for—and then break my word."

"I am not asking a whole lot."

"Not a whole lot to you, I know. But do you really mean that you don't want me ever to speak to you again?"

"If you must put it that way—yes."

"Well," he took a long breath, "there is one way to make sure of that. I'll tell you honestly I don't want to stand in the way of such a wish, if it's really yours. As you have said, it isn't fair, perhaps, for me to go against it. Got your pistol with you, Nan?"

"No."

"That is the way you take care of yourself, is it?"

"I'm not afraid of you."

"You ought to be ashamed of yourself not to be. And you don't even know whom you'll meet before you can lock the front door again. You promised me never to go out without it.

Strategy

Promise me that once more, will you?" She did as he asked her. "Now, give me your hand, please," he went on. "Take hold of this."

"What is it?"

"The butt of my revolver. Don't be afraid." She heard the slight click of the hammer with a thrill of strange apprehension. "What are you doing?" she demanded hurriedly.

"Put your finger on the trigger—so. It is cocked. Now pull."

She caught her breath. "What do you mean?"

He was holding the gun in his two hands, his fingers overlapping hers, the muzzle at the breast of his jacket. "Pull," he repeated, "that's all you have to do; I'm steadying it."

She snatched back her hand. "What do you mean?" she cried. "For me to kill you? Shame!"

"You are too excited—all I asked you was to take the trouble to crook your finger—and I'll never speak to you again—you'll have your wish forever."

"Shame!"

"Why shame?" he retorted. "I mean what I say. If you meant what you said, why don't you put it out of my power ever to speak to you? Do you want me to pull the trigger?"

"I told you once I'm not an assassin—how dare

233

you ask me to do such a thing?" she cried furiously.

"Call your uncle," he suggested coolly. "You may hold this meantime so you'll know he's in no danger. Take my gun and call your uncle——"

"Shame on you!"

"Call Gale—call any man in the Gap—they'll jump at the chance."

"You are a cold-blooded, brutal wretch—I'm sorry I ever helped you—I'm sorry I ever let you help me—I'm sorry I ever saw you!"

She sprang away before he could interpose a word. He stood stunned by the suddenness of her outburst, trying to listen and to breathe at the same time. He heard the front door close, and stood waiting. But no further sound from the house greeted his ears.

"And I thought," he muttered to himself, "that might calm her down a little. I'm certainly in wrong, now."

CHAPTER XVIII

HER BAD PENNY

NAN reached her room in a fever of excitement, angry at de Spain, bitterly angry at Gale, angry with the mountains, the world, and resentfully fighting the pillow on which she cried herself to sleep.

In the morning every nerve was on edge. When her Uncle Duke, with his chopping utterance, said something short to her at their very early breakfast he was surprised by an answer equally short. Her uncle retorted sharply. A second curt answer greeted his rebuff, and while he stared at her, Nan left the table and the room.

Duke, taking two of the men, started that morning for Sleepy Cat with a bunch of cattle. He rode a fractious horse, as he always did, and this time the horse, infuriated as his horses frequently were by his brutal treatment, bolted in a moment unguarded by his master, and flung Duke on his back in a strip of lava rocks.

The old man—in the mountains a man is called old after he passes forty—was heavy, and the fall a serious one. He picked himself up while the men were recovering his horse, knocked the horse over with a piece of jagged rock when the frightened beast was brought back, climbed into the saddle again, and rode all the way into town.

But when his business was done, Duke, too, was done. He could neither sit a horse, nor sit in a wagon. Doctor Torpy, after an examination, told him he was booked for the hospital. A stream of profane protest made no difference with his adviser, and, after many threats and hard words, to the hospital the hard-shelled mountaineer was taken. Sleepy Cat was stirred at the news, and that the man who had defied everybody in the mountains for twenty years should have been laid low and sent to the hospital by a mere bronco was the topic of many comments.

The men that had driven the cattle with Duke, having been paid off, were now past getting home, and there were no telephones in the Gap. De Spain, who was at Calabasas, knew Nan would not be alarmed should her uncle not return that night. But early in the morning a messenger from McAlpin rode to her with a note, telling her of the accident.

Whatever his vices, Duke had been a good protector to his dead brother's child. He had sent her to good schools and tried to revive in her, despite her untoward surroundings, the better tra-

Her Bad Penny

ditions of the family as it had once flourished in Kentucky. Nan took the saddle for Sleepy Cat in haste and alarm. When she reached her uncle's bedside she understood how seriously he had been hurt, and the doctor's warnings were not needed to convince her he must have care.

Duke refused to let her leave him, in any case, and Nan relieved the nurse, and what was of equal moment, made herself custodian of the cash in hand before Duke's town companions could get hold of it. Occasional trips to the Gap were necessary as the weeks passed and her uncle could not be moved. These Nan had feared as threatening an encounter either by accident, or on his part designed, with de Spain. But the impending encounter never took place. De Spain, attending closely to his own business, managed to keep accurate track of her whereabouts without getting in her way. She had come to Sleepy Cat dreading to meet him and fearing his influence over her, but this apprehension, with the passing of a curiously brief period, dissolved into a confidence in her ability to withstand further interference, on any one's part, with her feelings.

Gale Morgan rode into town frequently, and Nan at first painfully apprehended hearing some time of a deadly duel between her truculent Gap admirer and her persistent town courtier—who

237

was more considerate and better-mannered, but
no less dogged and, in fact, a good deal more difficult to handle.

As to the boisterous mountain-man, his resolute
little cousin made no secret of her detestation of
him. She denied and defied him as openly as a
girl could and heard his threats with continued
indifference. She was quite alone, too, in her
fear of any fatal meeting between the two men
who seemed determined to pursue her.

The truth was that after Calabasas, de Spain,
from Thief River to Sleepy Cat, was a marked
man. None sought to cross his path or his pur-
poses. Every one agreed he would yet be killed,
but not the hardiest of the men left to attack him
cared to undertake the job themselves. The
streets of the towns and the trails of the mountains were free as the wind to de Spain. And
neither the town haunts of Calabasas men nor
those of their Morgan Gap sympathizers had any
champion disposed to follow too closely the alert
Medicine Bend railroader.

In and about the hospital, and in the town
itself, Nan found the chief obstacle to her peace
of mind in the talk she could not always avoid
hearing about de Spain. Convalescents in the cor-
ridors, practically all of them men, never gathered in sunny corners or at the tables in the din-

Her Bad Penny

ing-room without de Spain's name coming in some way into the talk, to be followed with varying circumstantial accounts of what really had happened that day at Calabasas.

And with all the known escapades in which he had figured, exhausted as topics, by long-winded commentators, more or less hazy stories of his earlier experiences at Medicine Bend in the company of Whispering Smith were dragged into the talk. One convalescent stage-guard at the hospital told a story one night at supper about him that chilled Nan again with strange fears, for she knew it to be true. He had had it from McAlpin himself, so the guard said, that de Spain's father had long ago been shot down from ambush by a cattleman and that Henry de Spain had sworn to find that man and kill him. And it was hinted pretty strongly that de Spain had information when he consented to come to Sleepy Cat that the assassin still lived, and lived somewhere around the head of the Sinks.

That night, Nan dreamed. She dreamed of a sinister mark on a face that she had never before seen—a face going into bronzed young manhood with quick brown eyes looking eagerly at her. And before her wondering look it faded, dream-like, into a soft mist, and where it had been, a man lay, lifting himself on one arm from the ground—

his sleeve tattered, his collar torn, his eyes half-living, half-dead, his hair clotted, his lips stiffened and distended, his face drawn. And all of this dissolved into an image of de Spain on horseback, sudden, alert, threatening, looking through the mist at an enemy. Then Nan heard the sharp report of a rifle and saw him whirl half around—struck—in his saddle, and fall. But he fell into her arms, and she woke sobbing violently.

She was upset for the whole day, moody and apprehensive, with a premonition that she should soon see de Spain—and, perhaps, hurt again. The dream unnerved her every time she thought of him. That evening the doctor came late. When he walked in he asked her if she knew it was Frontier Day, and reminded her that just a year ago she had shot against Henry de Spain and beaten the most dangerous man and the deadliest shot on the mountain divide in her rifle match. How he had grown in the imagination of Sleepy Cat and Music Mountain, she said to herself—while the doctor talked to her uncle—since that day a year ago! Then he was no more than an unknown and discomfited marksman from Medicine Bend, beaten by a mountain girl: now the most talked-of man in the high country. And the suspicion would sometimes obtrude itself with pride into her mind, that she who never mentioned his name when it was discussed before her, really knew and understood him better than any of those that talked so much—that she had at least one great secret with him alone.

When leaving, the doctor wished to send over from his office medicine for her uncle. Nan offered to go with him, but the doctor said it was pretty late and Main Street pretty noisy: he preferred to find a messenger.

Nan was sitting in the sick-room a little later—B-19 in the old wing of the hospital, facing the mountains—when there came a rap on the half-open door. She went forward to take the medicine from the messenger and saw, standing before her in the hall, de Spain.

She shrank back as if struck. She tried to speak. Her tongue refused its office. De Spain held a package out in his hand. "Doctor Torpy asked me to give you this."

"Doctor Torpy? What is it?"

"I really don't know—I suppose it is medicine." She heard her uncle turn in his bed at the sound of voices. Thinking only that he must not at any cost see de Spain, Nan stepped quickly into the hall and faced the messenger. "I was over at the doctor's office just now," continued her visitor evenly, "he asked me to bring this down for your uncle." She took the package with an

incoherent acknowledgment. Without letting her
eyes meet his, she was conscious of how fresh and
clean and strong he looked, dressed in a livelier
manner than usual—a partly cowboy effect, with
a broader Stetson and a gayer tie than he ordinarily affected. De Spain kept on speaking:
"The telephone girl in the office down-stairs told
me to come right up. How is your uncle?"

She regarded him wonderingly: "He has a
good deal of pain," she answered quietly.

"Too bad he should have been hurt in such a
way. Are you pretty well, Nan?" She thanked
him.

"Have you got over being mad at me?" he
asked.

"No," she averred resolutely.

"I'm glad you're not," he returned, "I'm not
over being mad at myself. Haven't seen you
for a long time. Stay here a good deal, do you?"

"All the time."

"I'll bet you don't know what day this is?"

Nan looked up the corridor, but she answered
to the point: "You'd lose."

"It's our anniversary." She darted a look of
indignant disclaimer at him. But in doing so
she met his eyes. "Have you seen the decora-
tions in Main Street?" he asked indifferently.
"Come out for a minute and look at them."

Her Bad Penny

She shook her head: "I don't care to," she answered, looking restlessly, this time, down the corridor.

"Come to the door just a minute and see the way they've lighted the arches." She knew just the expression of his eyes that went with that tone. She looked vexedly at him to confirm her suspicion. Sure enough there in the brown part and in the lids, it was, the most troublesome possible kind of an expression—hard to be resolute against. Her eyes fell away, but some damage had been done. He did not say another word. None seemed necessary. He just kept still and something—no one could have said just what—seemed to talk for him to poor defenseless Nan. She hesitated helplessly: "I can't leave uncle," she objected at last.

"Ask him to come along."

Her eyes fluttered about the dimly lighted hall: de Spain gazed on her as steadily as a charmer. "I ought not to leave even for a minute," she protested weakly.

"I'll stay here at the door while you go."

Irresolute, she let her eyes rest again for a fraction of a second on his eyes; when she drew a breath after that pause everything was over. "I'd better give him his medicine first," she said, looking toward the sick-room door.

Nan of Music Mountain

His monosyllabic answer was calm: "Do."
Then as she laid her hand on the knob of the
door to enter the room: "Can I help any?"

"Oh, no!" she cried indignantly.

He laughed silently: "I'll stay here."

Nan disappeared. Lounging against the win-
dow-sill opposite the door, he waited. After a
long time the door was stealthily reopened. Nan
tiptoed out. She closed it softly behind her: "I
waited for him to go to sleep," she explained as she
started down the corridor with de Spain. "He's
had so much pain to-day: I hope he will sleep."

"I hope so, too," exclaimed de Spain fervently.

Nan ignored the implication. She looked
straight ahead. She had nothing to say. De
Spain, walking beside her, devoured her with his
eyes; listened to her footfalls; tried to make
talk; but Nan was silent.

Standing on the wide veranda outside the
front door, she assented to the beauty of the distant illumination but not enthusiastically. De
Spain declared it could be seen very much better
from the street below. Nan thought she could
see very well where they stood. But by this
time she was answering questions—dryly, it is
true and in monosyllables, but answering. De
Spain leading the way a step or two forward at a
time, coaxed her down the driveway.

244

Her Bad Penny

She stood again irresolute, he drinking in the fragrance of her presence after the long separation and playing her reluctance guardedly. "Do you know," she exclaimed with sudden resentment, "you make it awfully hard to be mean to you?"

With a laugh he caught her hand and made her walk down the hospital steps. "You may be as mean as you like," he answered indifferently. "Only, never ask me to be mean to you."

"I wish to heaven you would be," she retorted.

"Do you remember," he asked, "what we were doing a year ago to-day?"

"No." Before he could speak again she changed her answer: "Yes, I do remember. If I said 'no' you'd be sure to remind me of what we were doing. We can't see as well here as we could from the steps."

"But from here, you have the best view in Sleepy Cat of Music Mountain."

"We didn't come out here to see Music Mountain."

"I come here often to look at it. You won't let me see you—what can I do but look at where you live? How long are you going to keep me away from you?"

Nan did not answer. He urged her to speak.

245

"You know very well it is my people that will never be friendly with you," she replied. "How can I be?"

They were passing a lawn settee. He sat down. She would not follow. She stood in a sort of protest at his side, but he did not release her hand. "I'll tell you how you can be," he returned. "Make me one of your people."

"That never can be," she declared stubbornly. "You know it as well as I do. Why do you say such things?" she demanded, drawing away her hand.

"Do you want to know?"

"No."

"It's because I love you."

She strove to command herself: "Whether you do or not can't make any difference," she returned steadily. "We are separated by everything. There's a gulf between us. It never can be crossed. We should both of us be wretched if it ever were crossed."

He had risen from the bench and caught her hand: "It's because we haven't crossed it we're wretched," he said determinedly. "Cross it with me now!" He caught her in his arms. She struggled to escape. She knew what was coming and fought to keep her face from him. With resistless strength and yet carefully as a mother

Her Bad Penny

with an obstinate child, he held her slight body against his breast, relentlessly drawing her head closer. "Let me go!" she panted, twisting her averted head from the hollow of his arm. Drinking in the wine of her frightened breath, he bent over her in the darkness until his pulsing eagerness linked her warm lips to his own. She had surrendered to his first kiss.

He spoke. "The gulf's crossed. Are you so awfully wretched?"

They sank together down on the bench. "What," she faltered, "will become of me now?"

"You are better off now than you ever were, Nan. You've gained this moment a big brother, a lover you can drag around the world after you with a piece of thread."

"You act as if I could!"

"I mean it: it's true. I'm pledged to you forever—you, to me, forever. We'll keep our secret till we can manage things; and we *will* manage them. Everything will come right, Nan, because everything must come right."

"I only hope you are not wrong," she murmured, her eyes turned toward the sombre mountains.

CHAPTER XIX

DANGER

WITH never such apprehension, never such stealth, never so heavy a secret, so sensible a burning in cheek and eye, as when she tiptoed into her uncle's room at midnight, Nan's heart beat as the wings of a bird beat from the broken door of a cage into a forbidden sky of happiness. She had left the room a girl; she came back to it a woman.

Sleep she did not expect or even ask for; the night was all too short to think of those tense, fearful moments that had pledged her to her lover. When the anxieties of her situation overwhelmed her, as they would again and again, she felt herself in the arms of this strange, resolute man whom all her own hated and whom she knew she already loved beyond all power to put away. In her heart, she had tried this more than once: she knew she could not, would not ever do it, or even try to do it, again.

She rejoiced in his love. She trusted. When he spoke she believed this man whom no one around her would believe; and she, who never had

believed what other men avowed, and who detested their avowals, believed de Spain, and secretly, guiltily, glowed in every word of his devotion and breathed faint in its every caress.

Night could hardly come fast enough, after
the next long day. A hundred times during that
day she reminded herself, while the slow, majestic sun shone simmering on the hot desert, that
she had promised to steal out into the grounds the
minute darkness fell—he would be waiting. A
hundred times in the long afternoon, Nan looked
into the cloudless western sky and with puny
eager hands would have pushed the lagging orb
on its course that she might sooner give herself
into the arms where she felt her place so sure, her
honor so safe, her helplessness so protected, herself so loved.

How her cheeks burned after supper when she
asked her uncle for leave to post a letter down-
town! How breathless with apprehension she
halted as de Spain stepped from the shadow of
the trees and drew her importunately beneath
them for the kiss that had burned on her troubled
lips all day! How, girl-like, knowing his caresses
were all her own—knowing she could at an instant call forth enough to smother her—she
tyrannized his importuning and, like a lovely
miser, hoarded her responsiveness under calm

249

eyes and laconic whispers until, when she did give back his eagerness, she made his senses reel.

How dreamily she listened to every word he let fall in his outpouring of devotion; how gravely she put up her hand to restrain his busy intrusion, and asked if he knew that no man in the world, least of all her fierce and burly cousin, had ever touched her lips until he himself forced a kiss on them the night before: "And now!" She hid her face against his shoulder. "Oh, Henry, how I love you! I'm so ashamed, I couldn't tell you if it weren't night: I'll never look you in the face again in the daytime."

And when he told her how little he himself had had to do with, and how little he knew about girls, even from boyhood, how she feigned not to believe, and believed him still! They were two children raised in the magic of an hour to the supreme height of life and dizzy together on its summit.

"I don't see how you can care for *me*, Henry. Oh, I mean it," she protested, holding her head resolutely up. "You know who we are, away off there in the mountains. Every one hates us; I suppose they've plenty of reason to: we hate everybody else. And why shouldn't we? We're at war with every one. You know, better than I do, what goes on in the Gap. I don't want to know; I try not to know; Uncle Duke tries to keep things from me. When you began to act— as if you cared for me—that day on Music—I couldn't believe you meant it at all. And yet— I'm afraid I liked to try to think you did. When you looked at me I felt as if you could see right through me."

Confidences never came to an end.

And diplomacy came into its own almost at once in de Spain's efforts to improve his relations with the implacable Duke. The day came when Nan's uncle could be taken home. De Spain sent to him a soft-spoken emissary, Bob Scott, offering to provide a light stage, with his compliments, for the trip. The intractable mountaineer, with his refusal to accept the olive-branch, blew Bob out of the room. Nan was crushed by the result, but de Spain was not to be dismayed.

Lefever came to him the day after Nan had got her uncle home. "Henry," he began without any preliminaries, "there is one thing about your precipitate ride up Music Mountain that I never got clear in my mind. After the fight, your cartridge-belt was hanging up in the barn at Calabasas for two weeks. You walked in to us that morning with your belt buckled on. You told us you put it on before you came up-stairs. What? Oh, yes, I know, Henry. But that belt wasn't hanging down-stairs with your coat earlier in the evening. No, Henry: it wasn't, not when I looked. Don't tell me such things, because—I don't know. Where was the belt when you found it?"

"Some distance from the coat, John. I admit that. I'll tell you: some one had moved the belt. It was not where I left it. I was hurried the morning I rode in and I can't tell you just where I found it."

Lefever never batted an eyelash. "I know you can't, Henry. Because you won't. That Scotch hybrid McAlpin knows a few things, too, that he won't tell. All I want to say is, you can trust that man too far. He's got all my recent salary. Every time Jeffries raises my pay that hairy-pawed horse-doctor reduces it just so much a month. And he does it with one pack of fifty-two small cards that you could stick into your vest pocket."

"McAlpin has a wife and children to support," suggested de Spain.

"Don't think for a moment he does it," returned Lefever vehemently. "I support his wife and children, myself."

"You shouldn't play cards, John."

"It was by playing cards that I located Sassoon, just the same. A little game with your

friend Bull Page, by the way. And say, that man
blew into Calabasas one day here lately with a
twenty-dollar bill; it's a fact. Now, where do
you suppose he got twenty dollars in one bill?
I know *I* had it two hours after he got there and
then in fifteen minutes that blamed bull-whacker
you pay thirty-two a week to took it away from
me. But I got Sassoon spotted. And where do
you suppose Split-lips is this minute?"

"Morgan's Gap."

"Quite so—and been there all the time. Now,
Bob has the old warrant for him: the question
is, how to get him out."

De Spain reflected a moment before replying:
"John, I'd let him alone just for the present,"
he said at length.

Lefever's eyes bulged: "Let Sassoon alone?"

"He will keep—for a while, anyway."

"What do you mean?"

"I don't want to stir things up too strong over
that way just at the minute, John."

"Why not?"

De Spain shuffled a little: "Well, Jeffries
thinks we might let things rest till Duke Morgan and the others get over some of their soreness."

Lefever, astonished at the indifference of de
Spain to the opportunity of nabbing Sassoon,

253

while he could be found, expostulated strongly. When de Spain persisted, Lefever, huffed, confided to Bob Scott that when the general manager got ready he could catch Sassoon himself.

De Spain wanted for Nan's sake, as well as his own, to see what could be done to pacify her uncle and his relatives so that a wedge might be driven in between them and their notorious henchman, and Sassoon brought to book with their consent; on this point, however, he was not quite bold-faced enough to take his friends into his confidence.

De Spain, as fiery a lover as he was a fighter, stayed none of his courting because circumstances put Music Mountain between him and his mistress. And Nan, after she had once surrendered, was nothing behind in the chances she unhesitatingly took to arrange her meetings with de Spain. He found in her, once her girlish timidity was overcome and a woman's confidence had replaced it, a disregard of consequences, so far as their own plans were concerned, that sometimes took away his breath.

The very day after she had got her uncle home, with the aid of Satterlee Morgan and an antiquated spring wagon, Nan rode, later in the afternoon, over to Calabasas. The two that would not be restrained had made their appointment at the lower lava beds half-way between the Gap and Calabasas. The sun was sinking behind the mountain when de Spain galloped out of the rocks as Nan turned from the trail and rode toward the black and weather-beaten meeting-place.

They could hardly slip from their saddles fast enough to reach each other's arms—Nan, trim as a model in fresh khaki, trying with a handkerchief hardly larger than a postage-stamp to wipe the flecks of dust from her pink cheeks, while de Spain, between dabs, covered them with importunate greetings. Looking engrossed into each other's eyes, and both, in their eagerness, talking at once, they led their horses into hiding and sat down to try to tell all that had happened since their parting. Wars and rumors of wars, feuds and raidings, fights and pursuits were no more to them than to babes in the woods. All that mattered to them—sitting or pacing together and absorbed, in the path of the long-cold volcanic stream buried in the shifting sands of the desert—was that they should clasp each other's clinging hands, listen each to the other's answering voice, look unrestrained into each other's questioning eyes.

They met in both the lava beds—the upper lay between the Gap and town—more than once.

Nan of Music Mountain

And one day came a scare. They were sitting
on a little ledge well up in the rocks where de
Spain could overlook the trail east and west, and
were talking about a bungalow some day to be in
Sleepy Cat, when they saw men riding from the
west toward Calabasas. There were three in the
party, one lagging well behind. The two men
leading, Nan and de Spain made out to be Gale
Morgan and Page. They saw the man coming
on behind stop his horse and lean forward, his
head bent over the trail. He was examining the
sand and halted quite a minute to study something. Both knew what he was studying—the
hoof-prints of Nan's pony heading toward the
lava. Nan shrank back and with de Spain moved
a little to where they could watch the intruder
without being seen. Nan whispered first: "It's
Sassoon." De Spain nodded. "What shall we
do?" breathed Nan.

"Nothing yet," returned her lover, watching
the horseman, whose eyes were still fixed on the
pony's trail, but who was now less than a half
mile away and riding straight toward them.

De Spain, his eyes on the danger and his hand
laid behind Nan's waist, led the way guardedly
down to where their horses stood. Nan, needing
no instructions for the emergency, took the lines
of the horses, and de Spain, standing beside his

Danger

own horse, reached his right hand over in front of the pommel and, regarding Sassoon all the while, drew his rifle slowly from its scabbard. The blood fled Nan's cheeks. She said nothing. Without looking at her, de Spain drew her own rifle from her horse's side, passed it into her hand and, moving over in front of the horses, laid his left hand reassuringly on her waist again. At that moment, little knowing what eyes were on him in the black fragments ahead, Sassoon looked up. Then he rode more slowly forward. The color returned to Nan's cheeks: "Do you want me to use this?" she murmured, indicating the rifle.

"Certainly not. But if the others turn back, I may need it. Stay right here with the horses. He will lose the trail in a minute now. When he reaches the rock I'll go down and keep him from getting off his horse—he won't fight from the saddle."

But with an instinct better than knowledge, Sassoon, like a wolf scenting danger, stopped again. He scanned the broken and forbidding hump in front, now less than a quarter of a mile from him, questioningly. His eyes seemed to rove inquisitively over the lava pile as if asking why a Morgan Gap pony had visited it. In another moment he wheeled his horse and spurred rapidly after his companions.

The two drew a deep breath. De Spain laughed: "What we don't know, never hurts us." He drew Nan to him. Holding the rifle muzzle at arm's length as the butt rested on the ground, she looked up from the shoulder to which she was drawn: "What should you have done if he had come?"

"Taken you to the Gap and then taken him to Sleepy Cat, where he belongs."

"But, Henry, suppose——"

"There wouldn't have been any 'suppose.'"

"Suppose the others had come."

"With one rifle, here, a man could stand off a regiment. Nan, do you know, you fit into my arm as if you were made for it?"

His courage was contagious. When he had tired her with fresh importunities he unpinned her felt hat and held it out of reach while he kissed and toyed with and disarranged her hair. In revenge, she snatched from his pocket his little black memorandum-book and some letters and read, or pretended to read them, and seizing her opportunity she broke from him and ran with the utmost fleetness up into the rocks.

In two minutes they had forgotten the episode almost as completely as if it never had been. But when they left for home, they agreed they would not meet there again. They knew that

258

Danger

Sassoon, like a jackal, would surely come back, and more than once, until he found out just what that trail or any subsequent trail leading into the beds meant. The lovers laughed the jackal's spying to scorn and rode away, bantering, racing, and chasing each other in the saddle, as solely concerned in their happiness as if there were nothing else of moment in the whole wide world.

CHAPTER XX

THEY had not underestimated the dange from Sassoon's suspicious malevolence. H returned next morning to read what further h could among the rocks. It was little, but i spelled a meeting of two people—Nan and an other—and he was stimulated to keep his eye and ears open for further discoveries. Moreove continuing ease in seeing each other, undetecte by hostile eyes, gradually rendered the lovers les cautious in their arrangements. The one thin; that possessed their energies was to be together.

De Spain, naturally reckless, had won in Na: a girl hardly more concerned. Self-reliant, botl of them, and instinctively vigilant, they spent s much time together that Scott and Lefever, whc before a fortnight had passed after Duke's retur: home, surmised that de Spain must be carryin on some sort of a clandestine affair hinting towar the Gap, only questioned how long it would b before something happened, and only hoped i would not be, in their own word, unpleasant. I was not theirs in any case to admonish d

Facing the Music

Spain, nor to dog the movements of so capable a friend even when his safety was concerned, so long as he preferred to keep his own counsel—there are limits within which no man welcomes uninvited assistance. And de Spain, in his long and frequent rides, his protracted absences, indifference to the details of business and careless humor, had evidently passed within these limits.

What was stage traffic to him compared to the sunshine on Nan's hair; what attraction had schedules to offer against a moment of her eyes; what pleasing connection could there be between bad-order wheels and her low laugh?

The two felt they must meet to discuss their constant perplexities and the problems of their difficult situation; but when they reached their trysting-places, there was more of gayety than gravity, more of nonchalance than concern, more of looking into each other's hearts than looking into the troublesome future. And there was hardly an inviting spot within miles of Music Mountain that one or the other of the two had not waited near.

There were, of course, disappointments, but there were only a few failures in their arrangements. The difficulties of these fell chiefly on Nan. How she overcame them was a source of surprise to de Spain, who marvelled at her innocent resource in escaping the demands at home and making her way, despite an array of obstacles, to his distant impatience.

Midway between Music Mountain and Sleepy Cat a low-lying wall of lava rock, in part sand-covered and in part exposed, parallels and sometimes crosses the principal trail. This undulating ridge was a favorite with de Spain and Nan, because they could ride in and out of hiding-places without more than just leaving the trail itself. To the west of this ridge, and commanding it, rose rather more than a mile away the cone called Black Cap.

"Suppose," said Nan one afternoon, looking from de Spain's side toward the mountains, "some one should be spying on us from Black Cap?" She pointed to the solitary rock.

"If any one has been, Nan, with a good glass he must have seen exchanges of confidence over here that would make him gnash his teeth. I know if I ever saw anything like it I'd go hang. But the country around there is too rough for a horse. Nobody even hides around Black Cap, except some tramp hold-up man that's crowded in his get-away. Bob Scott says there are dozens of mountain-lions over there."

But Sassoon had the unpleasant patience of a mountain-lion and its dogged persistence, and,

Facing the Music

hiding himself on Black Cap, he made certain one day of what he had long been convinced—that Nan was meeting de Spain.

The day after she had mentioned Black Cap to her lover, Nan rode over to Calabasas to get a bridle mended. Galloping back, she encountered Sassoon just inside the Gap. Nan so detested him that she never spoke when she could avoid it. On his part he pretended not to see her as she passed. When she reached home she found her Uncle Duke and Gale standing in front of the fireplace in the living-room. The two appeared from their manner to have been in a heated discussion, one that had stopped suddenly on her appearance. Both looked at Nan. The expression on their faces forewarned her. She threw her quirt on the table, drew off her riding-gloves, and began to unpin her hat; but she knew a storm was impending.

Gale had been made for a long time to know that he was an unwelcome visitor, and Nan's greeting of him was the merest contemptuous nod. "Well, uncle," she said, glancing at Duke, "I'm late again. Have you had supper?"

Duke always spoke curtly; to-night his heavy voice was as sharp as an axe. "Been late a good deal lately."

Nan laid her hat on the table and, glancing

composedly from one suspicious face to the other, put her hands up to rearrange her hair. "I'm going to try to do better. I'll go out and get my supper if you've had yours." She started toward the dining-room.

"Hold on!" Nan paused at her uncle's ferocious command. She looked at him either really or feignedly surprised, her expression changing to one of indignation, and waited for him to speak. Since he did no more than glare angrily at her, Nan lifted her brows a little. "What do you want, uncle?"

"Where did you go this afternoon?"

"Over to Calabasas," she answered innocently.

"Who'd you meet there?" Duke's tone snapped with anger. He was working himself into a fury, but Nan saw it must be faced. "The same people I usually meet—why?"

"Did you meet Henry de Spain there this afternoon?"

Nan looked squarely at her cousin and returned his triumphant expression defiantly before she turned her eyes on her uncle. "No," she said collectedly. "Why?"

"Do you deny it?" he thundered.

"Yes, I deny it. Why?"

"Did you see de Spain at Calabasas this afternoon?"

Facing the Music

"No."

"See him anywhere else?"

"No, I did not. What do you mean? What," demanded his niece with spirit, "do you want to know? What are you trying to find out?"

Duke turned in his rage on Gale. "There! You hear that—what have you got to say now?" he demanded with an abusive oath.

Gale, who had been hardly able to refrain from breaking in, answered fast. "What have I got to say?" he roared. "I say I know what I'm talking about. I say she's lying, Duke."

Nan's face turned white with anger. Before she could speak her uncle took up the words. "Hold on," he shouted. "Don't tell me she lies." He launched another hot expletive. "I know she doesn't lie!"

Gale jumped forward, his finger pointed at Nan. "Look here, do you deny you are meeting Henry de Spain all over the desert?"

Nan's anger supported her without a tremor. "Who are you to ask me whom I meet or don't meet?"

"You've been meeting de Spain right along, haven't you? You met him down the Sleepy Cat trail near Black Cap, didn't you?"

Nan stood with her back against the end of the table where her uncle's first words had stopped

265

her, and she looked sidewise toward her cousin. In her answer he heard as much contempt as a girl's voice could carry to a rejected lover. "So you've turned sneak!"

Gale roared a string of bad words.

"You hire that coyote, Sassoon, to spy for you, do you?" demanded Nan coolly. "Aren't you proud of your manly relation, uncle?" Duke was choking with rage. He tried to speak to her, but he could not form his words. "What is it you want to know, uncle? Whether it is true that I meet Henry de Spain? It is. I do meet him, and we're engaged to be married when you give us permission, Uncle Duke—and not till then."

"There you have it," cried Gale. "There's the story. I told you so. I've known it for a week, I tell you." Nan's face set. "Not only," continued her cousin jeeringly, "meeting that——"

Almost before the vile epithet that followed had reached her ears, Nan caught up the whip. Before he could escape she cut Gale sharply across the face. "You coward," she cried, trembling so she could not control her voice. "If you ever dare use that word before me again, I'll horsewhip you. Go to Henry de Spain's face, you skulker, and say that if you dare."

"Put down that quirt, Nan," yelled her uncle.

"I won't put it down," she exclaimed defiantly.

Facing the Music

"And he will get a good lashing with it if he says one more word about Henry de Spain."

"Put down that quirt, I tell you," thundered her uncle.

She whirled. "I won't put it down. This hulking bully! I know him better than you do." She pointed a quivering finger at her cousin. "He insulted me as vilely as he could only a few months ago on Music Mountain. And if this very same Henry de Spain hadn't happened to be there to protect me, you would have found me dead next morning by my own hand. Do you understand?" she cried, panting and furious. "That's what *he* is!"

Her uncle tried to break in. "Stop!" she exclaimed, pointing at Gale. "*He* never told you that, did he?"

"No; nor you neither," snapped Duke hoarsely.

"I didn't tell you," retorted Nan, "because I've been trying to live with you here in peace among these thieves and cutthroats, and not keep you stirred up all the time. And Henry de Spain faced this big coward and protected me from him with an empty revolver! What business of yours is it whom I meet, or where I go?" she demanded, raining her words with flaming eyes on her belligerent cousin. "I will never marry you to save you from the hangman. Now leave this house." She stamped her foot. "Leave this house, and never come into it again!"

Gale, beside himself with rage, stood his ground. He poured all that he safely could of abuse on Nan's own head. She had appeased her wrath and made no attempt to retort, only looking at him with white face and burning eyes as she breathed defiance. Duke interfered. "Get out!" he said to Gale harshly. "I'll talk to her. Go home!"

Not ceasing to mutter threats, Gale picked up his hat and stamped out of the house, slamming the doors. Duke, exhausted by the quarrel, sat down, eying his niece. "Now what does this mean?" he demanded hoarsely.

She tried to tell him honestly and frankly all that her acquaintance with de Spain did mean—dwelling no more than was necessary on its beginning, but concealing nothing of its development and consequences, nothing of her love for de Spain, nor of his for her. But no part of what she could say on any point she urged softened her uncle's face. His square hard jaw from beginning to end looked like stone.

"So he's your lover?" he said harshly when she had done.

"He wants to be your friend," returned Nan, determined not to give up.

Facing the Music

Duke looked at her uncompromisingly: "That man can't ever be any friend of mine—understand that! He can't ever marry you. If he ever tries to, so help me God, I'll kill him if I hang for it. I know his game. I know what he wants. He doesn't care a pinch of snuff about you. He thinks he can hit me a blow by getting you away from me."

"Nothing could be further from the truth," exclaimed Nan hopelessly.

Duke struck the table a smashing blow with his fist. "I'll show Mr. de Spain and his friends where they get off."

"Uncle Duke, if you won't listen to reason, you must listen to sense. Think of what a position you put me in. I love you for all your care of me. I love him for his affection for me and consideration of me—because he knows how to treat a woman. I know he wouldn't harm a hair on your head, for my sake, yet you talk now of bloodshed between you two. I know what your words mean—that one of you, or both of you are to be killed for a senseless feud. He will not stand up and let any man shoot him down without resistance. If you lay your blood on his head, you know it would put a stain between him and me that never could be washed out as long as we lived. If you kill him I could never stay here

269

with you. His blood would cry out every day and night against you."

Duke's violent finger shot out at her. "And you're the gal I took from your mammy and promised I'd bring up a decent woman. You've got none o' her blood in you—not a drop. You're the brat of that damned, mincing brother of mine, that was always riding horseback and showing off in town while I was weeding the tobacco-beds."

Nan clasped her hands. "Don't blame me because I'm your brother's child. Blame me because I'm a woman, because I have a heart, because I want to live and see you live, and to see you live in peace instead of what we do live in—suspicion, distrust, feuds, alarms, and worse. I'm not ungrateful, as you plainly say I am. I want you to get out of what you are in here—I want to be out of it. I'd rather be dead now than to live and die in it. And what is this anger all for? Nothing. He offers you his friendship—"
She could speak no further. Her uncle with a curse left her alone. When she arose in the early morning he had already gone away.

CHAPTER XXI

A TRY OUT

SLEEPY CAT is not so large a place that one would ordinarily have much trouble in finding a man in it if one searched well. But Duke Morgan drove into town next morning and had to stay for three days waiting for a chance to meet de Spain. Duke was not a man to talk much when he had anything of moment to put through, and he had left home determined, before he came back, to finish for good with his enemy.

De Spain himself had been putting off for weeks every business that would bear putting off, and had been forced at length to run down to Medicine Bend to buy horses. Nan, after her uncle left home—justly apprehensive of his intentions—made frantic efforts to get word to de Spain of what was impending. She could not telegraph—a publicity that she dreaded would have followed at once. De Spain had expected to be back in two days. Such a letter as she could have sent would not reach him at Medicine Bend.

As it was, a distressing amount of talk did attend Duke's efforts to get track of de Spain.

271

Nan of Music Mountain

Sleepy Cat had but one interpretation for his inquiries—and a fight, if one occurred between these men, it was conceded would be historic in the annals of the town. Its anticipation was food for all of the rumors of three days of suspense. For the town they were three days of thrilling expectation; for Nan, isolated, without a confidant, not knowing what to do or which way to turn, they were the three bitterest days of anxiety she had ever known.

Desperate with suspense at the close of the second day—wild for a scrap of news, yet dreading one—she saddled her pony and rode alone into Sleepy Cat after nightfall to meet the train on which de Spain had told her he would return from the east. She rode straight to the hospital, instead of going to the livery-barn, and leaving her horse, got supper and walked by way of unfrequented streets down-town to the station to wait for the train.

Never had she felt so miserable, so helpless, so forsaken, so alone. With the thought of her nearest relative, the man who had been a father to her and provided a home for her as long as she could remember, seeking to kill him whose devotion had given her all the happiness she had ever known, and whose safety meant her only pledge of happiness for the future—her heart sank.

A Try Out

When the big train drew slowly, almost noise-lessly, in, Nan took her place where no incoming passenger could escape her gaze and waited for de Spain. Scanning eagerly the figures of the men that walked up the long platform and approached the station exit, the fear that she should not see him battled with the hope that he would still appear. But when all the arrivals had been accounted for, he had not come.

She turned, heavy-hearted, to walk back up-town, trying to think of whom she might seek some information concerning de Spain's whereabouts, when her eye fell on a man standing not ten feet away at the door of the baggage-room. He was alone and seemed to be watching the changing of the engines, but Nan thought she knew him by sight. The rather long, straight, black hair under the broad-brimmed Stetson hat marked the man known and hated in the Gap as "the Indian." Here, she said to herself, was a chance. De Spain, she recalled, spoke of no one oftener than this man. He seemed wholly disengaged.

Repressing her nervous timidity, Nan walked over to him. "Aren't you Mr. Scott?" she asked abruptly.

Scott, turning to her, touched his hat as if quite unaware until that moment of her existence.

273

Nan of Music Mountain

"Did Mr. de Spain get off this train?" she asked, as Scott acknowledged his identity.

"I didn't see him. I guess he didn't come to-night." Nan noticed the impassive manner of his speaking and the low, even tones. "I was kind of looking for him myself."

"Is there another train to-night he could come on?"

"I don't think he will be back now before to-morrow night."

Nan, much disappointed, looked up the line and down. "I rode in this afternoon from Music Mountain especially to see him." Scott, without commenting, smiled with understanding and encouragement, and Nan was so filled with anxiety that she welcomed a chance to talk to somebody. "I've often heard him speak of you," she ventured, searching the dark eyes, and watching the open, kindly smile characteristic of the man. Scott put his right hand out at his side. "I've ridden with that boy since he was so high."

"I know he thinks everything of you."

"I think a lot of him."

"You don't know me?" she said tentatively.

His answer concealed all that was necessary. "Not to speak to, no."

"I am Nan Morgan."

A Try Out

"I know your name pretty well," he explained; nothing seemed to disturb his smile.

"And I came in—because I was worried over something and wanted to see Mr. de Spain."

"He is buying horses north of Medicine Bend. The rain-storm yesterday likely kept him back some. I don't think you need worry much over anything though."

"I don't mean I am worrying about Mr. de Spain at Medicine Bend," disclaimed Nan with a trace of embarrassment.

"I know what you mean," smiled Bob Scott. She regarded him questioningly. He returned her gaze reassuringly as if he was confident of his ground. "Did your pony come along all right after you left the foot-hills this afternoon?"

Nan opened her eyes. "How did you know I came through the foot-hills?"

"I was over that way to-day." Something in the continuous smile enlightened her more than the word. "I noticed your pony went lame. You stopped to look at his foot."

"You were behind me," exclaimed Nan.

"I didn't see you," he countered prudently.

She seemed to fathom something from the expression of his face. "You couldn't have known I was coming in," she said quickly.

"No." He paused. Her eyes seemed to invite a further confidence. "But after you started it would be a pity if any harm came to you on the road."

"You knew Uncle Duke was in town?" Scott nodded. "Do you know why I came?"

"I made a guess at it. I don't think you need worry over anything."

"Has Uncle Duke been talking?"

"Your Uncle Duke doesn't talk much, you know. But he had to ask questions."

"Did you follow me down from the hospital to-night?"

"I was coming from my house after supper. I only kept close enough to you to be handy."

"Oh, I understand. And you are very kind. I don't know what to do now."

"Go back to the hospital for the night. I will send Henry de Spain up there just as soon as he comes to town."

"Suppose Uncle Duke sees him first."

"I'll see that he doesn't see him first."

"Where is Uncle Duke to-night, do you know?"

"Lefever says he is up-street somewhere."

"That means Tenison's," said Nan. "You need not be afraid to speak plainly, as I must. Uncle Duke is very angry—I am deathly afraid of their meeting."

Even de Spain himself, when he came back the

next night, seemed hardly able to reassure her.
Nan, who had stayed at the hospital, awaited
him there, whither Scott had directed him, with
her burden of anxiety still upon her. When she
had told all her story, de Spain laughed at her
fears. "I'll bring that man around, Nan, don't
worry. Don't believe we shall ever fight. I may
not be able to bring him around to-morrow, or
next week, but I'll do it. It takes two to quarrel,
you know."

"But you don't know how unreasoning Uncle
Duke is when he is angry," said Nan mournfully.
"He won't listen to *any*body. He always would
listen to me until now. Now, he says, I have gone
back on him, and he doesn't care what happens.
Think, Henry, where it would put me if either of
you should kill the other. Henry, I've been
thinking it all over for three days now. I see
what must come. It will break both our hearts,
I know, but they will be broken anyway. There
is no way out, Henry—none."

"Nan, what do you mean?"

"You must give me up."

They were sitting in the hospital garden, he
at her side on the bench that he called their
bench. It was here he had made his unrebuked
avowal—here, he had afterward told her, that he
began to live. "Give you up," he echoed with

gentleness. "How could I do that? You're like the morning for me, Nan. Without you there's no day; you're the kiss of the mountain wind and the light of the stars to me. Without the thought of you I'd sicken and faint in the saddle, I'd lose my way in the hills; without you there would be no to-morrow. No matter where I am, no matter how I feel, if I think of you strength wells into my heart like a spring. I never could give you up."

He told her all would be well because it must be well; that she *must* trust him; that he would bring her safe through every danger and every storm, if she would only stick to him. And Nan, sobbing her fears one by one out on his breast, put her arms around his neck and whispered that for life or death, she *would* stick.

It was not hard for de Spain next morning to find Duke Morgan. He was anxious on Nan's account to meet him early. The difficulty was to meet him without the mob of hangers-on whose appetite had been whetted with the prospect of a death, and perhaps more than one, in the meeting of men whose supremacy with the gun had never been successfully disputed. It required all the diplomacy of Lefever to "pull off" a conference between the two which should not from the start be hopeless, because of a crowd of Duke's

A Try Out

partisans whose presence would egg him on, in spite of everything, to a combat. But toward eleven o'clock in the morning, de Spain having been concealed like a circus performer every minute earlier, Duke Morgan was found, alone, in a barber's hands in the Mountain House. At the moment Duke left the revolving-chair and walked to the cigar stand to pay his check, de Spain entered the shop through the rear door opening from the hotel office.

Passing with an easy step the row of barbers lined up in waiting beside their chairs, de Spain walked straight down the open aisle, behind Morgan's back. While Duke bent over the case to select a cigar, de Spain, passing, placed himself at the mountain-man's side and between him and the street sunshine. It was taking an advantage, de Spain was well aware, but under the circumstances he thought himself entitled to a good light on Duke's eye.

De Spain wore an ordinary sack street suit, with no sign of a weapon about him; but none of those who considered themselves favored spectators of a long-awaited encounter felt any doubt as to his ability to put his hand on one at incomparably short notice. There was, however, no trace of hostility or suspicion in de Spain's greeting.

"Hello, Duke Morgan," he said frankly. Morgan looked around. His face hardened when he saw de Spain, and he involuntarily took a short step backward. De Spain, with his left hand lying carelessly on the cigar case, faced him. "I heard you wanted to see me," continued de Spain. "I want to see you. How's your back since you went home?"

Morgan eyed him with a mixture of suspicion and animosity. He took what was to him the most significant part of de Spain's greeting first and threw his response into words as short as words could be chopped: "What do you want to see me about?"

"Nothing unpleasant, I hope," returned de Spain. "Let's sit down a minute."

"Say what you got to say."

"Well, don't take my head off, Duke. I was sorry to hear you were hurt. And I've been trying to figure out how to make it easier for you to get to and from town while you are getting strong. Jeffries and I both feel there's been a lot of unnecessary hard feeling between the Morgans and the company, and we want to ask you to accept this to show some of it's ended." De Spain put his left hand into his side pocket and held out an unsealed envelope to Morgan. Duke, taking the envelope, eyed it distrustfully.

A Try Out

"What's this?" he demanded, opening it and drawing out a card.

"Something for easier riding. An annual pass for you and one over the stage line between Calabasas and Sleepy Cat—with Mr. Jeffries's compliments."

Like a flash, Morgan tore the card pass in two and threw it angrily to the floor. "Tell 'Mr.' Jeffries," he exclaimed violently, "to——"

The man that chanced at that moment to be lying in the nearest chair slid quietly but imperiously out from under the razor and started with the barbers for the rear door, wiping the lather from one unshaven side of his face with a neck towel as he took his hasty way. At the back of the shop a fat man, sitting in a chair on the high, shoe-shining platform, while a negro boy polished him, rose at Morgan's imprecation and tried to step over the bootblack's head to the floor below. The boy, trying to get out of the way, jumped back, and the fat man fell, or pretended to fall, over him—for it might be seen that the man, despite his size, had lighted like a cat on his feet and was instantly half-way up to the front of the shop, exclaiming profanely but collectedly at the lad's awkwardness, before de Spain had had time to reply to the insult.

The noise and confusion of the incident were

considerable. Morgan was too old a fighter to look behind him at a critical moment. No man could say he had meant to draw when he stamped the card underfoot, but de Spain read it in his eye and knew that Lefever's sudden diversion at the rear had made him hesitate; the crisis passed like a flash. "Sorry you feel that way, Duke," returned de Spain, undisturbed. "It is a courtesy we were glad to extend. And I want to speak to you about Nan, too."

Morgan's face was livid. "What about her?"

"She has given me permission to ask your consent to our marriage," said de Spain, "sometime in the reasonable future."

It was difficult for Duke to speak at all, he was so infuriated. "You can get my consent in just one way," he managed to say, "that's by getting me."

"Then I'm afraid I'll never get it, for I'll never 'get' you, Duke."

A torrent of oaths fell from Morgan's cracked lips. He tried to tell de Spain in his fury that he knew all about his underhanded work, he called him more than one hard name, made no secret of his deadly enmity, and challenged him to end their differences then and there.

De Spain did not move. His left hand again lay on the cigar case. "Duke," he said, when his antagonist had exhausted his vituperation, "I wouldn't fight you, anyway. You're crazy angry at me for no reason on earth. If you'll give me just one good reason for feeling the way you do toward me, and the way you've always acted toward me since I came up to this country, I'll fight you."

"Pull your gun," cried Morgan with an imprecation.

"I won't do it. You call me a coward. Ask these boys here in the shop whether they agree with you on that. You might as well call me an isosceles triangle. You're just crazy sore at me when I want to be friends with you. Instead of pulling my gun, Duke, I'll lay it out on the case, here, to show you that all I ask of you is to talk reason." De Spain, reaching with his left hand under the lapel of his coat, took a Colt's revolver from its breast harness and laid it, the muzzle toward himself, on the plate-glass top of the cigar stand. It reduced him to the necessity of a spring into Morgan for the smallest chance for his life if Morgan should draw; but de Spain was a desperate gambler in such matters even at twenty-eight, and he laid his wagers on what he could read in another's eye.

"There's more reasons than one why I shouldn't fight you," he said evenly. "Duke, you're old enough to be my father—do you realize that? What's the good of our shooting each other up?" he asked, ignoring Morgan's furious interruptions. "Who's to look after Nan when you go—as you must, before very many years? Have you ever asked yourself that? Do you want to leave her to that pack of wolves in the Gap? You know, just as well as I do, the Gap is no place for a high-bred, fine-grained girl like Nan Morgan. But the Gap is your home, and you've done right to keep her under your roof and under your eye. Do you think *I'd* like to pull a trigger on a man that's been a father to Nan? Damnation, Duke, could you expect me to do it, willingly? Nan is a queen. The best in the world isn't good enough for her—I'm not good enough, I know that. She's dear to you, she is dear to me. If you really want to see me try to use a gun, send me a man that will insult or abuse her. If you want to use your own gun, use it on me if I ever insult or abuse her—is that fair?"

"Damn your fine words," exclaimed Morgan slowly and implacably. "They don't pull any wool over my eyes. I know you, de Spain—I know your breed——"

"What's that?"

Morgan checked himself at that tone. "You can't sneak into my affairs any deeper," he cried.

A Try Out

"Keep away from my blood! I know how to take care of my own. I'll do it. So help me God, if you ever take any one of my kin away from me—it'll be over my dead body!" He ended with a bitter oath and a final taunt: "Is that fair?"

"No," retorted de Spain good-naturedly, "it's not fair. And some day, Duke, you'll be the first to say so. You won't shake hands with me now, I know, so I'll go. But the day will come when you will."

He covered his revolver with his left hand, and replaced it under his coat. The fat man who had been leaning patiently against a barber's chair ten feet from the disputants, stepped forward again lightly as a cat. "Henry," he exclaimed, in a low but urgent tone, his hand extended, "just a minute. There's a long-distance telephone call on the wire for you." He pointed to the office door. "Take the first booth, Henry. Hello, Duke," he added, greeting Morgan with an extended hand, as de Spain walked back. "How are you making it, old man?"

Duke Morgan grunted.

"Sorry to interrupt your talk," continued Lefever. "But the barns at Calabasas are burning —telephone wires from there cut, too—they had to pick up the Thief River trunk line to get a

285

message through. Makes it bad, doesn't it?" Lefever pulled a wry face. "Duke, there's somebody yet around Calabasas that needs hanging, isn't there? Yes."

CHAPTER XXII

GALE PERSISTS

WHEN within an hour de Spain joined Nan, tense with suspense and anxiety, at the hospital, she tried hard to read his news in his face.

"Have you seen him?" she asked eagerly. De Spain nodded. "What does he say?"

"Nothing very reasonable."

Her face fell. "I knew he wouldn't. Tell me all about it, Henry—everything."

She listened keenly to each word. De Spain gave her a pretty accurate recital of the interview, and Nan's apprehension grew with her hearing of it.

"I knew it," she repeated with conviction. "I know him better than you know him. *What* shall we do?"

De Spain took both her hands. He held them against his breast and stood looking into her eyes. When he regarded her in such a way her doubts and fears seemed mean and trivial. He spoke only one word, but there was a world of confidence in his tone: "Stick."

287

She arched her brows as she returned his gaze, and with a little troubled laugh drew closer. "Stick, Nan," he repeated. "It will come out all right."

She paused a moment. "How can you know?"

"I know because it's got to. I talked it all over with my best friend in Medicine Bend, the other day."

"Who, Henry?"

"Whispering Smith. He laughed at your uncle's opposing us. He said if your uncle only knew it, it's the best thing that could happen for him. And he said if all the marriages opposed by old folks had been stopped, there wouldn't be young folks enough left to milk the cows."

"Henry, what is this report about the Calabasas barns burning?"

"The old Number One barn is gone and some of the old stages. We didn't lose any horses, and the other barns are all right. Some of our Calabasas or Gap friends, probably. No matter, we'll get them all rounded up after a while, Nan. Then, some fine day, we're going to get married."

De Spain rode that night to Calabasas to look into the story of the fire.

McAlpin, swathed in bandages, made no bones about accusing the common enemy. No witnesses could be found to throw any more light on

Gale Persists

the inquiry than the barn boss himself. And de
Spain made only a pretense of a formal investigation. If he had had any doubts about the origin
of the fire they would have been resolved by an
anonymous scrawl, sent through the mail, promis-
ing more if he didn't get out of the country.

But instead of getting out of the country, de
Spain continued as a matter of energetic policy
to get into it. He rode the deserts stripped, so
to say, for action and walked the streets of Sleepy
Cat welcoming every chance to meet men from
Music Mountain or the Sinks. It was on Nan
that the real hardships of the situation fell, and
Nan who had to bear them alone and almost
unaided.

Duke came home a day or two later without a
word for Nan concerning his encounter with de
Spain. He was shorter in the grain than ever,
crustier to every one than she had ever known
him—and toward Nan herself fiercely resentful.
Sassoon was in his company a great deal, and
Nan knew of old that Sassoon was a bad symptom.
Gale, too, came often, and the three were much
together. In some way, Nan felt that she herself was in part the subject of their talks, but no
information concerning them could she ever get.

One morning she sat on the porch sewing when
Gale rode up. He asked for her uncle. Bonita

289

told him Duke had gone to Calabasas. Gale announced he was bound for Calabasas himself, and dismounted near Nan, professedly to cinch his saddle. He fussed with the straps for a minute, trying to engage Nan in the interval, without success, in conversation. "Look here, Nan," he said at length, studiously amiable, "don't you think you're pretty hard on me, lately?"

"No, I don't," she answered. "If Uncle Duke didn't make me, I'd never look at you, or speak to you—or live in the same mountains with you."

"I don't think when a fellow cares for you as much as I do, and gets out of patience once in a while, just because he loves a girl the way a red-blooded man can't help loving her, she ought to hold it against him forever. Think she ought to, Nan?" he demanded after a pause. She was sewing and had kept silence.

"I think," she responded, showing her aversion in every syllable, "before a man begins to talk red-blood rot, he ought to find out whether the girl cares for him, or just loathes the sight of him."

He regarded her fixedly. Paying no attention to him, but bending in the sunshine over her sewing, her hand flying with the needle, her masses of brown hair sweeping back around her pink ears and curling in stray ringlets that the wind danced with while she worked, she inflamed her brawny cousin's ardor afresh. "You used to care for me, Nan. You can't deny that." Her silence was irritating. "Can you?" he demanded. "Come, put up your work and talk it out. I didn't use to have to coax you for a word and a smile. What's come over you?"

"Nothing has come over me, Gale. I did use to like you—when I first came back from school. You seemed so big and fine then, and were so nice to me. I did like you."

"Why didn't you keep on liking me?"

Nan made no answer. Her cousin persisted. "You used to talk about thinking the world of me," she said at last; "then I saw you one Frontier Day, riding around Sleepy Cat with a carriage full of women."

Gale burst into a huge laugh. Nan's face flushed. She bent over her work. "Oh, that's what's the matter with you, is it?" he demanded jocularly. "You never mentioned *that* before."

"That isn't the only thing," she continued after a pause.

"Why, that was just some Frontier Day fun, Nan. A man's got to be a little bit of a sport once in a while, hasn't he?"

"Not if he likes me." She spoke with an ominous distinctness, but under her breath. He caught her words and laughed again. "Pshaw, I didn't think you'd get jealous over a little thing like that, Nan. When there's a celebration on in town, everybody's friendly with everybody else. If you lay a little thing like that up against me, where would the rest of the men get off? Your strawberry-faced Medicine Bend friend is celebrating in town most of the time."

Her face turned white. "What a falsehood!" she exclaimed hotly. Looking at her, satisfied, he laughed whole-heartedly again. She rose, furious. "It's a falsehood," she repeated, "and I know it."

"I suppose," retorted Gale, regarding her jocosely, "you asked him about it."

He had never seen her so angry. She stamped her foot. "How dare you say such a thing! One of those women was at the hospital—she is there yet, and she is going to die there. She told Uncle Duke's nurse the men they knew, and whom they didn't know, at that place. And Henry de Spain, when he heard this miserable creature had been taken to the hospital, and Doctor Torpy said she could never get well, told the Sister to take care of her and send the bills to him, because he knew her father and mother in Medicine Bend and went to school with her there when she was a decent girl. Go and hear what *she* has to say about Henry de Spain, you contemptible falsifier."

Gale Persists

Gale laughed sardonically. "That's right. I like to see a girl stick to her friends. De Spain ought to take care of her. Good story."

"And she has other good stories, too, you ought to hear," continued Nan undismayed. "Most of them about you and your fine friends in town. She told the nurse it's *you* who ought to be paying her bills till she dies."

Gale made a disclaiming face and a deprecating gesture. "No, no, Nan—let de Spain take care of his own. Be a sport yourself, girlie, right now." He stepped nearer her. Nan retreated. "Kiss and make up," he exclaimed with a laugh. But she knew he was angry, and knew what to guard against. Still laughing, he sprang toward her and tried to catch her arm.

"Don't touch me!" she cried, jumping away with her hand in her blouse.

"You little vixen," he exclaimed with an oath, "what have you got there?" But he halted at her gesture, and Nan, panting, stood her ground.

"Keep away!" she cried.

"Where did you get that knife?" thundered Gale.

"From one who showed me how to use it on a coward!"

He affected amusement and tried to pass the

incident off as a joke. But his dissimulation was more dangerous, she knew, than his brutality, and he left her the prey to more than one alarm and the renewed resolve never to be taken off her guard. That night he came back. He told her uncle, glancing admiringly at Nan as he recounted the story, how she had stood her ground against him in the morning.

Nor did Nan like the way her uncle acted while he listened—and afterward. He talked a good deal about Gale and the way she was treating her cousin. When Nan declared she never would have anything to do with him, her uncle told her with disconcerting bluntness to get all that out of her head, for she was going to marry him. When she protested she never would, Duke told her, with many harsh oaths, that she should never marry de Spain even if he had to kill him or get killed to stop it, and that if she had any sense she would get ready to marry her cousin peaceably, adding, that if she didn't have sense, he would see himself it was provided for her.

His threats left Nan aghast. For two days she thought them all over. Then she dressed to go to town. On her way to the barn her uncle intercepted her. "Where you going?"

"To Sleepy Cat," returned Nan, regarding him collectedly.

Gale Persists

"No, you're not," he announced bluntly.

Nan looked at him in silence. "I don't want you running to town any more to meet de Spain," added Duke, without any attempt to soften his injunction.

"But I've got to go to town once in a while, whether I meet Henry de Spain or not, Uncle Duke."

"What do you have to go for?"

"Why, for mail, supplies—everything."

"Pardaloe can attend to all that."

Nan shook her head. "Whether he can or not, I'm not going to be cut off from going to Sleepy Cat, Uncle Duke—nor from seeing Henry de Spain."

"Meaning to say you won't obey, eh?"

"When I'm going to marry a man it isn't right to forbid me seeing him."

"You're not going to marry him; you're going to marry Gale, and the quicker you make up your mind to it the better."

"You might better tell me I am going to marry Bull Page—I would marry him first. I will never marry Gale Morgan in the living world, and I've told you so more than once."

He regarded his niece a moment wrathfully and, without replying, walked back to the house. Nan, upset but resolute, went on to the barn and asked Pardaloe to saddle her pony. Pardaloe shuffled around in an obliging way, but at the end of some evasion admitted he had orders not to do it. Nan flamed at the information. She disliked Pardaloe anyway, not for any reason she could assign beyond the fact that he had once been a chum of Gale's. But she was too high-spirited to dispute with him, and returned to the house pink with indignation. Going straight to her uncle, she protested against such tyranny. Duke was insensible alike to her pleas and her threats.

But next morning Nan was up at three o'clock. She made her way into the barn before a soul was stirring, and at daybreak was well on her way to Sleepy Cat. She telephoned to de Spain's office from the hospital and went to breakfast. De Spain joined her before she had finished, and when they left the dining-room she explained why she had disappointed him the day before. He heard the story with misgivings.

"I'll tell you how it looks to me, Nan," he said when she had done. "You are like a person that's being bound tighter every day by invisible cords. You don't see them because you are fear-less. You are too fearless, Nan," he added, with apprehension reflected in the expression of his face. "I'll tell you what I wish you'd do, and I say it knowing you won't do it," he concluded.

Gale Persists

She made light of his fears, twisting his right hand till it was helpless in her two hands and laughing at him. "How do you know I won't do it?"

"Because I've asked you before. This is it: marry me, now, here, to-day, and don't take any more chances out there."

"But, Henry," protested Nan, "I can't marry you now and just run away from poor Uncle Duke. If you will just be patient, I'll bring him around to our side."

"Never, Nan."

"Don't be so sure. I know him better than you do, and when he comes for anybody, he comes all at once. Why, it's funny, Henry. Now that I'm picking up courage, you're losing it!"

He shook his head. "I don't like the way things are going."

"Dearie," she urged, "should I be any safer at home if I were your wife, than I am as your sweetheart. I don't want to start a horrible family war by running away, and that is just what I certainly should do."

De Spain was unconvinced. But apprehension is short-lived in young hearts. The sun shone, the sky spread a speckless blue over desert and mountain, the day was for them together. They did not promise all of it to themselves at once—

they filched its sweetness bit by bit, moment by moment, and hour by hour, declaring to each other they must part, and dulling the pain of parting with the anodyne of procrastination. Thus, the whole day went to their castles and dreams. In a retired corner of the cool dining-room at the Mountain House, they lingered together over a long-drawn-out dinner. The better-informed guests by asides indicated their presence to others. They described them as the hardy couple who had first met in a stiff Frontier Day rifle match, which the girl had won. Her defeated rival—the man now most regarded and feared in the mountain country—was the man with the reticent mouth, mild eyes, curious birthmark, and with the two little, perplexed wrinkles visible most of the time just between his dark eyebrows, the man listening intently to every syllable that fell from the lips of the trimly bloused, active girl opposite him, leaning forward in her eagerness to tell him things. Her jacket hung over the back of her chair, and she herself was referred to by the more fanciful as queen of the outlaw camp at Music Mountain.

They two were seen together that day about town by many, for the story of their courtship was still veiled in mystery and afforded ground for the widest speculation, while that of their difficulties, and such particulars as de Spain's fruitless efforts to conciliate Duke Morgan and Duke's open threats against de Spain's life were widely known. All these details made the movement and the fate of the young couple the object of keenly curious comment.

In the late afternoon the two rode almost the whole length of Main Street together on their way to the river bridge. Every one knew the horseflesh they bestrode—none cleaner-limbed, hardier, or faster in the high country. Those that watched them amble slowly past, laughing and talking, intent only on each other, erect, poised, and motionless, as if moulded to their saddles, often spoke of having seen Nan and her lover that day. It was a long time before they were seen riding down Main Street together again.

CHAPTER XXIII

DE SPAIN WORRIES

THEY parted that evening under the shadow
of Music Mountain. Nan believed she could
at least win her Uncle Duke over from any effort
of Gale's to coerce her. Her influence over her
uncle had never yet failed, and she was firm in
the conviction she could gain him to her side,
since he had everything to win and nothing to
lose by siding against Gale, whom he disliked and
distrusted, anyway.

For de Spain there was manifestly nothing to
do but doubtfully to let Nan try out her influence. They agreed to meet in Calabasas just as
soon as Nan could get away. She hoped, she
told him, to bring good news. De Spain arranged
his business to wait at Calabasas for her, and was
there, after two days, doing little but waiting and
listening to McAlpin's stories about the fire and
surmises as to strange men that lurked in and
about the place. But de Spain, knowing Jeffries
was making an independent investigation into
the affair, gave no heed to McAlpin's suspicions.

To get away from the barn boss, de Spain took

300

De Spain Worries

refuge in riding. The season was drawing on toward winter, and rain clouds drifting at intervals down from the mountains made the saddle a less dependable escape from the monotony of Calabasas. Several days passed with no sight of Nan and no word from her. De Spain, as the hours and days went by, scanned the horizon with increasing solicitude. When he woke on the sixth morning, he was resolved to send a scout into the Gap to learn what he could of the situation. The long silence, de Spain knew, portended nothing good. And the vexing feature of his predicament was that he had at hand no trustworthy spy to despatch for information; to secure one would be a matter of delay. He was schooled, however, to making use of such material as he had at hand, and when he had made up his mind, he sent to the stable for Bull Page.

The shambling barn man, summoned gruffly by McAlpin, hesitated as he appeared at the office door and seemed to regard the situation with suspicion. He looked at de Spain tentatively, as if ready either for the discharge with which he was daily threatened or for a renewal of his earlier, friendly relations with the man who had been queer enough to make a place for him. De Spain set Bull down before him in the stuffy little office.

"Bull," he began with apparent frankness, "I want to know how you like your job."

Wiping his mouth guardedly with his hand to play for time and as an introduction to a carefully worded reply, Bull parried. "Mr. de Spain, I want to ask you just one fair question."

"Go ahead, Bull."

Bull plunged promptly into the suspicion uppermost in his mind. "Has that slat-eyed, flat-headed, sun-sapped sneak of a Scotchman been complaining of my work? *That*, Mr. de Spain," emphasized Bull, leaning forward, "is what I want to know first—is it a fair question?"

"Bull," returned de Spain with corresponding and ceremonial emphasis, "it is a fair question between man and man. I admit it; it *is* a fair question. And I answer, no, Bull. McAlpin has had nothing on the face of the desert to do with my sending for you. And I add this because I know you want to hear it: he says he couldn't complain of your work, because you never do any."

"That man," persisted Bull, reinforced by the hearty tone and not clearly catching the drift of the very last words, "drinks more liquor than I do."

"He must be some tank, Bull."

"And I don't hide it, Mr. de Spain."

De Spain Worries

"You'd have to crawl under Music Mountain to do that. What I want to know is, do you like your job?"

On this point it was impossible to get an expression from Bull. He felt convinced that de Spain was pressing for an answer only as a preliminary to his discharge. "No matter," interposed the latter, cutting Bull's ramblings short, "drop it, Bull. I want you to do something for me, and I'll pay for it."

Bull, with a palsied smile and a deep, quavering note of gratitude, put up his shaky hand. "Say what. That's all. I've been paid."

"You know you're a sot, Bull."

Bull nodded. "I know it."

"A disgrace to the Maker whose image you were made in."

Bull started, but seemed, on reflection, to consider this a point on which he need not commit himself.

"Still, I believe there's a man in you yet. Something, at any rate, you couldn't completely kill with whiskey, Bull—what?"

Bull lifted his weak and watery eyes. His whiskey-seamed face brightened into the ghost of a smile. "What I'm going to ask you to do," continued de Spain, "is a man's job. You can get into the Gap without trouble. You are the

303

only man I can put my hand on just now, that
can. I want you to ride over this morning and
hang out around Duke Morgan's place till you
can get a chance to see Miss Nan——"

At the mention of her name, Bull shook his
head a moment in affirmative approval. "She's
a queen!" he exclaimed with admiring but pun-
gent expletives. "A queen!"

"I think so, Bull. But she is in troublesome
circumstances. You know Nan and I——"

Bull winked in many ways.

"And her Uncle Duke is making us trouble,
Bull. I want you to find her, speak with her,
and bring word to me as to what the situation is.
That doesn't mean you're to get drunk over there
—in fact, I don't think anybody over there would
give you a drink——"

"Don't believe they would."

"And you are to ride back here with what you
can find out just as quick, after you get into the
clear, as a horse will bring you."

Bull passed his hand over his mouth with a
show of resolution. It indicated that he was pulling himself together. Within half an hour he was
on his way to the Gap.

For de Spain hours never dragged as did the
hours between his starting and the setting of the
sun that night without his return. And the sun

De Spain Worries

set behind Music Mountain in a drift of heavy clouds that brought rain. All evening it fell steadily. At eleven o'clock de Spain had given up hope of seeing his emissary before morning and was sitting alone before the stove in the office when he heard the sound of hoofs. In another moment Bull Page stood at the door.

He was a sorry sight. Soaked to the skin by the steady downpour; rain dripping intermittently from his frayed hat, his ragged beard, and tattered coat; shaking with the cold as if gripped by an ague, Bull, picking his staggering steps to the fire, and sinking in a heap into a chair, symbolized the uttermost tribute of manhood to the ravages of whiskey. He was not drunk. He had not even been drinking; but his vitality was gone. He tried to speak. It was impossible. His tongue would not frame words, nor his throat utter them. He could only look helplessly at de Spain as de Spain hastily made him stand up on his shaking knees, threw a big blanket around him, sat him down, kicked open the stove drafts, and called to McAlpin for more whiskey to steady the wreck of it crouching over the fire.

McAlpin after considerable and reluctant search produced a bottle, and unwilling, for more reasons than one, to trust it to Bull's uncertain possession, brought a dipper. Bull held the dipper while de

305

Spain poured. McAlpin, behind the stove, hopped
first on one foot and then on the other as de Spain
recklessly continued to pour.   When the liquor
half filled the cup, McAlpin put out unmistakable
distress signals, but Bull, watching the brown
stream, his eyes galvanized at the sight, held fast
to the handle and made no sign to stop.   "Bull!"
thundered the barn boss with an emphatic word.
"That is Elpaso's bottle.   What are you dreaming
of, man? Mr. de Spain, you'll kill him.   Don't
ye see he can't tell ye to stop?"

Bull, with the last flickering spark of vitality
still left within him, looked steadily up and winked
at de Spain. McAlpin, outraged, stamped out
of the room.   Steadying the dipper in both hands,
Bull with an effort passed one hand at the final
moment preliminarily over his mouth, and, raising
the bowl, emptied it.   The poison electrified him
into utterance.   "I seen her," he declared, holding
his chin well down and in, and speaking in a par-
donably proud throat.

"Good, Bull!"

"They've got things tied up for fair over there."
He spoke slowly and brokenly.   "I never got inside the house till after supper.   Toward night
I helped Pardaloe put up the stock. He let me
into the kitchen after my coaxing for a cup of
coffee—he's an ornery, cold-blooded guy, that

De Spain Worries

Pardaloe. Old Duke and Sassoon think the sun rises and sets on the top of his head—funny, ain't it ?"

De Spain made no comment. "Whilst I was drinking my coffee——"

"Who gave it to you ?"

"Old Bunny, the Mex. Pardaloe goes out to the bunk-house; I sits down to my supper, alone, with Bunny at the stove. All of a sudden who comes a-trippin' in from the front of the house but Nan. I jumped up as strong as I could, but I was too cold and stiff to jump up real strong. She seen me, but didn't pay no attention. I dropped my spoon on the floor. It didn't do no good, neither, so I pushed a hot plate of ham gravy off the table. It hit the dog 'n' he jumped like kingdom come. Old Bunny sails into me, Nan a-watchin', and while Mex was pickin' up and cleanin' up, I sneaks over to the stove and winks at Nan. Say, you oughter seen her look mad at me. She was hot, but I kept a-winkin' and I says to her kind of husky-like: 'Got any letters for Calabasas to-night ?' Say, she looked at me as if she'd bore holes into me, but I stood right up and glared back at the little girl. 'Come from there this mornin',' says I, low, 'going back to-night. Some one waiting there for news.'

"By jing! Just as I got the words out o' my

mouth who comes a-stalking in but Gale Morgan. The minute he seen me, he lit on me to beat the band—called me everything he could lay his tongue to. I let on I was drunk, but that didn't help. He ordered me off the premises. 'N' the worst of it was, Nan chimed right in and began to scold Bunny for lettin' me in—and leaves the room, quick-like. Bunny put it on Pardaloe, and she and Gale had it, and b' jing, Gale put me out —said he'd pepper me. But wait till I tell y' how she fooled him. It was rainin' like hell, 'n' it looked as if I was booked for a ride through it and hadn't half drunk my second cup of coffee at that. I starts for the barn, when some one in the dark on the porch grabs my arm, spins me around like a top, throws a flasher up into my face, and there was Nan. 'Bull,' she says, 'I'm sorry. I don't want to see you ride out in this with nothing to eat; come this way quick.'

"She took me down cellar from the outside, under the kitchen. When Gale goes out again she flings up the trap-door, speaks to Mex, pulls all the kitchen shades down, locks the doors, and I sets down on the trap-door steps 'n' eats a pipin' hot supper; say! Well, I reckon I drank a couple o' quarts of coffee. 'Bull,' she says, 'I never done you no harm, did I?' 'Never,' says I, 'and I never done you none, neither, did I? And

what's more, I never will do you none.' Then I
up and told her. 'Tell him,' says she, 'I can't
get hold of a horse, nor a pen, nor a piece of paper
—I can't leave the house but what I am watched
every minute. They keep track of me day and
night. Tell him,' she says, 'I can protect myself;
they think they'll break me—make me do what
they want me to—marry—but they can't break
me, and I'll never do it—tell him that.'

"'But,' says I, 'that ain't the whole case, Miss
Nan. What he'll ask me, when he's borin'
through me with *his* eyes like the way you're
borin' me through with yours, is: When will you
see him—when will he see you?'

"She looked worrit for a minit. Then she
looks around, grabs up the cover of an empty
'bacco box and a fork and begins a-writing inside." Bull, with as much of a smile as he could
call into life from his broken nerves, opened up
his blanket, drew carefully from an inside coat
pocket an oilskin package, unwrapped from it the
flat, square top of a tin tobacco box on which
Nan had scratched a message, and handed it
triumphantly to de Spain.

He read her words eagerly:

"Wait; don't have trouble. I can stand anything better than bloodshed, Henry. Be patient."

While de Spain, standing close to the lantern,

deciphered the brief note, Bull, wrapping his blanket about him with the air of one whose responsibility is well ended, held out his hands toward the blazing stove. De Spain went over the words one by one, and the letters again and again. It was, after all their months of ardent meetings, the first written message he had ever had from Nan. He flamed angrily at the news that she was prisoner in her own home. But there was much to weigh in her etched words, much to think about concerning her feelings— not alone concerning his own.

He dropped into his chair and, oblivious for a moment of his companion's presence, stared into the fire. When he started from his revery Bull was asleep. De Spain picked him up, carried him in his blanket over to a cot, cut the wet rags off him, and, rolling him in a second blanket, walked out into the barn and ordered up a team and light wagon for Sleepy Cat. The rain fell all night.

CHAPTER XXIV

AN OMINOUS MESSAGE

FEW men bear suspense well; de Spain took his turn at it very hard. For the first time in his life he found himself braved by men of a type whose defiance he despised—whose lawlessness he ordinarily warred on without compunction—but himself without the freedom that had always been his to act. Every impulse to take the bit in his teeth was met with the same insurmountable obstacle—Nan's feelings—and the unpleasant possibility that might involve him in bloodshed with her kinspeople.

"Patience." He repeated the word to himself a thousand times to deaden his suspense and apprehension. Business affairs took much of his time, but Nan's situation took most of his thought. For the first time he told John Lefever the story of Nan's finding him on Music Mountain, of her aid in his escape, and the sequel of their friendship. Lefever gave it to Bob Scott in Jeffries's office.

"What did I tell you, John?" demanded Bob mildly.

"No matter what you told me," retorted Le-
fever. "The question is: What's he to do to get
Nan away from there without shooting up the
Morgans?"

De Spain had gone that morning to Medicine
Bend. He got back late and, after a supper at
the Mountain House, went directly to his room.

The telephone-bell was ringing when he unlocked and threw open his door. Entering the
room, he turned on a light, closed the door behind
him, and sat down to answer the call.

"Is this Henry de Spain?" came a voice, slowly
pronouncing the words over the wire.

"Yes."

"I have a message for you."

"What is it?"

"From Music Mountain."

"Go ahead."

"The message is like this: 'Take me away from
here as soon as you can.'"

"Whom is that message from?"

"I can't call any names."

"Who are you?"

"I can't tell you that."

"What do you mean?"

"Just what I say. Good-by."

"Hold on. Where are you talking from?"

"About a block from your office."

An Ominous Message

"Do you think it a fair way to treat a man to——"

"I have to be fair to myself."

"Give me the message again."

"'Take me away from here as soon as you can.'"

"Where does it come from?"

"Music Mountain."

"If you're treating me fair—and I believe you mean to—come over to my room a minute."

"No."

"Let me come to where you are?"

"No."

"Let me wait for you—anywhere?"

"No."

"Do you know me?"

"By sight."

"How did you know I was in town to-night?"

"I saw you get off the train."

"You were looking for me, then?"

"To deliver my message."

"Do you think that message means what it says?"

"I know it does."

"Do you know what it means for me to undertake?"

"I have a pretty stiff idea."

"Did you get it direct from the party who sent it?"

"I can't talk all night. Take it or leave it just where it is."

De Spain heard him close. He closed his own instrument and began feverishly signalling central. "This is 101. Henry de Spain talking," he said briskly. "You just called me. Ten dollars for you, operator, if you can locate that call, quick!"

There was a moment of delay at the central office, then the answer: "It came from 234—Tenison's saloon."

"Give me your name, operator. Good. Now give me 22 as quick as the Lord will let you, and ring the neck off the bell."

Lefever answered the call on number 22. The talk was quick and sharp. Messengers were instantly pressed into service from the despatcher's office. Telephone wires hummed, and every man available on the special agent's force was brought into action. Livery-stables were covered, the public resorts were put under observation, horsemen clattered up and down the street. Within an incredibly short time the town was rounded up, every outgoing trail watched, and search was under way for any one from Morgan's Gap, and especially for the sender of the telephone message.

De Spain, after instructing Lefever, hastened

An Ominous Message

to Tenison's. His rapid questioning of the few habitués of the place and the bartender elicited only the information that a man had used the telephone-booth within a few minutes. Nobody knew him or, if they did know him, refused to describe him in any but vague terms. He had come in by the front door and slipped out probably by the rear door—at all events, unnoticed by those questioned. By a series of eliminating inquiries, de Spain made out only that the man was not a Morgan. Outside, Bob Scott in the saddle waited with a led horse. The two men rode straight and hard for the river bridge. They roused an old hunter who lived in a near-by hut, on the town side, and asked whether any horseman had crossed the bridge. The hunter admitted gruffly that he *had* heard a horse's hoof recently on the bridge. Within how long? The hunter, after taking a full precious minute to decide, said thirty minutes; moreover, he insisted that the horseman he had heard had ridden into town, and not out.

Sceptical of the correctness of the information, Scott and de Spain clattered out on the Sinks. Their horseflesh was good and they felt they could overtake any man not suspecting pursuit. The sky was overcast, and speed was their only resource. After two miles of riding, the pursuers reined up on a ridge, and Scott, springing from the saddle, listened for sounds. He rose from the ground, declaring he could hear the strides of a running horse. Again the two dashed ahead.

The chase was bootless. Whoever rode before them easily eluded pursuit. The next time the scout dropped from his saddle to listen, not the faintest sound rewarded his attention. De Spain was impatient. "He could easily slip us," Scott explained, "by leaving the trail for a minute while we rode past—if he knows his business— and I guess he does."

"If the old man was right, that man could have ridden in town and out, too, within half to three-quarters of an hour," said de Spain. But how could he have got out without being heard?"

"Maybe," suggested Scott, "he forded the river."

"Could he do it?"

"It's a man's job," returned Scott, reflecting, "but it could be done."

"If a man thought it necessary."

"If he knew you by sight," responded Scott unmoved, "he might have thought it necessary."

Undeterred by his failure to overtake the fugitive, de Spain rode rapidly back to town to look for other clews. Nothing further was found to throw light on the message or messenger. No one had been found anywhere in town from Mor-

An Ominous Message

gan's Gap; whoever had taken a chance in delivering the message had escaped undetected.

Even after the search had been abandoned the significance of the incident remained to be weighed. De Spain was much upset. A conference with Scott, whose judgment in any affair was marked by good sense, and with Lefever, who, like a woman, reached by intuition a conclusion at which Scott or de Spain arrived by process of thought, only revealed the fact that all three, as Lefever confessed, were nonplussed.

"It's one of two things," declared Lefever, whose eyes were never dulled by late hours. "Either they've sent this to lure you into the Gap and 'get' you, or else—and that's a great big 'or else'—she needs you. Henry, did that message —I mean the way it was worded—sound like Nan Morgan?"

De Spain could hardly answer. "It did, and it didn't," he said finally. "But—" his companions saw during the pause by which his lips expressed the resolve he had finally reached that he was not likely to be turned from it—"I am going to act just as if the word came from Nan and she does need me."

More than one scheme for getting quickly into touch with Nan was proposed and rejected within the next ten minutes. And when Lefever, after

317

conferring with Scott, put up to de Spain a proposal that the three should ride into the Gap
together and demand Nan at the hands of Duke
Morgan, de Spain had reached another conclusion.

"I know you are willing to take more than your
share, John, of any game I play. In the first
place it isn't right to take you and Bob in where
I am going on my own personal affair. And I
know Nan wouldn't enjoy the prospect of an all-
around fight on her account. Fighting is a horror
to that girl. I've got her feelings to think about
as well as my own. I've decided what to do,
John. I'm going in alone."

"You're going in alone!"

"To-night. Now, I'll tell you what I'd like
you to do if you want to: ride with me and wait
till morning, outside El Capitan. If you don't
hear from me by ten o'clock, ride back to Calabasas and notify Jeffries to look for a new manager."

"On the contrary, if we don't hear from you
by ten o'clock, Henry, we will blaze our way in
and drag out your body." Lefever put up his
hand to cut off any rejoinder. "Don't discuss it.
What happens after ten o'clock to-morrow morning, if we don't hear from you before that, can't
possibly be of any interest to you or make any

difference." He paused, but de Spain saw that he was not done. When he resumed, he spoke in a tone different from that which de Spain usually associated with him. "Henry, when I was a youngster and going to Sunday-school, my old Aunt Lou often told me a story about a pitcher that used to go to the well. And she told me it went many, many times, safe and sound; but my Aunt Lou told me, further, the pitcher got so used to going to the well safe and sound that it finally went once too many times, just once too often, and got smashed all to hell. Aunt Lou didn't say it exactly in that way—but such was the substance of the moral.

"You've pulled a good many tough games in this country, Henry. No man knows better than I that you never pulled one for the looks of the thing or to make people talk—or that you ever took a chance you didn't feel you had to take. But, it isn't humanly possible you can keep this up for all time; it *can't* go on forever. The pitcher goes to the well once too often, Henry; there comes a time when it doesn't come back.

"Understand—I'm not saying this to attempt to dissuade you from the worst job you ever started in on. I know your mind is made up. You won't listen to me; you won't listen to Scott; and I'm too good an Indian not to know where I

get off, or not to do what I'm told. But this is
what I have been thinking of a long, long time;
and this is what I feel I ought to say, here and
now."

The two men were sitting in de Spain's room.
De Spain was staring through the broad south
window at the white-capped peaks of the distant
range. He was silent for a time. "I believe
you're right, John," he said after a while. "I
know you are. In this case I am tied up more
than I've ever been tied before; but I've got to
see it through as best I can, and take what comes
without whining. My mind is made up and,
strange as it may sound to you, I feel that I *am*
coming back. Not but what I know it's due me,
John. Not but what I expect to get it sometime.
And maybe I'm wrong now; but I don't feel as
if it's coming till I've given all the protection to
that girl that a man can give to a woman."

CHAPTER XXV

A SURPRISING SLIP

SCOTT was called by Lefever to conclude in secret the final arrangements. The ground about the quaking asp grove, and nearest El Capitan, afforded the best concealment close to the Gap. And to this point Scott was directed to bring what men he could before daybreak the following morning.

"It's a short notice to get many men together —of the kind we want," admitted Lefever. "You'll have to skirmish some between now and midnight. What do you think you can do?"

Scott had already made up a tentative list. He named four: first, Farrell Kennedy, who was in town, and said nobody should go if he didn't; Frank Elpaso, the Texan; the Englishman, Tommie Meggeson; and Wickwire, if he could be located—any one of them, Lefever knew, could give an account of himself under all circumstances.

While Scott was getting his men together, de Spain, accompanied by Lefever, was riding toward Music Mountain. Scott had urged on them but one parting caution—not to leave the aspens until rain began falling. When he spoke there was not a cloud in the sky. "It's going to rain to-night, just the same," predicted Scott. "Don't leave the trees till it gets going. Those Gap scouts will get under cover and be hunting for a drink the minute it gets cold—I know them. You can ride right over their toes, if you'll be patient."

The sun set across the range in a drift of grayish-black, low-lying clouds, which seemed only to await its disappearance to envelop the mountains and empty their moisture on the desert. By the time de Spain and Lefever reached the end of their long ride a misty rain was drifting down from the west. The two men had just ridden into the quaking asps when a man coming out of the Gap almost rode into them. The intruders had halted and were sufficiently hidden to escape notice, had not Lefever's horse indiscreetly coughed. The man from the Gap reined up and called out. Lefever answered.

"It's Bull Page," declared de Spain, after the exchange of a few words, calling to Bull at the same time to come over to the shelter of the trees.

"What's going on in there, Bull?" asked de Spain after Bull had told him that Gale had driven him out, and he was heading for Calabasas.

"You tell," retorted Page. "Looks to me like old Duke's getting ready to die. Gale says he's

A Surprising Slip

going to draw his will to-night, and don't want nobody around—got old Judge Druel in there."

De Spain pricked up his ears. "What's that, Druel?" he demanded. Bull repeated his declaration. Lefever broke into violent language at the Sleepy Cat jurist's expense, and ended by declaring that no will should be drawn in the Gap that night by Duke Morgan or anybody else, unless he and Bull were made legatees.

Beyond this nothing could be learned from Bull, who was persuaded without difficulty by Lefever to abandon the idea of riding to Calabasas through the rain, and to spend the night with him in the neighborhood, wherever fancy, the rain, and the wind—which was rising—should dictate.

While the two were talking de Spain tried to slip away, unobserved by Lefever, on his errand. He failed, as he expected to, and after some familiar abuse, rode off alone, fortified by every possible suggestion at the hands of a man to whom the slightest precaution was usually a joke.

Mountains never look blacker than when one rides into them conscious of the presence of enemies and alert for signs and sounds. But custom dulls the edge of apprehension. De Spain rode slowly up the main road without expecting to meet any one, and he reached the rise where the trail forked to Duke's ranch unchallenged. Here he stopped his horse and looked down toward the roof that sheltered Nan. Night had fallen everywhere, and the increasing rain obscured even the outline of the house. But a light shone through one uncurtained window. He waited some time for a sound of life, for a door to open or close, or for the dog to bark— he heard nothing. Slipping out of the wet saddle, he led his horse in the darkness under the shelter of the lone pine-tree and, securing him, walked slowly toward the house.

The light came from a window in the living-room. Up-stairs and toward the kitchen everything was dark. De Spain walked gingerly around to where he could command the living-room window. He could see within, the figures of three men but, owing to the dim light and the distance at which he stood, he could identify none of them with certainty. Mindful of the admonitions he had been loaded with, he tramped around the house in narrowing circles, pausing at times to look and listen. In like manner he circled the barn and stables, until he had made sure there was no ambush and that he was alone outside. He then went among the horses and, working with a flash-light, found Nan's pony, a bridle and, after an ineffectual search for a saddle, led the bareback horse out to where his own

A Surprising Slip

stood. Walking over to Nan's window he signalled and called to her. Getting no answer, he tossed a bit of gravel up against her window. His signal met with no response and, caching his rifle under the kitchen porch, he stepped around to the front of the house, where, screened by a bit of shrubbery, he could peer at close range into the living-room.

Standing before the fire burning in the open hearth, and with his back to it, he now saw Gale Morgan. Sitting bolt upright beside the table, square-jawed and obdurate, his stubby brier pipe supported by his hand and gripped in his great teeth, Duke Morgan looked uncompromisingly past his belligerent nephew into the fire. A third and elderly man, heavy, red-faced, and almost toothless as he spoke, sat to the right of the table in a rocking-chair, and looked at Duke; this was the old lawyer and justice from Sleepy Cat, the sheriff's brother—Judge Druel.

Nan was not to be seen. Gale, big and aggressive, was doing most of the talking, and energetically, as was his habit. Duke listened thoughtfully, but seemingly with coldness. Druel looked from Gale to Duke, and appeared occasionally to put in a word to carry the argument along.

De Spain suspected nothing of what they were talking about, but he was uneasy concerning Nan,

325

and was not to be balked, by any combination, of his purpose of finding her. To secure information concerning her was not possible, unless he should enter the house, and this, with scant hesitation, he decided to do.

He wore a snug-fitting leathern coat. He unbuttoned this and threw it open as he stepped noiselessly up to the door. Laying his hand on the knob, he paused, then, finding the door unlocked, he pushed it slowly open.

The wind, rushing in, upset his calculations and blew open the door leading from the hall into the living-room. A stream of light in turn shot through the open door, across the hall. Instantly de Spain stepped inside and directly behind the front door—which he now realized he dare not close—and stood expectant in the darkness. Gale Morgan, with an impatient exclamation, strode from the fireplace to close the front door.

As he walked into the hall and slammed the front door shut, he could have touched with his hand the man standing in the shadow behind it. De Spain, not hoping to escape, stood with folded arms, but under the elbow of his left arm was hidden the long muzzle of his revolver. Holding his breath, he waited. Gale's mind was apparently filled with other things. He did not suspect the presence of an intruder, and he walked back into the living-room, partly closing the second door. De Spain, following almost on his heels, stepped past this door, past the hall stairs opposite it, and through a curtained opening at the end of the hall into the dining-room. Barely ten feet from him, this room opened through an arch into the living-room, and where he stood he could hear all that was said.

"Who's there?" demanded Duke gruffly.

"Nobody," said Gale. "Go on, Druel."

"That door never opened itself," persisted Duke.

"The wind blew it open," said Gale impatiently.

"I tell y' it didn't," responded Duke sternly; "somebody came in there, or went out. Maybe she's slipped y'."

"Go up-stairs and see," bellowed Gale at his uncle.

Duke walked slowly out into the hall and, with some difficulty, owing to his injured back, up the stairs. A curtain hung beside the arch where de Spain stood, and this he now drew around him. Gale walked into the hall again, searched it, and waited at the foot of the stairs. De Spain could hear Duke's rough voice up-stairs, but could neither distinguish his words nor hear any response to them. Within a moment the elder man tramped heavily down again, saying only, "She's there," and, followed by Gale, returned to the living-room.

"Now go on, Druel," exclaimed Gale, sitting down impatiently, "and talk quick."

Druel talked softly and through his nose: "I was only going to say it would be a good idea to have two witnesses."

"Nita," suggested Gale.

Duke was profane. "You couldn't keep the girl in the room if she had Nita to help her. And I want it understood, Gale, between you and me, fair and square, that Nan's goin' to live right here with me after this marriage till I'm satisfied she's willing to go to you—otherwise it can't take place, now nor never."

De Spain opened his ears. Gale felt the hard, cold tone of his crusty relative, and answered with like harshness: "What do you keep harping on that for? You've got my word. All I want of you is to keep yours—understand?"

"Come, come," interposed Druel. "There's no need of hard words. But we need two witnesses. Who's going to be the other witness?"

Before any one could answer de Spain stepped out into the open archway before the three men. "I'll act as the second witness," he said.

With a common roar the Morgans bounded to their feet. They were not unused to sudden onslaughts, nor was either of them a man to shrink from a fight at short quarters, if it came to that, but blank astonishment overwhelmed both. De Spain, standing slightly sidewise, his coat lapels flapped wide open, his arms akimbo, and his hands on his hips, faced the three in an attitude of readiness only. He had reckoned on the instant of indecision which at times, when coupled with apprehension, paralyzes the will of two men acting together. Under the circumstances either of the Morgans alone would have whipped a gun on de Spain at sight. Together, and knowing that to do so meant death to the one that took the first shot from the archway, each waited for the other; that fraction of a second unsettled their purpose. Instead of bullets, each launched curses at the intruder, and every second that passed led away from a fight.

De Spain took their oaths, demands, and abuse without batting an eye. "I'm here for the second witness," was all he repeated, covering both men with short glances. Druel, his face muddily white as the whiskey bloat deserted it, shrunk inside his shabby clothes. He seemed, every time de Spain darted a look at him, to grow visibly smaller, until his loose bulk had shrivelled inside an armchair hardly large enough normally to contain it.

De Spain with each epithet hurled at him took a dreaded forward step toward Gale, and Druel, in the line of fire, brought his knees up and his head down till he curled like a porcupine. Gale, game as he undoubtedly was, cornered, felt perhaps recollections of Calabasas and close quarters with the brown eyes and the burning face. What they might mean in this little room, which de Spain was crossing step by step, was food for thought. Nor did de Spain break his obstinate silence until their burst of rage had blown. "You've arranged your marriage," he said at length. "Now pull it."

"My cousin's ready to marry me, and she's goin' to do it to-night," cried Gale violently.

Duke, towering with rage, looked at de Spain and pointed to the hall door. "You hear that! Get out of my house!" he cried, launching a vicious epithet with the words.

"This isn't your house," retorted de Spain angrily. "This house is Nan's, not yours. When she orders me out I'll go. Bring her down," he thundered, raising his voice to shut off Duke, who had redoubled his abuse. "Bring her into this room," he repeated. "We'll see whether she wants to get married. If she does, I'll marry her. If she doesn't, and you've been putting this up to force her into marrying, so help me God, you'll

be carried out of this room to-night, or I will."
He whirled on her uncle with an accusing finger.
"You used to be a man, Duke. I've taken from
you here to-night what I would take from no man
on earth but for the sake of Nan Morgan. She
asked me never to touch you. But if you've gone
into this thing to trap your own flesh and blood,
your dead brother's girl, living under your own
protection, you don't deserve mercy, and to-night
you shall have what's coming to you. I've fought
you both fair, too fair. Now—before I leave—
it's my girl or both of you."

He was standing near Druel. Without taking
his eyes off the other men, he caught Druel with
his left hand by the coat collar, and threw him
half-way across the room. "Get up-stairs, you
old carrion, and tell Nan Morgan, Henry de Spain
is here to talk to her."

Druel, frightened to death, scrambled into the
hall. He turned on de Spain. "I'm an officer
of the law. I arrest you for trespass and assault,"
he shouted, shaking with fear.

"Arrest *me?*" echoed de Spain contemptuously.
"You scoundrel, if you don't climb those stairs
I'll send you to the penitentiary the day I get
back to town. Up-stairs with your message!"

"It isn't necessary," said a low voice in the
hall, and with the words Nan appeared in the

open doorway. Her face was white, but there was
no sign of haste or panic in it; de Spain choked
back a breath; to him she never had looked in
her silence so awe-inspiring.

He addressed her, holding his left hand out
with his plea. "Nan," he said, controlling his
voice, "these men were getting ready to marry
you to Gale Morgan. No matter how you feel
toward me now, you know me well enough to
know that all I want is the truth: Was this with
your consent?"

She stepped into the line of fire between her
cousin and de Spain as she answered. "No.
You know I shall never marry any man but you.
This vile bully," she turned a little to look at her
angry cousin, "has influenced Uncle Duke—who
never before tried to persecute or betray me—
into joining him in this thing. They never could
have dragged me into it alive. And they've kept
me locked for three days in a room up-stairs,
hoping to break me down."

"Stand back, Nan."

If de Spain's words of warning struck her with
terror of a situation she could not control, she did
not reveal it. "No," she said resolutely. "If
anybody here is to be shot, I'll be first. Uncle
Duke, you have always protected me from Gale
Morgan; now you join hands with him. You

drive me from this roof because I don't know how I can protect myself under it."

Gale looked steadily at her. "You promised to marry me," he muttered truculently. "I'll find a way to make you keep your word."

A loud knocking interrupted him, and, without waiting to be admitted, Pardaloe, the cowboy, opened the front door and stalked boldly in from the hall.

If the situation in the room surprised him he gave no evidence of it. And as he walked in Nan disappeared. Pardaloe was drenched with rain, and, taking off his hat as he crossed the room to the fire, he shook it hard into the blazing wood.

"What do you want, Pardaloe?" snapped Duke.

Pardaloe shook his hat once more and turned a few steps so that he stood between the uncurtained window and the light. "The creek's up," he said to Duke in his peculiarly slow, steady tone. "Some of Satt's boys are trying to get the cattle out of the lower corral." He fingered his hat, looked first at Duke, then at Gale, then at de Spain. "Guess they'll need a little help, so I asked Sassoon to come over—" Pardaloe jerked his head indicatively toward the front. "He's outside with some of the boys now."

"Tell Sassoon to come in here!" thundered Gale.

Nan of Music Mountain

De Spain's left arm shot out. "Hold on, Pardaloe; pull down that curtain behind you!"

"Don't touch that curtain, Pardaloe!" shouted Gale Morgan.

"Pardaloe," said de Spain, his left arm pointing menacingly and walking instantly toward him, "pull that curtain or pull your gun, quick." At that moment Nan, in hat and coat, reappeared in the archway behind de Spain. Pardaloe jerked down the curtain and started for the door. De Spain had backed up again. "Stop, Pardaloe," he called. "My men are outside that door. Stand where you are," he ordered, still enforcing his commands with his right hand covering the holster at his hip. "I leave this room first. Nan, are you ready?" he asked, without looking at her.

"Yes."

Her uncle's face whitened. "Don't leave this house to-night, Nan," he said menacingly.

"You've forced me to, Uncle Duke."

"Don't leave this house to-night."

"I can't protect myself in it."

"Don't leave this house—most of all, with that man!" He pointed at de Spain with a frenzy of hatred. Without answering, the two were retreating into the semidarkness of the dining-room. "Nan," came her uncle's voice, hoarse with feeling, "you're saying good-by to me forever."

A Surprising Slip

"No, uncle," she cried. "I am only doing what I have to do."

"I tell you I don't want to drive you from this roof, girl."

A rush of wind from an opening door was the only answer from the dark dining-room. The two Morgans started forward together. The sudden gust sucked the flame of the living-room lamp up into the chimney and after a brief, sharp struggle extinguished it. In the confusion it was a moment before a match could be found. When the lamp was relighted the Morgans ran into the dining-room. The wind and rain poured in through the open north door. But the room was empty.

Duke turned on his nephew with a choking curse. "This," he cried, beside himself with fury, "is your work!"

CHAPTER XXVI

FLIGHT

IT was a forbidding night. Moisture-laden clouds, drifting over the Superstition Range, emptied their fulness against the face of the mountains in a downpour and buried the Gap in impenetrable darkness. De Spain, catching Nan's arm, spoke hurriedly, and they hastened outside toward the kitchen. "We must get away quick," he said as she buttoned her coat. And, knowing how she suffered in what she was doing, he drew her into the shelter of the porch and caught her close to him. "It had to come, Nan. Don't shed a tear. I'll take you straight to Mrs. Jeffries. When you are ready, you'll marry me; we'll make our peace with your Uncle Duke together. Great God! What a night! This way, dearie."

"No, to the stable, Henry! Where's your horse?"

"Under the pine, and yours, too. I found the pony, but I couldn't find your saddle, Nan."

"I know where it's hidden. Let's get the horses."

"Just a minute. I stuck my rifle under this

336

porch." He stooped and felt below the stringer. Rising in a moment with the weapon on his arm, the two hurried around the end of the house toward the pine-tree. They had almost reached this when a murmur unlike the sounds of the storm made de Spain halt his companion.

"What is it?" she whispered. He listened intently. While they stood still the front door of the house was opened hurriedly. A man ran out along the porch toward the stable. Neither Nan nor de Spain could make out who it was, but de Spain heard again the suspicious sound that had checked him. Without speaking, he took Nan and retreated to the corner of the house. "There is somebody in that pine," he whispered, "waiting for me to come after the horses. Sassoon may have found them. I'll try it out, anyway, before I take a chance. Stand back here, Nan."

He put her behind the corner of the house, threw his rifle to his shoulder, and fired as nearly as he could in the darkness toward and just above the pine. Without an instant's hesitation a pistol-shot answered from the direction in which he had fired, and in another moment a small fusillade followed. "By the Almighty," muttered de Spain, "we must have our horses, Nan. Stay right here. I'll try driving those fellows off their perch."

She caught his arm. "What are you going to do?"

"Run in on them from cover, wherever I can find it, Nan, and push them back. We've got to have those horses."

"Henry, we can get others from the stable."

"There may be more men waiting there for us."

"If we could only get away without a fight!"

"This is Sassoon and his gang, Nan. You heard Pardaloe. These are not your people. I've got to drive 'em, or we're gone, Nan."

"Then I go with you."

"No."

"Yes!" Her tone was unmistakable.

"Nan, you can't do it," whispered de Spain energetically. "A chance bullet——"

She spoke with decision: "I go with you. I can use a rifle. Better both of us be killed than one. Help me up on this roof. I've climbed it a hundred times. My rifle is in my room. Quick, Henry."

Overruling his continued objections, she lifted her foot to his hand, caught hold of the corner-post, and springing upward got her hands on the low end of the roof boards. With the agility of a cat, she put her second foot on de Spain's shoulder, gained the sloping roof, and scrambled on her hands and knees up toward the window of her

Flight

room. The heavy rain and the slippery boards made progress uncertain, but with scarcely any delay, she reached her window and pushed open the casement sash. A far-off peal of thunder echoed down from the mountains. Luckily, no flash had preceded it, and Nan, rifle in hand, slid safely down to the end of the lean-to, where de Spain, waiting, caught one foot on his shoulder, and helped her to the ground. He tried again to make her stay behind the house. Finding his efforts vain, he directed her how to make a zigzag advance, how to utilize for cover every rock and tree she could find in the line toward the pine, and, above all, to throw herself flat and sidewise after every shot—and not to fire often.

In this way, amid the falling of rain and the uncharted dangers of the darkness, they advanced on the pine-tree. Surprisingly little effort seemed necessary to drive off whoever held it. De Spain made his way slowly but safely to the disputed point and then understood—the horses were gone.

He had hardly rejoined Nan, who waited at a safe distance, and told her the bad news, when a fresh discharge of shots came from two directions —seemingly from the house and the stable. A moment later they heard sharp firing far down the Gap. This was their sole avenue of escape. It was bad enough, under the circumstances, to nego-

339

tiate the trail on horseback—but to expose Nan, who had but just put herself under his protection, to death from a chance bullet while stumbling along on foot, surrounded by enemies—who could follow the flash of their own shots if they were forced to use their rifles, and close in on them at will—was an undertaking not to be faced.

They withdrew to the shelter of a large rock familiar to Nan even in the dark. While de Spain was debating in his mind how to meet the emergency, she stood at his side, his equal, he knew, in courage, daring, and resource, and answered his rapid questions as to possible gateways of escape. The rain, which had been abating, now ceased, but from every fissure in the mountains came the roar of rushing water, and little openings of rock and waterway that might have offered a chance when dry were now out of the question. In fact, it was Nan's belief that before morning water would be running over the main trail itself.

"Yet," said de Spain finally, "before morning we must be a long way from this particular spot, Nan. Lefever is down there—I haven't the slightest doubt of that. Sassoon has posted men at the neck of the Gap—that's the first thing he would do. And if John heard my rifle when I first shot, he would be for breaking in here, and his men, if they've come up, would bump into

Flight

Sassoon's. It would be insane for us to try to get out over the trail with Sassoon holding it against Lefever—we might easily be hit by our friends instead of our enemies. I'll tell you what, Nan, suppose I scout down that way alone and see what I can find out?"

He put the proposal very lightly, realizing almost as soon as he made it what her answer would be. "Better we go together," she answered in the steady tone he loved to hear. "If you were killed, what would become of me? I should rather be shot than fall into his hands after this —if there was ever a chance for it before, there'd be no mercy now. Let's go together."

He would not consent, and she knew he was right. But what was right for one was right, she told him, for both, and what was wrong for one was wrong for both. "Then, I'll tell you," he said suddenly, as when after long uncertainty and anxious doubt one chooses an alternative and hastens to follow it. "Retreat is the thing for us, Nan. Let's make for Music Mountain and crawl into our cave till morning. Lefever will get in here some time to-morrow. Then we can connect with him."

They discussed the move a little further, but there seemed no escape from the necessity of it, despite the hardship involved in reaching the

341

refuge; and, realizing that no time was to be lost, they set out on the long journey. Every foot of the troublesome way offered difficulties. Water impeded them continually. It lay in shallow pools underfoot and slipped in running sheets over the sloping rocks that lay in their obscure path. Sometimes de Spain led, sometimes Nan picked their trail. But for her perfect familiarity with every foot of the ground they could not have got to the mountain at all.

Even before they succeeded in reaching the foot of it their ears warned them of a more serious obstacle ahead. When they got to the mountain trail itself they heard the roar of the stream that made the waterfall above the ledge they were trying to reach. Climbing hardly a dozen steps, they found their way swept by a mad rush of falling water, its deafening roar punctured by fragments of loosened rock which, swept downward from ledge to ledge, split and thundered as they dashed themselves against the mountainside. On a protected floor the two stood for a moment, listening to the roar of the cataract that had cut them off their refuge.

"No use, Nan," said de Spain. "There isn't any other trail, is there?"

She told him there was no other. "And this will run all night," she added. "Sometimes it runs like this for days. I ought to have known there would be a flood here. But it all depends on which side of the mountain the heavy rain falls. Henry," she said, turning to him and as if thinking of a question she wanted to ask, "how did you happen to come to me just to-night when I wanted you so?"

"I came because you sent for me," he answered, surprised.

"But I didn't send for you."

He stopped, dumfounded. "What do you mean, Nan?" he demanded uneasily. "I got your message on the telephone to come at once and take you away."

"Henry! I didn't send any message—when did you get one?"

"Last night, in my office in Sleepy Cat, from a man that refused to give his name."

"I never sent any message to you," she insisted in growing wonderment. "I have been locked in a room for three days, dearie. The Lord knows I wanted to send you word. Who ever telephoned a message like that? Was it a trap to get you in here?"

He told her the story—of the strenuous efforts he had made to discover the identity of the messenger—and how he had been balked. "No matter," said Nan, at last. "It couldn't have been a trap. It must have been a friend, surely, not an enemy."

"Or," said de Spain, bending over her as if he were afraid she might escape, and putting his face close to hers, "some mildly curious person, some idle devil, Nan, that wanted to see what two timid men would look like, mixed up in a real fight over the one girl in the mountains both are trying to marry at once."

"Henry," every time she repeated his name de Spain cared less for what should happen in the rest of the world, "what are we going to do now? We can't stay here all night—and take what they will greet us with in the morning."

He answered her question with another: "What about trying to get out by El Capitan?"

She started in spite of herself. "I mean," he added, "just to have a look over there, Nan."

"How could you even have a look a night like this?" she asked, overcome at the thought of the dizzy cliff. "It would be certain death, Henry."

"I don't mean at the worst to try to cross it till we get a glimpse of daylight. But it's quite a way over there. I remember some good hiding-places along that trail. We may find one where I can build a little fire and dry you out. I'm more worried over you being wet all night

344

than the rest of it. The question is, Can we find a trail up to where we want to go?"

"I know two or three," she answered, "if they are only not flooded."

The storm seemed to have passed, but the darkness was intense, and from above the northern Superstitions came low mutterings of thunder. Compelled to strike out over the rocks to get up to any of the trails toward El Capitan, Nan, helped by de Spain when he could help, led the ascent toward the first ledge they could hope to follow on their dangerous course.

The point at which the two climbed almost five hundred feet that night up Music Mountain is still pointed out in the Gap. An upturned rock at the foot, a stunted cedar jutting from the ledge at the point they finally gained, marked the beginning and end of their effort. No person, looking at that confused wall, willingly believes it could ever have been scaled in the dead of night. Torn, bruised, and exhausted, Nan, handed up by her lover, threw herself at last prostrate on the ledge at the real beginning of their trail, and from that vantage-point they made their way along the eastern side of Music Mountain for two miles before they stopped again to rest.

It was already well after midnight. A favoring spot was seized on by de Spain for the resting-

place he wanted. A dry recess beneath an overhanging wall made a shelter for the fire that he
insisted on building to warm Nan in her soaked
clothing. He found cedar roots in the dark and
soon had a blaze going. It was dangerous, both
realized, to start a fire, but they concealed the
blaze as best they could and took the chance—a
chance that more nearly than any that had gone
before, cost them their lives. But what still lay
ahead of the two justified in de Spain's mind what
he was doing. He acted deliberately in risking
the exposure of their position to unfriendly eyes
far distant.

CHAPTER XXVII

EL CAPITAN

THE mutterings above the mountains now
grew rapidly louder and while the two hov-
ered over the fire, a thunder-squall, rolling wildly
down the eastern slope, burst over the Gap. Its
sudden fury put aside for a time all question of
moving, and Nan's face took on a grave expression as she looked in the firelight at her companion, thinking of how far such a storm might
imperil their situation, how far cut off their already narrow chance of escape.

De Spain—reclining close beside her, looking
into the depths of her eyes as the flickering blaze
revealed them, drying himself in their warmth
and light, eating and drinking of their presence
on the mountainside alone with him, and pledged
to him, his protection, and his fortunes against
the world—apparently thought of nothing beyond the satisfaction of the moment. The wind
drove the storm against the west side of the huge
granite peak under which they were sheltered and
gave them no present trouble in their slender
recess. But Nan knew even better than her com-

347

panion the fickle fury of a range storm, and understood uncomfortably well how a sudden shift might, at any moment, lay their entire path open to its fierceness. She warned de Spain they must be moving, and, freshened by the brief rest, they set out toward El Capitan.

Their trail lay along granite levels of comparatively good going and, fleeing from the squall, they had covered more than half the distance that separated them from the cliff, when a second thunder-storm, seeming to rush in from the desert, burst above their heads. Drenched with rain, they were forced to draw back under a projecting rock. In another moment the two storms, meeting in the Gap, crashed together. Bolt upon bolt of lightning split the falling sheets of water, and thunder, exploding in their faces, stunned and deafened them.

Mountain peaks, played on by the wild light, leaped like spectres out of the black, and granite crags, searched by blazing shafts, printed themselves in ghostly flames on the retina; thunder, searching unnumbered gorges, echoed beneath the sharper crashes in one long, unending roll, and far out beyond the mountains the flooded desert tossed on a dancing screen into the glare, rippled like a madcap sea, and flashed in countless sheets of blinding facets. As if an unseen hand had touched a thousand granite springs above the Gap, every slender crevice spouted a stream that shot foaming out from the mountainsides. The sound of moving waters rose in a dull, vast roar, broken by the unseen boom of distant falls, launching huge masses of water into caverns far below. The storm-laden wind tore and swirled among the crowded peaks, and above all the angry sky moaned and quivered in the rage of the elements.

Nan leaned within de Spain's arm. "If this keeps up," he said after some time, "our best play is to give up crossing to-night. We might hide somewhere on the mountain to-morrow, and try it toward evening."

"Yes, if we have to," she answered. But he perceived her reluctant assent. "What I am afraid of, Henry, is, if they were to find us. You know what I mean."

"Then we won't hide," he replied. "The minute we get the chance we will run for it. This is too fierce to last long."

"Oh, but it's November!" Nan reminded him apprehensively. "It's winter; that's what makes it so cold. You never can tell in November."

"It won't last all night, anyway," he answered with confidence.

Despite his assurance, however, it did last all

night, and it was only the lulls between the sharp squalls that enabled them to cover the trail before daylight. When they paused before El Capitan the fury of the night seemed largely to have exhausted itself, but the overcharged air hung above the mountains, trembling and moaning like a bruised and stricken thing. Lightning, playing across the inky heavens, blazed in constant sheets from end to end of the horizon. Its quivering glare turned the wild night into a kind of ghastly, uncertain day. Thunder, hoarse with invective, and hurled mercilessly back and forth by the fitful wind, drew farther and farther into the recess of the mountains, only to launch its anger against its own imprisoned echoes. Under it all the two refugees, high on the mountainside, looked down on the flooding Gap.

Their flight was almost ended. Only the sheer cliff ahead blocked their descent to the aspen grove. De Spain himself had already crossed El Capitan once, and he had done it at night—but it was not, he was compelled to remind himself, on a night like this. It seemed now a madman's venture and, without letting himself appear to do so, he watched Nan's face as the lightning played over it, to read if he could, unsuspected, whether she still had courage for the undertaking. She regarded him so collectedly, whether answering a question or asking one, that he marvelled at her strength and purpose. Hardly a moment passed after they had started until the eastern sky lightened before the retreating storm, and with the first glimmer of daylight, the two were at the beginning of the narrow foothold which lay for half a mile between them and safety.

Here the El Capitan trail follows the face of the almost vertical wall which, rising two thousand feet in the air, fronts the gateway of Morgan's Gap.

They started forward, de Spain ahead. There was nothing now to hurry them unduly, and everything to invite caution. The footholds were slippery, rivulets still crossed the uncertain path, and fragments of rock that had washed down on the trail, made almost every step a new hazard. The face of El Capitan presents, midway, a sharp convex. Just where it is thrown forward in this keen angle, the trail runs out almost to a knife-edge, and the mountain is so nearly vertical that it appears to overhang the floor of the valley.

They made half the stretch of this angle with hardly a misstep, but the advance for a part of the way was a climb, and de Spain, turning once to speak to Nan, asked her for her rifle, that he might carry it with his own. What their story might have been had she given it to him, none

can tell. But Nan, holding back, refused to let
him relieve her. The dreaded angle which had
haunted de Spain all night was safely turned on
hands and knees and, as they rounded it toward
the east, clouds scudding over the open desert
broke and shot the light of dawn against the
beetling arête.

De Spain turned in some relief to point to the
coming day. As he did so a gust of wind, sweeping against the sheer wall, caught him off his
guard. He regained his balance, but a stone,
slipping underfoot, tipped him sidewise, and he
threw himself on his knees to avoid the dizzy
edge. As he fell forward he threw up his hand
to save his hat, and in doing so released his rifle,
which lay under his hand on the rock. Before
he could recover it the rifle slipped from reach.
In the next instant he heard it bouncing from
rock to rock, five hundred feet below.

Greatly annoyed and humiliated, he regained
his feet and spoke with a laugh to reassure Nan.
Just as she answered not to worry, a little singing
scream struck their ears; something splashed suddenly close at hand against the rock wall; chips
scattered between them. From below, the sound
of a rifle report cracked against the face of the
cliff. They were so startled, so completely amazed
that they stood motionless. De Spain looked

down and over the uneven floor of the Gap. The ranch-houses, spread like toys in the long perspective, lay peacefully revealed in the gray of the morning. Among the dark pine-trees he could discern Nan's own home. Striving with the utmost keenness of vision to detect where the shot had come from, de Spain could discover no sign of life around any of the houses. But in another moment the little singing scream came again, the blow of the heavy slug against the splintering rock was repeated, the distant report of the rifle followed.

"Under fire," muttered de Spain. He looked questioningly at Nan. She herself, gazing across the dizzy depths, was searching for the danger-point. A third shot followed at a seemingly regular interval—the deliberate interval needed by a painstaking marksman working out his range and taking his time to find it. De Spain watched Nan's search anxiously. "We'd better keep moving," he said. "Come! whoever is shooting can follow us a hundred yards either way." In front of de Spain a fourth bullet struck the rock. "Nan," he muttered, "I've got you into a fix. If we can't stop that fellow he is liable to stop us. Can you see anything?" he asked, waiting for her to come up.

"Henry!" She was looking straight down into

the valley, and laid her hand on de Spain's shoulder. "Is there anything moving on the ridge—over there—see—just east of Sassoon's ranchhouse?"

De Spain, his eyes bent on the point Nan indicated, drew her forward to a dip in the trail which, to one stretched flat, afforded a slight protection. He made her lie down, and just beyond her refuge chose a point where the path, broadening a little and rising instead of sloping toward the outer edge, gave him a chance to brace himself between two rocks. Flattened there like a target in midair, he threw his hat down to Nan and, resting on one knee, waited for the shot that should tumble him down El Capitan or betray the man bent on killing him. Squalls of wind, sweeping into the Gap and sucked upward on the huge expanse of rock below, tossed his hair and ballooned his coat as he buttoned it. Another bullet, deliberately aimed, chipped the rock above him. Nan, agonizing in her suspense, cried out she must join him and go with him if he went. He steadied her apprehension and with a few words reminded her, as a riflewoman, what a gamble every shot at a height such as they occupied, and with such a wind, must be. He reminded her, too, it was much easier to shoot down than up, but all the time he was searching for the flash that should point the assassin. A bullet struck again viciously close between them. De Spain spoke slowly: "Give me your rifle." Without turning his head he held out his hand, keeping his eyes rigidly on the suspicious spot on the ridge. "How far is it to that road, Nan?"

She looked toward the faint line that lay in the deep shadows below. "Three hundred yards."

"Nan, if it wasn't for you, I couldn't travel this country at all," he remarked with studious unconcern. "Last time I had no ammunition— this time, no rifle—you always have what's needed. How high are we, Nan?"

"Seven hundred feet."

"Elevate for me, Nan, will you?"

"Remember the wind," she faltered, adjusting the sight as he had asked.

With the cautioning words she passed the burnished weapon, glittering yet with the rain-drops, into his hand. A flash came from the distant ridge. Throwing the rifle to his shoulder, de Spain covered a hardly perceptible black object on the trail midway between Sassoon's ranch-house and a little bridge which he well remembered —he had crossed it the night he dragged Sassoon into town. It seemed a long time that he pressed the rifle back against his shoulder and held his eye along the barrel. He was wondering as he

covered the crouching man with the deadly sight
which of his enemies this might be. He even
slipped the rifle from his shoulder and looked long
and silently at the black speck before he drew the
weapon back again into place. Then he fired before Nan could believe he had lined the sights.
Once, twice, three times his hand fell and rose
sharply on the lever, with every mark of pre-
cision, yet so rapidly Nan could not understand
how he could discover what his shots were doing.

The fire came steadily back, and deliberately,
without the least intimation of being affected by
de Spain's return. It was a duel shorn of every
element of equality, with an assassin at one end
of the range, and a man flattened half-way up the
clouds against El Capitan at the other, each determined to kill the other before he should stir
one more foot.

Far above, an eagle, in morning flight, soared
majestically out from a jutting crag and circled
again and again in front of El Capitan, while the
air sang with the whining dice that two gamblers
against death threw across the gulf between them.
Nan, half hidden in her trough of rock, watched
the great bird poise and wheel above the deadly
firing, and tried to close her eyes to the figure of
de Spain above her, fighting for her life and his
own.

El Capitan

She had never before seen a man shooting to kill another. The very horror of watching de Spain, at bay among the rocks, fascinated her. Since the first day they had met she had hardly seen a rifle in his hands.

Realizing how slightly she had given thought to him or to his skill at that time, she saw now, spellbound, how a challenge to death, benumbing her with fear, had transformed him into a silent, pitiless foeman, fighting with a lightning-like decision that charged every motion with a fatality for his treacherous enemy. Her rifle, at his shoulder, no longer a mere mechanism, seemed in his hands something weightless, sensible, alive, a deadly part of his arm and eye and brain. There was no question, no thought of adjusting or handling or haste in his fire, but only an incredible swiftness and sureness that sent across the thin-aired chasm a stream of deadly messengers to seek a human life. She could only hope and pray, without even forming the words, that none of her blood were behind the other rifle, for she felt that, whoever was, could never escape.

She tried not to look. The butt of the heating rifle lay close against the red-marked cheek she knew so well, and to the tips of the fingers every particle of the man's being was alive with strength and resource. Some strange fascination drew her senses out toward him as he knelt and threw shot after shot at the distant figure hidden on the ridge. She wanted to climb closer, to throw herself between him and the bullets meant for him. She held out her arms and clasped her hands toward him in an act of devotion. Then while she looked, breathlessly, he took his eyes an instant from the sights. "He's running!" exclaimed de Spain as the rifle butt went instantly back to his cheek. "Whoever he is, God help him now!"

The words were more fearful to Nan than an imprecation. He had driven his enemy from the scant cover of a rut in the trail, and the man was fleeing for new cover and for life. The speck of black in the field of intense vision was moving rapidly toward the ranch-house. Bullet after bullet pitilessly led the escaping wretch. Death dogged every eager footfall. Suddenly de Spain jerked the rifle from his cheek, threw back his head, and swept his left hand across his straining eyes. Once more the rifle came up to place and, waiting for a heartbeat, to press the trigger, he paused an instant. Flame shot again in the gray morning light from the hot muzzle. The rifle fell away from the shoulder. The black speck running toward the ranch-house stumbled, as if stricken by an axe, and sprawled headlong on the trail. Throwing the lever again like lightning, de Spain held the rifle back to his cheek.

He did not fire. Second after second he waited, Nan, lying very still, watching, mute, the dull-red mark above the wet rifle butt. No one had need to tell her what had happened. Too well she read the story in de Spain's face and in what she saw, as he knelt, perfectly still, only waiting to be sure there was no ruse. She watched the rifle come slowly down, unfired, and saw his drawn face slowly relax. Without taking his eyes off the sprawling speck, he rose stiffly to his feet. As if in a dream she saw his hand stretched toward her and heard, as he looked across the far gulf, one word: "Come!"

They reached the end of the trail. De Spain, rifle in hand, looked back. The sun, bursting in splendor across the great desert, splashed the valley and the low-lying ridge with ribboned gold. Farther up the Gap, horsemen, stirred by the firing, were riding rapidly down toward Sassoon's ranch-house. But the black thing in the sunshine lay quite still.

CHAPTER XXVIII

LEFEVER TO THE RESCUE

LEFEVER, chafing in the aspen grove under the restraint of waiting in the storm, was ready long before daylight to break orders and ride in to find de Spain.

With the first peep of dawn, and with his men facing him in their saddles, Lefever made a short explanation.

"I don't want any man to go into the Gap with me this morning under any misunderstanding or any false pretense," he began cheerfully. "Bob Scott and Bull will stay right here. If, by any chance, de Spain makes his way out while the rest of us are hunting for him, you'll be here to signal us—three shots, Bob—or to ride in with de Spain to help carry the rest of us out. Now, it's like this," he added, addressing the others. "You, all of you know, or ought to know—everybody 'twixt here and the railroad knows—that de Spain and Nan Morgan have fastened up to each other for the long ride down the dusty trail together. That, I take it, is their business. But

360

Lefever to the Rescue

her uncle, old Duke, and Gale, and the whole bunch, I hear, turned dead sore on it, and have fixed it up to beat them. You all know the Morgans. They're some bunch—and they stick for one another like hornets, and all hold together in a fight. So I don't want any man to ride in there with me thinking he's going to a wedding. He isn't. He may or may not be going to a funeral, but he's *not* going to a shivaree."

Frank Elpaso glanced sourly at his companions. "I guess everybody here is wise, John."

"I know *you* are, Frank," retorted Lefever testily; "that's all right. I'm only explaining. And I don't want *you* to get sore on me if I *don't* show you a fight." Frank Elpaso grunted. "I am under orders." John waved his hand. "And I can't do anything——"

"But talk," growled Frank Elpaso, not waving his hand.

Lefever started hotly forward in his saddle. "Now look here, Frank." He pointed his finger at the objecting ranger. "I'm here for business, not for pleasure. Any time I'm free you can talk to me——"

"Not till somebody gags you, John," interposed Elpaso moodily.

"Look here, Elpaso," demanded Lefever, spurring his horse smartly toward the Texan, "are

361

you looking for a fight with me right here and now?"

"Yes, here and now," declared Elpaso fiercely.

"Or, there and then," interposed Kennedy, ironically, "some time, somewhere, or no time, nowhere. Having heard all of which, a hundred and fifty times from you two fellows, let us have peace. You've pulled it so often, over at Sleepy Cat, they've got it in double-faced, red-seal records. Let's get started."

"Right you are, Farrell," assented Lefever, "but——"

"Second verse, John. You're boss here; what are we going to do? That's all we want to know."

"Henry's orders were to wait here till ten o'clock this morning. There's been firing inside twice since twelve o'clock last night. He told me to pay no attention to that. But if the whole place hadn't been under water all night, I'd have gone in, anyway. This last time it was two high-powered guns, picking at long range and, if I'm any judge of rifles and the men probably behind them, some one must have got hurt. It's all a guess—but I'm going in there, peaceably if I can, to look for Henry de Spain; if we are fired on—we've got to fight for it. And if there's any talking to be done——"

"You can do it," grunted Elpaso.

Lefever to the Rescue

"Thank you, Frank. And I will do it. I need not say that Kennedy will ride ahead with me, Elpaso and Wickwire with Tommie Meggeson."

Leaving Scott in the trees, the little party trotted smartly up the road, picking their way through the pools and across the brawling streams that tore over the trail toward Duke Morgan's place. The condition of the trail broke their formation continually and Lefever, in the circumstances, was not sorry. His only anxiety was to keep Elpaso from riding ahead far enough to embroil them in a quarrel before he himself should come up.

Half-way to Duke's house they found a small bridge had gone out. It cut off the direct road, and, at Elpaso's suggestion, they crossed over to follow the ridge up the valley. Swimming their horses through the backwater that covered the depression to the south, they gained the elevation and proceeded, unmolested, on their way. As they approached Sassoon's place, Elpaso, riding ahead, drew up his horse and sat a moment studying the trail and casting an occasional glance in the direction of the ranch-house, which lay under the brow of a hill ahead.

When Lefever rode up to him, he saw the story that Elpaso was reading in the roadway. It told of a man shot in his tracks as he was running toward the house—and, in the judgment of these men, fatally shot—for, while his companions spread like a fan in front of him, Lefever got off his horse and, bending intently over the sudden page torn out of a man's life, recast the scene that had taken place, where he stood, half an hour earlier. Some little time Lefever spent patiently deciphering the story printed in the rutted road, and marked by a wide crimson splash in the middle of it. He rose from his study at length and followed back the trail of the running feet that had been stricken at the pool. He stopped in front of a fragment of rock jutting up beside the road, studied it a while and, looking about, picked up a number of empty cartridge-shells, examined them, and tossed them away. Then he straightened up and looked searchingly across the Gap. Only the great, silent face of El Capitan confronted him. It told no tales.

"If this was Henry de Spain," muttered Elpaso, when Lefever rejoined his companions, "he won't care whether you join him now, or at ten o'clock, or never."

"That is not Henry," asserted Lefever with his usual cheer. "Not within forty rows of apple-trees. It's not Henry's gun, not Henry's heels, not Henry's hair, and thereby, not Henry's head that was hit that time. But it was to a finish

Lefever to the Rescue

—and blamed if at first it didn't scare me. I thought it *might* be Henry. Hang it, get down and see for yourselves, boys."

Elpaso answered his invitation with an inquiry. "Who was this fellow fighting with?"

"That, also, is a question. Certainly not with Henry de Spain, because the other fellow, I think, was using soft-nosed bullets. No white man does that, much less de Spain."

"Unless he used another rifle," suggested Kennedy.

"Tell me how they could get his own rifle away from him if he could fire a gun at all. I don't put Henry quite as high with a rifle as with a revolver—if you want to split hairs—mind, I say, if you want to split hairs. But no man that's ever seen him handle either would want to try to take any kind of a gun from him. Whoever it was," Lefever got up into his saddle again, "threw some ounces of lead into that piece of rock back there, though I don't understand how any one could see a man lying behind it.

"Anyway, whoever was hit here has been carried down the road. We'll try Sassoon's ranchhouse for news, if they don't open on us with rifles before we get there."

In the sunshine a man in shirt sleeves, and leaning against the jamb, stood in the open doorway

365

of Sassoon's shack, watching the invaders as they rode around the hill and gingerly approached. Lefever recognized Satt Morgan. He flung a greeting to him from the saddle.

Satt answered in kind, but he eyed the horsemen with reserve when they drew up, and he seemed to Lefever altogether less responsive than usual. John sparred with him for information, and Satterlee gave back words without any.

"Can't tell us anything about de Spain, eh?" echoed Lefever at length. "All right, Satt, we'll find somebody that can. Is there a bridge over to Duke's on this trail?"

Satt's nose wrinkled into his normal smile. "There is a bridge—" The report of three shots fired in the distance, seemingly from the mouth of the Gap, interrupted him. He paused in his utterance. There were no further shots, and he resumed: "There is a bridge that way, yes, but it was washed out last night. They're blockaded. Duke and Gale are over there. They're pretty sore on your man de Spain. You'd better keep away from 'em this morning unless you're looking for trouble."

Lefever, having all needed information from Scott's signal, raised his hand quickly. "Not at all," he exclaimed, leaning forward to emphasize his words and adding the full orbit of his eye to

366

his sincerity of manner. "Not at all, Satt. This is all friendly, all friendly. But," he coughed slightly, as if in apology, "if Henry shouldn't turn up all right, we'll—ahem—be back."

None of his companions needed to be told how to get prudently away. At a nod from Lefever Tommie Meggeson, Elpaso, and Wickwire wheeled their horses, rode rapidly back to the turn near the hill and, facing about, halted, with their rifles across their arms. Lefever and Kennedy followed leisurely, and the party withdrew leaving Satterlee, unmoved, in the sunny doorway. Once out of sight, Lefever led the way rapidly down the Gap to the rendezvous.

Of all the confused impressions that crowded Nan's memory after the wild night on Music Mountain, the most vivid was that of a noticeably light-stepping and not ungraceful fat man advancing, hat in hand, to greet her as she stood with de Spain, weary and bedraggled in the aspen grove.

A smile flamed from her eyes when, turning at once, he rebuked de Spain with dignity for not introducing him to Nan, and while de Spain made apologies Lefever introduced himself.

"And is this," murmured Nan, looking at him quizzically, "really Mr. John Lefever whom I've heard so many stories about?"

She was conscious of his pleasing eyes and even teeth as he smiled again. "If they have come from Mr. de Spain—I warn you," said John, "take them with all reserve."

"But they haven't all come from Mr. de Spain."

"If they come from any of my friends, discredit them in advance. You could believe what my enemies say," he ran on; then added ingenuously, "if I had any enemies!" To de Spain he talked very little. It seemed to take but few words to exchange the news. Lefever asked gingerly about the fight. He made no mention whatever of the crimson pool in the road near Sassoon's hut.

CHAPTER XXIX

PUPPETS OF FATE

THE house in the Gap that had sheltered Nan for many years seemed never so empty as the night she left it with de Spain. In spite of his vacillation, her uncle was deeply attached to her. She made his home for him. He had never quite understood it before, but the realization came only too soon after he had lost her. And his resentment against Gale as the cause of her leaving deepened with every hour that he sat next day with his stubborn pipe before the fire. Duke had acceded with much reluctance to the undertaking that was to force her into a marriage. Gale had only partly convinced him that once taken, the step would save her from de Spain and end their domestic troubles. The failure of the scheme left Duke sullen, and his nephew sore, with humiliation.

In spite of the alarms and excitement of the night, of Gale's determination that de Spain should never leave the Gap with Nan, and of the rousing of every man within it to cut off their

escape, Duke stubbornly refused to pursue the
man he so hated or even to leave the house in
any effort to balk his escape. But Gale, and Sassoon who had even keener reason for hating de
Spain, left Duke to sulk as he would, and set
about getting the enemy without any help from
the head of the house. In spite of the caution
with which de Spain had covered his movements,
and the flood and darkness of the night, Sassoon
by a mere chance had got wind through one of
his men of de Spain's appearance at Duke
Morgan's, and had begun to plan, before Nan and
de Spain had got out of the house, how to trap
him.

Duke heard from Pardaloe, during the night and
the early morning, every report with indifference.
He only sat and smoked, hour after hour, in silence. But after it became known that de Spain
had, beyond doubt, made good his escape, and
had Nan with him, the old man's sullenness
turned into rage, and when Gale, rankling with
defeat, stormed in to see him in the morning, he
caught the full force of Duke's wrath. The
younger man taken aback by the outbreak and
in drink himself, returned his abuse without hesitation or restraint. Pardaloe came between them
before harm was done, but the two men parted
with the anger of their quarrel deepened.

Puppets of Fate

When Nan rode with de Spain into Sleepy Cat that morning, Lefever had already told their story to Jeffries over the telephone from Calabasas, and Mrs. Jeffries had thrown open her house to receive Nan. Weary from exposure, confusion, and hunger, Nan was only too grateful for a refuge.

On the evening of the second day de Spain was invited to join the family at supper. In the evening the Jeffrieses went down-town.

De Spain was talking with Nan in the living-room when the telephone-bell rang in the library.

De Spain took the call, and a man's voice answered his salutation. The speaker asked for Mr. de Spain and seemed particular to make sure of his identity.

"This," repeated de Spain more than once, and somewhat testily, "is Henry de Spain speaking."

"I'd like to have a little talk with you, Mr. de Spain."

"Go ahead."

"I don't mean over the telephone. Could you make it convenient to come down-town somewhere, say to Tenison's, any time this evening?"

The thought of a possible ambuscade deterred the listener less than the thought of leaving Nan, from whom he was unwilling to separate himself for a moment. Likewise, the possibility of an

attempt to kidnap her in his absence was not
overlooked. On the other hand, if the message
came from Duke and bore some suggestion of a
compromise in the situation, de Spain was unwilling to lose it. With these considerations turning in his mind, he answered the man brusquely:
"Who are you?"

The vein of sharpness in the question met with
no deviation from the slow, even tone of the voice
at the other end of the wire. "I am not in position to give you my name," came the answer,
"at least, not over the wire."

A vague impression suddenly crossed de Spain's
mind that somewhere he had heard the voice
before. "I can't come down-town to-night," returned de Spain abruptly. "If you'll come to
my office to-morrow morning at nine, I'll talk
with you."

A pause preceded the answer. "It wouldn't
hardly do for me to come to your office in daylight. But if it would, I couldn't do it to-morrow,
because I shan't be in town in the morning."

"Where are you talking from now?"

"I'm at Tenison's place."

"Hang you," said de Spain instantly, "I know
you now." But he said the words to himself,
not aloud.

"Do you suppose I could come up to where

you are to-night for a few minutes' talk?" continued the man coolly.

"Not unless you have something very important."

"What I have is more important to you than to me."

De Spain took an instant to decide. "All right," he said impatiently; "come along. Only—" he paused to let the word sink in, "—if this is a game you're springing——"

"I'm springing no game," returned the man evenly.

"You're liable to be one of the men hurt."

"That's fair enough."

"Come along, then."

"Mr. Jeffries's place is west of the courthouse?"

"Directly west. Now, I'll tell you just how to get here. Do you hear?"

"I'm listening."

"Leave Main Street at Rancherio Street. Follow Rancherio north four blocks, turn west into Grant Avenue. Mr. Jeffries's house is on the corner."

"I'll find it."

"Don't come any other way. If you do, you won't see me."

"I'm not afraid of you, Mr. de Spain, and I'll

373

come as you say. There's only one thing I should like to ask. It would be as much as my life is worth to be seen talking to you. And there are other good reasons why I shouldn't like to have it known I *had* talked to you. Would you mind putting out the lights before I come up—I mean, in the front of the house and in the room where we talk?"

"Not in the least. I mean—I am always willing to take a chance against any other man's. But I warn you, come prepared to take care of yourself."

"If you will do as I ask, no harm will come to any one."

De Spain heard the receiver hung up at the other end of the wire. He signalled the operator hastily, called for his office, asked for Lefever, and, failing to get him, got hold of Bob Scott. To him he explained rapidly what had occurred, and what he wanted. "Get up to Grant and Rancherio, Bob, as quick as the Lord will let you. Come by the back streets. There's a high mulberry hedge at the southwest corner you can get behind. This chap may have been talking for somebody else. Anyway, look the man over when he passes under the arc-light. If it is Sassoon or Gale Morgan, come into Jeffries's house by the rear door. Wait in the kitchen for my call from the living-room, or a shot. I'll arrange for your getting in."

Leaving the telephone, de Spain rejoined Nan in the living-room. He told her briefly of the expected visit and explained, laughingly, that his caller had asked to have the lights out and to see him alone.

Nan, standing close to him, her own hand on his shoulder and her curling hair against his scarred cheek, asked questions about the incident because he seemed to be holding something back. She professed to be satisfied when he requested her to go up to her room and explained it was probably one of the men coming to tell about some petty thieving on the line or of a strike brewing among the drivers. He made so little of the incident that Nan walked up the stairs on de Spain's arm reassured. When he kissed her at her room door and turned down the stairs again, she leaned in the half-light over the banister, waving one hand at him and murmuring the last caution: "Be careful, Henry, won't you?"

"Dearie, I'm always careful."

"'Cause you're all I've got now," she whispered.

"You're all I've got, Nan, girl."

"I haven't got any home—or anything—just you. Don't go to the door yourself. Leave the

375

front door open. Stand behind the end of the piano till you are awfully sure who it is."

"What a head, Nan!"

De Spain cut off the lights, threw open the front door, and in the darkness sat down on the piano stool. A heavy step on the porch, a little while later, was followed by a knock on the open door.

"Come in!" called de Spain roughly. The bulk of a large man filled and obscured for an instant the opening, then the visitor stepped carefully over the threshold. "What do you want?" asked de Spain without changing his tone. He awaited with keenness the sound of the answer.

"Is Henry de Spain here?"

The voice was not familiar to de Spain's ear. He told himself the man was unknown to him. "I am Henry de Spain," he returned without hesitation. "What do you want?"

The visitor's deliberation was reflected in his measured speaking. "I am from Thief River," he began, and his reverberating voice was low and distinct. "I left there some time ago to do some work in Morgan's Gap. I guess you know, full as well as I do, that the general office at Medicine Bend has its own investigators, aside from the division men. I was sent in to Morgan's Gap some time ago to find out who burned the Calabasas barn."

Puppets of Fate

"Railroad man, eh?"

"For about six years."

"And you report to—— ?"

"Kennedy."

De Spain paused in spite of his resolve to push the questions. While he listened a fresh conviction had flashed across his mind. "You called me up on the telephone one night last week," he said suddenly.

The answer came without evasion. "I did."

"I chased you across the river?"

"You did."

"You gave me a message from Nan Morgan that she never gave you."

"I did. I thought she needed you right off. She didn't know me as I rightly am. I knew what was going on. I rode into town that evening and rode out again. It was not my business, and I couldn't let it interfere with the business I'm paid to look after. That's the reason I dodged you."

"There is a chair at the left of the door; sit down. What's your name?"

The man feeling around slowly, deposited his angular bulk with care upon the little chair. "My name"—in the tenseness of the dark the words seemed to carry added mystery—"is Pardaloe."

"Where from?"

377

"My home is southwest of the Superstition Mountains."

"You've got a brother—Joe Pardaloe?" suggested de Spain to trap him.

"No, I've got no brother. I am just plain Jim Pardaloe."

"Say what you have got to say, Jim."

"The only job I could get in the Gap was with old Duke Morgan—I've been working for him, off and on, and spending the rest of my time with Gale and Dave Sassoon. There were three men in the barn-burning. Dave Sassoon put up the job."

"Where is Dave Sassoon now?"

"Dead."

"What do you mean?"

"I mean what I say."

Both men were silent for a moment.

"Yesterday morning's fight?" asked de Spain reluctantly.

"Yes, sir."

"How did he happen to catch us on El Capitan?"

"He saw a fire on Music Mountain and watched the lower end of the Gap all night. Sassoon was a wide-awake man."

"Well, I'm sorry, Pardaloe," continued de Spain after a moment. "Nobody could call it my fault. It was either he or I—or the life of a woman who never harmed a hair of his head, and a woman I'm bound to protect. He was running when he was hit. If he had got to cover again there was nothing to stop him from picking both of us off. I shot low—most of the lead must have gone into the ground."

"He was hit in the head."

De Spain was silent.

"It was a soft-nose bullet," continued Pardaloe.

Again there was a pause. "I'll tell you about that, too, Pardaloe," de Spain went on collectedly. "I lost my rifle before that man opened fire on us. Nan happened to have her rifle with her—if she hadn't, he'd 've dropped one or both of us off El Capitan. We were pinned against the wall like a couple of targets. If there were soft-nose bullets in her rifle it's because she uses them on game—bobcats and mountain-lions. I never thought of it till this minute. That is it."

"What I came up to tell you has to do with Dave Sassoon. From what happened to-day in the Gap I thought you ought to know it now. Gale and Duke quarrelled yesterday over the way things turned out; they were pretty bitter. This afternoon Gale took it up again with his uncle, and it ended in Duke's driving him clean out of the Gap."

"Where has he gone?"

"Nobody knows yet. Ed Wickwire told me once that your father was shot from ambush a good many years ago. It was north of Medicine Bend, on a ranch near the Peace River; that you never found out who killed him, and that one reason why you came up into this country was to keep an eye out for a clew."

"What about it?" asked de Spain, his tone hardening.

"I was riding home one night about a month ago from Calabasas with Sassoon. He'd been drinking. I let him do the talking. He began cussing you out, and talked pretty hard about what you'd done, and what he'd done, and what he was going to do—" Nothing, it seemed, would hurry the story. "Finally, Sassoon says: 'That hound don't know yet who got his dad. It was Duke Morgan; that's who got him. I was with Duke when he turned the trick. We rode down to de Spain's ranch one night to look up a rustler.' That," concluded Pardaloe, "was all Sassoon would say."

He stopped. He seemed to wait. There was no word of answer, none of comment from the man sitting near him. But, for one, at least, who heard the passionless, monotonous recital of a murder of the long ago, there followed a silence as

Puppets of Fate

relentless as fate, a silence shrouded in the mystery of the darkness and striking despair into two hearts—a silence more fearful than any word.

Pardaloe shuffled his feet. He coughed, but he evoked no response. "I thought you was entitled to know," he said finally, "now that Sassoon will never talk any more."

De Spain moistened his lips. When he spoke his voice was cracked and harsh, as if with what he had heard he had suddenly grown old.

"You are right, Pardaloe. I thank you. I—when I—in the morning. Pardaloe, for the present, go back to the Gap. I will talk with Wickwire—to-morrow."

"Good night, Mr. de Spain."

"Good night, Pardaloe."

Bending forward, limp, in his chair, supporting his head vacantly on his hands, trying to think and fearing to think, de Spain heard Pardaloe's measured tread on the descending steps, and listened mechanically to the retreating echoes of his footsteps down the shaded street. Minute after minute passed. De Spain made no move. A step so light that it could only have been the step of a delicate girlhood, a step free as the footfall of youth, poised as the tread of womanhood and beauty, came down the stairs. Slight as she was, and silent as he was, she walked straight to him in the darkness, and, sinking between his feet, wound her hands through his two arms. "I heard everything, Henry," she murmured, looking up. An involuntary start of protest was his only response. "I was afraid of a plot against you. I stayed at the head of the stairs. Henry, I told you long ago some dreadful thing would come between us—something not our fault. And now it comes to dash our cup of happiness when it is filling. Something told me, Henry, it would come to-night—some bad news, some horror laid up against us out of a past that neither you nor I are to blame for. In all my sorrow I am sorriest, Henry, for you. Why did I ever cross your path to make you unhappy when blood lay between your people and mine? My wretched uncle! I never dreamed he had murder on his soul—and of all others, that murder! I knew he did wrong —I knew some of his associates were criminals. But he has been a father and mother to me since I could creep—I never knew any father or mother."

She stopped, hoping perhaps he would say some little word, that he would even pat her head, or press her hand, but he sat like one stunned. "If it could have been anything but this!" she pleaded, low and sorrowfully. "Oh, why did you not listen to me before we were en-

Puppets of Fate

gulfed! My dear Henry! You who've given me all the happiness I have ever had—that the blood of my own should come against you and yours!" The emotion she struggled with, and fought back with all the strength of her nature, rose in a resistless tide that swept her on, in the face of his ominous silence, to despair. She clasped her hands in silent misery, losing hope with every moment of his stoniness that she could move him to restraint or pity toward her wretched foster-father. She recalled the merciless words he had spoken on the mountain when he told her of his father's death. Her tortured imagination pictured the horror of the sequel, in which the son of the murdered man should meet him who had taken his father's life. The fate of it, the hopelessness of escape from its awful consequence, overcame her. Her breath, no longer controlled, came brokenly, and her voice trembled.

"You have been very kind to me, Henry— you've been the only man I've ever known that always, everywhere, thought of me first. I told you I didn't deserve it, I wasn't worthy of it——"

His hands slipped silently over her hands. He gathered her close into his arms, and his tears fell on her upturned face.

CHAPTER XXX

HOPE FORLORN

THERE were hours in that night that each had reason long to remember; a night that seemed to bring them, in spite of their devotion, to the end of their dream. They parted late, each trying to soften the blow as it fell on the other, each professing a courage which, in the face of the revelation, neither could clearly feel.

In the morning Jeffries brought down to de Spain, who had spent a sleepless night at the office, a letter from Nan.

De Spain opened it with acute misgivings. Hardly able to believe his eyes, he slowly read:

DEAREST:

A wild hope has come to me. Perhaps we don't know the truth of this terrible story as it really is. Suppose we should be condemning poor Uncle Duke without having the real facts? Sassoon was a wretch, Henry, if ever one lived —a curse to every one. What purpose he could serve by repeating this story, which he must have kept very secret till now, I don't know; but there was some reason. I *must* know the whole truth—I feel that I, alone, can get hold of it, and that you would approve what I am doing if you were here with me in this little room, where I am writing at daybreak, to show you my heart.

384

Hope Forlorn

Long before you get this I shall be speeding toward the Gap. I am going to Uncle Duke to get from him the exact truth. Uncle Duke is breaking—has broken—and now that the very worst has come, and we must face it, he will tell me what I ask. Whether I can get him to repeat this to you, to come to you, to throw himself on your pity, my dearest one, I don't know. But it is for this I am going to try, and for this I beg of your love—the love of which I have been so proud!—that you will let me stay with him until I at least learn everything and can bring the whole story to you. If I can bring him, I will.

And I shall be safe with him—perfectly safe. Gale has been driven away. Pardaloe, I know I can trust, and he will be under the roof with me. *Please, do not try to come to me.* It might ruin everything. Only forgive me, and I shall be back with what I hope for, or what I fear, very, very soon. Not till then can I bear to look into your eyes. You have a better right than anyone in the world to know the whole truth, cost what it may. Be patient for only a little while with

NAN.

It was Jeffries who said, afterward, he hoped never again to be the bearer of a letter such as that. Never until he had read and grasped the contents of Nan's note had Jeffries seen the bundle of resource and nerve and sinew, that men called Henry de Spain, go to pieces. For once, trouble overbore him.

When he was able to speak he told Jeffries everything. "It is my fault," he said hopelessly. "I was so crippled, so stunned, she must have thought—I see it now—that I was making ready

385

to ride out by daybreak and shoot Duke down on sight. It's the price a man must pay, Jeffries, for the ability to defend himself against this bunch of hold-up men and assassins. Because they can't get me, I'm a 'gunman'——"

"No, you're not a 'gunman.'"

"A gunman and nothing else. That's what everybody, friends and enemies, reckon me—a gunman. You put me here to clean out this Calabasas gang, not because of my good looks, but because I've been, so far, a fraction of a second quicker on a trigger than these double-damned crooks.

"I don't get any fun out of standing for ten minutes at a time with a sixty-pound safety-valve dragging on my heart, watching a man's eye to see whether he is going to pull a gun on me and knock me down with a slug before I can pull one and knock him down. I don't care for that kind of thing, Jeff. Hell's delight! I'd rather have a little ranch with a little patch of alfalfa—enough alfalfa to feed a little bunch of cattle, a hundred miles from every living soul. What I would like to do is to own a piece of land under a ten-cent ditch, and watch the wheat sprout out of the desert."

Jeffries, from behind his pipe, regarded de Spain's random talk calmly.

"I do feel hard over my father's death," he

went on moodily. "Who wouldn't? If God meant me to forget it, why did he put this mark on my face, Jeff? I did talk pretty strong to Nan about it on Music Mountain. She accused me then of being a gunman. It made me hot to be set down for a gunman by her. I guess I did give it back to her too strong. That's the trouble —my bark is worse than my bite—I'm always putting things too strong. I didn't know when I was talking to her then that Sandusky and Logan were dead. Of course, she thought I was a butcher. But how could I help it?

"I did feel, for a long time, I'd like to kill with my own hands the man that murdered my father, Jeff. My mother must have realized that her babe, if a man-child, was doomed to a life of blood-shed. I've been trying to think most of the night what she'd want me to do now. I don't know what I *can* do, or can't do, when I set eyes on that old scoundrel. He's got to tell the truth— that's all I say now. If he lies, after what he made my mother suffer, he ought to die like a dog—no matter who he is.

"I don't want to break Nan's heart. What can I do? Hanging him here in Sleepy Cat, if I could do it, wouldn't help her feelings a whole lot. If I could see the fellow—" de Spain's hands, spread before him on the table, drew up

tight, "if I could get my fingers on his throat, for
a minute, and talk to him, tell him what I think
of him—I might know what I would want to do
—Nan might be there to see and judge between
us. I'd be almost willing to leave things to her
to settle herself. I only want what's right.
But," the oath that recorded his closing threat
was collected and pitiless, "if any harm comes to
that girl now from this wild trip back among
those wolves—God pity the men that put it over.
I'll wipe out the whole accursed clan, if I have to
swing for it right here in Sleepy Cat!"

John Lefever, Jeffries, Scott in turn took him
in hand to hold him during three days, to restrain
the fury of his resentment, and keep him from
riding to the Gap in a temper that each of them
knew would mean only a tragedy worse than
what had gone before. Mountain-men who happened in and out of Sleepy Cat during those three
days remember how it seemed for that time as
if the attention of every man and woman in the
whole country was fixed on the new situation that
balked de Spain. They knew only that Nan had
gone back to her people, not why she had gone
back; but the air was eager with surmise and
rumor as to what had happened, and in this complete overturning of all de Spain's hopes, what
would happen before the story ended.

Hope Forlorn

Even three days of tactful representation and patient admonition from cool-headed counsellors did not accomplish all they hoped for in de Spain's attitude. His rage subsided, but only to be followed by a settled gloom that they knew might burst into uncontrollable anger at any moment.

A report reached McAlpin that Gale Morgan was making ready to return to Music Mountain with the remnant of Sandusky's gang, to make a demand on Duke for certain property and partnership adjustments. This rumor he telephoned to Jeffries. Before talking with de Spain, Jeffries went over the information with Lefever. The two agreed it was right, in the circumstances, that de Spain should be nearer than Sleepy Cat to Nan. Moreover, the period of waiting she had enjoined on him was almost complete.

Without giving de Spain the story fully, the two men talking before him let the discussion drift toward a proposal on his part to go down to Calabasas, where he could more easily keep track of any movement to or from the Gap, and this they approved. De Spain, already chafing under a hardly endured restraint, lost no time in starting for Calabasas, directing Lefever to follow next day.

It added nothing to his peace of mind in the morning to learn definitely from McAlpin that

Nan of Music Mountain

Gale Morgan, within twenty-four hours, had really disappeared from Calabasas. No word of any kind had come from Music Mountain for days. No one at Calabasas was aware even that Nan had gone into the Gap again. Bob Scott was at Thief River. De Spain telephoned to him to come up on the early stage, and turned his attention toward getting information from Music Mountain without violating Nan's injunction not to frustrate her most delicate effort with her uncle.

As a possible scout to look into her present situation and report on it, McAlpin could point only to Bull Page. Bull was a ready instrument, but his present value as an assistant had become a matter of doubt, since practically every man in the Gap had threatened within the week to blow his head off—though Bull himself felt no scruples against making an attempt to reach Music Mountain and get back again. It was proposed by the canny McAlpin to send him in with a team and light wagon, ostensibly to bring out his trunk, which, if it had not been fed to the horses, was still in Duke's barn. As soon as a rig could be got up Page started out.

It was late November. A far, clear air drew the snow-capped ranges sharply down to the eye of the desert—as if the speckless sky, lighted by

Hope Forlorn

the radiant sun, were but a monster glass rigged to trick the credulous retina. De Spain, in the saddle in front of the barn, his broad hat brim set on the impassive level of the Western horseman, his lips seeming to compress his thoughts, his lines over his forearm, and his hands half-slipped into the pockets of his snug leather coat, watched Page with his light wagon and horses drive away.

Idling around the neighborhood of the barns in the saddle, de Spain saw him gradually recede into the long desert perspective, the perspective which almost alone enabled the watcher to realize as he curtained his eyes behind their long, steady lashes from the blazing sun, that it was a good bit of a way to the foot of the great outpost of the Superstition Range.

De Spain's restlessness prevented his remaining quietly anywhere for long. As the morning advanced he cantered out on the Music Mountain trail, thinking of and wishing for a sight of Nan. The deadly shock of Pardaloe's story had been dulled by days and nights of pain. His deep-rooted love and his loneliness had quieted his impulse for vengeance and overborne him with a profound sadness. He realized how different his feelings were now from what they had been when she knelt before him in the darkened room and, not daring to plead for mercy for her uncle, had asked him only for the pity for herself that he had seemed so slow to give. Something reproached him now for his coldness at the moment that he should have thought of her suffering before his own.

The crystal brightness of the day brought no elation to his thoughts. His attention fixed on nothing that did not revert to Nan and his hunger to see her again. If he regarded the majestic mountain before him, it was only to recall the day she had fed him at its foot, long before she loved him—he thought of that truth now—when he lay dying on it. If the black reaches of the lava beds came within view, it was only to remind him that, among those desolate rocks, this simple, blue-eyed girl, frail in his eyes as a cobweb despite her graceful strength, had intrusted all her life and happiness to him, given her fresh lips to his, endured without complaint the headstrong ardor of his caresses and, by the pretty mockery of her averted eyes, provoked his love to new adventure.

Memory seemed that morning as keen as the fickle air—so sharply did it bring back to him the overwhelming pictures of their happiness together. And out of his acute loneliness rose vague questionings and misgivings. He said to

Hope Forlorn

himself in bitter self-reproach that she would not have gone if he had been to her all he ought to have been in the crisis of that night. If harm should befall her now! How the thought clutched and dragged at his heart. Forebodings tortured him, and in the penumbra of his thoughts seemed to leave something he could not shake off—a vague, haunting fear, as if of some impending tragedy that should wreck their future.

It was while riding in this way that his eyes, reading mechanically the wagon trail he was aimlessly following—for no reason other than that it brought him, though forbidden, a little closer to her—arrested his attention. He checked his horse. Something, the trail told him, had happened. Page had stopped his horses. Page had met two men on horseback coming from the Gap. After a parley—for the horses had tramped around long enough for one—the wagon had turned completely from the trail and struck out across the desert, north; the two horsemen, or one with a led horse, had started back for the Gap.

All of this de Spain gathered without moving his horse outside a circle of thirty feet. What did it mean? Page might have fallen in with cronies from the Gap, abandoned his job, and started for Sleepy Cat, but this was unlikely. He might have encountered enemies, been point-

edly advised to keep away from the Gap, and pretended to start for Sleepy Cat, to avoid trouble
with them. Deeming the second the more prob-
able conclusion, de Spain, absorbed in his speculations, continued toward the Gap to see whether
he could not pick up the trail of Page's rig farther on.

Within a mile a further surprise awaited him.
The two horsemen, who had headed for the Gap
after stopping Page, had left the trail, turned
to the south, down a small draw, which would
screen them from sight, and set out across the
desert.

No trail and no habitation lay in the direction
they had taken—and it seemed clearer to de Spain
that the second horse was a led horse. There was
a story in the incident, but his interest lay in
following Page's movements, and he spurred
swiftly forward to see whether his messenger had
resumed the Gap trail and gone on with his mission. He followed this quest almost to the mountains, without recovering any trace of Page's rig.
He halted. It was certain now that Page had
not gone into the Gap.

Perplexed and annoyed, de Spain, from the
high ground on which he sat his horse, cast his
eyes far out over the desert. The brilliant sunshine flooded it as far as the eye could reach. He

scanned the vast space without detecting a sign of life anywhere, though none better than he knew that any abundance of it might be there. But his gaze caught something of interest on the farthest northern horizon, and on this his scrutiny rested a long time. A soft brown curtain rose just above the earth line against the blue sky. Toward the east it died away and toward the west it was cut off by the Superstition peaks.

De Spain, without giving the weather signs much thought, recognized their import, but his mind was filled with his own anxieties and he rode smartly back toward Calabasas, because he was not at ease over the puzzles in the trail. When he reached the depression where the horsemen had, without any apparent reason, turned south, he halted. Should he follow them or turn north to follow Page's wanderings? If Page had been scared away from the Gap, for a time, he probably had no information that de Spain wanted, and de Spain knew his cunning and persistence well enough to be confident he would be back on the Gap road, and within the cover of the mountains, before a storm should overtake him. On the north the brown curtain had risen fast and already enveloped the farthest peaks of the range. Letting his horse stretch its neck, he hesitated a moment longer trying to decide whether to fol-

low the men to the south or the wagon to the
north. A woman might have done better. But
no good angel was there to guide his decision,
and in another moment he was riding rapidly to
the south with the even, brown, misty cloud behind him rolling higher into the northern sky.

CHAPTER XXXI

DE SPAIN RIDES ALONE

HE had ridden the trail but a short time when it led him in a wide angle backward and around toward Calabasas, and he found, presently, that the men he was riding after were apparently heading for the stage barns. In the north the rising curtain had darkened. Toward Sleepy Cat the landscape was already obliterated. In the south the sun shone, but the air had grown suddenly cold, and in the sharp drop de Spain realized what was coming. His first thought was of the southern stages, which must be warned, and as he galloped up to the big barn, with this thought in mind he saw, standing in the doorway, Bull Page.

De Spain regarded him with astonishment. "How did you get here?" was his sharp question.

Page grinned. "Got what I was after, and c'm' back sooner'n I expected. Half-way over to the Gap, I met Duke and the young gal on horseback, headed for Calabasas. They pulled up. I pulled up. Old Duke looked kind o' ga'nted, and it seemed like Nan was in a considerable hurry to get to Sleepy Cat with him, and he couldn't stand the saddle. Anyway, they was heading for Calabasas to get a rig from McAlpin. I knowed McAlpin would never give old Duke a rig, not if he was a-dyin' in the saddle."

"They've got your rig!" cried de Spain.

"The gal asked me if I'd mind accommodatin' 'em," explained Bull deprecatingly, "to save time."

"They headed north!" exclaimed de Spain. The light from the fast-changing sky fell copper-colored across his horse and figure. McAlpin, followed by a hostler, appeared at the barn door.

Bull nodded to de Spain. "Said they wanted to get there quick. She fig'erd on savin' a few miles by strikin' the hill trail in. So I takes their horses and lets on I was headin' in for the Gap. When they got out of sight, I turned 'round——"

Even as he spoke, the swift-rolling curtain of mist overhead blotted the sun out of the sky.

De Spain sprang from his saddle with a ringing order to McAlpin. "Get up a fresh saddle-horse!"

"A horse!" cried the startled barn boss, whirling on the hostler. "The strongest legs in the stable, and don't lose a second! Lady Jane; up with her!" he yelled, bellowing his orders into the echoing barn with his hands to his mouth. "Up with her for Mr. de Spain in a second! Marmon! Becker! Lanzon! What in hell are you all doing?" he roared, rushing back with a fusillade of oaths. "Look alive, everybody!"

"Coming!" yelled one voice after another from the depths of the distant stalls.

De Spain ran into the office. Page caught his horse, stripped the rifle from its holster, and hurriedly began uncinching. Hostlers running through the barn called shrilly back and forth, and de Spain springing up the stairs to his room provided what he wanted for his hurried flight. When he dashed down with coats on his arm the hoofs of Lady Jane were clattering down the long gangway. A stable-boy slid from her back on one side as Bull Page threw the saddle across her from the other; hostlers caught at the cinches, while others hurriedly rubbed the legs of the quivering mare. De Spain, his hand on McAlpin's shoulder, was giving his parting injunctions, and the barn boss, head cocked down, and eyes cast furtively on the scattering snowflakes outside, was listening with an attention that recorded indelibly every uttered syllable.

Once only, he interrupted: "Henry, you're ridin' out into this thing alone—don't do it."

"I can't help it," snapped de Spain impatiently.

"It's a man killer."

"I can't help it."

"Bob Scott, if he w's here, 'ud never let you do

399

it. I'll ride wi' ye myself, Henry. I worked for
your father——"

"You're too old a man, Jim——"

"Henry——"

"Don't talk to me! Do as I tell you!" thundered de Spain.

McAlpin bowed his head.

"Ready!" yelled Page, buckling the rifle holster in place. Still talking, and with McAlpin
glued to his elbow, de Spain vaulted into the saddle, caught the lines from Bull's hands, and
steadied the Lady as she sidestepped nervously
—McAlpin following close and dodging the dancing hoofs as he looked earnestly up to catch the
last word. De Spain touched the horse with the
lines. She leaped through the doorway and he
raised a backward hand to those behind. Running outside the door, they yelled a chorus of
cries after the swift-moving horseman and, clus-
tered in an excited group, watched the Lady with
a dozen great strides round the Calabasas trail
and disappear with her rider into the whirling
snow.

She fell at once into an easy reaching step, and
de Spain, busy with his reflections, hardly gave
thought to what she was doing, and little more to
what was going on about him.

No moving figure reflects the impassive more
than a horseman of the mountains, on a long ride.

De Spain Rides Alone

Though never so swift-borne, the man, looking neither to the right nor to the left, moving evenly and statue-like against the sky, a part of the wiry beast under him, presents the very picture of indifference to the world around him. The great swift wind spreading over the desert emptied on it snow-laden puffs that whirled and wrapped a cloud of flakes about horse and rider in the symbol of a shroud. De Spain gave no heed to these skirmishing eddies, but he knew what was behind them, and for the wind, he only wished it might keep the snow in the air till he caught sight of Nan.

The even reach of the horse brought him to the point where Nan had changed to the stage wagon. Without a break in her long stride, Lady Jane took the hint of her swerving rider, put her nose into the wind, and headed north. De Spain, alive to the difficulties of his venture, set his hat lower and bent forward to follow the wagon along the sand. With the first of the white flurries passed, he found himself in a snowless pocket, as it were, of the advancing storm. He hoped for nothing from the prospect ahead; but every moment of respite from the blinding whirl was a gain, and with his eyes close on the trail that had carried Nan into danger, he urged the Lady on.

When the snow again closed down about him he calculated from the roughness of the country

that he should be within a mile of the road that
Nan was trying to reach, from the Gap to Sleepy
Cat. But the broken ground straight ahead
would prevent her from driving directly to it.
He knew she must hold to the right, and her
curving track, now becoming difficult to trail,
confirmed his conclusion.

A fresh drive of the wind buffeted him as he
turned directly north. Only at intervals could he
see any trace of the wagon wheels. The driving
snow compelled him more than once to dismount
and search for the trail. Each time he lost it
the effort to regain it was more prolonged. At
times he was compelled to ride the desert in wide
circles to find the tracks, and this cost time when
minutes might mean life. But as long as he could
he clung to the struggle to track her exactly.
He saw almost where the storm had struck the
two wayfarers. Neither, he knew, was insensible to its dangers. What amazed him was that
a man like Duke Morgan should be out in it.
He found a spot where they had halted and, with
a start that checked the beating of his heart, his
eyes fell on her footprint not yet obliterated,
beside the wagon track.

The sight of it was an electric shock. Throwing himself from his horse, he knelt over it in the
storm, oblivious for an instant of everything but
that this tracery meant her presence, where he

now bent, hardly half an hour before. He swung, after a moment's keen scrutiny, into his saddle, with fresh resolve. Pressed by the rising fury of the wind, the wayfarers had become from this point, de Spain saw too plainly, hardly more than fugitives. Good ground to the left, where their hope of safety lay, had been overlooked. Their tracks wandered on the open desert like those who, losing courage, lose their course in the confusion and fear of the impending peril.

And with this increasing uncertainty in their direction vanished de Spain's last hopes of tracking them. The wind swept the desert now as a hurricane sweeps the open sea, snatching the fallen snow from the face of the earth as the seagale, flattening the face of the waters, rips the foam from the frantic waves to drive it in wild, scudding fragments across them.

De Spain, urging his horse forward, unbuckled his rifle holster, threw away the scabbard, and holding the weapon up in one hand, fired shot after shot at measured intervals to attract the attention of the two he sought. He exhausted his rifle ammunition without eliciting any answer. The wind drove with a roar against which even a rifle report could hardly carry, and the snow swept down the Sinks in a mad blast. Flakes torn by the fury of the gale were stiffened by the bitter wind into powdered ice that stung horse and rider. Casting away the useless carbine, and pressing his horse to the limit of her strength and endurance, the unyielding pursuer rode in great coiling circles into the storm, to cut in, if possible, ahead of its victims, firing shot upon shot from his revolver, and putting his ear intently against the wind for the faint hope of an answer.

Suddenly the Lady. stumbled and, as he cruelly reined her, slid helpless and scrambling along the face of a flat rock. De Spain, leaping from her back, steadied her trembling and looked underfoot. The mare had struck the rock of the upper lava bed. Drawing his revolver, he fired signal shots from where he stood. It could not be far, he knew, from the junction of the two great desert trails—the Calabasas road and the Gap road. He felt sure Nan could not have got much north of this, for he had ridden in desperation to get abreast of or beyond her, and if she were south, where, he asked, in the name of God, could she be?

He climbed again into the saddle—the cold was gripping his limbs—and, watching the rocky landmarks narrowly, tried to circle the dead waste of the half-buried flow. With chilled, awkward fingers he filled the revolver again and rode on, discharging it every minute, and listening—hoping against hope for an answer. It was when he had almost completed, as well as he could compute, the wide circuit he had set out on, that a faint shot answered his continuing signals.

With the sound of that shot and those that followed it his courage all came back. But he had yet to trace through the confusion of the wind and the blinding snow the direction of the answering reports.

Hither and thither he rode, this way and that, testing out the location of the slowly repeated shots, and signalling at intervals in return. Slowly and doggedly he kept on, shooting, listening, wheeling, and advancing until, as he raised his revolver to fire it again, a cry close at hand came out of the storm. It was a woman's voice borne on the wind. Riding swiftly to the left, a horse's outline revealed itself at moments in the driving snow ahead.

De Spain cried out, and from behind the furious curtain heard his name, loudly called. He pushed his stumbling horse on. The dim outline of a second horse, the background of a wagon, a storm-beaten man—all this passed his eyes unheeded. They were bent on a girlish figure running toward him as he slid stiffly from the saddle. The next instant Nan was in his arms.

CHAPTER XXXII

THE TRUTH

WITH the desperation of a joy born of despair she laid her burning cheek hysterically against his cheek. She rained kisses on his ice-crusted brows and snow-beaten eyes. Her arms held him rigidly. He could not move nor speak till she would let him. Transformed, this mountain girl who gave herself so shyly, forgot everything. Her words crowded on his ears. She repeated his name in an ecstasy of welcome, drew down his lips, laughed, rejoiced, knew no shamefacedness and no restraint—she was one freed from the stroke of a descending knife. A moment before she had faced death alone; it was still death she faced—she realized this—but it was death, at least, together, and her joy and tears rose from her heart in one stream.

De Spain comforted her, quieted her, cut away one of the coats from his horse, slipped it over her shoulders, incased her in the heavy fur, and turned his eyes to Duke.

The old man's set, square face surrendered

The Truth

nothing of implacability to the dangers confronting him. De Spain looked for none of that. He had known the Morgan record too long, and faced the Morgan men too often, to fancy they would flinch at the drum-beat of death.

The two men, in the deadly, driving snow, eyed each other. Out of the old man's deep-set eyes burned the resistance of a hundred storms faced before. But he was caught now like a wolf in a trap, and he knew he had little to hope for, little to fear. As de Spain regarded him, something like pity may have mixed with his hatred. The old outlaw was thinly clad. His open throat was beaten with snow and, standing beside the wagon, he held the team reins in a bare hand. De Spain cut the other coat from his saddle and held it out. Duke pretended not to see and, when not longer equal to keeping up the pretense, shook his head.

"Take it," said de Spain curtly.

"No."

"Take it, I say. You and I will settle our affairs when we get Nan out of this," he insisted.

"De Spain!" Duke's voice, as was its wont, cracked like a pistol, "I can say all I've got to say to you right here."

"No."

"Yes," cried the old man.

"Listen, Henry," pleaded Nan, seeking shelter from the furious blast within his arm, "just for a moment, listen!"

"Not now, I tell you!" cried de Spain.

"He was coming, Henry, all the way—and he is sick—just to say it to you. Let him say it here, now."

"Go on!" cried de Spain roughly. "Say it."

"I'm not afraid of you, de Spain!" shouted the old man, his neck bared to the flying ice. "Don't think it! You're a better man than I am, better than I ever was—don't think I don't know that. But I'm not afraid of e'er a man I faced, de Spain; they'll tell you that when I'm dead. All the trouble that ever come 'tween you and me come by an accident—come before you was born, and come through Dave Sassoon, and he's held it over me ever since you come up into this country. I was a young fellow. Sassoon worked for my father. The cattle and sheep war was on, north of Medicine Bend. The Peace River sheepmen raided our place—your father was with them. He never did us no harm, but my brother, Bay Morgan, was shot in that raid by a man name of Jennings. My brother was fifteen years old, de Spain. I started out to get the man that shot him. Sassoon trailed him to the Bar M, the old de Spain ranch, working for your father."

The Truth

The words fell fast and in a fury. They came as if they had been choked back till they strangled. "Sassoon took me over there. Toward night we got in sight of the ranch-house. We saw a man down at the corral. 'That's Jennings,' Sassoon says. I never laid eyes on him before—I never laid eyes on your father before. Both of us fired. Next day we heard your father was killed, and Jennings had left the country. Sassoon or I, one of us, killed your father, de Spain. If it was I, I did it never knowing who he was, never meaning to touch him. I was after the man that killed my brother. Sassoon didn't care a damn which it was, never did, then nor never. But he held it over me to make trouble sometime 'twixt you and me. I was a young fellow. I thought I was revenging my brother. And if your father was killed by a patched bullet, his blood is not on me, de Spain, and never was. Sassoon always shot a patched bullet. I never shot one in my life. And I'd never told you this of my own self. Nan said it was the whole truth from me to you, or her life. She's as much mine as she is yours. I nursed her. I took care of her when there weren't no other living soul to do it. *She got me and herself out into this, this morning. I'd never been caught like this if I'd had my way.* I told her 'fore we'd been out an hour we'd never see the end of

409

it. She said she'd rather die in it than you'd think she quit you. I told her I'd go on with her and do as she said—that's why we're here, and that's the whole truth, so help me God!

"I ain't afraid of you, de Spain. I'll give you whatever you think's coming to you with a rifle or a gun any time, anywhere—you're a better man than I am or ever was, I know that—and that ought to satisfy you. Or, I'll stand my trial, if you say so, and tell the truth."

The ice-laden wind, as de Spain stood still, swept past the little group with a sinister roar, insensible alike to its emotions and its deadly peril. Within the shelter of his arm he felt the yielding form of the indomitable girl who, by the power of love, had wrung from the outlaw his reluctant story—the story of the murder that had stained with its red strands the relations of each of their lives to both the others. He felt against his heart the faint trembling of her frail body. So, when a boy, he had held in his hand a fluttering bird and felt the whirring beat of its frightened heart against his strong, cruel fingers.

A sudden aversion to more bloodshed, a sickening of vengeance, swept over him as her heart mutely beat for mercy against his heart. She had done more than any man could do. Now she waited on him. Both his arms wrapped round

The Truth

her. In the breathless embrace that drew her closer she read her answer from him. She looked up into his eyes and waited. "There's more than what's between you and me, Duke, facing us now," said de Spain sternly, when he turned. "We've got to get Nan out of this—even if we don't get out ourselves. Where do you figure we are?" he cried.

"I figure we're two miles north of the lava beds, de Spain," shouted Morgan.

De Spain shook his head in dissent. "Then where are we?" demanded the older man rudely.

"I ought not to say, against you. But if I've got to guess, I say two miles east. Either way, we must try for Sleepy Cat. Is your team all right?"

"Team is all right. We tore a wheel near off getting out of the lava. The wagon's done for."

De Spain threw the fur coat at him. "Put it on," he said. "We'll look at the wheel."

They tried together to wrench it into shape, but worked without avail. In the end they lashed it, put Nan on the Lady, and walked behind while the team pushed into the pitiless wind. Morgan wanted to cut the wagon away and take to the horses, but de Spain said, not till they found a trail or the stage road.

So much snow had fallen that in spite of the

blizzard, driving with an unrelenting fury, the drifts were deepening, packing, and making all effort increasingly difficult. It was well-nigh impossible to head the horses into the storm, and de Spain looked with ever more anxious eyes at Nan. After half an hour's superhuman struggle to regain a trail that should restore their bearings, they halted, and de Spain, riding up to the wagon, spoke to Morgan, who was driving: "How long is this going to last?"

"All day and all night." Nan leaned closely over to hear the curt question and answer. Neither man spoke again for a moment.

"We'll have to have help," said de Spain after a pause.

"Help?" echoed Morgan scornfully. "Where's help coming from?"

De Spain's answer was not hurried. "One of us must go after it." Nan looked at him intently.

Duke set his hard jaw against the hurtling stream of ice that showered on the forlorn party. "I'll go for it," he snapped.

"No," returned de Spain. "Better for me to go."

"Go together," said Nan.

De Spain shook his head. Duke Morgan, too, said that only one should go; the other must stay. De Spain, while the storm rattled and

The Truth

shook at the two men, told why he should go
himself. "It's not claiming you are not entitled
to say who should go, Duke," he said evenly.
"Nor that our men, anywhere you reach, wouldn't
give you the same attention they would me.
And it isn't saying that you're not the better man
for the job—you've travelled the Sinks longer
than I have. But between you and me, Duke,
it's twenty-eight years against fifty. I ought to
hold out a while the longer, that's all. Let's
work farther to the east."

Quartering against the mad hurricane, they
drove and rode on until the team could hardly be
urged to further effort against the infuriated elements—de Spain riding at intervals as far to the
right and the left as he dared in vain quest of a
landmark. When he halted beside the wagon for
the last time he was a mass of snow and ice; horse
and rider were frozen to each other. He got down
to the ground with a visible effort, and in the
singing wind told Duke his plan and purpose.

He had chosen on the open desert a hollow falling somewhat abruptly from the north, and beneath its shoulder, while Morgan loosened the
horses, he scooped and kicked away a mass of
snow. The wagon had been drawn just above
the point of refuge, and the two men, with the aid
of the wind, dumped it over sidewise, making of

the body a windbreak over the hollow, a sort of roof, around which the snow, driven by the gale, would heap itself in hard waves. Within this shelter the men stowed Nan. The horses were driven down behind it, and from one of them de Spain took the collar, the tugs, and the whiffletree. He stuck a hitching-strap in his pocket, and while Morgan steadied the Lady's head, de Spain buckled the collar on her, doubled the tugs around the whiffletree, and fastened the roll at her side in front of the saddle.

Nan came out and stood beside him as he worked. When he had finished she put her hand on his sleeve. He held her close, Duke listening, to tell her what he meant to try to do. Each knew it well might be the last moment together. "One thing and another have kept us from marriage vows, Nan," said de Spain, beckoning at length to Morgan to step closer that he might clearly hear. "Nothing must keep us longer. Will you marry me?"

She looked up into his eyes. "I've promised you I would. I will promise every time you ask me. I never *could* have but one answer to that, Henry—it must always be yes!"

"Then take me, Henry," he said slowly, "here and now for your wedded husband. Will you do this, Nan?"

"I've promised you I would. I will promise every time you
ask me."

The Truth

Still looking into his eyes, she answered without surprise or fear: "Henry, I do take you."

"And I, Henry, take you, Nan, here and now for my wedded wife, for better for worse, for richer for poorer, from this day forward, until death us do part."

They sealed their pact with a silent embrace. De Spain turned to Duke. "You are the witness of this marriage, Duke. You will see, if an accident happens, that anything, everything I have —some personal property—my father's old ranch north of Medicine Bend—some little money in bank at Sleepy Cat—goes to my wife, Nan Morgan de Spain. Will you see to it?"

"I will. And if it comes to me—you, de Spain, will see to it that what stock I have in the Gap goes to my niece, Nan, your wife."

She looked from one to the other of the two men. "All that I have," she said in turn, "the lands in the Gap, everywhere around Music Mountain, go to you two equally together, or whichever survives. And if you both live, and I do not, remember my last message—bury the past in my grave."

Duke Morgan tested the cinches of the saddle on the Lady once more, unloosed the tugs once more from the horse's shoulder, examined each buckle of the collar and every inch of the two strips of leather, the reinforced fastenings on the whiffletree, rolled all up again, strapped it, and stood by the head till de Spain swung up into the saddle. He bent down once to whisper a last word of cheer to his wife and, without looking back, headed the Lady into the storm.

CHAPTER XXXIII

GAMBLING WITH DEATH

BEYOND giving his horse a safe headway from the shelter, de Spain made little effort to guide her. He had chosen the Lady, not because she was fresher, for she was not, but because he believed she possessed of the three horses the clearest instinct to bring her through the fight for the lives that were at stake. He did not deceive himself with the idea he could do anything to help the beast find a way to succor; that instinct rested wholly in the Lady's head, not in his. He only knew that if she could not get back to help, he could not. His own part in the effort was quite outside any aid to the Lady—it was no more than to reach alive whatever aid she could find, that he might direct it to where Nan and her companion would endure a few hours longer the fury of the storm.

His own struggle for life, he realized, was with the wind—the roaring wind that hurled its broadsides of frozen snow in monstrous waves across the maddened sky, challenging every living thing.

417

It drove icy knives into his face and ears, paralyzed in its swift grasp his muscles and sinews,
fought the stout flow of blood through his veins,
and searched his very heart to still it.

Encouraging the Lady with kind words, and
caressing her in her groping efforts as she turned
head and tail from the blinding sheets of snow and
ice, de Spain let her drift, hoping she might bring
them through, what he confessed in his heart to
be, the narrowest of chances.

He bent low in his saddle under the unending
blasts. He buffeted his legs and arms to fight
off the fatal cold. He slipped more than once
from his seat, and with a hand on the pommel
tramped beside the horse to revive his failing
circulation; there would come a time, he realized,
when he could no longer climb up again, but he
staved that issue off to the last possible moment
of endurance, because the Lady made better time
when he was on her back. When the struggle to
remount had been repeated until nature could
no longer by any staggering effort be made to
respond to his will, until his legs were no longer a
part of his benumbed being—until below his hips
he had no body answerable to his commands, but
only two insensible masses of lead that anchored
him to the ground—he still forced the frozen feet
to carry him, in a feeble, monstrous gait beside

the Lady, while he dragged with his hands on the saddle for her patient aid.

One by one every thought, as if congealed in their brain cells, deserted his mind—save the thought that he must not freeze to death. More than once he had hoped the insensate fury of the blizzard might abate. The Lady had long since ceased to try to face it—like a stripped vessel before a hurricane, she was drifting under it. De Spain realized that his helpless legs would not carry him farther. His hands, freezing to the pommel, no longer supported him. They finally slipped from it and he fell prostrate in the snow beside his horse. When he would cry out to her his frozen lips could mumble no words. It was the fight no longer of a man against nature, but only of an indomitable soul against a cruel, hateful death. He struggled to his feet only to fall again more heavily. He pulled himself up this time by the stirrup-strap, got his hands and arms up to the pommel, and clung to it for a few paces more. But he fell at last, and could no longer rise from the ground. The storm swept unceasingly on.

The Lady, checked by the lines wrapped on his arm, stopped. De Spain lay a moment, then backed her up a step, pulled her head down by the bridle, clasped his wooden arms around her

neck, spoke to her and, lifting her head, the mare
dragged him to his feet. Clumsily and helplessly
he loosened the tugs and the whiffletree, beat his
hands together with idiotic effort, hooked the
middle point of the whiffletree into the elbow of
his left arm, brought the forearm and hand up
flat against his shoulder, and with the hitching-
strap lashed his forearm and upper arm tightly
together around the whiffletree.

He drew the tugs stiffly over the Lady's back,
unloosed the cinches of the saddle, pushed it off
the horse and, sinking into the snow behind her,
struck with his free arm at her feet. Relieved of
the saddle, the Lady once more started, dragging
slowly behind her through the snow a still breathing human being. Less than an hour before it
had been a man. It was hardly more now, as
the Lady plodded on, than an insensate log.
But not even death could part it again from the
horse to which de Spain, alive, had fastened it.

The fearful pain from the tortured arm, torn
at times almost from its socket, the gradual snap-
ping of straining ligaments, the constant rupture
of capillaries and veins sustained his consciousness for a while. Then the torturing pain abated,
the rough dragging shattered the bruised body less.
It was as if the Lady and the storm together were
making easier for the slowly dying man his last

Gambling with Death

trail across the desert. He still struggled to keep
alive, by sheer will-power, flickering sparks of
consciousness, and to do so concentrated every
thought on Nan. It was a poignant happiness
to summon her picture to his fainting senses; he
knew he should hold to life as long as he could
think of her. Love, stronger than death, welled
in his heart. The bitter cold and the merciless
wind were kinder as he called her image from
out of the storm. She seemed to speak—to lift
him in her arms. Ahead, distant mountains rose,
white-peaked. The sun shone. He rode with her
through green fields, and a great peace rested on
his weary senses.

Lady Jane, pushing on and on, enlightened by
that instinct before which the reason of man is
weak and pitiful, seeing, as it were, through the
impenetrable curtain of the storm where refuge
lay, herself a slow-moving crust of frozen snow,
dragged to her journey's end—to the tight-shut
doors of the Calabasas barn—her unconscious
burden, and stood before them patiently waiting
until some one should open for her. It was one
of the heartbreaks of a tragic day that no one
ever knew just when the Lady reached the door
or how long she and her unconscious master waited
in the storm for admission. A startled exclama-

tion from John Lefever, who had periodically and anxiously left the red-hot stove in the office to walk moodily to the window, brought the men tumbling over one another as he ran from his companions to throw open the outer door and pull the drooping horse into the barn.

It was the Indian, Scott, who, reading first of all the men everything in the dread story, sprang forward with a stifled exclamation, as the horse dragged in the snow-covered log, whipped a knife from his pocket, cut the incumbered arm and white hand free from the whiffletree and, carrying the stiffened body into the office, began with insane haste to cut away the clothing.

Lefever, perceiving it was de Spain thus drawn to their feet, shouted, while he tore from the blade of Scott's knife the frozen garments, the orders for the snow, the heated water, the warm blankets, the alcohol and brandy, and, stripped to his waist, chafed the marble feet. The Indian, better than a staff of doctors, used the cunning of a sorcerer to revive the spark of inanimate life not yet extinguished by the storm. A fearful interval of suspense followed the silence into which the work settled, a silence broken only by the footsteps of men running to and from the couch over which Scott, Lefever, and McAlpin, half-naked, worked in mad concert.

Gambling with Death

De Spain opened his eyes to wander from one to the other of the faces. He half rose up, struggling in a frenzy with the hands that restrained him. While his companions pleaded to quiet him, he fought them until, restored to its seat of reason, his mind reasserted itself and, lying exhausted, he told them in his exquisite torture of whom he had left, and what must be done to find and bring them in.

While the relief wagons, equipped with straining teams and flanked by veteran horsemen, were dashing out of the barn, he lapsed into unconsciousness. But he had been able to hold Scott's hand long enough to tell him he must find Nan and bring her in, or never come back.

It was Scott who found her. In their gropings through the blizzard the three had wandered nearer Calabasas than any one of them dreamed. And on the open desert, far south and east of the upper lava beds, it was Scott's horse that put a foot through the bottom of the overturned wagon box. The suspected mound of snow, with the buried horses scrambling to their feet, rose upright at the crash. Duke crouched, half-conscious, under the rude shelter. Lying where he had placed her, snugly between the horses, Scott found Nan. He spoke to her when she opened her staring eyes, picked her up in his arms, called to his companions for the covered wagon, and began to restore her, without a moment of delay, to life. He even promised if she would drink the hateful draft he put to her lips and let him cut away her shoes and leggings and the big coat frozen on her, that in less than an hour she should see Henry de Spain alive and well.

CHAPTER XXXIV

AT SLEEPY CAT

NOTHING in nature, not even the storm itself, is so cruel as the beauty of the after
calm. In the radiance of the sunshine next day
de Spain, delirious and muttering, was taken to
the hospital at Sleepy Cat. In an adjoining room
lay Nan, moaning reproaches at those who were
torturing her reluctantly back to life. Day and
night the doctors worked over the three. The
town, the division, the stagemen, and the mountain-men watched the outcome of the struggle.
From as far as Medicine Bend railroad surgeons
came to aid in the fight.

De Spain cost the most acute anxiety. The
crux of the battle, after the three lives were held
safe, centred on the effort to save de Spain's arm
—the one he had chosen to lose, if he must lose
one, when he strapped it to the whiffletree. The
day the surgeons agreed that if his life were to be
saved the arm must come off at the shoulder a
gloom fell on the community.

In a lifetime of years there can come to the
greater part of us but a few days, a few hours,
sometimes no more than a single moment, to show

of what stuff we are really made. Such a crisis came that day to Nan. Already she had been wheeled more than once into de Spain's room, to sit where she could help to woo him back to life. The chief surgeon, in the morning, told Nan of the decision. In her hospital bed she rose bolt upright. "No!" she declared solemnly. "You shan't take his arm off!"

The surgeon met her rebellion tactfully. But he told Nan, at last, that de Spain must lose either his arm or his life. "No," she repeated without hesitation and without blanching, "you shan't take off his arm. He shan't lose his life."

The blood surged into her cheeks—better blood and redder than the doctors had been able to bring there—such blood as de Spain alone could call into them. Nan, with her nurse's help, dressed, joined de Spain, and talked long and earnestly. The doctors, too, laid the situation before him. When they asked him for his decision, he nodded toward Nan. "She will tell you, gentlemen, what we'll do."

And Nan did tell them what the two who had most at stake in the decision would do. Any man could have done as much as that. But Nan did more. She set herself out to save the arm and patient both, and, lest the doctors should change their tactics and move together on the arm surreptitiously, Nan stayed night and day with de Spain, until he was able to make such active use of either arm as to convince her that he, and not the surgeons, would soon need the most watching.

Afterward when Nan, in some doubt, asked the chaplain whether she was married or single, he obligingly offered to ratify and confirm the desert ceremony.

This affair was the occasion for an extraordinary round-up at Sleepy Cat. Two long-hostile elements—the stage and railroad men and the Calabasas-Morgan Gap contingent of mountain-men, for once at least, fraternized. Warrants were pigeonholed, suspicion suspended, side-arms neglected in their scabbards. The fighting men of both camps, in the presence of a ceremony that united de Spain and Nan Morgan, could not but feel a generous elation. Each party considered that it was contributing to the festivity in the bride and the groom the very best each could boast, and no false note disturbed the harmony of the notable day.

Gale Morgan, having given up the fight, had left the country. Satterlee Morgan danced till all the platforms in town gave way. John Lefever attended the groom, and Duke Morgan sternly, but without compunction, gave the bride.

Nan of Music Mountain

From Medicine Bend, Farrell Kennedy brought a notable company of de Spain's early associates for the event. It included Whispering Smith, whose visit to Sleepy Cat on this occasion was the first in years; George McCloud, who had come all the way from Omaha to join his early comrades in arms; Wickwire, who had lost none of his taciturn bluntness—and so many train-despatchers that the service on the division was crippled for the entire day.

A great company of self-appointed retainers gathered together from over all the country, rode behind the gayly decorated bridal-coach in procession from the church to Jeffries's house, where the feasts had been prepared. During the reception a modest man, dragged from an obscure corner among the guests, was made to take his place next Lefever on the receiving-line. It was Bob Scott, and he looked most uncomfortable until he found a chance to slip unobserved back to the side of the room where the distinguished Medicine Bend contingent, together with McAlpin, Pardaloe, Elpaso, and Bull Page, slightly unsteady, but extremely serious for the grave occasion, appeared vastly uncomfortable together.

The railroad has not yet been built across the Sinks to Thief River. But only those who lived

At Sleepy Cat

in Sleepy Cat in its really wild stage days are entitled to call themselves early settlers, or to tell stories more or less authentic about what then happened. The greater number of the Old Guard of that day, as cankering peace gradually reasserted itself along the Sinks, turned from the stage coach to the railroad coach; some of them may yet be met on the trains in the mountain country. Wherever you happen to find such a one, he will tell you of the days when Superintendent de Spain of the Western Division wore a gun in the mountains and used it, when necessary, on his wife's relations.

Whether it was this stern sense of discipline or not that endeared him to the men, these old-timers are, to a man, very loyal to the young couple who united in their marriage the two hostile mountain elements. One in especial, a white-haired old man, described by the fanciful as a retired outlaw, living yet on Nan's ranch in the Gap, always spends his time in town at the de Spain home, where he takes great interest in an active little boy, Morgan de Spain, who waits for his Uncle Duke's coming, and digs into his pockets for rattles captured along the trail from recent huge rattlesnakes. When his uncle happens to kill a big one—one with twelve or thirteen rings and a button—Morgan uses it to scare his younger

429

sister, Nan. And Duke, secretly rejoicing at his bravado, but scolding sharply, helps him adjust the old ammunition-belt dragged from the attic, and cuts fresh gashes in it to make it fit the childish waist. His mother doesn't like to see her son in warlike equipment, ambushing little Nan in the way Bob Scott says the Indians used to do. She threatens periodically to burn the belt up and throw the old rifles out of the house. But when she sees her uncle and her husband watching the boy and laughing at the parade together, she relents. It is only children, after all, that keep the world young.

9 781889 439099